PERISH
THE DAY

PERISH
THE DAY

A Thriller

JOHN FARROW

MINOTAUR BOOKS
A Thomas Dunne Book
New York

This is a work of fiction. All of the characters, organizations, and events portrayed in this novel are either products of the author's imagination or are used fictitiously.

A THOMAS DUNNE BOOK FOR MINOTAUR BOOKS.
An imprint of St. Martin's Press.

PERISH THE DAY. Copyright © 2017 by John Farrow Mysteries, Inc. All rights reserved.
Printed in the United States of America. For information, address St. Martin's Press,
175 Fifth Avenue, New York, N.Y. 10010.

www.thomasdunnebooks.com
www.minotaurbooks.com

Library of Congress Cataloging-in-Publication Data

Names: Farrow, John, 1947– author.
Title: Perish the day : a thriller / John Farrow.
Description: New York : Minotaur Books, 2017. | Series: The storm murders trilogy ; 3
Identifiers: LCCN 2017002190| ISBN 9781250057709 (hardcover) |
    ISBN 9781250112361 (ebook)
Subjects: LCSH: Police—Quebec (Province)—Montreal—Fiction. |
    Murder—Investigation—Fiction. | BISAC: FICTION / Mystery & Detective /
    General. | FICTION / Mystery & Detective / Police Procedural. |
    GSAFD: Suspense fiction. | Mystery fiction.
Classification: LCC PR9199.3.F455 P47 2017 | DDC 813/.54—dc23
LC record available at https://lccn.loc.gov/2017002190

Our books may be purchased in bulk for promotional, educational, or business use. Please contact
your local bookseller or the Macmillan Corporate and Premium Sales Department at
1-800-221-7945, extension 5442, or by e-mail at MacmillanSpecialMarkets@macmillan.com.

First Edition: May 2017

10 9 8 7 6 5 4 3 2 1

ACKNOWLEDGMENTS

On the occasion of my fortieth anniversary publishing novels (a longer time spent writing them), I'm dedicating this novel to my editors down through the years. In chronological order, this is for Dennis Lee, the late Gordon Montador, the late Ellen Seligman, Philippa Campsie, Ed Carson, Iris Tupholme, Barbara Berson, and most recently the joy that is Marcia Markland. I'm indebted to each of you and learned something of consequence—a truckload at times; sometimes a wee gem—from everyone. Thanks all.

PART 1

ONE

The clock in its tower. A watchful eye on campus.

He admires the mechanism, how the constant churning of the gears looms over the flawless serenity of his lover's spent form. That contrast. Its pace not measured by a rudimentary *tick-tock*, rather by a methodical *shhlunka-shhlunka* as the big hand cycles through the minutes. In the afterglow of the clock's exterior light, the young woman appears radiant to him. Her lips parted in anticipation of his farewell kiss. He's done his best for her. Attended to each exacting detail. Not only is she beautiful now—has she not always been lovely with her alabaster skin, dark tresses, and sultry black eyes?—at long last she lies before him as exquisite and perfectly serene.

That's the key, the wonder of it all: following their rapture, her serenity.

Shhlunka-shhlunka.

No time to dawdle. The more difficult task comes next.

The man regrets the vulgarity of this aspect, that he must lug her down the clock-tower stairs. Nothing about the transition will be elegant. Carry her in his arms, her limbs at a dangle, or hoist her over a

shoulder like a sack of . . . But he will not disparage her dignity with
that descriptor. He can no longer delay the job. She cannot be left high
and dry in the tower, undetected perhaps for weeks before being found
in unspeakable condition. An imperative, she must be discovered sooner,
not later, that others can be struck by her presentation. If nothing
else, her refined beauty is to be displayed as though for the first time.
His artistry will be appreciated then, validated, even revered.

Steep, old, and cracked, the wood stairs are best negotiated with
one hand on the railing. He chooses to bend his shoulder into her waist
and lift her that way, which keeps a hand free to hold on. Her head and
neck swing down, her hair gets mussed, and that's unfortunate, yet this
rude aspect will soon be over. Taking up the strain, he comforts her
with words.

For the first time he is aware of his own breathing, it's audible. He
grunts as he adjusts her position to secure his balance.

Together, they embark on the treacherous descent.

"Easy does it, my lovely. Gently down."

One careful step at a time.

Shhlunka–shhlunka.

He takes it slowly, not wanting to drop her. That would be a calamity. He guards against pitching forward, which might imperil his own
life.

The effort is not merely physical. He must also harness his emotions.
The force of the intimacy that flows between them arrives as a surprise. The faithful cooperation of her body with his own feels transformative. As though they have become one. His lover snuggles into the
crook of his shoulder, her form adjusting to accommodate his heroics,
to help make this journey safer and easier for them both. On the demanding descent, the intensity of his emotions revives, as when their passions
were conjoined, for is this not the ultimate act of love and expiation, the
letting go, the sacrifice inherent in his devotion to her and to her alone
for the sake of their ultimate freedom? Never can others understand
what they have known, what they have shared. His eyes well up. He
staggers, his knees quake, his thighs rebel with the weight and the
burden of their travail and his whole body aches with the solemnity of
this final rite.

Yet, she is not a burden, he will not think of her that way, for she bears for him the weightlessness of love, of surrender, of intimacy. Seemingly she evaporates off his back and shoulders on the steep stairs. Rather, it is the weight of a pathetic, sordid world that he must lug as he turns at each landing and prodigiously maneuvers to shuffle with care to the next level. Around and around and down they go, not conveniently in a spiral but in tight right-angled twists, each minute marked by the decreasing volume of the clock's accompaniment above them,

shhlunka–shhlunka,

until, at last, they achieve the base of the stairs.

The bottom step of the tower is located seven flights up. From here, an elevator ferries folks to the ground floor. He has no intention of making that descent with her. Here is where they must part. From now on, she'll require a different consort, and will probably be zipped in a banal body bag, poor thing, to descend farther.

Before that indignity is inflicted upon her, the man arranges her positioning for her to look her best when next revealed. The chic white dress is an inspired selection. The blue ribbon—synthetic, which is regrettable, yet silky to the touch—hangs from her waist as a sash, a subtle yet illuminating accessory, youthful and free, very laissez-faire. A devil-may-care attitude, yet elegant. Her white blouse and business attire, so unbecoming, has already been removed from the tower, exchanged for what suits her best. The blue of the sash repeated in her hair with a touch of lace. Her makeup redone. She's pleased, he's certain. Much care is taken with her clothing and look. The nylon stockings are from another era, true, but seriously, how much longer can a man apologize for that? Even though she gives him a hard time about it, he knows that she's secretly happy to play these dress-up games.

The demure bodice is enticing for its saucy reveal.

Silly girl, she likes it that way.

The blush created by a powder upon the shock of her white skin casts a glow.

What is left for him now remains vital. He needs to frame her properly, brush her hair again, arrange petals amid the strands and on the steps around her to permit her beauty to fully shine. His kit bag awaits by the exit door at the base of the stairs and he begins to execute these critical touches to her portraiture. He has rescued her from harm and vowed to sanctify her in this way. In the art and sweetness of death she will be revered, her beauty unblemished and now inextinguishable.

Let coarse people snap their photographs. Forensic scientists will sully her form with insensitive probes. Nothing is to be done about any of that except to disregard their primitive reactions, their pedestrian procedures. Despite their abundant ignorance, the fools will be unable to resist being impressed. They'll know soon enough what it is to stand in the presence of luminous art.

She is his finest creation. The embodiment of his life's work.

She deserves his best, he's certain.

He owes her that much, so gives his all.

His cunning, of course, will also be recognized as brilliant. Yet for the moment, somewhat to his surprise, it is of no special interest to him. Only his transcendental artistry counts now.

At the base of the tower the young woman is arranged in a pose, one hand by her hip, another adjusted above her head. Every gesture exhibits a proper attitude, one of lassitude and superiority, of ease and entitlement, of largesse and indulgence. She is positioned. None too soon. She is beginning to stiffen. The flowers are precisely posited around her and upon her, the results tested repeatedly from various angles. He fusses and tries again until everything is just so, then places a printed invitation to a cocktail party between the fingertips of her upper left hand to further confound the imbeciles. To entice them as well. To draw them into his sphere, then to revel in their defeat. He imparts one last holy farewell kiss upon the woman's lips, which lingers awhile.

The man breathes the empty cavity of her body and blows his own air into her lungs.

He must admit, then, to an error and apologize. He must not indulge himself again. He has a duty to remain above the emotional slurry, although it arrives more acutely than anticipated. Having smudged her lips, he must now repair and paint them more perfectly than before. The man wipes his own mouth clean, and sits upon the floor below her to gaze upward to best admire the view, as though she performs upon a stage and he has become her audience.

One final touch, now that all is done. A lasting grace. The ultimate gift to transport her through time and space, to commemorate the sanctity of their union—she has been his only perfect lover—that she might be carried upon angelic wings. He removes a felt cloth from the pocket of his kit bag which he unwraps to reveal a necklace, a shining, spiritual talisman. Bold, precise, the gemstones have been arranged in a manner to keep her alive, perhaps, even in death, or possibly through death into a next world. A nether life. Her vitality and her hope is embedded in the selection of stones, although one set curries favor for a request of his own. A petition for his own good health, a message for her to carry into the beyond.

Lovely for her to sacrifice herself this way.

He adjusts the necklace around her neck.

Perfect. Exquisite.

And now? Has the time come?

Not to go. Not to leave her. Not just yet.

Has the time come to switch off the light?

He will await the morning, when people flood the library seven floors below, where he will effect a disguise for the cameras and for his exit. He will await the morning, the crucial hour of her discovery.

The man sits in the light from a bare bulb, alone in the dead girl's company, content to honor the sanctity of her memory and slowly turn his gaze away. The deep, still stare of her dark eyes bores into him one last time. So absolute. So final. This moment. He shuts his own eyes, and summons to mind again the young woman in the throes of their mutual rapture.

She was glad, back then, that he had come to rescue her from debasement and oblivion, from the fury of this world.

Glad now that he comforts her in the next.

He does what he must do. He reaches up and turns off the light.

Shhlunka-shhlunka utters the clock in its tower. As though her heart still beats with a sacred rhapsody, with life's secret thrum. More faint down here, yet it beats on, rapturous in the dark, within their stillness.

Whispering, minute by minute, as the darkness takes hold.

Shhlunka-shhlunka.

She's surely at rest now, and if all goes well, at peace.

TWO

Roiling with thunder, shot through by lightning, burly black cloud rises above the eastern hills of Vermont to blot out the morning sun. The storm amasses forces on the mountaintops, then releases a booming barrage upon the valleys of New Hampshire where the Connecticut and White Rivers converge. Over the radio, a particularly poetic weatherwoman describes the event as "an anarchy of meteorological maneuvers hell-bent on reckless destruction." Tickled by her illustration, she giggles. Professor Philip Lars Toomey, listening in at seven-fifteen in the morning and brought up short by the quasi-hysterics, the lack of professionalism, suspects that the woman has not been to bed, and is probably inebriated.

Rather timidly, Toomey pokes his nose out the front door of his modest bungalow to judge the tempest for himself. A twitch of his nostrils and a glance up confirms the forecast of a deluge and widespread calamity. Rivers will flood their banks; sewers pitch off their manhole covers. Wind whips through the Norwegian maples on his front lawn. Leaves that sprouted relatively recently are suddenly everywhere, in the air and gallivanting down the sidewalk, while across the street the trunks of mature pines sway so erratically they might soon snap. Heavy rain is inevitable, yet a further prospect vexes him more. If he sprints to the carport immediately he'll make it without being soaked. If he drives off, does he want to be out on a highway when hail pelts down? A forty percent chance, according to the tipsy morning weatherwoman. Should he trust a drunk's forecast? Dare he risk a pockmarked hood? A dinged roof? His poor beloved Bimmer! Insurance will pay, but the hassle, the time, the aggravation of it all.

And of course, he'll be out of pocket for the deductible.

He has to think this through.

He's of two minds. Drive to work, get through the morning routine, lunch, exchange secret messages inside the bark of a ratty old hickory tree, then carry on to his lady love's abode to enjoy an afternoon of illicit passion. Scandalize himself. Afterward, review his day and perhaps tally the damage to his car while downing a pint in a favorite pub. Sounds good. Inviting. The alternative is to skip all that and stay home. Risk nothing. Enjoy little. Phone his girl and beg off. She'll understand. Then mope about it for a day which at least protects the BMW from golf balls hurtling out of the sky, and keeps his own life safe should the ice that descends prove to be the size of fists.

Out there, he could easily get clobbered.

Back when he was pushing himself from bed, the weatherwoman predicted an incessant downpour until midnight. "Epic," she promised, vowing: "Torrential." She giggled while sprinkling in words such as *teeming* and *relentless* and *extremely wet* to convey her perspective. She cheerily advised the morning news anchor that the day was bound to be "a soaker," morning traffic might be washed away and the deluge approach Noah's standards, a comment that apparently had her in stitches as her partner took over, all the while chuckling himself, although, in his case, nervously.

Toomey wants both of them sacked.

If she's not drunk she's on drugs.

Wrecking his day early in the morning, then laughing about it—the nerve of those two! He might write a letter. The male announcer is less giddy but he's definitely slurring his words.

Two choices. Go or stay. A third option for the day suggests that he wait, stay home until noon, write that letter, then either make a run for it into town or suppress his raging lust completely. Makes sense, except that he fundamentally distrusts third options.

During a lifetime of spy craft, the professor has never desired more than a pair of best choices in any circumstance. Third possibilities propagate confusion, which in turn creates danger whenever there's no time to think. If the best course of action in a given situation is to turn either right or left, then going straight ahead usually means over a cliff. A fourth escape route might work in theory and be the best one, yet inevitably leads to a paralysis of thinking. Limiting a decision to two options, whether they be agreeable or not, allows a man in the field to flip a mental coin and take his chances. Heads, he has a fifty-fifty shot of being right—better than that if he's lucky, and any spy worth his salt must rely on luck—or tails, and if that's the wrong choice, at least he knows which way to run.

Toomey has time to spare this morning, which might be the problem. He allows the thunder to force the issue—*Quick! Decide!*—before the next explosive rumble. Tossing a trench coat over his sports jacket, he clutches his messenger bag to use as an umbrella and bolts out the side door. By the time he starts up the BMW and pulls free of the carport, the rain has not only begun, the ferocity is stunning. The wipers scarcely keep up. All he's experiencing is wind and rain, no hail, and Toomey knows that if ice doesn't bombard him at the outset, he's probably safe. As is his Bimmer. *Whew.* He'll drive on, first to the Dowbiggin School of International Studies via a favorite coffee shop in Hanover and eventually into the randy quarrel of his lover's bed. He'll get some work done early then enjoy wicked sex. Crazy sex. Lovely sex. What a life. Storm aside, the day is setting up as ideal.

Under the waterfall pouring from a blackened sky, the pavement is difficult to discern in the headlights, although once on his way he desires nothing more than to be on the road, bound for the freeway, his life marginally at risk while driving through the fury. If anything, the prospect of making love in rhythm to the rain adds to the thrill. If the weather remains electric and cacophonous, so much the better.

Toomey is confident that no one suspects a thing.

That no one ever will.

While a number of professors are stuck teaching summer classes, he is unencumbered until the fall, yet chooses to trek onto the campus every morning to accomplish a modicum of work. Partly he suffers a need to justify his salary, as his income is a sinecure for a job well done in service to country. He's well paid but underworked. He also insists on keeping up appearances because the habits of spy craft do not easily release their grip. Subterfuge—pretending to work—comes naturally to him, and doesn't that hold him in good stead given that his new purpose, at long last, rightfully belongs to the craft of love? Secret love. True love, perhaps. Although a familiar doubt kicks in. *Is it love? Can I call it that?* Wipers lash the glass, the tempo evocative for him. *Not lust?* He muddles through the oblique equation. *Love and lust both, then. God help me, will I ever—will anyone ever—discern a difference?*

He can flip a coin to get his answer. He holds off, preferring to savor the moment. In the gloomy downpour, under the raucous thunder and startling lightning, Philip Lars Toomey enters the town of Hanover. Close to the Ivy League jewel of Dartmouth College he'll pull in for coffee, then on out of town to a lesser campus where he plies his trade in the gentle hamlet of Holyoake, New Hampshire.

THREE

Vernon Colchester is soaked to the skin. The peak of his ball cap keeps the rain out of his eyes, and that's all. His hair is wet. The permeable fabric merely filters the cascade. No point hurrying, no point worrying about it anymore, he has hit the magic moment when he cannot possibly be wetter. No different than taking a bath. The leisurely pace to his lope is admirable given the ferocity of the onslaught as he strolls across the soggy green of Dowbiggin. Headed for the library.

Given summer's quiet season and the violence of the storm he will not be sharing the building with many others. Inside, his wet shoes squeak as he passes posters of musicians who have played on the Dartmouth campus, although Dowbiggin undergrads were always welcomed. Joan Baez and Ray Charles, Bruce Springsteen and Jerry Garcia, Duke Ellington, Sly and the Family Stone, others, all before his time. When he first visited the Dowbiggin School for a summer orientation the posters impressed him. He felt he was enrolling in a four-year rock concert. Let the good times roll. Now that he's graduating he can attest that it was never like that. He didn't get to any memorable concerts himself. Regardless, he's enjoyed the place.

Of his time here, the only thing he'd change would be his love life. He's so wet, his clothes are saturated. He leaks as he walks.

Vernon Colchester has a friend who frequents the Washington Room, small and dim save for the table lamps. The friend once experienced a vivid dream where he met the love of his life at a table there, and so became a dedicated habitué, reading and studying in the space whenever time permitted, often from dawn to dusk. The initial dream-lover was an enchanting young woman; in the time since the dream the friend discovered that he was gay. He's been kidded that the love of his life might have shown up, but, male or female, he had his eyes on the wrong gender at the time. In any case, no soul mate has arrived for him yet, and today the weather may have kept his friend away from his morning reading, as the room is vacant.

Using a hand dryer and paper towels, he attempts to dry his head and face in the men's room. That helps, but he doesn't notice much improvement when he dabs his shirt and pants. Vernon goes up a spiral staircase to the second level. Table lamps with green glass shades and chairs covered in green leather denote the Oxford/Cambridge influence. Not to mention the blatant rip-off of Dartmouth. The Dowbiggin School was initially formed by a breakaway contingent from the more renowned institution. A question of policy. The junior school floundered, then miraculously revived with substantial funding, most of it covert and therefore believed to be governmental. What level or branch of government has always been a matter of conjecture; in any case funds were spent to emulate, on a smaller scale, the architecture, if not the prestige, of their formidable neighbor down the road.

A large round table in the center of the library's wood-paneled room is divided into study sections where Vernon Colchester takes a seat. He checks his phone, discreetly. He's expecting to meet someone, a stranger, a prospective employer. He'll have to protest that he doesn't always look like a drowned cat. The timing for the meeting has been set as approximate, the plan being that he is to arrive early, then wait.

He's arrived early. Now he waits.

He's soon bored, and peruses the books. Wherever he goes he creates puddles. Nothing he finds on the shelves today strikes his fancy. He enjoys browsing, though, reads a line or a paragraph, examines a lithograph or an illustration from volumes as diverse as scientific field journals from the nineteenth century and recent children's stories. He senses a subliminal ache, for this is different, now that he's graduating, now that he's on the cusp of his chosen career. Riffling through books, he grasps how elusive knowledge can be, that the best that anyone can hope to learn is the tiniest fraction of what is known, and with the best of luck discover something fresh to add to a field. To wit, he's probably not read a single book in this particular library, reading many from others, and has learned a great deal, all of which adds up to a smidgen.

Enough to know that he knows very little.

His cell phone vibrates in his pants front pocket.

A text.

Something wrong. Change of plan. Meet you in the caf.

Why would anything be wrong? What constitutes *wrong*? He was to meet a man in a library, the library is empty, how does that hold potential for something to be wrong?

He's feeling alert now, tense, thinking that perhaps this is a test. Vernon Colchester goes downstairs. He's a tall and lanky youth who will fill out someday and be substantial, physically imposing. For now, he comes across as skinny. Despite a giraffelike quality augmented by red hair and freckles, he's remarkably coordinated in his movements, coming down the stairs at a clip. Any observer might think that his feet merely shuffle, that his hips, torso, and dangling arms soon will ease into a tap dance worthy of Fred Astaire.

The Lincoln Library's cafeteria that lies below the main level has distinguished itself from rudimentary campus eateries by accumulating statues and busts of twentieth-century figures, placing them amid a forest of sculptures from the era. Vernon Colchester moves from the West Wing, which chronicles the Gay Nineties through the Roaring Twenties, with little more than a nod to the First World War, and into the East Wing, where the struggles of the Dirty Thirties and the Second World War are memorialized. Familiar with the room, Vernon feels anxious in it today. He assumes that the meeting, its portent and its mysteriousness, is to blame. In the dark surrounds of factory workers in ruins and soldiers in both agony and triumph, his introductory meeting is taking on an increased measure of foreboding.

The wait lasts nearly an hour.

The phone bumps in his pocket again.

Police to seventh floor Lincoln. Death @ Dowbiggin.
Check it out.

This time, he hurries. He *is* being tested, he deduces that now. Back on the ground floor he sees cops asking for directions. Knowing where to go he beats them to the elevators. He disembarks on the sixth floor as the seventh is restricted: the elevator doors won't open for him there. The police will have to come this way and already campus security is preparing for their arrival. They seem stressed. Vernon sneaks back among the book stacks and waits, to eavesdrop and to see whatever he can, to *check it out,* as instructed. He's not been hired yet and he wants to impress his unknown boss. He's a spy-in-training, potentially anyway. He waits to see and hear whatever can be gleaned.

FOUR

Seated for a late breakfast, Sandra and Émile Cinq-Mars are noticeably subdued. Their time in New Hampshire has been hectic, not without' troubles and emotional pitfalls, and shortly a pleasant bedlam will consume them: Sandra's niece and her niece's girlfriends are to arrive. In the interim they're content to sip coffee, await croissants and jam, and enjoy precious downtime with their own thoughts.

For Sandra, recent days have been a hardship. Her eighty-nine-year-old mom is in palliative care and family members have been preparing for the demise of their matriarch. Adding to the sadness of failing physical health marked by an almost daily diminishment of organ function, the matriarch's mental state has dwindled from formidable to frail in the blink of an eye. In coming down to New Hampshire, Sandra expected to share old memories with her mom, final thoughts and her deepest expressions of love. All that has been taken away. As natural as an impending death for an aged and frail person may be, she's finding herself affected far more than she expected, in large measure because this sudden decline in her mom's faculties has made the last days wretched. Being on the cusp of her passing has released a welter of emotions. *No one can prepare for the loss of a parent.* Having spoken such words to others on occasion, she now needs to repeat them to herself.

They've arrived ahead of time. Sandra remains within herself, while Émile looks through the morning paper, subdued as well, although they both intend to be chipper once the girls show up. The next two weeks lead to the commencement ceremony at the Dowbiggin School of International Studies, which Émile and Sandra are attending to honor their niece Caroline's graduation. As the young woman and her chums will be harnessed to their own madcap social agenda as the big day draws near, uncle and aunt are treating them to a breakfast gathering early on. Unsaid, yet understood by all, the couple may be more involved with a funeral and with grieving by the time commencement day arrives. For that added reason they've elected to celebrate in advance.

While the couple showed up before the appointed hour, expecting to be on their own for a bit, their guests are now officially late. Sandra stretches. She feels a need to rouse herself from a sluggish disposition, and inquires if anything is interesting. She means in the news.

Her husband—Émile Cinq-Mars, the famous and now retired detective—stately at sixty-six even at this fresh hour of the morning, is more than willing to be attentive. He's glad to be sharing a meal with her while she's not reduced to weeping.

"Remarkably, no. I suppose that's a good thing. Today's main topic is the weather."

"No wonder. Is it ever coming down. It's teeming!"

"Hmm," Émile says.

She interprets his tone. Her detective-husband's noncommittal expression to denote his disagreement with prevailing opinion is, if not legendary, all too familiar.

"You don't agree?" she probes. "That it's raining? Or is your semigrunt an indication that you don't think it's raining particularly hard?"

"It wasn't a semigrunt," he objects.

"All right." Sandra has always enjoyed being feisty in debate. Utilizing a hockey metaphor, Émile has told her that she's tough along the boards, that she gets her elbows up in the corners. His intellectual and intuitive strengths may actually be legendary, although she knows his buttons and how to press them. As a consequence, their verbal jousts usually turn out to be fair fights. He doesn't get that from many people, and now that he's a little older, and she remains nineteen years his junior and probably sharper, she prevails more often than once she did. "A full-fledged grunt then."

He recognizes that she's being as playful as possible under the circumstances. Folding the paper, he welcomes another sip of joe before responding. "I agree that it's raining. I also agree that it's raining hard. Where I disagree—"

"You see? I knew it. Here it comes."

"Where I disagree is with your comment 'no wonder.'"

She's puzzled. "You don't think a newspaper should write about the weather?"

"I didn't say that. I simply find it remarkable, and a *wonder*, that they are writing about the weather *before* the weather actually happens. It's here now. The paper was printed overnight. They're not reporting on the news, they're *predicting* the news, the weather, before it gets here. See? All of which tells me that they had a very slow news day. No murders—"

"Why should there be murders? Because you showed up? Why do you check newspapers for murders, Émile?"

"No murders," he repeats. "Nor am I looking for any. I'm just pointing out. No traffic accidents. No local political scandals. All they could find to write about is the *prediction* of violent weather and make that the news. Which, in the greater scheme of things, is probably welcome."

She's amused, and that's welcome, too. Lately it's been difficult to lighten up. The change in their mood has come at an opportune moment, for Caroline and two of her friends are bursting into the restaurant with much laughter and shrieking from being out in the torrent. It's a dramatic entrance, which garners the attention and amusement of other patrons. People notice their flattened hair and wet tangles, their plight, and grin.

One soaked girl is feeling exposed.

"What'll I do?" she cries in a half-whisper, her arms desperately crisscrossed over her chest.

"My uncle Émile won't look."

"He's not the only person in here exactly."

"Kali, I'll spoon-feed you. Keep your arms crossed until you dry out."

More laughter, these girls don't let one another off the hook easily. "Slut, don't play innocent. When you left the house you knew this would happen. Anyway, you're wearing a bra, what's the big deal?"

"I'm poking through!" She peeks down at her chest, and patrons are looking too, despite her whispering. "The rain's made me cold! I'm shivering."

"Oh no," the lone blonde among the three remarks.

"What?"

"Addie's not here yet."

"Drear. Where is that girl?"

They bounce on over to Émile and Sandra's table.

In the flurry of greetings, Caroline takes a moment to place a hand on her aunt Sandra's shoulder, look her in the eyes, and convey an ongoing sympathy for their circumstances. She's about to lose a grandmother she's been close to from birth. The two women acknowledge the cloud they are under even as they break off and enter the festivity of the morning.

"My God, this rain!" Kali exclaims. She accepts Caroline's light jacket to maintain her modesty, and there's more laughter about that as Émile stares at the ceiling while she puts it on. She can finally uncross her arms and Caroline makes a comment that it's too bad she won't uncross her legs which has everyone groaning and Émile adopting an artificially censorious expression. Anastasia, then, needs to be introduced, as she is the one friend the older couple hasn't met since arriving back in New Hampshire. Émile is immediately drawn to her bubbly personality and innate cheerfulness. She's a tad short and happily plump, a marginal chubbiness that bequeaths to her the bright cheeks of a cherub. Her eyes have a way of jumping around that expresses a buoyant spirit. She's smart and in love with life, he can tell. He thinks that if he was ever blessed with a daughter and allowed to choose, if that's how procreation worked, he'd want her to turn out like this one. Or be this one.

"Where's Addie?" Sandra inquires.

"That's the question of the hour," Caroline reveals. Émile and Sandra's niece, she's the tall one, slender, and carries herself with the posture of a girl who's been on horseback since birth. Like her aunt, she has a highly competitive streak, and she's ridden a few mounts in the hunting class that did well in New England meets. She's also a swimmer who lacked the upper-body strength—and the desire to acquire it—to bring home ribbons. The boys love her, although she's strict with them. She tends to gain the upper hand early in any relationship. Once a boyfriend understands the lay of the land, he either moves on or is moved along, at least that's the pattern she's confided to her aunt Sandra. She expects to be a CEO one day and is off to law school in the fall, this time at Boston University. "We haven't heard from Addie since yesterday. She's gone. Poof! Vanished."

"Is that typical behavior?" Émile asks, his tone reverting to his days as a detective before retirement.

"Not typical. Not without precedent." Aware that she's talking to a professional sleuth, she catches the tenor of his interest. "Addie tends to turn into a ditz whenever she meets a new guy she likes. It's just that we haven't heard that that's happened."

"Unlike Kali, Addie doesn't waste time," Anastasia adds. She manages to be tongue-in-cheek while also deferring to the seriousness of the retired cop's query.

"She also has that other thing," Kali brings up.

Anastasia promptly squelches the subject. "Not happening," she says, a bit stridently, a bit too forcefully, and Émile has the impression that sharp kicks on Kali's shins have occurred under the table.

"I'm sure she's fine," Sandra says, then looks down, as though to acknowledge that it's illogical that her desire for all to be well should trump their legitimate worries. Yet the girls don't seem overly concerned, either.

"Call Vernon yet?" Kali asks. She keeps tugging the jacket more tightly around herself, unnecessarily, as though still feeling half-naked.

"Putting it off," Caroline admits, then explains to her aunt and uncle, "Vernon's her ex. One of. The one who'd rather not be an ex. See why I don't want to involve him? She was supposed to show up at a party last night but never did. We were hoping she'd be here, she knows where to come. She may still show up. She's just way late. We're way late. Sorry about that. The rain."

"Text Vernon," Kali suggests. "You'll worry otherwise. She's probably hungover. Or maybe she had a relapse and they're back together."

"She'd keep that to herself, wouldn't she?" Anastasia tacks on, agreeing, again being serious with a humorous undercurrent. Émile loves her already.

Caroline concedes, mutters, "Okay," and taps out a message on her phone as the waitress comes by with menus and to confirm, as it turns out, that everyone wants to start with orange juice and coffee.

"This morning," Émile warns, "each of you is on a splurge diet."

They're fine with that, and Anastasia, his new favorite, scrunches up her face and pumps both fists while mouthing the word *yes!* These three are young women of privilege, possessed of intellect, talent, and refinement. They've also applied themselves to their studies as elite students and are exulting now in a cloudburst of freedom and adventure pending the rest of their lives.

As coffee for the girls and juice is brought to the table, the senior couple is informed of summer plans and career choices. Anastasia will be backpacking through Europe. Her parents are on their way in from Oregon, "to find out if they got their money's worth," then after commencement she flies to Amsterdam, "boyfriend in tow. I'll see if I can't do a student exchange along the way."

"You want to return to school in Europe?" Émile asks, unaware that he's being slow. He looks up into that bright laughing smile.

"No, sir, I mean, I'll see if I can't find a new and improved boyfriend along the way. I was thinking Italian. Maybe French. I'm open to anything, really."

After that, she'd like to work on third-world agricultural concerns, and may take another year or two of study for that. No specific plan as yet, although she's aware of her options while being open to anything. Émile could take her home right now and show her off. "I wonder if your parents, when they fly in from Oregon, would consider, I don't know, giving you up. What do you think, Sandra?"

His wife is puzzled, but Kali gets it. "I'm officially jealous."

Anastasia gets it, too. "My folks say they're willing to take on a chunk of my student loan. If you're willing to make them an offer . . .

they might be persuaded. I did work my way through school, scored a scholarship or two—"

"Or four," Kali corrects her.

"Or four. The debt's not too bad. You can swing it."

"Actually, we've been thinking of selling the farm. I could take a look at my credit line." Émile's happy to have his remarks rewarded with a laugh. He and Sandra exchange quick smiles, as it's true about the farm. And moving here.

Everyone pauses as Caroline's mobile device announces a response. Her look is soon distressed. "Oh my God," she whispers.

"What?" Anastasia rests a hand in the crook of Caroline's elbow and leans in to get a peek at the iPhone screen.

"Death at—" She draws the letter *a* in the air and circles it, to indicate the *at* sign on a computer keyboard. "Dowbiggin. That's his subject line."

"What's that about?"

"Something's happened." Caroline reads the text. "Vernon says a girl's been found on campus."

"What do you mean, *found*?"

Anastasia's question goes unanswered as the phone suddenly plays a hard-rock song. Caroline checks the screen, answers, and says, "Vernon?" She listens. "Oh my God." The phrase is spoken quietly.

"What is it, Caroline?" Émile Cinq-Mars asks.

The girl continues on with her caller. "It can't be, that can't be. No, we haven't seen her—" She listens and she's fidgeting now and when her eyes pass over her uncle's she's clearly upset, verging on panic. "Find out!" she commands her caller. "Ask them! Find out, Vernon!"

He has apparently signed off, and Caroline taps a button to conclude her end of the conversation. The others await news. Her eyes look hurt.

"A girl's been found on campus. Dead. Vernon heard someone say there wasn't any blood, so maybe she fell down the stairs."

"What stairs?" Kali asks.

"I don't know what stairs!" Caroline snaps back. She implores her uncle with her eyes. "Vernon says the library's been evacuated. By the police. Uncle Émile?"

He's the one who's lived these scenes before, who's investigated murders, who's taken biker gangs apart, if the myths be true, with his teeth. He's plowed the Mafia underground in his home city of Montreal where once they were kingpins, where once they governed the darker alleys. Given all that myth and hearsay, she wants to know, and pleads through her facial expression, if he will help. Can her uncle, the retired policeman, discover what's going on? Why is there a dead girl on campus, and more importantly, who is she?

"I have no standing here," Émile demurs. That's not good enough, of course, a judgment reflected on the faces of the four women, including his wife's. A wait-and-see attitude will only compound their worry. Appearances count for something, as does action, and Émile concludes that in this circumstance it's probably beneficial to appear to be helping out. Especially with four women waiting for him to act, not because he's the only man, as they're not inclined to lean on men, but because he's in the business. "Okay. To be on the safe side, let's go over there. Me and you, Caroline. Find out what's up."

"Everything will be fine, I'm sure," Sandra adds, and understands why she's saying that even as the words spill out. She can handle only so much sadness right now and has already maxed out her limit.

Caroline retrieves her jacket from Kali, who crosses her arms again, then she and Émile wend their way back through the café, pausing at the front door where they brace themselves for the ferocity of the storm.

FIVE

Philip Lars Toomey can count on the atmosphere to be convivial, the coffee at the Green Briar Café to be piping hot, to set him on a proper footing for the day.

In the muggy air of the shop the professor makes his first contact of the morning with a campus crowd, less active now that school is not in full swing. Students are noticeably more relaxed, most likely for the same reason. He eases into an enjoyable mix of casual fashion and flare, pretty faces and ambient conversation sprinkled with laughter, not all of it self-conscious. Animated by the storm, people enjoy being safely indoors and in the company of others. Toomey's professorship has not been earned through academic slogging; four years after his retirement from the front lines, time taken up instead by classroom duty, the pleasure of a college atmosphere has not lost its impetus. Spending time, legitimately, among the young spared him from being mothballed, resuscitating his life in other ways.

He counts himself lucky.

Although he's the oldest in the room at the moment, in his mind he's not old, a hale fifty-four, his next birthday pending in the oncoming month of June. From the age of fifteen he's been more broad across the middle than the chest, yet he won't call himself overweight, either. He admits to being pear-shaped in a vaguely feminine way. Early in life, a receding hairline marked his appearance without ever proving extensive. Five feet nine, Toomey does not feel tall, yet hates to think of himself as average. He's never known how to quantify himself. Not receiving the image in a mirror he'd hoped for as an adolescent, he chose a frumpiness of attire and augmented that with a grumpiness of disposition, an odd compensation. He then sloughed that off in his fifties when he hit upon the realization that women his age weren't looking for the same attributes they were avid about in their twenties. As a consequence, he might be able to compete now. Among other improvements, his bachelorhood stands out as a plus these days rather than being a stigma, or at least a detail that provokes suspicion. Currently, his dress and demeanor strike others as more mid-management in style than professorial, not in the least spy-like, and certainly Toomey is more attentive to his haberdashery than when his sole purpose in putting on clothes, in grooming himself, was to go unnoticed. Living undercover, perpetually in the shadows, he developed good technique and the persona to pass through the world with apparent invisibility. Freed from that rigor and having discovered a desire to do so, he's been nurturing a personal, yet salient, élan. He calls it conservative, not wanting to come across as some idiotic aging man desperate to rediscover his youth—privately, he concedes that that is exactly how he ought to be pegged—but conservative, with a touch, *a soupçon,* of dash.

I've got dash, he bolstered himself one morning, the thought taking him by surprise, and since that moment he dresses to that sartorial threshold.

Coffee in hand, Toomey sips as he walks out, then gets blasted by the wind and huddles among others beneath a canopy. Everyone is getting wet anyway. With his messenger bag over his head and his cup and a little brown sack in hand he makes a run for the BMW, two cars down. Brutal. Behind the wheel again, he knows he'll dry off. Sips his coffee and breaks apart a chocolate chip muffin. The more difficult foray will be between the parking lot on campus and the building that houses his office. And yet, he finds the storm invigorating. Its nature is treacherous and wild. He has no class to teach, no schedule to maintain, he's free to enjoy it, and Toomey does exactly that.

Everywhere, people scamper about, twenty feet from car to store, or from a bus stop to the shelter of an awning. Any attempt to stay dry is hopeless, and Toomey delights in those students who concede defeat and let the rain soak them to the bone, twirling and dancing in the cascade, flinching, then laughing under the startling flashes of light. Thunder causes the ground they prance upon to tremble.

He must watch out for them, the carefree, and also for those who mindlessly burst into a sprint, as it's difficult to see through the rain and the attention of those caught out is compromised. He wends his way out of Hanover onto a country road. He locates the taillights of a car ahead, a driver does the same behind him, and cautiously the vehicles, at reduced speed, motor through the deluge. Lights on in homes indicate their arrival in Holyoake and Professor Toomey makes it onto the campus safely. He continues to be circumspect driving down a side of the green—a smaller replica of the famous one in Hanover—and on to his parking spot behind the initial threshold of buildings. Toomey notices in his rearview mirror the arrival of police cars behind him, their lights flashing, and he's tempted for a moment to pull over in case they're following him for some picayune infraction. Yet they veer off, he carries on, and in the rear parking lot he sits in the car a while, chewing more of his muffin and mulling his twin choices—stay or run—hoping for a letup, which the voices over the car radio have reiterated will not happen anytime soon. The announcer, a sober one now, might as well be speaking to him directly, "Professor, man up, get out of the car, get wet, you will survive."

Such a voice never does address him, but that's the advice he follows.

He's running. Out the corner of his eye he's struck once again by the beauty of the campus. Classic Ivy League, or, in this case, imitation Ivy League, and wouldn't it be grand to reincarnate as a student here? As he puddle-hops his way to a back door and into his building, Toomey reminds himself that teaching here isn't half bad either, and in this lifetime, too, even if his credentials are sketchy.

Inside, he creates a pond where he shakes the water off.

Philip Toomey's office is cramped, a typical professor's digs. A studied look, given that the hundreds of books on the shelves have gone largely unread. A select few have been scoured multiple times. He will not bother with the rest. He also possesses bound documents up the wazoo, inscribed in officialese. A few of these he's authored himself. Bundles of papers and more piles of books limit his view of the Green, although on sunny days the tall windows admit a dusty glow. Today, the glass is smeared with condensation, he feels he's inside a fishbowl. Putting his cup and messenger bag down, he removes his trench coat and uses the inner fabric to dry his face and fluff his hair, then sits, finishes the coffee, and ditches the paper cup into a waste bin that holds debris from the last three days, to be emptied overnight eventually. He swivels in his seat one way, then the other, and tilts back. Overall, he feels pretty good. He clasps his hands behind his head and revels in his contentment.

He's safe now. He's survived a dangerous life. He's lucky to be alive and luckier still to be in love.

Or lust.

Or lust.

Smiling at the voices in his head, the professor gets cracking on his work.

The untidiness across his desk he keeps under surveillance if not entirely under control. Resting on a stack lies the transcript of an interview a colleague in criminology recently gave to a television station in Boston. On Mother's Day, a week and a half ago, a young man in New Orleans fired a gun into a crowded public space, causing terror and a stampede. The shooter, who luckily, some say miraculously, didn't kill anyone, eluded police officers nearby who were hampered in their pursuit by the dense, panicked crowd. The outraged colleague of Toomey's decried on Boston television "the vegetative lives of a subset of a subset of humanity" that American cities tolerated, who lived, he claimed, without morals or the slightest regard for human life.

His colleague's thesis on what could be done about the matter asserted that the only hope for the nation depended upon superior parenting.

Like that was going to happen anytime soon.

As a spy, even as a former spy, Toomey was nothing if not self-aware. He knew exactly what was going on with himself. He wanted out of the woodwork. When TV required an expert, they should not be dialing his dumb-assed colleague with his theories on subsets and a pundit's desire for better mommy-son relations on Mother's Day, even when the mother was on drugs and the son may never have met her. He wanted to be the one the networks called—the local stations, at least—when things went wrong, to propose the tough and logistical standards necessary whenever young men fired guns into crowds with cops nearby, in some cities with frequency and apparent impunity. Politically difficult, he still wanted to show what could be done, that even in this age of gangs and a reactionary component in society, where there was a will there may yet be a way to make certain that a gun would never rest in the hands of a miscreant at a Mother's Day celebration again. Or, if one showed up, that the carrier of the weapon was incarcerated until both his generation and the next were pensioned off. If the gun was fired, of course, that required a whole other level of response.

His ideas might not work either, nor would they be popular, nor were they fully formed yet, the subject having nothing to do with his field of expertise. At least he'd spare himself listening to subset babble and bad-mommy talk.

Although it's more than that. He is, after all, self-aware.

He has lived as a spy for most of his adult life, and done the shadowy work, that now he wants to be front and center, to have his say in public. That's all there is to it. Out from the dark side of the street, having lived as a shade, he wants to stand in the light, be noticed. While he hoped for a cool posting in the State Department when the time came to step back from the fray, a fun job at a university is proving to be an interesting second choice. The only downside is that his job lacks the exposure that, rather suddenly and surprisingly, especially with his new sense of style, he now craves.

Is it wise to desire public attention? Especially these days, when he's continuing to make a contribution? And when, as it happens, he has a secret lover in her nest? He has to ask the questions and live with being unsure of the answers. He keeps a notebook, composing what he might say if he finds himself free to express his mind while also possessing an appropriate venue—as on local television. Or he might keep his theories to himself as time goes by. Yet this constitutes his first private discourse with himself this morning, before moving on to more substantive matters. "The Role of Police in Crowd Protection," subtitled "The Anticipation of an Incident," awaits him. He might make it a paper, then see that the media receives copies. Or not. For now, he'll scratch a few notes and judge over time how well his ideas are formulating.

Or, he'll flip a coin.

If he does get on TV, he won't speak with a frog in his throat, as did his subset of a subset vegetative colleague. Nor will he look utterly self-conscious as that man did. The Boston station has to be looking for a more viable, more impressive alternative, and Toomey spies an opportunity in the making.

He is able to keep himself both stimulated and occupied with his morning labors, but as the clock ticks around and the rain is incessant against the windows other stirrings emerge. *Oh lust.* Suppressed for so long. He wants to think about that more deeply, it has become a preoccupation, lust. He suspects that love and lust need not be considered mutually exclusive whenever the lust side of the quotient is clearly the more pressing, the more powerful and overwhelming. Love, in comparison, seems little more than an inkling, lurking as a fugitive in the bushes waiting for him to pass by. Maybe holding a knife to his throat. In these matters, he happily acknowledges both his lack of experience—that must be why it's fun!—and his general flailing ineptitude. And yet, for all that, he is enjoying success with his new enterprise.

He's taken lovers before. On occasion his job predicated an involvement with a woman, and once with women in general when he had had to fake a weakness for prostitutes. He's been in what he was willing to call love on three occasions since adolescence—once with an enemy, once with a colleague, and once with a mystery woman whom he had loved but not trusted. In each case, he had been burdened by an inner conjecture, namely that he was insufficiently handsome or adept to be considered a desirable man, that the best he could hope for was a favor granted. True love, or its complement, true passion, would remain but a fable to him, an illusion, decidedly elusive. Time and good fortune might be teaching him otherwise, and the moment arrives on this day to risk the rain again, grab a quick bite, complete his usual Friday errand in the cemetery, then visit Malory.

Toomey packs his bag, stuffing the diary into a side pocket but omitting the book on Chinese industrial development he brought from home which he's concluded is inadequate and now assigns to the ignominy of an office shelf alongside the largely unread. He checks his look in the mirror that hangs on the back of the door. Does he have it today? Oh yes: *dash!* Even in this circumstance, being wet, he's pleased with himself. *Accennn-tuate the positive!* Wide-set brown eyes. Thick, darkly pensive eyebrows. A nose bending straight down from the bridge, suggestively pugilistic. *E-limmm-inate the negative:* a sad-sack mouth that's learning to smile, to show off those pearly whites. What an amazing change to his fortunes. Incredible what a pressed shirt can do for his morale! Who knew? Although the key is the constant company of a girlfriend he's agog for. Toomey grins to the hilt back at himself, and decamps, knowing that he will be passing through a lengthy building for a while before braving the tempest outside.

In his judgment, this is what no one suspects, that in driving onto the campus, a benign daily sojourn, that in working here awhile, and in walking right on through the campus hours later, first for lunch and an errand—his secret exchange—then to his car to depart Holyoake and embark across the river to White River Junction, Vermont, into a shabby neighborhood on the opposite side of the Connecticut River, he is becoming his own man at long last. He is giving the bum's rush to the false identities of a lifetime and finding his own heart's blood, aware of his own pulse for a change.

The thrill of it is already overwhelming as he steps outside into the teeth of a whole gale. Thunder sucks the air right out of him, vibrating the ground he's running on, the earth he's slipping and sliding on.

SIX

They drive onto the Dowbiggin campus in Émile's white Cadillac Escalade, a gift in lieu of payment from a case he solved close to a year ago. Given the drama of a report that the library is being evacuated, he expects a crowd. Classes, though, are not in session, and foul weather has tempted neither students nor faculty to stroll on over. For those who have left the building, lingering outside under the relentlessly pelting rain does not appeal when nothing is to be gleaned.

Police vehicles continue to arrive. The former detective judges that the situation is dire given their numbers and the fact that both Hanover and New Hampshire state police are involved. Holyoake's department is restricted to a single officer, and he's probably here, too, although he operates under the aegis of the Hanover Police Department. Émile cannot say with conviction that a black sedan is FBI. He has a hunch it might be. He pulls in where parking is normally not permitted, close to the police perimeter, and asserts a certain official authority.

He hands his keys to Caroline.

"My chances of gaining access are remote. I'll need to bluff my way through."

"I'm coming with you."

"That reduces our chances exponentially."

"Excuse me? I need to get in," Caroline insists.

"Actually," he points out, "you don't. Being upset only reinforces that. I'm not legally parked. If someone wants you to move, say you're with the police. Tell them your uncle's an off-duty cop who's inside. If that's not good enough, drive off and I'll call you later for a pickup."

Reluctantly, she agrees. At least they're about to do *something*, which is as much as she can expect.

Émile tugs on a ball cap, climbs out and slams the door behind him. His waist-length jacket is considered rain resistant, not water-proof, which in this torrent means next to useless. He does a quick trot through the blinding sheets to where an officer stands guard, uncomfortably.

"Sir?" the young man in uniform challenges. He must yell as the rain smacking the pavement is loud. Draped in clear plastic, his cap funnels water onto Émile's ankles and shoes.

"I'm a homicide detective!" Émile Cinq-Mars shouts back.

"Sir? Who with?"

Bluff number one, tripped up out of the gate.

"Retired!" Cinq-Mars admits.

"I can't admit you, sir."

"I thought I might lend my expertise! Probably I've covered more homicides than all these men combined!"

"Who with, sir?" the cop asks again. He's a good man, Cinq-Mars can tell. He'd welcome him on his own team, if he still had a team. He'd have to teach him, though, not to be tricked. Unofficially, the young cop may have confirmed, without being aware of it, that the investigation concerns a homicide.

"I'm from Montreal! Quebec!" loudly, the former detective declares. He knows how well that's going to go over anywhere in the United States. In his experience, the smaller the town, the less an impression such a comment will make. He adds, rather helplessly, "Canada!"

He can tell that the uniform is straining not to laugh.

"Okay, sir," the guy manages to shout back instead of chuckling, "you'll have to leave. I saw where you parked. You need to move your vehicle, sir. You understand." He's able to get his point across without straining his vocal cords.

Émile tries that, to be loud without shouting at the top of his lungs. "Unfortunately, I do. Who's in charge?" he demands to know. The lowest rank on the scene isn't going to break the rules for him, especially when a car pulls in, unmarked, and the bearing of the man in the passenger seat catches their attention. "Him?"

"Hanover chief of police," the officer admits. "Sir, you should get out of this weather. I would if I could. Our officers and the state troopers have the situation under control."

"FBI? Are they here?"

"Sir. Please."

Émile reads the information off the badge on the patrol officer's campaign-style hat. He's with the town's police department, and will do everything by the book with his boss on the scene. Émile gives the man a nod and heads across the front steps to intercept the police chief rushing into the building. Whether the man is intent on hurrying to the scene of a major crime or merely wants out of the rain is impossible to determine. Most likely both. With his eyes protected by the brim of his Smoky the Bear, the man nearly bumps into him, then looks up, startled.

"Chief," Cinq-Mars says, interrupting his sprint. The man's rank is declared on his blue hat. Uncommon for municipal police, the hats are the Hanover department's choice.

"Who're you?" A bark of a voice. Despite that, he projects a pleasant, avuncular look, as though to indicate that his bark is worse than his bite, or that he doesn't have much of a bark, either. He's white, about fifty, and his eyes squint as he tries to bring another person into focus through the rain.

"Sir, I'm a retired homicide detective from Montreal." Émile hedges on that point. While he's solved a significant number of murders in his day, much to the chagrin of homicide detectives, he was never a member of their department. He doesn't need to explain that here, his standing flimsy enough as it is.

"Congratulations," the man remarks. If not actually dripping with sarcasm, the officer is not above avoiding the attitude. "On your retirement, I mean. I'm happy for you. Sorry, no time to chat."

"May I go inside with you?"

"Actually, no. You can't."

"I may be able to lend a hand."

"You're not getting the message here, are you? How do you want me to say this? I know a few different ways. Let me think now. No, just two different ways. One you heard. Should I say the other one?"

"Seriously, I might be useful inside."

"Why's that?" The policeman is brushing past him, not waiting for an answer. Cinq-Mars matches his gait. Being a tall man, his stride easily keeps pace with the chief's, and he takes two steps at a time.

"It's my area of expertise, that's true, sir. That's not all. There's something you need to know."

"What's that?" The chief stops. He means to prevent Cinq-Mars from taking a step closer to the front door.

"I'm here because my niece's girlfriend is missing. She's a student at Dowbiggin, she's been gone all night. If you need to make a positive identification, if it's the missing friend—I pray it's not—then I can help with that."

The Hanover police chief grants Cinq-Mars a closer examination through the downpour. "First off, who said anything about a homicide?"

"Nobody but me. Word is going around about a body. We both know that college students don't fall down stairs and die as a general rule. If one did, that would be tragic. I'm not sure the event would attract this many marked and unmarked vehicles. Unless you do things differently down here."

"I'm sure we do things differently down here. Who said anything about needing an ID?" His eyes wander over to the duty officer as if it was him.

"Absolutely no one, sir. Unless you just did? Does the dead girl not have ID? I last saw the missing girl two days ago. Her image is very fresh in my mind. Also, look, I've got a few desperate kids that I need to help out. They're frantic that the dead girl and their missing friend might be one and the same. Let me find that out, for their sake. They're counting on me. Frankly, I'm hoping that I can't help you, that it's somebody else in there, but if we can spare my niece and her friends a whole lot of worry and upset, then why not? That helps us look for the missing girl elsewhere, you get to cross her off a list. On the other side of the ledger, if you need an ID on your victim and I happen to provide it, doesn't that put you one step ahead of the game that much sooner?"

Cinq-Mars knows that if he was on the job and presented with a similar rant by a guy he didn't know, he'd be suspicious enough to keep him around if for no other reason than to check him out. He would also eye him closely, up and down, as if placing him under a mental microscope to find out how he thrives under the scrutiny, exactly as this cop is doing right now. If he was the guardian at the gate, he'd then ask for his ID and let him through while keeping his suspicions handy. Long experience, however, has taught him that the next logical step for a cop to take is not necessarily what comes down the pike, at least not nearly as often as anyone might hope, expect, or prefer.

He waits with patience and suffers the man's keen gaze.

"All right," the chief concedes at last. "Let's get out of the rain. Inside, you can show me your ID."

Good man. "Thanks."

"Whatever." He's keeping his suspicions on hold, too. Good cop.

They go through the proud library doors, opened for them by campus security. Once inside, the foyer doesn't draw attention to itself. The beauty of the interior, the woodwork, the windows, the eloquence of the ceiling and the charm of the space is hinted at along the periphery.

The height of the ceiling inflicts the hushed tones of a library on him.

The chief of police is signaling with one finger for a plainclothes detective to come over and, after Émile extracts his ID from his wallet, has him check out his story. He reads the name aloud to the other officer, "Émile Cinq-Mars, is that how you pronounce it?" He doesn't wait for an answer, spelling the name out as the other cop nods. Then the chief remarks, "It's familiar. Tell you what. Google him on that fancy phone of yours. Show me what comes up." While his underling checks him out, he flips through Émile's various ID cards, which confirms that he's a retired detective.

"If you're here for commencement, you're early."

"I don't recall saying that. It's true, I'm here for commencement. I'm here early because my wife is from the area. Her mother's dying. Not long to go."

The man seems suddenly quiet. "Sorry to hear that," he says eventually, an odd delay. A thought seems to have occurred to him and caused a change of attitude. He hands the wallet back. "Where'd you say you were staying?"

He hadn't mentioned it, of course. Cinq-Mars detects that the question only sounds casual. It's intended to suss him out. "I didn't. I've been put up at my mother-in-law's house. She lives on a horse farm. Or did. She won't be coming home, we're told."

"I know who that sounds like," the sheriff reveals.

"Who?"

"Why don't you tell me?"

"Mary Lowndes."

The chief checks him with a glance again. He's gone up in stature. The man knows the name.

Émile elevates several more notches when the officer's detective shows him what's come up on the screen of his smartphone. He probably didn't expect that Émile's fame is known on the Internet. What's online is as much myth as reality, but there it is, the dismemberment of the Hells Angels, the scorched-earth policy with respect to the Mafia, a legendary detective busting the bad guys.

"You've got a rep," the cop confirms, flipping through screen pages with his thumb, then hands the phone back to his officer. "Look at that. A handsome guy when you were younger."

"Always with the nose, though."

"Can't be hid."

"People tell me they never notice."

"People lie," the chief deadpans.

"Most do," Cinq-Mars concurs. While he made peace with his impressive honker eons ago, it's an adjustment for others in his presence. He doesn't mind helping them along.

"Let's go see what trouble has come to our sweet town," the chief suggests. "I can warn you that it's tragic news." Although he's warning up to him, Cinq-Mars finds himself suspicious of that. Perhaps it's a dose of fame causing folks to treat him differently, yet he senses that in this instance something else is going on. He's puzzled by this cop.

They walk at a clip through the library. Cinq-Mars wishes he could muffle their footsteps. Their wet shoes squeak as they go.

"Who's here?" Cinq-Mars asks. "State troopers. FBI. Anybody else?"

The cop gives him a look. "Why would FBI be here?"

"I saw a car. It had that FBI look."

"One of ours, maybe," the chief tells him. "We try to look good." Then he holds out his hand. "My apologies. Bad manners. Alex Till."

"Pleased to meet you, Chief."

"With all due respect to your record, this will be in and out. Give us an ID if you can, then go. You understand. As it is, I'll be jammed up with state troopers."

"Whose jurisdiction is this?"

"Starts with me. Some will say it's too big for my department. Let alone for my britches. State will take over."

"Who decides?"

"The governor. I'm all out of influence in his office. Never had much to begin with. Troopers stake a claim to influence. Point of fact, they own this governor."

"If I see anything, I'll take it to you. Let you know."

"What do you mean, see anything?"

"I'm not putting anybody down. At times I catch a detail, that's all. I've worked a lot of scenes."

"All due respect, Émile—may I call you Émile?"

"Please."

"All due respect, don't meddle."

He might as well ask him not to look both ways when crossing a street. It can be done, but why live like that?

As they walk through a gauntlet then upstairs, the chief refers to everyone by name, including a few members of the library staff who've been asked to stay behind. They ascend in an elevator, then pass through a gate in a grille. *A fence,* Cinq-Mars is thinking, *indoors.* They enter through a doorway at the base of the clock tower. Amid the hubbub of officers, they see, lying on the stairs as though posing for a fashion shoot, with flower petals littered across her body, a deceased young woman. The one he was hoping not to find. The ramifications will stagger his household, as he has the worst news to report.

"Well?" Chief Till inquires.

Cinq-Mars nods. "Think so," he says, a lie. He knows so. "May I take a closer look?"

"You think you have a name?"

"Ninety percent. Can I step up? People keep blocking my view."

"Yeah. Sure. Coming through!" he calls out. "Let us through, I may have an ID here."

The comment clears a path and other officers and a forensics crew step clear to give Émile access. He squats down. He knows whom he's looking at, but seeks to maintain as accurate a visual memory of the scene as possible. He takes his time. He studies the girl's form, her dress which is totally out of place, the sash, the ribbon in her hair, the exacting makeup, the ligature marks on her throat, the substantial necklace, the lipstick shade, the absence of life in her eyes, a kind of calling card betwixt her fingers. He's accustomed to being in the company of the dead. Nonetheless, if he stares at this young woman for very long it'll break his heart.

"Detective Cinq-Mars?" Till asks him. Everyone knows that he's had more than enough time to positively identify the victim.

He stands. "Her name is Addie. I believe that's short for Adele. Her last name is Langford. My niece can tell you more. I understand that she's from Michigan. She's to graduate this year."

Giving her a name and a background sketch causes the professionals to take a moment of commemoration. All that promise and intelligence and beauty, gone.

"Thanks," Chief Till remarks. "Sorry about this."

"My niece is outside. In my car. You may want to talk to her. Let me break the news first. Give her a minute to adjust. As best she can, that is. This will be a shock."

"Sure, Émile. We do have to talk to her, of course. Let me give the troopers a heads-up. We'll take it from here. They'll want to talk to her the same time I do, I expect."

"Go easy," Émile whispers, with intensity. He knows that he'll have no influence on how they conduct themselves. He's assuming that the sadness that now pervades the room, which will soon extend across the campus and include the town, will govern how the first interviews are to be conducted.

Before he departs, Émile takes one last look at the room, and at the deceased young woman. The most striking element is her pose. He can't believe that her wardrobe or her positioning is accidental. This is what he's expected to see, and he tries to look past the elaborate presentation. This has been planned, suggesting a manic-compulsive at work. Criminals who are like that—being tight, controlled, and meticulous in their planning and execution—can be difficult to shake loose. None of which is welcome news. Killers like this one are rare and that will enhance the difficulties for investigators. The young woman's regular clothes have been disposed of, something Till will want to study. If he doesn't think to ask what she was wearing before being dressed up in a costume, he'll make sure he does.

He wonders what's on that calling card.

Till is gone awhile, receiving and vetting information. When he returns, Cinq-Mars inquires, "Strangulation?"

"Looks like."

"Rape?" he requests under his breath. He almost doesn't want to know.

"To be determined. Except for the bruising on her throat, she looks untouched. Unblemished, although nobody's lifted her dress yet."

"Hmm," Cinq-Mars grunts. Had his wife been present, she'd identify his utterance as a distinctive note of contention.

Apparently, the chief also holds to a dissenting view. "That'll likely fall apart, of course. She's been dolled up. Ever hear of a rapist-killer who dresses his victim to the nines and tidies her up *after the fact* then puts her on display?"

"Can't say I have," Cinq-Mars admits.

"Think again, sir," Till relates. "You have now."

SEVEN

Her jet-blackness, Professor Philip Toomey ruminates, and her brains, causes the experience to feel strange and simultaneously wonderful. A substantial body, that's another aspect that he can't explain. Powerful, round, inexplicably firm and soft at the same moment. She stands an inch taller than him and is equally heavy, and her shape, her dimensions were never previously inside his mental docket, which makes the whole of the experience flat-out surprising. Initially, anyway. As well, the woman is so tough-world, backstreet smart, which is new to him, and he loves that part, too. And yet, somewhat to his consternation, the real surprise is the sheer blackness of her, for him an otherworldliness where his senses get lost. Not only lost in her, lost in this otherworldliness, beginning with the neighborhood, the stark faces, the veneer of suffering, the subset of a subset of a vegetative misery and lament, and he wants to kill his colleague for those profane remarks and imagines that particular murder as a warm act of love, of contrition, of expiation and personal forgiveness, a debt paid, a bounty collected, although even his warm murderous latent intent is inexplicable and confounding. Not that it matters. He isn't going to kill anybody. Not when the fleshy heat of her is upon him and he smothers himself in her folds and rhythms, slathers her, moistures her slick perspirations, and feels himself lifted and slammed down again by her whimsy, her own courtship of him both unfathomable and wholly redeeming. Somehow. Some way. She doesn't meet smart men in her world as an equal, and he supposes that that is the reverse attraction for her. She gets it on with him mentally. Walking through the rain he feels the tug in his trousers and the bulge in his heart and lungs, as if it's *her* blood now that's pumping through his veins, about to deliver him to an inexplicable and brazen sense of himself.

A joyous self. He's impudent now. Different.

Joy is both ruthless and awkward in his life. A midnight strangler with a chokehold on him now.

As always, Professor Toomey delays. A familiar digression given his long-term marriage to routine.

First, he needs to complete a morning chore.

He carries a sandwich with him. Chicken, one he's roasted himself, with a celery-nut mixture. A small can of V8 for starters, as a nod to good health, then he scatters his best intentions with a Diet Coke to quaff it all down. The former came from home and is warm although he doesn't mind, the latter cool, plucked from a vending machine on his way out. He eludes the rain under a porch overhang and while it isn't anywhere near noon proceeds to consume his meal.

Nourishment and energy for the rambunctious task ahead.

Then the sprint to his Bimmer.

Toomey drives through the avenues that wind between the school and the Connecticut River before parking along a road in a favored spot. He's out in the rain again getting soaked along a wooded hiking trail, then reverses direction onto a modest civic lane to the cemetery. He looks around once he's through the gates, as if for a gravestone, as if he's here to pay his respects, all of which is both subterfuge and old habit. An exercise that's futile today. The grounds and trails are usually well traveled with lovers and baby strollers, with loners and groups of students taking the air. Not a single soul today, not under this endless cloudburst, not even a manic jogger. A lightning flash startles him, and moments later a thunderclap is deafening. He's in an alcove of trees, dangerous turf in these conditions, and prefers not to linger. The former spy strides past a young tree that an accident of nature has shaped to resemble a snake charmer's viper rising to a flute's hypnotic tune, at least in his imagination, and three trees along is the shaggy-bark hickory. Again he glances around but this time makes it look as though he's dropped something. Mere ploy. Futile, still. Even if he's not alone, no one will be able to discern his movements through the sheets of rain.

He's so wet he could swim home.

Another lightning strike makes him bounce.

Drenched, he's reminded of slippery sexual contortions that will go on all afternoon. Toomey slides a page from the inside of his coat pocket that will mean nothing to anyone save for a rare few. Innocuous drivel, essentially, but imbedded in the text are a few lines that count, the critical, coded thoughts he means to communicate, primarily to see if his correspondent can work through the code. Leaning over to afford the paper protection from the rain, he folds it in half. Priority green. In half again. Priority blue. Then to a quarter its initial size. Priority red. He surreptitiously guides the folded page through a gap of the shaggy bark that gives the tree its name and into a plastic pouch that's wholly sheltered from the elements, then reaches higher and extracts a similar sheet in the same slick motion. The deft moves are tempered in such a way that anyone observing him with only a casual interest will be unlikely to perceive that he has exchanged papers with a tree trunk. The casual observer will see only that he leaned against the trunk briefly while with his free hand he scratched an itch at the back of his thigh. He then returns to the lane, then a walking trail again, and picks up the pace back to his car. He drops the new communication into an outer pocket of his bag on the passenger seat, and proceeds toward his rendezvous with love.

Or, as goes the general drift to his thinking today, with lust. His hair is flattened, his toes feel squishy in his leaking shoes, while his heart joyfully thumps with the anticipation of his pending carnal privilege.

Toomey drives off campus then out of Holyoake. Once on the freeway his speed never climbs above thirty-five miles an hour. Even at that rate, as he passes a pair of transport trucks the backsplash from their wheels is blinding. After that he stays a safe distance behind a big pickup—close enough to glimpse its taillights, far enough back that the torrent coming off its wheels doesn't add to the deluge from the skies. As he crosses the bridge over the Connecticut River, traffic slows to a crawl into Vermont on the other side.

All anybody wants is to get off the highway.

The route into White River Junction is circuitous and not remotely intuitive. Toomey knows it well and anticipates each freeway turn and circle despite the diminished visibility. A good thing on a day like today. The darkness is shocking for the hour, then lightning reflects off a rock outcropping for an instant and the sudden brightness is disorienting. Once he's heading downhill from the outlying industrial district of hotels, diners, and gas stations into the old town, he knows he'll be all right. The town's heyday lies in its distant past, when the railroad ruled and the forest and mill industries flourished. That's no longer the case, and being situated off the highways keeps the old town depressed and showing its age.

Which helps project an indigent charm.

He sails on by the Calvin Coolidge Hotel, which has been modestly spruced up through time, although the establishment next door projects a large, simple sign to entice a portion of the proud hotel's clientele—ROOM WITH BATH—as though rooms without baths might still persist in the modern age. An arrow points to the entrance up the block. If travelers harbor further qualms as to the quality of the digs, a second large sign at the building's opposite end reassures the doubtful by announcing the availability of both cold *and* hot water. Right with the times.

Across the railway tracks, homes display their poverty, and on the edge of this neighborhood, Professor Toomey parks his BMW. It's not that he doesn't want his car to be left on the sketchy streets—it's no safer where it is—he doesn't want anyone to know his precise whereabouts at this time of day. Even in walking to Malory's place, he will follow a route similar to a figure-eight highway ramp. Any man intent on following him might suddenly discover him at his back.

Toomey makes a point to never exit the car promptly, in case others are on his tail. Routine technique, and the baseline of spy craft is to be obsessed with technique. Situated in the car, he's secretly a keen observer of his surroundings, although visibility is highly restricted today. All the more reason to go slow.

Killing time, he checks the note extracted from the hickory's bark.

Folded to a quarter its size: *priority red*.

Interesting.

He unfolds the paper, reads, and the whole of his body goes still. He feels himself thrust back into another time and place, when danger lurked in the very air he breathed.

Typed, an imperative:

Breached
Run!

Only that. He sits there, stunned a moment, constantly rereading. The words never change no matter how often he scans them.

Breached

Written without a period, as though in haste.

Run!

Emphasized by an adolescent exclamation mark.

Despite the command, Toomey does not know what to do. Run? He can't run. And why? He has to know why first. He's not involved in anything serious enough to warrant this edict. Or is that not true? He thinks about starting up the car again and going straight back to the hickory tree, retrieving the note he'd left, substituting another, and asking questions. But no, if there is a problem at his confederate's end, even if it's a mistake, their drop might be compromised.

Run! What does anyone mean by that?

Where to? How far? From what?

He looks up. The neighborhood waits in its familiar disposition, only wet. Normally, he might see kids on bicycles. The infirm whiling away their time on a stone fence, yapping, are a common sight, too. He'd expect a few cars to come and go, though not today. Everything looks the same and yet everything is different and that difference is accentuated by the darkness of midday and by the rhythmic thump of his heartbeat. And by this new urgency. *Run!* He's been in tight spots before, but doesn't know if this constitutes a tight spot. Likely, the message is merely an overreaction. A misunderstanding. What he has to do now is precisely not run. Running is nothing but careless and possibly dangerous and against his better instincts not to mention against his training, experience, and expertise. He's probably been alerted by an inexperienced young man in a panic. If this is a game, it's a facile test. If it's something ominous, the author of the message is probably overwrought. No. He'll not run. He'll carry on with his day. Obliterate himself in Malory's passionate mournful intensity and emerge with the reminder that he is now merely a professor, a quiet academic, he is no longer risking his life out in the field. He's fled that world and is living in comfort beyond the range of enemy fire. His correspondent is probably feeling nothing more than the risk of friendly fire. He himself no longer gets mired in such weary internecine battles. Oh, he keeps a hand in, but nothing more. *Breached?* If somebody panics due to a lack of experience or a lapse in judgment, then such a reaction remains to be accessed in the fullness of time. As for himself, he's off to make love to his woman. Nothing more matters right now.

Run? Hardly.

In his favor, when he climbs out of the car again, the rain is merely steady, nothing severe.

Walking, his habit is to constantly create confusion by making his movements obscure and unpredictable, even if, ultimately, they're routine. A learned discipline, one he maintains to keep his skills up.

He's had reason to maintain his foray as secret.

For some, that he's white and she's black is a barrier for them to be accepted as a couple, even in this day and age, although it goes beyond that. She is black and poor, while he is white and prosperous, which for many makes it less acceptable. Moreover, he is white, prosperous, and a professor at Dowbiggin, while she is black, poor, and a member of the custodial staff at the same institution. She cleans toilets and waxes floors. He's as clean as a whistle while she smokes dope. He hobnobs with political, corporate, and academic elites while she hangs with the few blacks in the region, who happen to be older jazz musicians who suffer from serious arthritis. Society's acceptance of them as a couple in small-town New England—*northern* New England, in white New Hampshire—is questionable, and surely it'll be trouble, possibly nasty trouble, at school.

Yet, doesn't that make it all the more fun? All the more, in a way, miraculous? The adventure is grand.

He mulls over the note as he walks his twisty route. What was meant by *breached*? By *run*? The words were generated by a computer's printer. The author, then, was not in such a mad scramble that he resorted to a quick handwritten scribble. But no. *Think!* Computer-generated means that the handwriting can never be traced, that this tip, if that's what it is, once delivered, remains anonymous forever. That's why it's not handwritten—but why no further information? Because nothing more is known? Only that something has been breached—their method of communication, perhaps, in the cemetery? Or something more sinister? For his correspondent, the initial reaction is flight. And to command that he run himself when, usually, running is the worst possible strategy. He will not until he knows more, or until someone gives him valid reason.

Or scares him into it.

That hasn't happened yet.

Toomey intentionally heads the wrong way to circle around. Shrinking concentric rings. He keeps up a sweat-popping pace in the ridiculously humid air. The current street has a rare attribute for the area as it's one-way to traffic, an advantage for the moment. Drivers are less observant of people when passing them from behind, and in the rain he's not invisible but he's virtually unidentifiable. No one who bothers to take note of him will be able to validate a description later.

He usually takes this much care every time he crosses the river for sex. Part of the excitement, perhaps. Certainly, part of the game.

Finally, he's close to Malory's flat.

The exterior is an eyesore with peeling, cracked blue paint. The walls of the house look scabby and shorn. Around the downstairs porch stands an intricate, rusting wrought-iron filigree, which speaks to a time when the modest home possessed a notion of flair. Other homes on the block exhibit a higher level of attention, although the tiny one next door is a tossed salad of yellow and orange, green and various reds. Malory's resembles a shipwreck cast upon a derelict shore. As a tenant, she lives upstairs. The window high above her entrance is shaded by an awning, the fabric disintegrating from sunlight although presently it admits the rain. An edge of the screen on the exterior door is curling, flies slip inside on warm sunny days, while the inner is patched, discolored, and dog-clawed ages ago. Toomey doesn't bother to ring. What's the point? He knows she's home, ready to admit him. He can count on her to be waiting for him.

In a pose, perhaps, to solicit love.

This constitutes the major change in his life, that suddenly he can depend on what he cannot fathom. A woman's love for him.

Or lust.

He goes up the shabby dark stairs and through the top door to find the woman he adores lying on the living room sofa. She's been shot through the head, and that's not the first horror he sees.

EIGHT

Before Émile Cinq-Mars reaches his car with a pair of detectives on his heels, Caroline, his niece, has assumed the worst. Why would these men be racing over to talk to her if not to inquire after her friend? Émile expects her to stay in the vehicle, instead she staggers through the rain toward him, saying, "No, Uncle Émile. No." She wants to punch him, to beat his chest, to combat whatever he has to say. They clasp each other and that's when she knows for sure, without a word being spoken, that one of her dear friends is dead.

"Let's go inside," Cinq-Mars suggests while remaining in her tight embrace. They come apart awkwardly, and Caroline clutches her belly.

"No," she recites. "Uncle Émile? It can't be. Not Addie. No."

The two policemen come up, and Émile keeps an arm around her as they guide them both back toward the library entrance.

"We'll sit a while, okay, then these two gentlemen will jot down some information. You'll have to be strong now, sweetie. This won't be easy."

"I can't believe it. I can't believe this is happening. Why Addie?"

"These men will try to find that out."

"Did she fall?"

"No, sweetie. She didn't fall."

"Can I see her?"

"Absolutely not. Even if one of these men suggests it, you are not to see her. Do you understand? You are not to see her."

She may or may not understand, but Caroline nods in agreement. If he can, she wants her uncle to help her through this, and she wants a sudden, twisting hurt to go away. She clutches herself suddenly, and appears to suffer a spasm that strikes along her stomach and lungs. Caroline gasps. Émile holds her more tightly, and the police chief, in sympathy to her shock and torment, speeds up his gait to get ahead and hold open the door.

Inside, they seat themselves on a bench away from anyone else, a place where students commonly converse. The other officer with them, a state trooper, fetches water in a pointy paper cup. Émile pleads for time. Caroline accepts that idea at first, only to argue against it a minute later. She downs the water in a single gulp. "Let them ask questions." She insists on it, and Émile inquires if he can stay. As a family member. As a former cop. The two officers consent to that.

The trooper qualifies, "For the time being."

The first questions are the right ones, easing the witness into talking freely and easily. What is Caroline's full name and where is she from, where does she go to school? A stupid question in this instance, but necessary. Confirm the basics. Where is Addie from? How long has she known her? When did she last see her? What was she wearing?

"She's always in jeans."

The chief asks if she owns a white dress.

"Dress?" Caroline responds, curiously. "What kind of white dress?"

The cop does his best to describe it.

Caroline is puzzled. "She doesn't own anything like that. If she did, she didn't have any reason to wear it. Not that I know of. Not last night."

"Did she wear nylons?"

"What do you mean nylons? You mean pantyhose? Sure, she wears pantyhose."

The trooper keeps his voice gentle. "I mean hosiery. Nylons, you know, with a garter belt and like that."

Rather than answer, Caroline asks Émile, "Are you sure the girl is Addie?"

"I can show you a picture," Chief Till lets her know.

"Okay," Caroline agrees over Émile's protests.

"I rather you didn't."

The trooper intervenes. "Why not?"

"I don't want it to be her last memory of her friend."

The men understand, although that's not a concern for them. Caroline thinks it over, decides that this is important, and assures her uncle that she'll be okay. He suspects that she won't be, but Caro has always had a mind of her own. As she should have. Chief Till shows her the headshot on a tablet of the young dead woman.

As Émile anticipated, Caroline crumbles and shakes, and starts to cry.

They give her a few minutes. At the very least, with nothing being said, identification has been doubly confirmed. Then Caroline surprises them. "She didn't wear her hair like that. That's not her makeup. She doesn't have that shade of lipstick, unless it's a bad picture. What's that around her neck?"

The three men each take turns looking at the tablet again, with Émile being the last one to see it. He and Till communicate with a silent nod, and he passes it back to Caroline. "What do you mean?" Till probes. "What about the necklace?"

The young woman studies the photo more carefully this time, less emotionally, then reiterates, "It's not hers. Me and Addie share everything. That necklace isn't hers. She has a thing about jewelry anyway. She doesn't approve."

"Approve? How do you mean?"

"She thinks it's wrong. Morally. Occasionally, okay, she'll put something on, ordinary colored glass or carved wood, but nothing like this. I don't know what the gemstones are, but diamonds? Addie would never wear diamonds or anything that might look like diamonds. Not even if she knew for a fact that none of them were blood diamonds. She used to ask: How can anybody know for sure? She'd say: Nobody should wear diamonds even if they're fake because that's like free advertising. People will desire them and that makes blood diamonds more common. Which makes us all culpable. Those are *her* arguments. She'd never put that necklace on."

Caroline is left alone for a minute. The three men consult. Émile is introduced to the state trooper, whose name is Hammond. While he and the town cop appreciate that he's given them a head start on a few things, now they want him gone. Hammond does, anyway.

"Sir, you've helped us out. Thanks. You've been on the job in the past. We respect that. We do. There's a point where we keep this in-house."

"You're saying that you've reached that point."

"We have, yes."

"Actually, you haven't."

"Excuse me?"

Émile gives him a penetrating look down the ski slope of his impressive schnoz. "I'll step aside—in a moment. I knew the dead girl, therefore I know a few questions that need to be asked right away. After that, I promise to be good. I'll take a hike."

Making eye contact, the chief and the trooper arrive at an agreement.

"You'll be brief?" the trooper asks, but it's not a question.

The three return to Caroline's side and sit with her. She seems more relaxed when it's her uncle who poses the next query.

"You mentioned this morning that your friend Addie could be, let's say, impetuous when it came to boys."

"Sure. She loses her head over a new guy. Happens quite often. She seems to only—" Caroline hesitates as her lips quiver. Suddenly she's reminded that her friend will never be in love again. They'll never laugh about that again, and she won't wind up weeping over a catastrophic breakup again, either. Coming out of it, Caroline casts her eyes about, not looking at any of the three, as if she's contemplating a quick exit.

The trooper nods to Cinq-Mars, and the two of them walk off a short distance together.

"Good question," the officer compliments him. "We've got this. You're her uncle. A family member. As a professional, you know how that can have a bearing on a witness's responses."

Cinq-Mars does know, although he's not inclined to welcome the other man's condescending attitude. "All right. Look, I'm calling my wife. She's sitting with two more of Addie's friends. If you have no objection, I'll pick them up, tell them the news, then bring them over. I presume you'll want to talk to them as well."

"Of course. Thank you for your cooperation."

Looking back over his shoulder, Émile sees Caroline accepting a tissue from Till. She blows her nose, dabs her eyes, then goes on talking. These two are probably right. She's more likely to speak of certain intimacies shared among friends in the company of strangers.

Someone else will ply her with the tricky questions.

He takes out his phone.

He walks farther away, and deeply exhales.

This is not a call he wants to make.

Twenty minutes later Émile Cinq-Mars is leading two teary young women and his wife into the library. Sandra stays with the girls who are met there by Caroline. They're granted a bit of time. Chief Till peels away from State Trooper Hammond to speak privately to Émile.

"Thanks for that. Bringing them over."

"Go easy on the girls, Chief. I'm sure you will. They've never experienced anything like this."

"Can't make any promises. The governor's edict has already come down."

"That was fast."

"I'm to remain an informed party, which means I'll have no more say in this investigation than you will."

"I'm sorry to hear that."

"No skin off your nose," Till points out to him.

"Instinct," Cinq-Mars tells him. "You give me confidence I don't feel in Trooper Hammond."

"You mean you figured out that I'm more likely to cooperate with you." The chief smiles and shrugs. "Maybe that's true, too, but it's not to be. Spilt milk."

"Did my niece impart any deep dark secrets?"

"A few."

Émile's surprised. "Seriously?"

Till shrugs once more. "She told us that the dead girl was also into girls. Once in a while anyway. Crazy about boys. Still, she switched over from time to time. I think that's what she was shy about saying in front of you."

Cinq-Mars takes that in. At times he's not pleased with his worldly knowledge, which he chooses to share in this instance. "I'm told that very few young women can get a degree in English literature these days without a certain amount of experimentation."

"Where you come from maybe," Till opines.

"Social patterns in Canada tend to follow the American lead, not the other way around. I've heard this has been going on in the Ivy League for a long time, although I don't know who tracks these things."

This time the policeman seems willing to concede ground. "The deceased girl, I just found out, studied international finance. Her major. Not English lit."

"I was making a generalized comment—"

"I know. What she was studying isn't the point. From what your niece said, Addie Langford was crazy about boys. She was open about that and shared the intimate details with her friends. When she had a fling with a girl though, she went into a shell. Slipped into hiding. She didn't emerge until the relationship was no longer current. When she went missing overnight, your niece says that that's what they were secretly worried about, that she'd found a girl, was having a thing, that they might not see her for a week or two. They might not have her attention, or find her in good humor, for that length of time."

"Wrecking their plans for commencement."

"Pretty much. Caroline told us about a recent ex-boyfriend."

"Vernon."

"You know him?"

"*Of* him. We've not met."

"Hammond called the boy. We'll talk to him soon. I mean, the troopers will."

"You're out of the loop, Chief? It is your town."

"Actually, Hanover's my town. I have administrative jurisdiction over Holyoake, as well. Because of that I'm assured of the troopers' total cooperation." The way he says it—deadpan—a listener might not cotton on to the underlying sarcasm. Émile recognizes what's dripping from his hat. This time, it's not outdoor rain.

"Good luck with that," Émile commiserates, and thinks that the two of them are about to part company when he notices that the chief is hesitating.

"What you said before," Till remarks.

Cinq-Mars gives him his full attention.

"Struck me as rude."

Cinq-Mars is flummoxed, then asks, "About female English majors?"

"That was also rude and I'm not going to believe it's true." He gives him a sharp glance, followed by a formal shrug. "I have a daughter who's an English major. We can't afford Dartmouth, no way. She's at Wisconsin. A son at Boston College. Mind you, he's threatening to become a priest. I don't know what scares me more between those two scenarios."

"I've been threatening to become a priest my whole life," Cinq-Mars tacks on, and while Till has no reason to think he's not joking, he takes him at his word.

"Instead, you chose to become a cop. Not sure I like that option, either. Not in the world we live in. Not after a morning like this."

"I hear that," Émile concurs. He knows that the man has something on his mind that might be significant, although he can't fathom what it might be. "When and how was I rude?" he wonders.

"You told me that if you catch a detail, you'll let me know, as if the rest of us are blind, deaf, and dumber than wallboard."

"Yeah," the older detective admits, "that was rude."

"I'm asking now. Since I'm officially the low man on the totem pole, any help is not a hindrance. I'm only asking. You do have more experience at murder scenes than me. More than anyone I know. So. Did you? See anything?"

Émile knows what's going on. The chief of police has been shoved off the case due to the superior political maneuvering of others, and any involvement he's permitted from now on will be nothing more than window dressing. He's looking for any way off the shelf that he can find.

"Actually, Chief, you called it accurately before."

"How's that?"

"A murderer who dresses up his victim after the fact is a rarity. But Caroline pointed out another thing."

"The necklace."

"Exactly. It doesn't belong to the victim. Yet it looks valuable to me. A rapist, a murderer, might be tempted to remove an item of value from a victim. Natural human avarice, let's say, or souvenir collecting. Or a killer might leave something behind because he doesn't want to get caught with it in his possession later. In this case, in addition to the makeup and the clothes, it's possible that the perpetrator placed an object of considerable value around the victim's neck. Who does that? I suggest that doing everything possible to trace that necklace might yield a clue or two. If the necklace has meaning, some secret significance, that also might point to our killer. The value of the necklace suggests that we're looking for a person of means."

Till seems to agree with that, although his body language indicates that he feels stymied. "Like the troopers will give it up to me anytime soon."

"High-quality digital photographs, Chief Till. Why not? While you're at it, e-mail me a set. I'll give you my card."

Eager to rush off and get on to a study of the jewelry, it's all the chief can do to delay another second to receive the card. He clicks it against his forehead in a gesture of thanks, and dashes off.

Émile, then, feels eyes upon him, turns, and spies Sandra in emotional distress. He goes to her and they embrace. They've not had children of their own, coming together a bit late in life for that, and this death of a family member's friend is hitting them as grievous in a personal way.

NINE

Malory, his love, is visible to him, draped across the sofa, a hip and one leg askew. Tangled in her own clothes she looks deformed. She's a bloody mess. A dark stream crossed the warped wood floorboards and pooled close to the professor's shoes where he stands by the door. Dry now. More blood lies splattered across the wall and upon an abstract painting of a sunny meadow.

He despised that painting.

Phil Toomey stands frozen in place. Wretched. Displaced.

In shock.

He's spotted the bullet hole in her head. First he saw the gaping wound that nearly separates her left shoulder from an arm, while other injuries, slices and stabs, mar her torso. He hunts for any special alarm or panic on her face, which is tilted toward him, seeing only that she is dead. Her mouth agape. Nothing to interpret in her gaze, nothing to seize upon as a final communication.

Professor Toomey is suddenly compelled by his own need to breathe, and gulps air. He snaps at the waist. His breath accelerates. He tries to measure each inhale and exhale, calm his heart rate before he hyperventilates.

He needs to believe that the appalling scene before him is real.

He needs to breathe and react. Do something.

She's clothed. At least, the thought strikes him, it wasn't that.

That solitary coherent notion severs his shock and his brain starts clicking again and suddenly he's returned to himself. Not calm but capable of functioning.

In the old days, Toomey was never required to commit an overt act of aggression, let alone a murder. Nor did he ever plan such a thing or cause an event like this to happen on his watch, nor had he been part of any discussion in which any similar deed was contemplated or devised. He never witnessed what people in his office liked to call extreme prejudice. Twice, however, the task of cleaning up a room—once with a corpse still in it—had been assigned to him. He had accomplished his chores with equanimity and dispatch. Even, he had to admit, with vague excitement. The first time, he understood why he'd been asked, he was the only agent handy in a remote theater of operations. The second request made no sense. When, eventually, he was able to confront his bosses, their response was both surprising and an object lesson. One that he committed to memory. From then on, he was careful about which tasks he performed exceptionally well. If given an unsavory chore he'd rather not repeat, he learned to botch it the first time.

Walk no closer. Instinctively, he knows this. He thinks he can make it to her but he mustn't risk blood on his shoes to either trace his steps or identify the pattern on his soles. Suddenly, his body rebels against him, he's on the verge of a scream. He fights to repress the reflex as his nerves recoil and rebound. Gasping, he dry heaves repeatedly and all seems lost.

He needs to grasp control of himself once again, then hang on. He's worked in the shadows but the darkest work was left to others. He passes through another moment when the whole of his being wants only to call out her name, to summon her back among the living, to rock her in his arms again, to be smothered by her embrace. He has to forcibly restrain himself, pin himself to reality, face this, and see exactly what's before him.

See her, but he must not touch her.

Blood's everywhere. Soaked into the floor. This has been atrocious.

From outside, Toomey hears car doors slam shut.

What to do?

Careful to step only on clear spots, he works his way to his right and a window there. He glances outside at the edge of a lace curtain. He almost expects to see this, too. Cops. Guesses that they're cops, anyway. Detectives. They're in no hurry. Should he receive them, with Malory savaged? Allow himself to be found on the scene? Proof of his innocence is indicated by his white spiffy shirt, blood-free, and his clean, pressed pants. No one could possible think that he was involved in the carnage. Not the spiffy professor. On the other hand, the cops are showing up within a minute of his arrival and, as an academic, what is he doing here? Did he need to see her—in her home—about having his desk dusted? Toomey has been a witness to how things work. If he's being set up, cops can easily orchestrate his personal defamation—cause him to appear bloody and bruised in a moment. As it is, his fingerprints and DNA are indelible throughout this apartment. His DNA from a day ago sleeps inside her, if that still counts, he doesn't know, and dried secretions undoubtedly are on the bedsheets and on her clothing and panties and mopped up by Kleenex and tossed in wastebaskets in the bathroom and bedroom and who knows where else.

They've ransacked each other all over this apartment, leaving evidence behind.

Run! The message had warned him to run.

If this is a setup—the early arrival of the cops, if they're cops, suggests that it might be—then he's toast. Even if it's not, he's still easy to frame, a lazy cop's wet dream. What jury in America, white, black, mixed, biased, or fair would sympathize with the rich white professor having it on with a poor black cleaner lady, who is now violated, savaged, and dead?

No one in court will mention how secretly smart she was or think it mattered. What mention can he make of a latent Eros without sounding the fool, or degrading the good opinion of himself that others might hold?

He does not want to leave poor Malory to the devices of the authorities. Not like this. He even has the thought that if she has family he wants to grieve with them. Properly. Publicly. Out of the shadows. And yet, if this is as it seems, a brutal crime of passion and the killer is a former lover or a new jealous one, or if it is a random homicidal-madman incident, a vegetative subset of a subset intrusion, then to stand there and implicate himself will only muddy the investigation and be helpful to no one. Least of all to himself. His fingerprints and DNA are on file, just not in any data bank local police can access. Still, who knows where this will lead, or where it began, or how, or if, he's been implicated. He's free to run and escape scot-free. He's also free to stay and suffer the ignominy of all that.

There's a third option, and how he hates third options. The additional alternative maintains that he's imperiled and caught in a trap. He can neither surrender nor flee without either option being construed differently. He has a note in his pocket that contains a dictum. Pure warning. Which he failed to heed.

Breached
Run!

He didn't follow the advice granted to him and now he's trapped. Don't move, don't speak, don't surrender, don't run, figure it out over the long haul.

He hates third options.

Such is the urgency of the moment that his full deliberations take no more than a hurried second. An eye blink. The police aren't bothering to ring the outside bell. They've opened the door. Maybe they're not cops. Killers? They're mounting the stairs. Phil Toomey steps carefully over the blood and approaches his lover. He still drips rainwater from his clothes. He desires to kiss her, hold her, bring her back to life. Those times that he performed well cleaning up a scene that involved extreme prejudice, he impressed his bosses by merely following his instincts. He does that now. He loves her. Lust is gone, vanished. At the end he understands what defeated him at the beginning. He loves her. He does not recognize what he takes from her. He's never seen it before. As he had removed intimate identifiers previously, in other theaters of operation—rings, a watch, a medical bracelet—he now takes the necklace from around her neck. Change what is. Skew the comprehension of a scene. Cause the exceptional to look mundane, gift the ordinary with intrigue. He removes a shoe of hers as well, and will drop it on his way through the kitchen. A blood-soaked cushion he'll drag down the hall. Hoist a sharp knife from the dripping tray by the sink and stab it into the floor. Figure that one out, coppers. He knows to do this but his motives are also more complex. He wants anything of hers and has no time to look around. The necklace. He hears the slow mounting of stairs. He had a key. They must have picked the lock. What cop does that? Who are they? He will not ever be back here. He removes his key to this apartment from his pocket, rips off a sheet of paper towel, wipes his prints off the key and places it on the radiator. Holding the towel, he takes two plastic apples from the kitchen table's decorative setting. Behind him, the steps have turned on a landing, are almost at the upper door. He strides quickly, silently, to the back exit, lifts the locking latch. He leaves, and while closing the door gently slips the plastic apples back inside, where they would have been knocked aside had anyone gone out that way. He departs by the exterior staircase down to the backyard and the shelter of the pouring rain.

In the time it takes to draw a breath, he's thinking, I'm out of here. I'm gone.

Yet he needs to go somewhere. He needs to weep until his lungs ache and his heart submits to being shattered. He also needs to know: Did he cause this to happen? Is there anything about him, mired in his past or a thing unknown, a breach, a failure to run, that precipitated his beloved's death? If it comes down to that and he has to forgive himself for a personal failing, Professor Phil Toomey has already sworn that he will not.

He runs in a straight line, no deceptive circles this time.

PART 2

TEN

The four women and Émile Cinq-Mars pile into his Escalade. Texts, e-mails, and voice messages exchanged on their mobile devices have convinced the girls that wherever they go they'll be inundated with queries and dramatic reactions. They consent to accompany Sandra and Émile back to the farm, to take a quiet hour or two to permit news of the tragedy to settle, both within themselves and throughout the community.

The girls never did get around to eating a full breakfast, and the police wore them out with repetitive questioning. Even amid their current distress they're ready for lunch. The three sound apologetic for being hungry. For the first time in their lives they've been staggered by a sudden and incomprehensible sorrow, and possess no road map on how to react. A simple need for food feels embarrassing, as if attending to the necessities of life betrays their lost friend. On the drive over they're sullen, and yet, by the time they enter the farmhouse, they've pulled themselves together enough to pitch in. Sandra attempts to thwart their initiative and take on the lunch preparations by herself, only to discover that letting them loose in the kitchen is the best tonic for the younger women. That's fine, except that she discovers herself stuck with time on her hands.

Sandra puts a call through to her sister, Charlotte, Caroline's mother, who's taking her turn at the palliative care center.

She's informed that their aged mom is tired and uncommunicative. The most significant signs of life come from the machines plugged into her. As grim as that report may be she is obliged to trump her sister's sad news. She tells Charlotte about the murder.

"Is she all right?" She means Caroline, although Sandra is sufficiently disoriented on the day to be confused for a few seconds. Charlotte realizes her verbal miscue first, adding, "I mean Caro. How is she? *Where* is she?"

"Right here. She's upset. The girls have endured the shock of their lives."

"Can I speak to her?"

"Of course."

Sandra intuits the result of that conversation. After the hushed tones and an exchange of information, more tears are shed. Caroline can barely believe the news that she's obliged to relay. Listening in from the next room, her aunt is reminded that this is how the process works, that in speaking of what cannot be fathomed, reality finds a way to take hold, to be present. The unbelievable gradually becomes apparent. She's proud of her niece, of how she manages to carry on talking even as tears flood her eyes and she gasps for a breath now and then as the tragedy simmers inside her. She sees for herself the inherent strength of this young woman.

Turning away, Sandra notices that while she was assessing Caroline, Anastasia has been observing her. Perhaps drawing a similar conclusion, perhaps admiring her own inner strength. The two manage a faint smile of encouragement. Sandra's guessing that whatever the girl has on her mind will emerge in due course. For the nonce the student returns to halving cherry tomatoes for the salad.

Off to find Émile, she discovers him standing by the front bay window. Hands in his pockets, staring out at the rain. Not much to see today, other than the havoc of the wind in the trees. Sandra comes up to him and presses against his side, hugging him and pinning both his arms in place.

"Don't say it," Émile cautions.

She's uncertain what he means.

He adds, "I know. I know. I know. One more murder."

"The question that begs an answer," Sandra ponders, with a note of whimsy in her voice, despite everything, "do murders occur because you happen to be in the vicinity, or do they occur everywhere constantly. You can't help be around when they do?"

"Hmm," Cinq-Mars grunts. In a way, he's forced to, she's squeezing so hard.

"What?" Sandra pushes him.

"There's a third possibility."

"With you, there always is."

"Maybe it's not a coincidence that murders occur wherever I go."

"Oh, so God arranges this? You're religious, but you've never been a silly fatalist."

"That's it. I may be forced to become that sort of fatalist."

He seems depressed by this latest death in his vicinity. "People do seem to die around you, dear. Still, I prefer the option behind Door Number Four."

"Which is?" She releases him, and in permitting her husband to be more flexible he leans down to receive a peck on his cheek.

"What you said. Coincidence. Bad stuff happens. You make it your habit to be around when it does. Only this time . . . that poor girl. Addie was so bright. I feel sorry for Caroline and the others. In a way, I feel guilty. This is going to be hard on them. I don't think they know how much yet."

"Why guilty?" Émile asks.

"My woes about Mom are put into perspective. This hardship tells me to buck up. Mom's death is not tragic. Intellectually, I've known it about my mother, that it's time. Emotionally—it's a hard river to cross. But this, Addie's murder. My God, it's horrific. She's so young. Mom, when she passes, that's nature taking its course after a long life, fully lived, well blessed. Sad, but I'm ready for it. Mom is not being robbed of her life. Addie has been."

Émile gives his wife a kiss on the forehead as he tucks her more firmly into his side. He knows what she's saying. They hold each other awhile.

Like her, Émile has also been taken by the inner fortitude of the young women. He has not always been enamored with the character and the resiliency shown by the sons and daughters of the privileged: This group contradicts his customary bias. Changing the subject to strike a more positive note, he remarks, "They're holding up well, the girls. I'm impressed."

"I noticed."

"Meaning?"

"You would've made a great dad, Émile. I'm sorry that it never happened."

She means the comment to take them in another direction, still, Émile strikes out on a different tangent altogether. "I was wondering a moment ago if there's not a kind of psychic exchange that goes on. A form of compensation. If I had kids, would I have spent my life getting mixed up in all this nastiness? Probably not. There'd be less time for it anyway. I know this sounds weird. Not having kids, does that put me in position to help the people who do, particularly the ones who suffer tragedies? Somehow, it seems to be what I've been given to do. For the sake of a family, I figure out who killed a mother or a father or a sibling or . . ." He hesitates, not wanting to finish the thought, but a truth confronts him. "Or a child."

Sandra pats his back. "You've done good work."

He straightens up. "Takes a toll," he mentions.

"Not only on you," she reminds him. The stresses on her and on their marriage have come between them.

Anastasia is in the room. She's overheard a portion of their conversation. Noticing her, they can tell that she's been waiting for the right moment. The coed manages a smile, and reports, "Lunch is ready if you are."

They step through to the dining room, gathering up Caroline along the way as she concludes with her mother. She and Sandra hug, then enter.

————

After lunch, another girlfriend, this one with a car, arrives to return the others back to their dorm rooms and apartments. It's hard for the young women to separate from one another, but necessary. They weep again as they depart, Caroline hugging each friend in turn. Suddenly they're gone and that's when the day's tragedy hits home. For a while she needs company, then solitude, and later in the afternoon she seeks out her uncle Émile. She finds him ensconced in an upstairs room used as a home office, sitting at the desk facing a laptop, the machine asleep. He's either deep in contemplation or half-asleep himself, while his wife naps in the next room. The young woman curls up in a wicker love seat along the wall opposite him and pulls a cushion over her knees. In response to her silent attention, Émile folds down the clamshell screen on his computer and returns her gaze.

"Dowbiggin will step up," she tells him. "A vigil. A memorial." Public opportunity for remembrance feels vital.

"Good. Good. That will be good." Sympathy is evident in his tone.

She makes a gesture with her lips that's difficult to decipher. He gathers that she doesn't have small talk on her mind.

"You're a detective, Uncle Émile," she points out to him.

"A more accurate statement when delivered in the past tense."

"Not what I heard."

True. He has kept a hand in, even postretirement.

She wants to know, "Are you going to be involved in this case?" The question sounds like a challenge.

"That won't be possible, Caro."

"Why not?"

"There's no way I can be."

"Why not?"

He separates his hands, as though to emphasize that there's nothing he can do. "Policemen guard their jurisdictions as avidly as a jealous lover guards a sweetheart. Imagine a guy going to another guy, the jealous type, asking if he'd mind lending out his girlfriend."

"Gross."

"Bad illustration maybe."

"More than maybe. Has that stopped you before?"

"A bad illustration?"

"Police jurisdiction."

"Not necessarily," he admits. "I have no traction here. I won't be able to get anywhere. Making any sort of clear headway will be impossible unless I'm invited onto the investigation. That's not going to happen anytime soon. Not in my lifetime, anyway. If I'm not invited in and still try to investigate on my own, I'll be cut off at the knees."

"Not necessarily," she counters, perhaps using his own words with deliberate intent.

"How do you figure that?"

Caroline has long made her ambitions well known, and has organized her life accordingly. If invited to a party, she's more likely to attend if she knows who's going, and if she feels that whoever's going might be beneficial to her future career. She'll avoid a party if the guest list is uninspiring, no matter the promise of fun or entertainment. Even while she's sitting with a relaxed posture on the sofa, Émile notices that she's intent, wanting to gain something in this talk.

"What did those cops do?" she asks him.

"What do you mean, *do*?"

"A few were running around dusting for fingerprints or whatever those technicians busy themselves with, but the detectives, the ones who are responsible for the actual investigating, the ones asking questions, what did they do? Who did they talk to?"

He's rarely at a loss in such a conversation. He feels that he's missing the point with his niece.

"Tell me," Émile suggests.

"They interviewed us. Me, Kali, and Anastasia."

She lets that point, a good one, hang in the air.

"And what did you tell them?" he wonders.

"Ask us and find out."

"I see what you're getting at."

Her intelligence has always been augmented by her drive, her interest in making her own way in the world. Sandra explained to him once, when Caro was much younger, that her niece was a talented rider, but that she would never be a great one. Her reasoning? Following the family business would never be sufficiently challenging for her. Instead, she followed a compulsion to do things differently, and do different things.

Émile can tell that she perceives that she's beat him on this point. "You might have your own questions, no? You're supposed to be a great detective, right? Even if you ask the same questions and we give you the same answers, you might understand them differently. Isn't that possible? Maybe you should ask us and see what that does. I mean, if it helps find Addie's killer, why not? If it doesn't"—she shrugs—"no damage."

The office chair is on wheels and Émile, remaining seated, rolls it away from the desk and places his hands behind his head. "Do you ever think about staying in law, forgetting about being a CEO?"

"Nope. I'd be bored. Why?"

"I'm trying to compliment you on being a strong proponent for your side in a discussion. All right, I'll start with you."

She smiles. She likes this victory.

"Did any of the questions asked by the other detectives surprise you, or did any of your answers to any question at all either surprise you or make you uncomfortable or surprise them?"

She shrugs. "No."

"I don't need to go over the common ground. I know what they must have asked. I can guess how you answered."

She's inclined to believe him.

"Do you think Addie brought this on herself?" Émile puts forward.

"What?"

"I'm asking."

"That's not fair. You're blaming the victim? That's wrong."

"Do you want fair or do you want the perpetrator caught? I only blame the killer, by the way. He's not here. I can't ask him any questions. The only other person in the room is you and you knew the victim. I'll try again. Do you think there's any possibility that Addie brought this on herself?"

She's fuming, a reaction that subsides, and rather than return Émile's penetrating stare she gazes out the window at the rain on the glass.

"I can rephrase the question," Émile offers.

"Can you? I think I'd appreciate that."

"Imagine the four friends together, including Addie. Let's say a year ago. A seer looks into a crystal ball and tells you that this will happen. One of your group will be murdered. Back then, whom do you guess it might be?"

"Addie," Caroline says, without hesitating.

"Why?"

"Aren't you the bastard?" she says.

"The truth can be a bastard, Caro. That's what we're interested in here."

She concedes with a slight head bob. "Addie's impetuous. Semi-reckless. I mean, come on, anybody our age is. If you're twenty-two you should be allowed to be twenty-two, right? Her danger filter is a lot more porous—*was* more porous—than, say, mine, or Anastasia's. Forget about Kali's, she's chickenhearted. I'll walk down a dark alley when I'm curious or excited about the alley. If I'm genuinely apprehensive, or scared shitless, or if I happen to know better, I either don't go down or keep a very watchful eye. Keep an escape route clear. Mentally, I wear running shoes. With Addie, it's almost as though she likes to be scared shitless. Wild side? A dabbler, I'd say, not a commitment thing. She dabbled when it suited her, and it suited her more than the rest of us. You know, the police never asked me any of this."

The furniture in this room is old and sits uncommonly low to the floor. Émile, reluctant still, reminds himself that this interview of a witness is no different than any other. His first task in such an inquisition is to remove the comfort level of the person being questioned. Comfortable people tell lies and are better at it than those under duress. Caroline might believe that she'll only speak the truth, but if he strikes a raw nerve or two, she might change her mind in a twinkling. He remembers how she didn't want to talk in front of him back at the library.

"They should have," he points out to her. He's not down on them. He knows they may have taken an entirely different tack to suit the circumstances and garnered results Caroline may be unaware of. "Your friend was murdered in your school. Whether you like it or not, that puts you closer to an understanding of what happened than any investigator can be at the outset. *Your friend. Your personal knowledge. Your turf.* You may not know that the truth is around you, it's close to you, it may flow through you. The police would have been remiss not to question you at length. Perhaps they were being kind. They may get back to you. Caro, this may not have occurred to you yet. You or one of your friends may have been the last person to see her alive. At least while she was still safe. More than anyone else, you have knowledge of her contacts, her habits, her situation, and her whereabouts except for obvious limitations. The key to this could lie with you. If it doesn't lie directly with you, it could well lie within your scope. Within your wider circle of friends, for instance—"

"I can't believe that any friend would do this," Caro interjected.

"That's not something that anyone anywhere wants to believe or can ever accept," Émile points out to her. "Yet friends kill friends every day, and here's a greater statistic: family members kill within the family. Let's hope the case is resolved and the perpetrator is put away. The harsh reality is, no matter who did this—or how or why or what happened— you aren't going to like what you learn. Right at this moment, you probably can't imagine what has occurred. Prepare yourself for that. Prepare your friends. You can walk away, get on with your lives. You're free to appreciate with fondness and sadness your good memories of Addie. If you trouble yourself to get to the bottom of what happened, then, when the truth comes out, that reality will haunt you for the rest of your days. You might never get over it. Be forewarned. Never say that a friend or a lover could not have done this. Feel free to hope otherwise, just never rule out any scenario or any person until you are dissuaded by irrefutable proof."

He lets her absorb that off-the-cuff lecture. Émile, though, is sensing a sea change here. As though he's rising to the challenge that she's been outlining. While he may be articulating how things might go, and they might not go well, Caroline's initiative has ignited a willingness to proceed.

"Truth is a bastard," she quotes him.

"Expect that," Cinq-Mars concurs.

He's frightened her a little, enough to make her more tentative.

"I'll give you an example," the retired detective says. "This morning I heard the name Vernon. Ex-boyfriend."

"No way." Caroline fights him on this. "It wasn't him."

"We don't need to make that judgment right away, do we?" he asks. "If he's innocent, fine, what's the problem? But consider. Ex-boyfriend may hold a grudge. Ex-boyfriend knows intimacies that even you do not. Ex-boyfriend was around Addie a lot in recent times and what did he see that did not seem important at the time, perhaps, or what did he overhear? Did Addie ever say anything about someone else *to* someone else that didn't seem to matter at the time? Now it might. Ex-boyfriend was on the scene this morning, he's the one who told us that a body had been found at the library. He may have had motive, he may have had opportunity, and failing that, he may possess critical secondary knowledge that hasn't even occurred to him yet. I'll guarantee you that the police will interview him. They'll be aggressive with him, too. That's how it has to be."

She gets that. "Okay," Caroline says, and asks, "What should I do?"

"Do? Don't do a thing." Cinq-Mars wheels his chair completely out from behind the desk, into the room's center. "Take no action whatsoever. I want you to be safe. To take care. To avoid any situation in the future where you're alone or unprotected until this gets figured out. We don't know what we're dealing with here. And yes, I do want you to be serious about that and not brush it off, Caro."

"But I want to help," Caroline protests. "I'm sure my friends do, too."

He evaluates her level of seriousness. Her return gaze carries an intensity and resolve that's unmistakable.

"One of the things you'll be doing over the next few days is talking to Vernon. That's only natural. Keep your senses wide open when you do. If the opportunity comes up, pick at his memory banks, search for anything that might have seemed amiss in recent days. It might be important. Approach any similar talk with anyone else with sensitivity and smarts. Assume nothing."

They nod to each other, as if making a pact.

"As mentioned," Émile goes on, "it's your milieu. In the coming days, you can do two things. Think through every moment you've spent with Addie recently, and try to see what or who was lurking in the shadows, even when, perhaps, you weren't paying attention. She had girlfriends. You know what I mean. You told the police that this morning. They told me. She had boyfriends—"

"You don't think a girl did this!" Caroline objects.

"Actually, I don't. Not by the way she was dressed, or dressed up. Also because that's rare. But do you see what I'm driving at? I can't rule it out. For a woman to be responsible might not be the norm, and it might not be politically correct in your mind, and it might be highly unlikely, but I can't rule anything out without evidence. Do you see? Does Addie have a roommate?" Caro affirms that with a nod. "Not one of your friends who were over today?" A shake of her head. "The police will talk to her, too. You should, too."

"She and Addie didn't like each other much."

"Even better."

"Why better?" Caro asks.

"Not being close friends, the roommate will be less inclined to protect her. That makes her more inclined to speak freely. She'll spill secrets. Such as, does she keep garter belts and nylon stockings in her bureau? She was wearing a pair when she was found. Are they hers? Or did someone dress her up? Ask Vernon. Did she ever dress up for him in garters and stockings? It's an intimate question. He might tell *you* the truth then fib to the police. Or vice versa. Or the police might not ask. You see?"

She did see.

"When you ask him anything, think about what he says and how he says it. Is he embarrassed? Shocked? Mortified? Upset, because that provokes another thought or jealousy? You see?"

The phone rings. Before Émile can wheel back to the desk to pick it up, they hear Sandra in the next room answering. He figures it's probably for her anyway, as nobody knows he's in New Hampshire. Or it might be for his mother-in-law, if an old friend hasn't learned of her illness.

"The point being, you'll be talking to a number of people over the next few days. People who knew Addie. Many of them will be in pain, and that will be genuine, and a few will show you that they're in pain where it's not necessarily genuine. Some won't know how to behave in this situation. They're not faking, they just don't know how to deal with this. Others won't be in pain, and you'll think that they're aloof. Really, they're mature enough *not* to fake it. Don't hold it against them. Grief is not a club. If you think of different levels of grief as clothes on a line—emotional disarray at one end, cool and collected at the other— who, if anyone, is suspicious because their behavior strikes you as odd? Bear in mind, there's a difference between odd and merely self-conscious. Among young people, you'll get a lot of the latter. If someone who is emoting strikes you as odd, or someone who is placid also strikes you as odd, then take note. What's that person's connection, if any, to Addie? If you want to help the police, be alert to things like that. If you want me to help, tell me what you hear and I'll vet it as best I can."

They check with each other, and through fleeting eye contact reach an agreement. Their commitment goes unspoken: They are willing to do this.

"Uncle Émile," Caroline asks, with a sly grin, "have you ruled us out, or are we on your list of suspects?"

He maintains a serious look. "You were with each other last night. Addie was already missing by then, you said, because she didn't show up to join you. I don't have a time of death as yet. I'm guessing that it wasn't last night, but early this morning. You're off the hook for murder, Caroline, but not entirely."

"Seriously?"

"The truth is a bastard. You know your involvement. I don't. I can believe you, but belief is not irrefutable proof. Not even a close cousin."

Sandra is slouching in the doorway. She yawns, having been awakened from sleep by the telephone, and leans against the jamb. "Sorry to interrupt your confab. You look like you're having a deep talk."

Émile gazes at her, and wonders if she's had news about her mother. "Who was on the phone? The hospital?"

She shakes her head. "A Chief Till? Do you know him? I guess you do, because he's coming over."

"Oh? Maybe he wants to share some news."

"I don't think so. Or that's not the only reason."

The statement is curious. Émile awaits her explanation.

"I agreed to this on your behalf, Émile. Get ready to go back out in the rain. Chief Till is coming over to pick you up."

"Why?"

"He wants you to visit a crime scene. A new one."

ELEVEN

The ball cap he was wearing earlier in the day has a soggy feel to it now, and Émile Cinq-Mars selects another. This gray one was favored by his mother-in-law in her garden for many years. Although frayed and stained it's flashy. Émile relaxes the band to make it fit and further bends the peak to deflect the rain. The orange neon stripe along one side is inexplicable to him. Caroline has no clue what it means either but comments that he'll show up in a car's headlights.

"Like a cat's eyes. I won't be able to prowl around in the dark all that discreetly."

She's smiling, a bit coyly. "Humble pie," she says.

"Excuse me?"

"Chow down. You're not always right, you know, for such a famous detective."

"I'm not following." She has a trick up her sleeve, he knows that much.

"You said, and I quote, not in your lifetime."

He catches her reference. "I haven't been invited onto the case yet, Caro. This Chief Till? He himself has already been booted off it. I don't know what he wants with me. I'm sure this is a—" He can't fill in the blank. He has no clue why Till is picking him up.

"Not in your lifetime," she repeats in a singsong voice, not hiding her friendly mockery. "Anyway, I've already invited you onto the case even if the chief won't."

Silently, he agrees. True enough.

Chief Till doesn't bother to climb out of his squad car when he arrives. The rain has let up considerably, enough to be called light, but he's been soaked to the skin six times that day. He flashes his high beams and honks, as if picking up a high school prom date, and the former detective from Canada dashes out to join him.

They travel slowly off the farm property. Many of the flooded potholes are immense and in the headlights it's impossible to differentiate deeper puddles from the shallow. Bouncing on the bad road, they find it difficult to talk without their words cracking on their lips. They only speak properly again when they're out on the smooth highway.

"What's up?" Émile asks. Tires swish on the wet asphalt. He enjoys that sound.

"You'll want to see this."

"Don't be so sure. I retired for a bunch of reasons. Not only on account of old age and a pension."

"Not what I heard."

"You don't think I had my reasons?"

"I don't think you retired. In name only, maybe. Not fully."

Do people tweet his every move now? Are bloggers on his case? He's unaware of anyone's scrutiny, although he does admit, "People keep saying that to me." But by *people*, he means his wife.

"I checked you out again. More carefully this time."

"There's nothing to check out that's current. Anyway, don't believe everything you read on the Internet. Sometimes I think the whole apparatus is a medium for fanatics."

"The earnest talk loudly, that is true. If you can call typing *loud*."

Till is comfortable behind the wheel. He's a man who enjoys being in a car in motion. They're alike that way. This man could drive to Washington State tomorrow and be in heaven all along the route. Émile appreciates that and also the way he substituted the word *earnest* for his word *fanatics*. He didn't call them wackos or nutcases or bozos. He comes across as a man who's fair.

"Nevertheless," the chief waxes on, "I can still do a tally. Take me. I'm mentioned on the Internet in about ten articles. Fluffy pieces. I could show you a picture of myself at a charity golf tournament even though I don't remember showing up for it, let alone teeing off. But you. Your name comes up *ten thousand times* and your picture maybe a hundred times and not once are you holding a golf club. One time it's a pistol in your hand. A couple of times you're holding a fugitive by his shirt collar and in neither case was he smiling for the camera. You look ornery in those photos, Émile. Like you wanted to throw the miscreant off a cliff. Not your best side, I suppose. People on the Internet have their opinions about you, Émile. I like a man who's willing to piss folks off. Seems like you managed to charm a few others."

"Ten thousand? That's another thing about the Internet. There's a lot of repetition. A ton of duplication."

"Oh yeah, and there's this one snapshot where you got a shotgun across your forearm. Blood on your coat."

"I think it was red wine."

"Some pic, that was. You've put big-time people away, my man."

"Never was it not a team effort. Did that not get written?"

"Bullshit. You go bowling and gangsters fall like tenpins. By the way," Till ruminates, then his remark stalls.

"By the way what?" Émile asks him after a moment's silence.

"That's a flashy hat. You're lighting up my interior here."

Émile was hoping he'd change the subject, glad when he does. He takes the ball cap off and examines it and explains that it belongs to his mother-in-law. He repeats that she's at the end of her life. Till confirms that he knows her and offers his sympathies. In the streetlights as they come to the edge of town, his cap back on, he glances over and studies the chief's visage. He wonders if he's a man he can trust, and if so, how far?

The officer projects a different look without his campaign hat, which has been tossed onto the backseat. Hatless, he comes across as even less assertive than usual, a man who'd be happiest sitting on a porch with his pooch. Uncle Mike. What a guy. Hat on, he still doesn't look all that hard. He'll never be mistaken for a boot-camp drill sergeant. Yet a sticker on his dash proclaims that he's ex-marine. *Semper fidelis.* Always faithful. Forever loyal. A man of the corps to the core. Cinq-Mars wants to run that wordplay by him but minds his tongue. Having the hat removed reveals the chief's sloped-back forehead, an uncommon feature, one that suggests a difficult birthing. He still has hair but it's thin and gray. The result both softens his look and confers an innate intelligence. The latter thought strikes Émile as being counterintuitive— smaller head size, smaller brain—and even though he knows that that's rarely true, the impression sticks.

"Do you have Indian blood in you, Chief Till?"

"Hope so. You?"

"Hope so, too. Bound to have, I suppose, back in time."

"My bloodlines include the Green Mountain Boys, I know that much. Nobody comes out and says it but I'm convinced they lived the wild life. Cross-fertilized the population if you take my meaning."

Driving through the rain-drenched night they both seem to be contemplating that frontier time.

Till breaks the silence. "We've got another one."

"Another what?"

"Murder."

This Cinq-Mars does not expect. Not in this sleepy collegiate town. "Don't tell me. Not another student."

"Nope. Thank God. Not a student and no correlation between the two as far as my officers on the scene can tell. Haven't been there myself." Till eases to a stop at a sign. No other traffic is visible, but he takes the opportunity to stay stopped as if a caravan of ghosts passes in front of them. He gives Cinq-Mars an intense look. "That is to say, no correlation at first glance. What a second glance reveals, that'll be up to us to decipher."

Cinq-Mars interprets his look, its intensity. Till is wondering if he can trust him, and if so, how far. They're both sounding the other out. Cinq-Mars comes at him from a different angle. "What is it you're not telling me?"

"Method to my madness, Émile. I don't want to affect how you see things. Observe your reaction type thing. I'll mind my peace for now."

He finally drives on.

"Are you on this new case?" Cinq-Mars inquires. The way Till rocks his head from side to side appears deliberately noncommittal. The displaced Montreal detective thinks about that a moment before he concludes, "Then you haven't told them yet, the troopers."

"Haven't got around to it, no. Hey, I haven't been on the scene myself. Not yet. For now, I'm delaying reports from my officers until I've had my own go look-see."

"How does this sound to anybody, Chief Till? You haven't told the state troopers that there's been another murder, yet here you are, telling me."

Till is nodding as though he's alone in the squad car, rummaging through private thoughts. "Put it this way," he explains eventually. "I'm still in shock. I can't believe how quickly they dumped me from the Dowbiggin murder, as if I don't live and serve here or couldn't possibly have anything to contribute to the investigation. Lightning speed. I also can't believe how sparse their communication has been since then, as if we don't have a gentleman's agreement among colleagues. If they want to be as quick as a hare in getting rid of me, should anyone be surprised if I'm as slow as a tortoise in alerting them to a new case? Personally, I think not. I might take my own sweet time. We'll have to see how that goes."

"What about my involvement?" Cinq-Mars inquires. He suspects he knows the answer to that one.

"You bring something to the table, Émile. Expertise. Experience beyond the norm. You helped me out this morning, perhaps you can give me a boost on the new case tonight. No pressure. A long shot, I know, but the way things stand, I don't have much else going on."

"That's not it," he tells him. "Not all of it anyway."

Till glances over. Once, twice, then he chuckles lightly to himself.

"What?" Cinq-Mars probes.

"You're right. You're right. You're a smart man. I'm letting you in on this first thing, even before I get out there myself, because when the troopers find out that I brought you in they'll be so pissed off they'll wet themselves. They'll have to go change their shorts. Won't be a damn thing they can do about it though, am I right? If they come away from the experience so irritated with me they'll want to spit in public, then maybe it'll occur to them why that is. Next time they might slow down a tad before calling the governor to give me the heave-ho. Not that anybody wants a next time to take place."

"Except, you already have one," Cinq-Mars points out to him.

"What's that?"

"A next time."

"See what I mean? A man needs to plan ahead. Look, Émile, I don't believe I'm obstructing. The contrary. From what I saw this morning, me and you taking our time with this investigation will only help things along. Not hinder. I'm not bringing you in *only* to piss off the troopers, teach them to mind their manners. That's part of it, I'll cop to that, but I know about you. If you can help me get a quick start, then who knows? This might work out."

That still doesn't seem completely coherent to Cinq-Mars. Something else is going on—what is it that this man is not saying?—yet he holds his doubts in abeyance. They drive on, and as they do he rehearses how he'll explain this to Caroline after claiming that such an invitation would not be forthcoming in his lifetime. He decides that he might reply by saying that he never expected to live this long, get a laugh that way.

"I'm connected to this town, Émile. Grew up near here. Still live here. I'm sworn to protect its citizens. That's all I care about. The troopers want to close this morning's murder, for sure, I don't doubt that for a second. I do, too. Mostly I want to protect this town, and the towns around us we serve. If you think about it, there's a difference. Trooper Hammond, he might say otherwise, but he's not showing me he gets the difference."

Émile doesn't recognize the neighborhood they're in, and can't figure out where they're headed. Even when a road sign comes up, it's next to impossible to decipher through the wet windshield. He gives up trying to map a suburb's twists and turns where all the homes have a similar look with matching yards, certainly in the dark, and entrusts his fate to Chief Till's hands. They stop amid a mess of patrol cars, with a few brave residents across the street standing out in the rain, watching, but nothing on the outside of the house seems worthy of anyone's attention other than the police presence. He and Till hurry inside out of the rain.

That the victim won't be a student is the extent of his knowledge as he enters, yet Cinq-Mars is geared to catalogue similarities or connections between the two murders occurring in nearby towns on the same day. Stepping into the home, he's struck by how one murder scene is so unlike the other.

He doesn't have far to go.

"Answered the doorbell," Till's lead officer remarks, walking them through the obvious part. The cop is wearing casual clothes, which is a little disconcerting. "Backed up a few steps, the way I see it, away from the gunman, takes a bullet through the neck. Nothing clean or neat about it. The bullet hit the far wall. Embedded there. The victim bled out. Or suffocated on his own blood, one of the two. Hard to say which came first. Not that it matters much."

"It matters," Cinq-Mars contradicts him.

The cop in jeans and a striped polo looks at him, then says, "To the vic, you mean."

"No," the retired investigator states, "it matters to us." Cinq-Mars met this officer briefly earlier in the day, they were introduced, although his name escapes him for the moment. Shilling, he wants to say, yet guesses that that's not right. "Have you been promoted to detective?"

"Sir?" the man asks, worried that he's being mocked.

"You're in plainclothes."

"No, sir. Off duty when I got the call."

"Just curious," Cinq-Mars says. "I didn't know towns this size even had detectives. Neighbors never heard a shot?"

"Who are you again?"

Till explains to his officer, "Old cop, having a look-see. Don't worry about it."

"The neighbors?" Cinq-Mars asks again.

"The door was probably closed by the time the gun was fired. Either way, with the rain, the sound gets muffled. He's been dead a while. Thunder and lightning at the same time as the gunshot maybe, or around the same time. It's all similar noise. Who'd notice an extra crack? Everybody's windows were shut tight to the storm anyway. Air conditioners were on. Plus, this looks cold-blooded, professional, don't think it was a robbery, so yeah, maybe he had a silencer, who knows?"

"No silencer," Cinq-Mars tells him. He can tell that the officer has been pleased to be running down the case, despite a total lack of experience. In a way he's sorry to upend his applecart.

The two town cops stay quiet an extra moment, looking at him. They find that the retired detective is absorbed in gazing at the corpse.

"Who found the body?" Cinq-Mars asks.

"Neighbor's teenage son. Came over to see if he knew anything about toilets. With the storm, his was backing up and his dad was up to his elbows in shit. Door was ajar. He peeked in. Bit of a shock."

Cinq-Mars seems to be exploring the walls, the ceiling.

"Ah, how do you know, sir, that there wasn't a silencer, if you don't mind my asking?" the off-duty officer asks him.

Till wants to know the same thing.

Cinq-Mars looks at them both, notes their confusion. "A killer with a silencer would've shot him again. Put him out of his misery. That's also why how he died is meaningful to us. Through the throat the man isn't talking, right? He wasn't keeping him alive to have a conversation. He was flinching down on the floor, making a commotion as he died. Gagging on his own blood, fighting for his life. The killer's instinct would be to finish him, except he didn't want to take a chance on firing twice. One gunshot, if they hear it at all, the neighbors think a tree limb cracked off in the storm, like you said. One shot, they stand there listening. Two, they might get curious, storm or no storm, take a look outside. He let him die slowly because he didn't want to fire a second shot and he didn't want to fire because he didn't have a silencer. That he died gagging on his blood confirms that."

The two local men nod, and resume gazing at the corpse as well. They can visualize the sordid moments better now. Till asks his man, "Do you have a name?"

The officer, who's wearing nitrile gloves, produces a Ziploc bag from his pants pocket, and from the bag the victim's wallet. He opens it up to display the man's driving license. "Philip Lars Toomey. We're standing in his residence. Do you want to know where he works?"

"Do I?" Till asks.

"Dowbiggin," Cinq-Mars answers. "I'm sorry, I've forgotten your name."

"Dennis," the detective answers. "Sergeant Schiller."

"Right."

"How did you know?" Schiller asks him back.

"His lapel pin. He either has a child graduating from Dowbiggin or he works there. This place marks him as a bachelor, makes me think he works there. I take it I'm right?"

Schiller displays a card in the man's wallet without removing it from its sleeve. "Faculty. I guess he's a professor."

"What department?"

"Don't know," Schiller admits.

"There's a computer over there," Cinq-Mars points out. "Find out. Interesting to see if his department is the same as Addie's, the dead girl's."

Till gives a nod of consent and his officer goes over to the computer. He keeps his nitrile gloves on to type.

"What makes you think he's single?" Till asks his new adviser.

"Where's the grieving hysterical widow? I don't see her distraught presence anywhere in sight, do you? It's not the time of day to be working and it's not the sort of day to go out on a long walk. Besides. Where are the family photos if he has one? This is the room for that. Nowhere in sight. He's a bachelor, or divorced for such a long time he might as well have been single his whole life."

Cinq-Mars is looking around the room as Till leans over the corpse for a last look at him. "The throat," Till says. "Kind of a strange choice. Was he a bad shot, the killer, or was he just mean that way?"

"Could've been a shaky hand. More likely, your officer nailed it."

"How so?"

"He wanted the door closed. To muffle sound. Two things follow from that. The shooter was moving in the act of closing the door. And the victim, hands up, perhaps, obedient, perhaps—he hadn't turned to run away. He was probably scared shitless and somewhat of a moving target. The shooter missed, slightly. We can withhold a definitive opinion until the killer's in custody. That conversation will be interesting."

Schiller returns to them, beaming. "Diplomatic relations, that's his field. He's been at Dowbiggin for only two years."

"Before that?"

He finds out why Schiller is beaming. He has that answer, too, at the ready. "State Department."

"Really," Cinq-Mars muses. "What did he do there?"

The question rapidly diminishes Schiller's bright grin. "I'll check on that," he says, and is about to retreat back to the computer.

"Before you go," Cinq-Mars says. "The wallet. Where'd you find it?"

"Hip pocket."

The dead man is wearing trousers, a white shirt, a light mauve sweater where the lapel pin resides, socks and slippers. "Anything else in his pockets?"

"No, sir. Not a thing."

"Nothing? Not even keys?"

"No, sir."

Cinq-Mars puts a request to Till. "Send an officer outside. The vehicle in the carport, is it wet?"

"Wet?"

"It's been raining today, have you noticed? If the car was in use, I don't think it would've dried off in this humidity. If the car was out, he was out, but I don't believe these clothes have been wet today. Look at his hair. Fluffy. I bet he showered and shampooed before his death. If he wasn't wearing these clothes outside today, what clothes was he wearing, and what's in those pockets, anything? He could've transferred the wallet, but did he leave anything behind in the other pockets?"

"Okay, but how will we know what he wore today? By what's still wet, I suppose."

"That'll make it easy. Also, if he was good enough to drive his car today then leave his keys in his pockets, that'll confirm his outfit."

Till sends a uniform out to check on the car.

"Make and model," Émile calls to him as the uniform is going out the door.

Schiller returns from the computer. "Funny thing. I can't find what he did for the State Department. Maybe somebody better than me on computers can."

"You Googled him?"

"His name comes up as a professor at Dowbiggin and that's it."

Cinq-Mars thinks about that, then pulls out his cell phone and walks away from the others. They hear him say, "Hey, it's me . . . Yeah, it's been a while . . . Good, good, how are you doing?" Apparently that question requires a lengthy answer before they hear him make a request. "I need information on a guy. Formerly at the State Department." Another pause, and he says, "It's on his résumé, but not showing where you'd expect to find it." He listens, then says, "That's the thing, I know what it means. That's why I'm asking you."

He gives the particulars over the phone, thanks his contact, and concludes the call. When he comes back to their huddle, Chief Till asks, "Who was that?"

Cinq-Mars doesn't say. He acts as though he never heard the question.

The uniform returns from the carport.

"Looks like it's been standing in a car wash all day," he reports. "Just like we do." Then he addresses Émile directly. "BMW, 5 Series. Quite new. Silver-gray. Black interior."

Cinq-Mars appreciates the impulse to provide details, although it isn't necessary in this instance. "Was it locked?" he wants to know.

"Yes, sir." Good that he checked.

"Let's see if we can't find his keys. Start with his wardrobe."

Finding a pair of damp trousers, neatly hung on a hanger in his closet, doesn't take long. A wet shirt has been dropped into a laundry hamper. A sports jacket is also damp, and in it they find the car fob and house keys on separate rings. Chief Till pulls out a sheet of paper, folded into eighths, from the inside chest pocket. He passes it to Schiller, with his gloved hands, to unfold. He doesn't read the two words that have been computer-generated, instead holds up the sheet for the others to read for themselves.

Breached
Run!

"Curiouser and curiouser," Cinq-Mars relates.

"Alice in Wonderland," Till says back.

"You're well-read," Cinq-Mars deadpans. They've been feeling each other out this whole time. He passes the BMW fob to Officer Schiller.

"Check the interior, will you? Touch nothing. Observe everything. Then report back."

"Yes, sir," the man responds. He looks a little sheepishly at his actual boss, but Chief Till isn't miffed in the slightest, and gives him a nod that sends him on his way.

"Chief, you don't get to investigate murders routinely," Cinq-Mars mentions. "I understand that, and trust me, you don't want to if you think otherwise. What do you investigate around here? What's the worst of it?"

"The worst? Bar fights. Domestic abuse. The worst though, of late, has been rape on campus. Been a big issue. We've had demonstrations, vigils, the administration has taken heat for trying to keep the problem out of the media. Objectively, if not in the beginning, then of late, I think they've reacted well. Taken measures. By the way, we do have murders around here, only they're the kind where everybody and his uncle knows who the killer is, and it takes about ninety minutes to bring him in."

"All serious stuff," Émile notes. He looks around. "Outerwear, some-where," he directs, and they go off in search of a raincoat.

What they find provides no further information. The coat's still wet, the pockets yield only Kleenex tissues, used, and old credit card receipts, one from a Walmart and the other from a restaurant in town. "He ate alone," Émile points out. "Time of day suggests dinner. This place for under thirty bucks, that's one person only. Three weeks ago."

"Okay," Till says.

"Okay," Cinq-Mars concurs.

"If that's all we've got I'm calling in the state troopers."

Before he can do that, his phone rings. He walks off to take the call and then returns. In the meantime, Émile sifts through the victim's bedside table and the top of his bureau. He sees a card with formal printing on it, an invitation, which he saw before in the hand of the dead girl, and under the card is an envelope mailed from the Dowbig-gin School. Émile takes out his mobile phone, and taps information into the phone's note-taking feature. He's not accustomed to doing this and hopes he'll be able to retrieve it later. Then he takes a photograph of the card, also with his phone. He's still getting used to all these bells and whistles on his new device. He wanders farther through the bungalow to get a feel for the place, then returns to the living room at Till's bidding. "What's up?"

Till wants to talk to him alone, then protects their privacy by whispering. "We've got another one."

"Another what?" Émile asks, then catches on before the man has a chance to reply. "You're not serious."

"White River Junction. Not my jurisdiction. Not my town. Across the river—that's across the state line, too, in Vermont. Our state troopers won't directly be called in to that one, either."

"Nor will you be. Who called?"

"The chief of police over there. We're pals. Mostly he called to let me know that he has one of his own, because he heard about today's murder, obviously. I told him that I now have two. That made us both think that I better check his out, in case they're related. This one? We don't know yet. I guess the Dowbiggin connection is compelling."

"You're saying we're invited to the scene?"

"I am, anyway, and I'm inviting you along with me. Just don't announce it to the media."

Émile understands. "Or to the New Hampshire state troopers."

Dennis Schiller has returned from his inspection of the BMW's interior with a look on his face that's difficult to decipher. He's tickled about something. "Why the shit-eating grin? Any bodies in the trunk?" his chief of police inquires.

"Car's clean. Immaculate. I guess guys with cars like that take care of them."

"Anything of interest?" Cinq-Mars inquires.

"Hell, yeah. You'll like this. Locked in the glove box, sir."

He always hated it when officers make him crawl around to pick up bits of meaning off the floor. "Tell me."

"A necklace, sir. There's a necklace in his glove box. It sure looks a lot like the one this morning."

"Seriously? Describe it."

The junior officer does so, and while they have to push him to refine his memory of the details, it's clear that he might as well be describing the necklace worn by Addie Langford in her death pose.

That's enough, but Till asks the officer, "Anything else?"

"Yes, sir. Between the front buckets, he's got a mobile phone."

The chief and Cinq-Mars exchange a glance. They both know what this means—a treasure trove of information—but there's a limit to how far they can push the boundaries, and that limit has now been broached.

Till calls his officers into a circle. "Leave everything as it was before we got here. I think we have the note memorized. Put it back in the pocket where we found it. Dennis, if you haven't locked the BMW, lock it now. You can probably do that from inside, then put the fob back where we found it. I was never here for long. Do you understand? You had a look around, that's the truth. I showed up, then relayed the information to our state troopers. That's all true. I wasn't here for long if anybody asks and I didn't do a damn thing except call in the troopers and go home. Presumably to bed. When they arrive let them do their nose-around thing, see what they turn up. What we turned up, or less, or more, let them find that out on their own. If they miss something then we can help them along. Let them work it through first. Is all that clear enough? Sorry for the BS, guys, but we've got to play the game if we want involvement in this."

They all get it, and the chief makes his call through to the state police. Cinq-Mars waits for him by the door, then they depart. Only they know where they're headed, to the scene of the third murder of the day in the area. They are on their way across the river over the high bridge when they discover more about the victim they left behind. Cinq-Mars takes a call on his mobile, and at the end of it he's silent a few moments, then he tells the chief, "Toomey. The dead guy. Worked for the State Department in name only."

"What does that mean?" Till asks.

Cinq-Mars shrugs. "Probably means CIA. Or NSA. Like me, retired. He must've had clout to be handed a professorship on a platter."

Till is driving down the long slope into White River Junction before he gets up the gumption to ask what he's itching to know. "Émile, how the hell did you find that out so fast?"

He doesn't answer. He doesn't know this man well enough to explain it, although he's impressed that he seems willing to accept that.

"Oh great," Till fulminates, thinking it through. "We'll be totally out of the picture if this goes up the ladder."

"Hmm," Cinq-Mars murmurs, as though to contradict him. He explains himself no further, and observes the characteristics of the town they've entered, which is clearly in a different economic bracket than Hanover, where they left. Night and day. Till lets him in on what he knows about the next victim, and Émile hunches forward as they approach a rather sad-looking house where on the second floor a woman is reported to have been both shot and hacked to death. Till issues a warning before they climb a short flight up.

"Take a good gulp of clean air, Émile," he says. "This one's not pretty, I'm told."

Émile does take that deep breath, which is when he notices for the first time that the rain has finally ceased.

TWELVE

In the backstreet apartment in Vermont, where a fresh contingent of officers and a separate authority holds sway, they tread lightly. Chief Till puts on a happy face, although he's informed right off the bat that his counterpart caved, putting in a call to the Vermont state troopers. Fortunately, available detectives are not nearby and the pair assigned to investigate have reported that they plan to finish their evening meal before driving to White River Junction. Twenty minutes earlier they announced their ETA as an hour and a half. Time enough for the local cops and their guests to poke around.

Knowing that he's already fudging protocol, Chief Roy Horriza barely tolerates an introduction to Émile Cinq-Mars. The very temper of his handshake expresses a doubt concerning the wisdom of an outsider being on the scene, and he mumbles that he doesn't endorse this development. His counterpart from across the river and the state line, Chief Till, explains, "Google the guy. He's investigated more murders than we get in the North Country in a half century," which is such an exaggeration that Émile Cinq-Mars wants to whip him. Till adds, "How many killings have you worked through yourself, Roy, where it wasn't the boyfriend or the husband who did it? What fell out of the sky today is a complicated business. We can use this man's expertise. Before you say what I know you're going to say let me say something to the contrary."

"What's that?" Horriza is willing to listen. He has short red hair and a well-freckled neck. His eyes constantly dart around even when he's as still as a brick.

"Fuck the idiot troopers," Till postulates. "Your state and mine. In mine, I got shoved out the door with a broomstick up my rear. Told to go ticket jaywalkers. In effect. Do you think, Roy, you'll fare better?"

The explanation suits neither Chief Horriza nor Émile. The ex-detective from Montreal is tempted to bring up that he's only here because his niece is counting on him to intervene, that he'd rather be home with his fist around a nightcap, a thought that won't go over well, either. Since he's taken the trouble to be present, since no one is formally asking him to leave, and since a murdered and butchered woman is lying in front of him with her mouth agape, Émile merely grunts. He manages to do so with vague authority, and Horriza's concerns are gently ignored.

He has a good look around.

Initially, he only glances at the poor victim, then seems to forget about her; the two chiefs clearly believe that a lengthy examination of the corpse is warranted. What do they expect him to do? Measure the gaping wounds created by a cleaver? Stick his eyeball into the bullet hole in the woman's forehead? What is apparent here is apparent to all and he doesn't need to provoke nightmares over the savagery. Instead, he peruses the kitchen, the bedroom, the closets, the bathroom.

Unknowingly, he's agitating Chief Till, who feels that he's having a gander in precisely the places where he didn't bother to look in the previous house. When, eventually, his curiosity gets the better of him, the chief demands that Cinq-Mars explain himself.

"Toomey carefully controlled his environment," postulates the former big-city detective. "Not the case here. What we wanted in the other house was the contents of his pockets, anything that he hadn't disposed of yet or filed away. Chief Till, picture his wallet. Now ask yourself, how many men keep their billfold that neat and tidy, with nothing extrane-

ous in it? One gas card, one credit card, no receipts, no notes jotted
down along the way. Even a note buried in his pocket was meticulously
folded into eighths. The only exception was a couple of receipts in his
raincoat. Easy to forget the ones in there. Which reminds me, we have
to get a look at his office on campus, preferably before the troopers show
up ahead of us. This victim, on the other hand, does not tidy up as she
goes. I've already seen condoms with their welcome DNA awaiting our
analysis. Two toothbrushes, different colors. Who's her lover? Working
uniforms suitable for a cleaning lady hang behind the door in her bedroom and in her closet. Private or corporate? You might want to ask that
question, but I have the answer. I've seen her pay stubs, both on her
bureau and on the kitchen counter. As I said, she's messy that way."

"What's her name?" Till asks.

"Malory Earle."

"Who does she work for?"

"Dowbiggin School of International Studies."

"Holy—"

"Exactly. You may want to consider this an isolated incident, Chief
Horriza," Émile says as the other man joins them and picks up his
thread. "Go ahead. But the dots are beginning to connect. Not only do
we have three murders in the same region on the same day, we could
very well have three murders linked to the same institution."

"A student and a professor, I see that," Till mentions, "an easy link,
but a cleaning lady?"

"Start by ruling it a threesome. If that doesn't pan out, nothing's
lost. If you dismiss the connections off the bat you run the risk of wrecking the investigation before it's begun."

Neither chief needs to be convinced of that—and both resent being
told—but Horriza spots a roadblock or two along the way. "What will
happen when the New Hampshire and Vermont state troopers pool
their resources? That's a prescription not covered by Obamacare, let me
tell you. They'll mess it up."

"Hmm," Cinq-Mars notes, then helps him out with that concern.
"They may not get the chance."

Horriza raises a quizzical eyebrow, and Till lets him know how
things might change. "FBI. For better or worse."

"Seriously?"

Till can't explain it himself, and shrugs.

Cinq-Mars concludes his wanderings at the victim's feet. The other two arrive behind him.

"What's in her purse?" he asks.

He's probably surprised that Horriza can quickly run down a list although he doesn't let on. Hearing it all, he asks, "No keys?"

"Ah. Nope. Not in her purse."

Having learned a thing or two from the previous house, Till suggests that they check what she wore during the day, and her outerwear. They do a thorough examination, but nothing shows up. All this time, Émile Cinq-Mars is standing by the body as if waiting for the corpse to sit up and have a chat. The two police chiefs report back to say that no keys have been found.

"They must be hidden somewhere," Horriza maintains. "The place is a bit of a mess."

"Who lets themselves into their own apartment," Cinq-Mars wonders aloud, "then hides their keys? If they're not here, what other keys does she carry with her? Keys for Dowbiggin, for instance? And yes, I want to know—*you* want to know—does she clean the clock tower?"

"The clock tower?" Horriza inquires. He hasn't heard the details of the day's first murder, and Till draws him a mental picture.

"Christ's sake," he sums up. "Doesn't sound like these killings are connected from what you say. They're different."

"Way different," Chief Till agrees.

"All the same in one way," Cinq-Mars points out to them, and he smiles, knowing that he's going to make them roll their eyes and groan. "In each case, someone's dead."

They don't react exactly as he anticipated. Horriza flips the bird.

They seem to be waiting on their guest detective again, which only dawns on Cinq-Mars slowly. Drawing up a theory, he rocks his head to one side and back. "Whoever showed up, she wasn't expecting him. I imagine that the door was left open, because she didn't answer it. She was waiting, provocatively, I suspect, for a lover to make an appearance. That could have been who arrived, her lover, and he might've just stormed in and started hacking away. A pique of temper, always possible. Then he put one between her eyebrows for good measure. More likely, she didn't know the intruder, and it was over before she could react. She would have been screaming from the first moment. This happened during the storm. Thunder and lightning, heavy rain. Why the brutality? We don't know. Let's keep it in mind as being a question that may lend an insight. Might be important. We'll see. What do the neighbors say?"

Cinq-Mars is told that the victim was well liked, that she indeed worked as a cleaning lady, people weren't sure where, a few said Dowbiggin, and that she worked shifts.

"What shift?"

"Nobody's definitive about it. They say the midnight usually, but not always."

"Interesting," Cinq-Mars points out.

"How so?" Till asks.

"Explains the afternoon tryst. She's not home at night to receive her lover."

"You think he might be somebody slipping away."

"We're looking at a man with flexibility to his working hours. Assuming he worked days."

"You mean like a professor. Like Toomey?"

"Or a cop." He tacks on a quick grin. They know he's needling them. "The professor and this one don't match up to type. Not just black-white, but rich-poor, she's taller I'd say, and don't you think, Chief Till, having been in both their homes, that they seem culturally and socially at opposite ends of the spectrum?" Till feels obliged to concur. "Do you know where they do come together?" Émile asks them both.

Taking his question as a challenge, the policemen mull it through. Till notes that both victims, Toomey and the woman, are modestly overweight. Cinq-Mars agrees that that's true, but says that that's not it, although it's a good observation. Neither the man nor the woman reside at the top end of universal beauty, Till points out, but adds that there's no accounting for animal attraction. Cinq-Mars agrees with that as well, adding that intellectual attraction can't be dismissed, either.

"How so?" Horriza objects. "She's a cleaning lady. He's a prof."

"Have you checked out her library?"

Both men admit that that's not occurred to them. For them, books fill shelf space, and that's it.

"This lady reads," Cinq-Mars informs them, "at a professorial level. What she does for a living doesn't point to that. In any case, we don't have to worry too much about it. Whoever her lover is, his DNA is all over this place. All we need to have to make things happen is to get that information back from the state troopers—from whichever state—once they acquire it."

"My state," Horriza says. "I'll try to curry their favor. God knows, Till's guys won't be talking to him. He pisses everybody off."

They have their little dig at each other, although there's merit to what Horriza contends. A more amicable relationship with his troopers gives him an advantage over Till. At that moment one of his officers reports that he's found a set of house keys in the kitchen. They'd been in plain view.

"No better place to hide something," Cinq-Mars comments, and Horriza is mildly miffed. His crew has been formally chided by an old retired guy from Canada.

Cinq-Mars can see that he's overstayed his welcome.

"Chief," Cinq-Mars requests of Till, "what you said earlier is spot on. This isn't pretty. Do you mind driving me home?"

The senior officer is surprised and a trifle taken aback, then decides that he's happy to do so. This murder is not his investigation. He and Émile retreat and are on their way again.

THIRTEEN

On the way out of White River Junction, now that the rain has stopped, Émile Cinq-Mars and Chief Till have a clearer view of the storm's destruction. Hoses run from basement windows to the streets, pumping excess water. Gusts have lopped off big limbs and taken down trees and in the glow of streetlights low-lying lawns sparkle as ponds. Crews tend to power outages. Neither man can see the Connecticut River while traversing the highway bridge, yet both imagine it, that roaring, that spontaneous surge through the dark. Toppled trees spin and nose-dive in the frantic rapids, while overhead a pale moon peeks through the scud of clouds surfing a tailwind.

Not knowing the area well, Émile expects they'll take the ramp off the far end of the bridge into West Lebanon, New Hampshire, retracing the way they ventured out. Till carries on toward Lebanon proper instead to depart the highway there. The visitor notes again that the man is obedient to the rules of the road, as he keeps the speedometer bang on the legal limit, at sixty-five.

"What do you make of it, Émile?" Till ruminates. "We have our troubles now and again, even though Holyoake's a real quiet community. Hanover, too, for the most part. Everybody has problems, we have our own in a sporadic fashion, nothing you don't expect. Although we arrest more students than anywhere across the Ivy League. For us though, make no mistake, three murders in a single day puts us on the map as a war zone. Like we've been invaded by an occupying force."

"Or by aliens," Émile reflects, as though he's serious. "So we want to believe. Sorry, Chief, for your troubles, but people are wicked everywhere. I take your meaning. Visiting my wife's folks over the years, I've enjoyed the peace and quiet of the place."

"There you go."

"Which is why it makes more sense if I ask you the question you're asking me. What do *you* make of all this? You're the man with the heap of local knowledge."

"Beats the hell out of me. Can't make hide nor tail of it."

"Hmm," Cinq-Mars murmurs, dissatisfied with that response. Momentarily, he says, "Put it another way. What troubles have you had lately? Anything recurring, ongoing?"

The question carries Till into a different mood. One he'd rather not visit. "Campuses in the region have had rape issues. True for a lot of the country; we were singled out for extra publicity. A climate of fear took hold. That mess is in the past, we're telling people. We hope we're right. Measures were taken, we had demonstrations and the like which at first I didn't welcome. Not only were college administrations for at least three schools on the hook. Folks also condemned the police in general, and me in particular. We're seeing the value now, though. Young people coming out in public like that, the culture may have altered. I don't think you can change a rapist's sick mind, but you can make the perpetrators more fearful, less bold. Boys who fall out of line can put a check on themselves. All that helps."

"I suspect that's true, if only to a degree," Émile concurs.

"We're also hoping," Till goes on, "that whoever was responsible, however many individuals were involved, that they're graduating. Don't get me wrong. Sending them to prison is my preference, but if they're putting on a square-cornered cap and getting the hell out of here, then good riddance, I say. Be gone."

"They become someone else's problem," Cinq-Mars reminds him.

"Did I not mention that I preferred prison? My failure to bring the culprits to justice weighs pretty damn heavy. Might yet cost me my job, too, I dunno yet, though that's not the point. If our young women are safer because the son of a tycoon's gone home to sit around his country club in Georgia or be another dickhead on Wall Street or wherever the hell he goes, I'll take that for now."

"Not true today," Cinq-Mars points out, with a note of solemnity.

Till is quiet at first. "No, not true today," he admits. "This is my problem now."

"Unless," Émile speculates. A thought has occurred which he nurtures internally.

Till gives him time before prompting him. "Unless what?"

"Unless a perpetrator is getting in his final licks before graduation, knowing he'll be gone from the scene in a week or two, never to be located. This could be perceived as a good time to inflict harm, before leaving for good."

Till turns the prospect over in his head. "So we have to act quickly."

Although his remark could be framed as a question, Émile knows it's not. "We always do," he reminds him.

He could contest a few matters that the chief mentioned a moment ago, debating points with all the subtlety of a boot applied to a throat. He forgoes the vitriol. Wanting a rapist merely gone from the vicinity is a poor alternative to justice. And wanting to consider three murders in a day as an external war that's come their way, as if paratroopers have tumbled out of the sky with no connection to any local malaise, is a typically human response. *How can a series of murders be local?* the thinking usually goes. *This misfortune must've been imported.* He senses that Till is a loyal citizen standing up for the good name of his community rather than being the skeptical, insightful investigating detective he needs to be in this situation, although he's willing to concede that the pressures faced by small-town police chiefs are beyond his ken. Public exposure inherent to the position, the constant political and social stresses, differ from those experienced by representatives of large forces in cities where cops, even famous ones like himself, work anonymously through the course of their day. This man can't eat a grape without someone questioning why it's red and not green. Or from what country it arrived.

Or who picked it.

"What do you think so far, Émile? Anything?"

The query is the chief's way of admitting that he's confounded by events.

Émile elects to reassure him.

"It's curious, Chief. Might even be unprecedented. I don't envy you the challenge. We have three deaths. We can connect the victims to the same school, but not to one another. Why is a dead girl gifted with a necklace by her killer? Why did we find a similar one in Toomey's glove box? What's the meaning of the note urging him to take flight? Who told him to run? What's been breached? When we look at this case, those aspects stick out—the matching necklaces and the warning note. They're not clues exactly, or not ones that we can figure out. They can have import. They hold out the possibility of being an accident in our favor."

"How do you mean, accident?" A car swishes by them as if they're standing still, then brakes to slow down, the driver realizing at the last second that he's speeding past a cop. He doesn't know that this one has restricted authority on the highway, and falls in behind him. "Ding-bat," Till murmurs to himself.

Émile thinks the question through. "We can reasonably assume that the killer may never have known about the necklace in Toomey's car. If he had known, would that have made any difference whatsoever? Would the killer have taken it away? Maybe, maybe not. If yes, then for what reason, if any, beyond its commercial value? The necklace connects Toomey's death to Addie Langford's, and without the necklace we'd only be speculating about a connection. The killer may have wanted to leave us with nothing more than speculations, but instead we have a powerful link. That just might be a very lucky accident. The other woman—what's her name again? I have trouble remembering English names."

"Malory Earle."

"With respect to her, I believe we'll collect her lover's DNA. Which we can hope will prove telling. I have a hunch, though, that it won't answer as many questions as it asks. We have to prepare for that anyway."

"How so?" Till wonders. "I think it'll answer questions."

"Oh, let's say she has a regular lover. Maybe he's gone missing. That'll make things easy. Let's say Toomey's her lover. I'm only suggesting that because they're both dead. What's up with that? Did he kill Malory Earle first? Then another person did him in? Doubt that. We've seen his day clothes and they aren't bloody. I'm not counting on any link there. If Professor Toomey and Miss Earle were lovers, is there a third person in a triangle? Or does she have a lover and Toomey's the third? Any chance that Toomey killed Addie? The necklace in his glove box is incriminating, no? Was it him? Why does he end up dead himself? Did poor Malory witness what she was not meant to see and did that lead to her death? That'll be a supposition the troopers will make, I can guarantee it and they might be right. They *will* be right to check it out. Mentally, it's hard for me to put Professor Toomey and young Addie together as lovers, although it's also hard to put him and Miss Earle together. Maybe I can manage it. Addie, of course, could have been attracted to his mind, that happens, or it may have been a one-way obsession on Toomey's part, leading to a pathological murder. That also happens. I still want to push through the three murders as being conjoined before treating them as separate incidents."

"Or two might be linked, and one is off on its own."

"Anything's possible, but why are you saying that?"

Till mulls it over. "You're looking at what connects the killings. Fine. I get that. But I'm conscious of what separates them out. They're different. Night and day. Okay, a gunshot twice, and we'll wait on ballistics to see if it's the same weapon or not. One gunshot victim was brutalized with what must have been a cleaver, or a machete, and the other one was left to gag on his own blood after a single bullet. Otherwise, he wasn't touched. The first victim we found was strangled, and we have the whole weird, sick component thing going on with that one, the dressing up and the pose. How can we not think that we don't have three different killers on our hands?"

"Multiple killers doesn't mean the crimes aren't linked. Keep that in mind, too."

"How does that happen?"

"You link the killers."

"That's a puzzle. I get the impression we need a lucky break or we're toast."

"Hmm," Cinq-Mars opines.

"You disagree?" Till is catching on to his inflections.

"A lucky break, I'll take that. Or damn good detective work. That works, too."

"I hear you. Amen to that. I don't disagree. I just think it might be up to us."

They come off the highway at Lebanon, New Hampshire, and drive through the heart of that industrial town before heading along a winding road into the countryside. The speed limit is thirty-five and Till again makes a point of sticking to it, although he's in a squad car and this isn't his town or jurisdiction. He could get away with pushing the limit here but chooses not to. While Émile admires that, another thought has nothing to do with Till being a stickler for the letter of the law. Intuition tells him that the chief wants to stretch out their discourse for as long as possible.

Indeed, the man seems chagrined when they arrive at Émile's mother-in-law's place. He parks after the long and bumpy road ends at the farmhouse, then cuts the ignition, as though to invite Émile to stay and chat.

"I gotta get in," Émile says, two fingers on the rocker switch that opens the door.

"Hang on a second," Till tells him.

Émile forgives him for that. The man is accustomed to giving orders to underlings and has forgotten himself, neglecting the status of his passenger as an independent citizen. The chief's thinking processes appear to cause him general discomfort.

"Something you don't know, you should know," Till says. In a way, a riddle.

"What's that?"

Cinq-Mars doesn't expect to be surprised, but he is by what the man says next.

"Your mother-in-law, Mrs. Lowndes."

He never imagined she'd merit a mention in the context of their day.

"Yeah?" Why is the other man straining to get his words out?

"Just coming clean here," Till begins, then shuts down again.

"Okay," Émile says after a few moments have passed. "Come clean."

Suddenly, the dam breaks. "She's been good to me. Helped me out with work when I was a kid. Later, she took my side when we had an uprising against me, she fought to turn that tide. She was very kind when my wife fell ill. My wife recovered, thank God, when it was touch and go through the chemo and all that. She's contributed materially and in practical ways to the department, and to the fire department. Given us a financial boost from time to time."

Cinq-Mars doesn't quite know what to say, and ends up saying what strikes him as inane under the circumstances. "I still can't believe that American towns elect their sheriffs and police chiefs. I'll never get that."

"Bad and good to it," Till suggests. "A man who's hired can always be fired, I suppose, and not necessarily when he deserves to be. A man who's elected can always lose next time. Fortunately, they don't get kicked out all that often under either system."

"Or unfortunately, as the case may be," Cinq-Mars puts in, giving Till a chuckle.

"Right you are, Émile. I'm not, though. If that's what you think. Elected."

"No?"

"Selected. By a committee. Hired and fired by the mayor and town council."

"You're right. That can be its own political beast."

"If you're wondering why I invited you in on this case, it's partly because I owe a lot to your mother-in-law. She's been an important person in my career. In my life, too. I'll miss her when she's gone. At this point, if she wasn't in her current circumstances and you weren't around,

I could be talking to her about what's transpired, hoping she might share a few aspects with her genius son-in-law."

"You're not serious."

"Halfway serious, maybe."

Émile knows that he is. He remembers, only now, that from time to time he did hear from Mrs. Lowndes about certain crimes in and around Hanover. "Unfortunately, that wouldn't help you. Her mind is pretty much gone."

"Oh no."

"That's not the half of it."

"I'm sorry to hear that. She's spoken well of you often, Émile. I mean, back when she was one sharp lady. You made her proud."

This is a surprise as well. When the marriage commenced, the much older, French-speaking, crime-busting, *Canadian* husband for her daughter didn't live up to the woman's standard for an ideal candidate.

Till chuckles again. "I've heard both sides. Past and present. But she got to know you, Émile, and heard about your accomplishments as a detective. Over the years, her pride grew. She came to understand her daughter's choice of husband. She was happy you two were together. Told me quite a few stories. She thought I'd be interested in hearing about another cop's success."

"I guess she got that part wrong."

"Nobody's perfect. She had that one major flaw."

The exchange is fine as far as it goes, although Émile thinks to challenge him. "Chief, when we met this morning, you Googled me."

"Only for show." A third time, Till enjoys a laugh. "I didn't want you to know you had an *in* with the local chief of police. For one thing, I didn't know if I'd like you. Didn't know if you'd impose all that bona fide success on me. Rub my nose in it, maybe. And you have, a little. I didn't open up. I was aware of your rep, Émile. Truth be told, I was intimidated the moment you introduced yourself and I've been trying to stay above water ever since."

"That's not easy to do today," Émile says, and waits for Till to catch the reference and chuckle once more.

After a delay, he comes through.

"If you don't mind my asking," the visiting detective asks, "why was there an uprising against you?"

"Handing out parking tickets to the rich and powerful, refusing to rescind. A situation where it was the principle of the thing, because the rich and powerful were insistent that I ticket the poor and the not-so-powerful for holding a street party. So I did. Rules are rules. The poor were ticketed the next time they didn't comply, their pockets emptied. The rich felt that different rules applied to them, that they could park in a no-parking zone while playing bridge and having a few drinks through the evening, coming back out onto the streets a bit wobbly and getting in behind the wheel. They demanded that I needed to be replaced for ticketing them when, if I was doing my job properly, I should have pulled a few of them over on suspicion of DUI. I gave them a break and they tried to remove me for my insolence. My insubordination, the mayor called it. Mrs. Lowndes turned that tide. Got public support behind me. I'll always be grateful. I only regret that I never nailed a few for DUI. Next time, I will. Or not. Anyway," Till concludes, "I want you to know that you have my sincere sympathies, and your wife, of course, at this difficult hour. Your wife's mom will be sorely missed when she passes."

"Thank you. I'll let Sandra know you said that."

Émile clicks the car door open. He then removes his right hand from the armrest, offers it to Till, and the two men shake. Knowing why he's been graced with this attention, why he's been granted certain allowances, that it's a family connection, helps him feel better about his role in the investigation.

On his way into the house, Émile notices lights on in the upstairs bedrooms, and in the living room downstairs. He finds Sandra on her own on the sofa by the fireplace, kisses her, and crosses to the liquor cabinet for a nightcap.

"I thought you'd be inviting your new friend in," Sandra says. "You could have."

"We're weary. Him and me both. Do we have guests?"

Sandra nods. But does not speak.

Émile sits opposite her, in the best chair available for his back. It's good that he's been on his feet a lot, not stuck in a car seat, for when he gets tired his back is usually the first body part to proclaim its weariness. He smiles, not to express happiness, rather to acknowledge the comfort of her company, and their privacy, given all that's transpired.

Sandra inhales deeply.

"What's wrong?" Until this moment, he hasn't noticed the depth of the change in her.

"I got the call," she replies. She tilts her head up, and tries to hold his gaze even as her eyes water.

"Sandra."

"Mom's gone."

"Oh sweetie."

He crosses to her then, and she weeps again, not for the first time, he now realizes.

"I'm sorry I wasn't here."

"That's all right. Caro was here, and then her mom came over. We all had a good cry." Sandra shakes the tears away. "We talked. We're done in, too. In the end Caro and Charlotte chose to stay. Because it's Mom's house? I don't know. Saying good-bye for the night seemed too difficult. I suppose we're in that terribly difficult zone where we're hurting and also feeling partly relieved. We don't quite know what to do with that." She exhales a long sigh. "Tomorrow the planning starts. So much to do in the days ahead. Tonight, I want nothing more than to sit a while, then go to bed and sleep. My mom's gone. It was time. But she's gone. Hey, I'm an orphan now, you know?"

She's weepy again. Émile can see that she's taking this as well as can be expected. A few days ago he would not have predicted any such thing. Time has passed, the circumstances have changed. Her grief will be heartfelt and prolonged, but there's no need for histrionics, not after the day's tragedy, and the circumstances of her mother's passing have predicated this sense of relief. The key, if a need for a key exists, is not to feel guilty for experiencing an updraft of relief. A life has passed on. All over the world new lives are being welcomed and celebrated at that very moment. One cannot occur without the other, and the only tragedy, the only greater sadness, is reserved for the young life taken prematurely, and for those whose final end is violent, and not natural at all.

"How did your evening go?" Sandra inquires, wanting a change of subject.

Émile gestures with his chin. He retreats the few steps across the carpet to his scotch. As the change of pace to the conversation is Sandra's way of coping with the moment, he provides her with a comprehensive, and yet abbreviated, version of the night's events. That he went to visit not just one murder scene, but two, is chilling, and does help detract her from grief in an odd way.

"Two more murders," she states, not as a question, or even with surprise.

Émile sips his drink and considers a raid on the fridge.

"How do you explain that?"

He can't. "We have a connection between the murdered professor and Addie. They were both in possession of a similar necklace. The third murder may be incidental. We'll know better once forensics has had a chance to report. I have a question for Caro, but it can wait until morning."

"About?"

He rocks his head as though he's not sure. "To ask if she knew the dead guy, Professor Toomey. Is she aware of any connection between him and Addie?"

"What did he teach?"

"International affairs, along those lines. I don't recall what Addie was studying."

"Not a large institution, Émile. Pretty much everyone studied international something."

"Oh yeah. I did know that."

"Are you wondering if Addie was carrying on with a professor?"

That slight rock of his head again. "Caro described her as romantically adventuresome. So it's possible. Do you think we can move this talk into the kitchen?" Émile requests. "I haven't eaten."

Salami and cheese on rye becomes the sandwich that suits the hour, with a side of leftover salad. He returns to the other room for a whiskey refill. On his return, he finds that Caroline has come down the stairs and sits on a lower step.

"I guess all detectives drink whiskey," she notes.

"I believe in God," Cinq-Mars replies, which mystifies her.

"What's your point about that exactly?"

"It's not an exact point." He decides to test her. "Why do you think I said it?"

She doesn't arrive at a response, and Émile sees that it was unfair to ask. The girl is bone-tired, worn down by a double grief in her life. They remain in the hall between the kitchen and the den. Sandra comes partway toward them, leans against the wall.

"When I was a patrolman I didn't eat too many doughnuts. Hardly any, although they are a quick way to take the edge off your appetite. I'm a religious man. I attend mass regularly."

"You're not a cliché," Caroline surmises from all that. She gets his point now.

"I like to think I'm not. I drink whiskey. Sure. Many cops do. Others don't. Lots more people who aren't policemen also drink whiskey. I'm willing to do what other people do, and enjoy what other people enjoy. None of that makes me them or them me. We're all different. I'm different. Whiskey, yes, doughnuts, no. The God thing is a total surprise to most people in this day and age."

"Inexplicable, I'd say," Caroline attests. She supports an elbow on a kneecap, her chin on top of a loosely curled fist. "Frankly, Uncle Émile, no offense, but it's intellectually unsustainable." More sheepishly, she adds, "In this day and age."

"Someday we'll talk about it and I'll convert you."

"Not damn likely. Excuse my language, but that's just a fact."

"I agree with you."

"Huh?"

"The point is, what is unsustainable for you isn't for me. We're different. We're all the same, yet we're all unique. Not all detectives drink whiskey. This one does. And no, I won't try to convert you. In my universe, everybody crosses paths with God in their own way. They may, or may not, use different language and different identifiers and call the experience by another name. Like I said, another day. I'm having a sandwich, by the way, as well as my nightcap. Interested?"

"Depends on the sandwich," Caro says, which is not true. Grief and weeping have made her hungry, and prompted as well this need for company.

The three eat while standing in the kitchen, and everyone sips whiskey. They think about things, and remember Addie and Sandra's mother. Émile knows that Caroline will be the next to speak, as he sees her glancing at him and forming her thoughts. Her ideas take time to meld.

"What more can we do?" she asks him. "More than what we talked about before. We'll do that, too. Keep our ears open, our noses on the floor." She peers at him with deliberate intent, indicating that she will not be put off or easily mollified. "I know you don't want us interfering, and you have a point. We shouldn't interfere. That could wreck things. On the other hand, we need to help. Me and my friends. Keep our ears open, okay, you said that. We can do that. Find out what other people have seen and heard. I'm not belittling that. It's a good idea. We'll do it. But what else? I just feel in my bones that there's more ways for us to help."

"Allow the police to do their job," Émile confirms.

"I'm not talking about that. I mean, it's not good enough that we just report on what people say," she insists. "There must be something concrete. You're here to guide us. Something . . . I don't know, detectivey."

"That's not a word."

"It is now."

Émile has an idea, but he's uncertain of its wisdom. He'll let it go if she backs off on the intensity of her gaze for a second.

Caroline does not relent.

"All right," he concedes. "There is one thing that we can consider. I don't want to use an actual photograph, as that will be viewed in a negative light, as interference, by the police. Are any of your friends good at drawing?"

Kali is the artistic talent among them, apparently.

"Draw what, though?" Caro asks. "She's more landscape and objects. Not portraits."

"Not faces," Émile interrupts. "Earlier I received an e-mail on my phone from Chief Till, with a photograph of the necklace that Addie was wearing. Now, you and your friends could show the photo around, but that deprives Addie of her privacy, I think. Because it means showing her neck. People will be more fixated on the fact that she was strangled and not on what we want them to see. Do you think Kali could draw the necklace, just by itself, so we'd have that rather than the photograph?"

Caroline is certain she could.

"If Kali can draw a likeness of the necklace, the three of you can distribute the drawing on social media—you know more about that aspect than I do. Ask if it's familiar to anyone. If we can get that ball rolling, it could lead to a clue. The necklace is about all we have to go on right now. Let's see if the people in your world—in your cyberspace world—can help."

Caroline welcomes the chance. "We'll get on it."

"In the morning," Émile stipulates. "There's a lot of sadness in this house tonight. We'll all be quiet and go to sleep. That's what we need more than anything. Sleep."

Caroline recognizes that he's referring to Sandra in particular, and perhaps himself, and consents without further discussion. She's excited though, and will be on it first thing in the morning.

Émile finishes his drink, then goes up well behind the others. He finds his wife sitting in bed in ambient light. She smiles as he removes his watch and empties his pockets before unbuttoning his shirt. "Émile? You're on this case?"

"Just," he says, then doesn't quite know how to finish, "poking around the bushes. Seeing what flies out."

"You're on this case," Sandra tells him. She holds out her hand, which Émile accepts, sits down beside her. They hear Caroline and her mother whispering in the adjacent room that they've confiscated for themselves. To the tune of the extraneous voices the couple kisses. Émile stands to continue preparing for bed, and once he's in from the bathroom, having brushed his teeth and taken his pills, he gets under the covers and wraps his arms around his grieving wife. He holds her close. They both feel sad, their breathing irregular. Entwined in that way, Sandra will fall asleep, while Émile stares at the ceiling half the night through.

PART 3

FOURTEEN

Breakfast becomes a solemn gathering. Hardly a word is spoken before coffee. Sandra, her niece Caroline, and her sister Charlotte, inhabit a deeper rung of grief after sleeping, while Émile slips into a funk of his own. Revived by caffeine he emerges from it, and guides Caro into reciting the names of the dead girl's friends and acquaintances as he writes them down. She stumbles over one person, a lady professor by the name of Shedden. When he questions her hesitation, Caro explains that the professor and Addie seemed to have been friends for a while, though not of late. They may have had a falling-out.

"A falling-out," Cinq-Mars repeats.

Caro is uncomfortable. "They used to hang off campus. Seemed a bit creepy to me. Then it stopped. Addie never said why. She didn't want to talk about it."

"Creepy," her uncle notes. He tries to keep his inflection casual.

"You know what I mean," Caro says. "Addie was bi. So she said, anyway. Okay? But, you know, with a prof, who's older . . . that's what's creepy. But I don't know for sure. No one does. Addie talked way too much about her boyfriends. She had too many of them, too. Women, only a few. She said virtually nothing about them. That's how it was with her. Always. Embarrassed, maybe. I don't know."

"That's what you didn't want to talk about in front of me yesterday, but you told the police."

"You know. You're my uncle."

"So's Bob."

"Excuse me?"

"Nothing. Poor joke. It's early."

The arrival of State Trooper Hammond at the farmhouse doesn't lighten anyone's mood, but at least the officer arouses their curiosity.

Émile steps outside to greet him and the women follow, taking up positions along the front porch where they hope to eavesdrop. Caroline once dubbed the front porch the family swamp, a place to swat mosquitoes and complain about the weather. While it serves those purposes well, it's also an observation post when unexpected visitors show up, usually to buy a horse or to book riding lessons. The trooper is not interested in such activities, and as he extends his hand Émile is surprised that he remembers the man's name. "Trooper Hammond. Good morning."

The return salutation sounds terse to his ear: "Mr. Cinq-Mars." Émile senses that he won't welcome the man's purpose in being here.

"What's up?" he asks the visitor.

"We need to talk."

"This early in the morning?" He does his best to come across as friendly. "You might find me grumpy, sir, but sure thing. How can I help? Would you like to go inside? Have a coffee?"

The officer adjusts his Smoky the Bear and examines the house. He notices Sandra and the young woman he interviewed yesterday observing him.

"I think I can say what needs to be said out here," the trooper decides.

"Is there a problem?" Cinq-Mars inquires.

"Doesn't need to be," the trooper reflects. "Shouldn't be a problem as long as we can both agree that you're it."

"It? I'm the problem?" He's not entirely surprised. He didn't take to this man from the outset. The trooper crosses his arms as though to demonstrate that he will brook no challenge.

"You're a retired cop," the trooper points out.

Cinq-Mars flashes a smile. "Since when is that a crime? Or anybody's problem?"

Hammond ignores him. He looks over at the horses in the paddocks, then back again. "Emphasis on the word *retired*."

"A fact of life," Émile points out to him. He knows where this is headed. "I'm told it beats the alternative."

"Stop muddling."

Surely, Émile thinks, the word he means to say is *meddling*. While English is second nature to him now, he still encounters a gap or two, given that French is his first language. Perhaps both words fit. "Who's muddling? Or meddling, do you mean?"

"I'm not going to excuse you, a man with your credentials. You know better. Last night you were out to the scene of two different murders, not to mention worming your way onto the crime scene yesterday A.M. This might come as a shock to your system, sir, you're not needed here. Neither are you invited. Big surprise, we can manage without you."

"I wouldn't worry about any shocks to my system, Trooper Hammond. Good of you, though, to drive out here to let me know."

"It goes beyond that."

"Sure hope so."

"Not only are you not needed, you're not wanted, either."

"That's clear."

"I'll make this easy on you."

"Just don't shock my system."

"Don't be flip with me, sir."

"Don't call me 'sir.'"

"What?"

"You didn't hear me?"

"It's a term of respect."

"Only when said respectfully."

The trooper has unfurled his arms now, and moves his feet around and rotates his waist. He puts his hands on his hips. In another time, in another situation, without three women watching him, he might have been inclined to throw a punch, and still might do in this circumstance if Émile were two decades younger. "I'm not going to hit an old man," he whispers.

"Speak up. I can't hear you. Neither can my witnesses."

"Stay away from this investigation. Don't talk to anybody involved. You don't visit any crime scenes and you don't discuss the matter with Chief Till. That man's going to be in his own cesspool of trouble if he doesn't put his ass under a microscope. Are we clear on that? Is any of this too complicated for you? Go back to being retired. You're not on the job anymore and you never were around here. My advice? Invest in a magnifying glass to study your belly button instead. Otherwise, I'm placing you under arrest for obstruction of justice if there's even one more incident, I don't care how minor. Just so you know. Are we clear?"

"I don't know why people ask that question."

The trooper is baffled a moment. "What question?"

"Are we clear? Do you think it comes from that movie?"

The words are almost on Hammond's lips, "What movie?" before he rethinks their conversation.

"You've been warned," Hammond tells him. "That's out of respect for you being on the job in your time. This is not your time, sir. Or mister. Or whatever you want to be called. Old man. It won't be detective. This is not your time and it's not your country. It's not your case and your interference will not be tolerated."

Cinq-Mars knows that the trooper wants to be able to say it once more—is that clear?—but he declines, and gets back in his car.

As he drives off, Émile watches him go, then returns to the house. The women appear dispirited. Even contrite, as though they're taking blame upon themselves. He's had his knuckles rapped.

He stops before the porch and looks up at them.

"Sorry about that," Caroline commiserates. She now believes that any contribution to the investigation of her friend's murder that he might have made has been short-circuited. "I guess maybe we got you into trouble."

"Trouble? What? Him?" Émile fires back. "He's not trouble. Don't ever pay attention to a man like that. Three murders on his watch and what is he concerned about? Who might be stepping on a crack in his sidewalk. That's his main bugaboo. That tells me he's lost, without a prayer. Maybe he can whistle Dixie but he can't solve a major crime. Now then," he says to Caroline in particular.

"What?" she answers back, still confused.

"Why the heck are you hanging around here? If you're planning to lend a hand, do you have time to dilly-dally? Get a move on."

In a twinkling, her attitude turns, her mother and aunt grin, and the young woman is suddenly eager and focused. She beats it back into the house to get a few things together, then commandeers her grand-mother's old Ford. Émile, for his part, will head into town as well. He has work to do, too. Let Hammond try and stop him. Aware of his defiance, Sandra grins. She's even laughing a little behind her tears.

"What?" A vague snarl.

She puts her hands up to simulate compliance. She knows he's roy-ally ticked off.

The morning sun scales the mountains and ascends into a familiar sky, yet the village is sleepy as Émile wends his way into Hanover. He's decided that he likes it here. The quality of the sensory experience is one that he has previously tried to assess—what is it that makes an American town feel American? It's not only the flags. In affluent New England, the respect for architecture is generally more prevalent than it is back home in Canada, although European villages are artful in pre-serving the past, and tidier, so that's not it, at least not in its entirety. As people move through their routines, there's a feeling of relaxation particular to these Main Streets that he finds less evident in the rest of the world. Émile begs to differ with those Americans who might think they are the hard workers and the go-getters of the universe. He detects an atmosphere quite different in the morning air of small Yankee towns. People seem to believe that everything is right with the world and they're at ease with that. What might occur on any given day is only what everyone expects. Even on this rare morning, a troubling time in the aftermath of three murders, folks chat, perhaps more intently than usual, yet they drop into the post office, grab a cup of coffee from a shop, greet friends, juggle their purses and newspapers, adjust their backpacks, and somehow look and feel gifted with the art of living. A provenance is built into their confidence, a daily ratification that this is the moment that's been awaited, it's been foretold, this is the time that is and the time that has always been ordained. It's not the future nor even the mythic past. Our time is the present, they're saying, or thinking, or just living as if that's the case, which is what makes a place fine and livable, if not wholly perfect. That's the essence of what's different, Émile concludes. These pristine New England towns seem perpetually aware of their own pageantry, and whether it's in the architecture or in the tone of personal exchanges, citizens feel obliged to inhabit and inhale an atmosphere, one they both celebrate and rely upon to sustain them. As if they are standing in as icons on a postcard, or see themselves as the nostalgic relics of a future age, for is this not the only moment that counts? The present is not only now, it's here and it's forever and it's American, thank God. These folks don't do panic or consternation, Émile attests, or don't do it well, nor do they suffer threats to their well-being with dramatic concern. As long as the sun shines upon the shade trees, and the children skip, and the old folks nod from their park benches, and the coffee shops are open, and a Mercedes can pull in behind a jalopy and a cop can smudge both cars' tires with chalk, then the disposition of the people on the streets is congenial, all is well, and all will remain well today, a fine day that is bound to fold gently into tomorrow.

Storm-free.

Émile is less certain of that, of course, perhaps because he's not American, yet he finds the general temperament appealing, even if he tends to feel that he's treading through an alternate universe.

He ponders, also—and this is a more difficult notion to grapple— the *stillness* that persists as sunlight shines upon American towns. He's not experienced it elsewhere. In a meditative moment of his own, he wonders, not for the first time, if it's him. That is, if the stillness that he detects does not occupy a space inside him where previously his mind merrily computed away, ringing up calculations. An aging thing, perhaps. Is it that his focus is less intent than before, less geared to the task at hand? Is that why he was slow to get off the seat of his pants this morning? Chief Till is younger. He'll check him out. Perhaps he can hold him to a standard he's no longer able to fully attain himself.

Hell, he thinks. I'm retired. I'm allowed to hang back. Yet to continue in such a vein will only prove Hammond right, that he ought to keep his nose out of things. Once that conclusion snaps to mind he knows he won't allow it.

He parks near the police station and tramps inside.

Cinq-Mars is interested in taking the chief of police by surprise, to observe how he starts his day after being subjected to the darkest crimes of his career. Émile is aware that he's feeling the need for friends in high places, and while he's inclined to believe that Till is an honest cop and probably a half-decent example of one, he's anxious to find out how he conducts himself when circumstances demand more of him than what's been required previously. His counterpart among the troopers failed his first test, knotting his colon over nothing more than jurisdiction. Till may also fail. The man's a worry because he knuckled under rather quickly to the New Hampshire state trooper, managing only a passive-aggressive counterpunch in soliciting Émile's help. As well, Till's remarks indicated that he's had difficulty in the past being respected. He admitted that he once required an old lady— Émile's mother-in-law—to run interference for him to help keep his job. Those could be benign experiences, or they could be warning signs, and Émile needs to assess him further before placing his trust in the man. The first thing he must find out: does Chief Till respond to a crisis by sleeping in after a late night, then by taking a two-hour breakfast to think things over, or is he on the job at the crack of dawn as he ought to be?

He finds him at his desk when he's escorted there by a rookie constable. He looks busy enough. His toast-and-jam has scarcely been munched.

"Morning, Émile. Have you solved all three cases yet?"

"Have you?"

"You're the one with the huge rep, so I was hoping. Coffee?"

"Had mine, thanks. What's on tap for today?" Cinq-Mars tests him. Till makes a gesture with his hands in front of his face which Émile fails to comprehend. "What's that supposed to mean?"

"First thing I got to do is extract this boot from between my teeth."

Émile is willing to play along with the metaphor. "Who did the kicking?"

"Hammond."

"He gets around."

"You, too?"

"Kept my groin covered. Of course, I'm independent. A foreign national. A visitor. I'm not on anybody's payroll and under no one's authority. He has less freedom to lord it over me."

"He's got me greeting the parents this morning, when they land."

"Addie Langford's?"

"Pleasant job, huh?"

"The man's a coward. It's *his* case."

"That's why. He says. His time is too precious. Although he's got time to kick me in the head and bitch to you. I'm not allowed to talk to you, by the way."

"You accepted that?"

"I suggested he study the Constitution. That's when he kicked me in the teeth again, warned me that the upcoming elections favor the incumbent mayor. With a new mandate he might have another go at me. Your mother-in-law won't be around to bail me out. He's right, too. After that he went to see you, I guess."

"Sorry about that."

"I could care less. An order from him becomes a de facto order from the governor if I put up a stink. He's given me an order. Meet and greet the grieving folks. With Kleenex at hand, I suppose. I'll do my job."

"Hard duty," Émile commiserates.

"I could wiggle off that hook, shift it to a subordinate, but hell, might as well be me. Anyway, better me on the ground to meet them than that slice of bacon."

A perspective that's not without merit. Émile's impressed.

"What are you up to today?" Till inquires.

"Lying low, officially."

"Unofficially?"

"Lying low," Émile repeats.

"Which means what exactly?"

"Chief Till, you sound as though you don't believe me?"

"Detective Cinq-Mars, where are you plunking down your ass right at this exact moment? On a park bench? Lying low as you say? Are you not in the office of the local police chief, a man, I presume, you're forbidden to visit? What are you doing in his office?" Till answers his own question. "Testing him. How can you call that lying low?"

If he was required to rate this fellow on a scale that evaluated their compatibility to be cops in the field, Till was scoring high marks. Rather than being happy about that, Émile is growing nervous. Although he's liking this guy, it's too soon to trust him beyond his usual skepticism.

"I was hoping to make a social call," Cinq-Mars admits. "I don't mean this visit. I'm in your office because I hoped that you might make an introduction which would let me call on someone else. I'm presuming that the chief of police and the president of Dowbiggin are acquainted? Mutual cooperation has been necessary over time, I imagine, between your offices?"

Till requires a moment to let the request sink in. He even repeats it out loud. "You want me to introduce you, an outsider, a retired cop, to President Palmerich." He checks his watch. "I'm off to the airport shortly. Can't do it in person right away. I could pick up the phone. Set something up."

"I'd appreciate that." He suspects that a speed bump is coming.

"Ah, Émile, it's my neck that's being stuck out here."

"You mean Hammond?"

"No, I mean the president of the Dowbiggin School. No one in the state sits in a more prestigious chair than the president of Dartmouth College, not even the governor himself. Dowbiggin is a giant step down from that, of course, but it's still on the stairs. Between the two administrations, there is communication. There's protocol that a guy in my position needs to observe. If I'm to introduce you . . ."

He lets Émile fill in the blanks. "You want to know if I'll behave."

"Something like that. I want to know what you're up to, and . . . frankly . . . how you want me to handle the introduction. I'll be doing you a favor, fine, on that basis I'm willing. Will I be doing Josh Palmerich a favor? Or myself a favor? He and I have good relations. I could set it up and tell him to watch out, to tread carefully. A warning, essentially. Or say that it's in the school's best interest to cooperate with you. I can even suggest that he trust you. Whichever. After the meeting, I want him to agree with my assessment. The question is, what should my assessment be?"

Till has given him more to think about than anticipated. He has a point. The chief's primary concern is to protect an ongoing relationship with the president of Dowbiggin, and through him to the other powers in the state. He can do that whether Émile plans to be antagonistic or congenial, as long as no one is blindsided in the interview. In essence, Till is asking Émile to propose his strategy in advance of the conversation, then stick to it.

Of course, he may want to approve of his strategy first.

Émile is tempted to be tough on the issue of rape on campus with the college president. He anticipates a whitewash on that one, but if there is a line between those previous incidents and the current murders, then it must be drawn. He is also interested in establishing relationships in this town that may prove useful over the breadth of this case, so he has a decision to make.

"I'll be gentle," the visitor declares at last. "Our interests and the president's are mutually beneficial. Everyone wants to find out who killed a Dowbiggin student, a member of the faculty, and a custodian. The institution has been desecrated. Only the truth can help it now. I'll float your circumstances before him, Chief. Point out that your hands are tied. Talking to me is a way for the president to help us out, and himself out, before the troopers make a botch of it. You can't go see him. You've been officially told to bugger off. I've been told the same thing but nothing's official in my case. It's a free country, even for a tourist. I can talk to anybody I want. Go ahead, Chief, invoke my history to the president, make me look good, then ask him to grant me leeway. If things go badly, if evidence turns up that's harmful to Dowbiggin, I won't turn him against you or me without first giving you a healthy heads-up and him a fair warning."

Now it's Till's turn to trust him or not. As he mulls it over, Cinq-Mars gives him a modicum of further assurance.

"Listen, Chief, we have no choice. With Hammond on the warpath, you won't be allowed to talk to the people you should be talking to, and I can't let myself appear to be more than a blip on his radar screen. I won't be riling anyone, let alone people in power. Not even Hammond if I can help it. Think of it this way. We'll be using Hammond's sour mood to help us get on track with others and that will assist us in working through the case. You have to love the irony. His attitude is our opportunity. His bad mood opens doors for us."

That's an argument Till can buy. He picks up the phone. Before dialing, he remarks, "I caught it, by the way. What you just did."

"What did I do?"

"Made yourself necessary."

That may be true, but Cinq-Mars doesn't want him to be thinking that way, arousing suspicions. "Chief, we're necessary to each other. That's my take."

"Let's hope so," he responds, rather sternly. The remark expresses a genuine expectation while also standing as a subtle warning.

Till dials.

Prior to convocation, the agenda for President Joshua Palmerich has been hectic. The festivities require his time, as does the annual influx of key donors. Private meetings and public appearances abound. The sordid events on campus have complicated his schedule, and in advance of Émile's arrival he made it clear that their talk will be brief. In his previous life, Émile could blow past such constraints by flashing a badge, but now he both recognizes and accepts the altered circumstances. For him to question someone these days, he must first negotiate the right to do so, then keep people onside throughout the interview. No bullying. Lucky to have the meeting at all, he's prepared to make the most of his allotted time.

In being admitted to the president's office, then, he's surprised to find the man not the least abrasive. The contrary, he appears to be receptive to the intrusion. He comes across as remarkably relaxed for a man whose institution has been hit by three inexplicable murders.

"Needless to say," Palmerich notes, although Cinq-Mars is thinking the opposite, that the point is worth making, "I was glad to receive

Chief Till's call. A good man. We've had opportunity to work together in the past."

"Not to keep you, I'll come to the crux of the issue," Cinq-Mars responds. "Chief Till has been ordered off the case, to give the state troopers a clear run. That jurisdictional wrangle is largely political, governed more by ego than pragmatism. I don't agree that it's the best decision. I'm here in his stead and I will keep him apprised. In this way his office can work alongside the school and, hopefully, assist the troopers see this through to the right conclusion, and swiftly. We must . . . it's delicate, how shall I phrase this?"

President Palmerich lightly taps his desk to allay his fears. He is not a naturally distinguished-looking man, in Émile's opinion. He dresses well, and in keeping with his office his grooming is impeccable, and yet it's not a stretch to imagine him running a small grocery store or a gas station. A bagginess to his skin, especially under the eyes, nurtures a wearied look that's long-standing, as though it runs generations deep. The man's designer glasses exude a contemporary fashion flair, his tie is silk and his watch an expensive timepiece. Then again, the curvature of his spine and a higher than normal pitch to his voice weakens the overall presentation. Something in his appearance seems off. He's a man, Cinq-Mars surmises, who has survived on intelligence and dogged ambition throughout his career, not charisma.

"I spoke to Trooper Hammond yesterday at length," Palmerich relates. "Again this morning. Stressful conversations, in light of the events. Given my association with Chief Till, I was hoping to speak with him today. That you've arrived as his emissary, or as his surrogate, is welcome, Mr. Cinq-Mars. The governor also called and advised me to work with Trooper Hammond—insisted, might be the better word—and I will. I lobbied for Chief Till, but if this arrangement, your presence, grants the university the benefit of both men and both departments, then I view that as a positive."

"You understand, sir, that Hammond may take exception."

Palmerich shrugs. "Neither the governor nor Trooper Hammond need know if you and I happen to discuss affairs of state. I confess, I did a quick Google search of your name. A famous police detective with a degree in agriculture, majoring in animal husbandry—which, I admit, is a new one on me—with a penchant for theology, one newspaper account stated, and spirituality. What a mix, Detective! How could I not agree to see you? Chief Till's recommendation is enough for me, but I have to say that your credentials are both a curiosity and impressive, especially when it comes to incarcerating the wicked. Now, sir, how may I help?"

Cinq-Mars thinks he has to be wise in his approach to his first line of inquiry. "Incidents have occurred on campus previously, over the last year or two."

"Over four years, I'm sorry to say. Do you think they're related?"

"I'm not jumping to that conclusion, no. Yet the rapes cannot be ignored. You have far more knowledge about them than I do—I have none. Let me ask, do any of those events bear resemblance to any aspect of what happened yesterday, on or off campus?"

He summons a shrug that rises up through his torso. "Not to my mind. One or more of yesterday's victims may have suffered a rape. I haven't been officially informed of that. If so, that would be a connection. I'm not cognizant of any similarity, and certainly we've not had anything that violent."

"Previously, no knives, no guns, no attempts to choke?"

"Two incidents were more violent than others to be sure, in terms of physical force and physical injury, but minus those particular aspects."

While he'd love to isolate the murders from the rapes, that can only occur if they truly are unrelated. "Were any previous victims forced to dress up? Put on a costume?"

"To that I can categorically say no."

"Was the clock tower involved in any of the previous incidents?"

"No." Palmerich first looks at Émile, then away, then back at him with a concerned furl to his brow. "Actually," he says.

"Are you serious?"

"No one was raped in the clock tower. But one victim, after the fact . . . I read her transcript . . . complained that she suffered inappropriate touching during a public visit to the tower prior to her rape. This was long before she was abused and it was deemed inconsequential. We have a winter festival. A festival tradition is to open the clock tower to anyone who wants to make the climb and enjoy the view. She didn't

issue a complaint when the incident took place. At the time she got mad
and confronted her aggressor. The rape investigation brought it back to
her mind; she mentioned it in passing in her deposition. She herself did
not allege that the incident was connected to the rape, but it gave the
police a suspect to track down and question. I forgot about it until this
moment."

"I'll want to talk to her."

"Chief Till will need to conduct the interview himself. I'm obliged
to protect the victim's privacy. Thank you, by the way."

"For what?"

"For jogging my memory. Hammond brought up the rapes yesterday but by the end of our discussion, I believe he dismissed any possible
connection. Now you've made one. Or at least, connected inappropriate
touching to the tower."

Cinq-Mars is not inclined to believe that he has. Overturning
stones, to his mind. "Sir, it's tentative. We'll see how it plays out."

"I understand. Nevertheless, Detective, you've demonstrated to me
that this shadow investigation of yours may have merit."

In returning his gaze, Cinq-Mars realizes that a slight disconnect
that he's felt from this man—what has been off—is attributable to a
form of strabismus—his eyes cross. The man's gaze is slightly askew:
when he thought they were making eye contact they weren't, and when
he thought they weren't they might have been. Recognizing that helps
him to settle into the talk. Chief Till need not have warned him about
alienating this man. He has no such intention, and decides to under-
score their successful bond with a couple of easy requests before dig-
ging into a more difficult issue.

"I was hoping," he begins, "to gain access to a few places on campus.
The first would be Professor Toomey's office. Feel free to have a security
guard in the room with me. I promise to only look, not touch, and certainly not take anything away. I'll leave that for Hammond. That said,
I'd be happy to get into the room before him. I don't imagine he's been
there yet."

Palmerich's nod appears to confer consent, although Cinq-Mars isn't
sure. Perhaps the president is waiting to hear what else he will request.

"As well," Émile elaborates, "I'd like to visit Malory Earle's specific workplaces. I won't be talking to her coworkers, leaving that to Hammond. It would only confuse them anyway. My next request is undoubtedly more difficult. The clock tower remains cordoned off, I expect. In any case, it's normally out of bounds and the entire seventh floor is restricted. I entered the tower yesterday, at its base—if anyone can say that being seven stories up is a base. In any case, I'd like to revisit, to make the climb to the top, to see what that might provide."

Again, a noncommittal nod. Cinq-Mars continues on once more.

"Professor Toomey came to you from the State Department. Prior to that he was in something or other that was clandestine. Such as the CIA."

"How did you know?" Finally, a reaction.

"I put two and two together," Cinq-Mars tells him.

"An interesting computation. You're close. I'll say nothing more. Allow me to play this card: I can neither confirm nor deny that opinion."

The two men share a smile.

"With that in mind, if there is anything, past or present, that strikes you as a red flag connecting his past to his murder, or to the other murders, then I hope you'll share that information. With me, of course, but if you prefer, only with the police."

"I understand. Nothing pops to mind, Mr. Cinq-Mars. I'm sorry to have to say this: We have to move this interview along."

Cinq-Mars would prefer to be more circumspect as he arrives at a key objective. "I noticed that Professor Toomey was in possession of an invitation to a cocktail party on campus this week."

"You have an eye for such details, Mr. Cinq-Mars. If the invite came from this office, then I believe I know which one he's expected to attend. A party given annually for many of our principal donors."

"If I may be direct, why was he invited?"

"His State Department background, I suppose. If we're calling it that. Someone may have requested that he be included, or he may have asked to be included. I'd have to check. We do desire to have a number of professors there, showing the colors, an organizer may have thought it was his turn. I confess, though, that when I noticed his name on the list, I was surprised."

"Why?"

He pulls his hands apart, then knits them together again. "We like to have our most prestigious minds present. Along with those who know how to work a room. As well as those with a recent claim to fame to talk about. He doesn't fit any of the three categories, and in fact he's virtually obliged by duty to be circumspect. Not good party material. What would he talk about, for instance? State secrets?"

"I was wondering if I might go."

Palmerich is taken aback. "Excuse me? Go? Why?"

"Sir, you know that a valuable necklace was placed around the throat of the victim yesterday."

"I saw it. I saw the victim where she lay, for a moment."

"The necklace has monetary value and yet was left behind. Donated, perhaps, to enhance the image the killer was trying to project of the victim. This leads me to suspect that the perpetrator may be a person of means. You have a gathering planned for persons of means—"

"I'm sorry. I see where you're headed. That is speculation and it is a bit wild, Mr. Cinq-Mars."

"I'm accusing no one, of course, and have no reason to do so. But persons of means need to be considered—"

"Our donors specifically? That would be folly, if not suicide, for me to subject any of them to that sort of scrutiny."

"The scrutiny—which is too strong a word—I assure you will be covert. No one will suspect a thing. Mere reconnaissance."

"This is an affluent part of the world, sir. Those individuals traveling up for our convocation ceremonies will not be the only people of wealth on hand. With all due respect, that's a bit of a stretch."

"Sir, no one is being accused or is being considered a suspect. As you say, there will be other persons of means on hand. Yet, with respect to the wealthy people who live in the area, they have lived here without such crimes as we saw committed yesterday. That the killer, or one of multiple killers, is, in fact, an outsider, perhaps with connections to the university, and also a person of means, merits consideration. Your party brings together persons of wealth who are also, many of them, outsiders. That's a gathering I'd like to infiltrate, just to take notes. If my identity is mysteriously revealed by an unforeseen accident, we'll say that I'm on hand as an additional security detail, in light of what has transpired. People will understand. You won't be vilified for having me around, but commemorated, probably, should I be found out."

"I'm less concerned with being commemorated than I am with being tarred, feathered, and rolled down a mountainside in a barrel, if I'm lucky."

They enjoy a chuckle, but Cinq-Mars falls to a more serious tone. "I can manufacture an identity for myself, if you prefer. Look, one thing that happens if we segregate the earlier rapes from these murders is that it points more strongly to an outsider, or outsiders. Proper police work has to take the donors into consideration. I understand your predicament, but consider this. On the off chance that a donor is complicit, do you want that person to be discovered and then have it reported that you shielded him, along with the other contributors, from being investigated? More tar and feathers, I'd say. The allegations won't interest me, it's others who will take a hard look. My request puts you in a difficult bind here. I apologize for that, as I do appreciate the conundrum."

Palmerich looks agitated. He is, Cinq-Mars thinks, secretly furious. He's about to lose his support and must come up with a new idea quickly.

"Sir," Cinq-Mars begins, stalling for time.

"Yes?"

As if an intruder had dropped it on the floor, Cinq-Mars picks it up, and marvels: a bargaining chip. He's amazed by how the mind works. He had discussed with Chief Till that the head trooper's antagonism signaled an opportunity for their side, and now he can make use of his own thesis. "This slant to the investigation may well occur with me or without me. If it's official, then you can expect a more heavy-handed experience. Red flags might be public ones in that case, and the university may find itself uninformed. If I'm able to run through this angle quickly and discreetly, no one will ever know unless it's a matter of import. In which case, the spirit of cooperation the university fostered will be reciprocated, and that cooperative spirit will be what's reported in the press."

Cinq-Mars sees now that when the president is genuinely noncommittal he does not gratuitously nod. Instead, he holds him in a steady gaze. The retired detective is noted for the intensity of his own hard look. Criminals have been known to confess under the pressure of his glare. He sees that this man is equally as intimidating as he himself is deemed to be. Indeed, the man's strabismus makes the intensity of his gaze difficult to suffer, as the recipient doesn't know how to engage the hawklike stare. Cinq-Mars feels sympathy for any misbehaving student on the hot seat in this office, feeling like a morsel about to be chewed. He wants to reassure Palmerich that he hasn't issued a threat, only a friendly warning, but it's too late for that.

Although Palmerich relents, he continues to withhold his acquiescence. "Mr. Cinq-Mars, I shall give the matter serious thought and let you know, although my advice is to not get your hopes up. I shall grant your other requests. And yes, a security guard will accompany you as you move around on campus."

"I understand. Thank you, sir."

"Not at all. I consider the university fortunate to have you examining this matter." He interrupts himself and a smile plays on his lips. "I was going to say . . . examining this matter on our behalf . . . but I have no idea if that is correct."

Cinq-Mars stands. "I'd express it that way, sir. Essentially, I want the truth to come out on behalf of the victim, who was a good friend of my niece. You want the truth, I'm sure, on behalf of your student and your employees. Even, if I may say so, your donors. We're on the same page. Oh, and I'd like to ask further questions about Miss Earle, but I've taken far too much of your time already. Later on, perhaps."

"Later on, then. I know nothing of the poor soul, I fear. Mr. Cinq-Mars, there's something you should know. It's my suspicion that you don't know this already."

Émile waits.

"Regarding the invitation issued to Professor Toomey. The same invitation was held in the fingers of Addie Langford when she was put on display in the tower."

Cinq-Mars pretends he wasn't aware.

"Then I must attend that party," he attests, and stands.

"We shall see, Mr. Cinq-Mars. I'll take it under advisement. In the meantime, if you'll wait outside, I'll request a security guard to be your escort on campus."

The president stands as well, and the two men shake hands.

By holding back a question about Malory Earle, he has been able to finagle a second talk if he needs one. Cinq-Mars is happy with that. He's generally content with their progress together.

And yet, all he's thinking about as he departs is how he's going to crash that cocktail party, by hook or by crook.

FIFTEEN

He's awaiting the arrival of his campus security guard. Paces, sits, paces again, then stands by while she receives instructions directly from President Palmerich before they're on their way.

The guard is a handsome woman who carries her natural heaviness with confident prowess. Her name is Roberta, she tells him, and flashes a smile, and speaks in a husky, low voice that's uncannily clear. A lovely tone. Most anyone else speaking so quietly would go unheard, but the distinct clarity to her timbre overcomes the diminished volume. She smiles a lot, and Émile gauges early on that the woman possesses the right instincts. She thinks before she speaks. With a wry air that he finds admirable, she takes issue with his first request. Roberta asks, "Did you inquire about Professor Shedden with President Palmerich, sir? She's not identified on your list for a visit."

"It wasn't necessary, Roberta. Will I be examining her office? No. I'll be seeing her in person. Big difference." He garnered her name from his niece over breakfast. The implication was that Addie may have had a relationship with her, or at any rate, a friendship.

The guard knows he's up to something, while he can tell that she's on to him.

"Roberta, whose permission do I need to talk to another individual in these United States? Especially here, in the live-free-or-die state? Similarly, if Professor Shedden is not interested in talking to me, that's her prerogative. We'll leave."

She's trying to figure his angle. She's a black woman who has probably had to deal with a few shady white men in her day, but she concedes in the soft bell tones of her distinctive voice, "All righty then, sir, let's find your lady prof. It's still a free country. But—"

He bites on her baited hook. "But what, Roberta?"

"No fishy business."

She makes him smile, too. "I left my rod and reel behind."

"Like I believe you." Even that skepticism she conveys with a smile.

He's already enjoying this woman.

On the trek across campus Émile feels only mildly guilty for duping the system. He needs neither a security guard nor anyone's permission to talk to Professor Shedden, yet being escorted by someone in uniform improves his chances of being taken seriously, which improves the odds of having his questions answered. By walking in with a guard at his side, his inquiry will appear to be officially sanctioned when it's not. Suggesting to President Palmerich that he might be assigned a guard as a watchdog over his behavior, Émile kept that kernel of strategy to himself. A sleight of hand. In uniform, Roberta serves in lieu of the badge that he's no longer empowered to flash.

As they walk, he learns that she has two children, both in high school, both good kids although neither is an angel. She also reveals that campus security has been touchy since yesterday. "We take it personal. Nobody's pointing a finger, but when you put on the uniform what is it you want to do?"

Émile isn't sure, and thoughtfully purses his lips.

"Protect the young ones," she tells him. "That's a good purpose in your life. Right there, it's not about stopping people parking where they shouldn't, or shaming rich frosh to pick up their litter. What you want to do is keep the young ones *safe*. A good purpose in life. Yesterday, that didn't happen. This is going to hurt for a long, long time."

"Did you know any of the victims?"

"Can't tell you a thing about them. Maybe if somebody shows me a picture I'll recognize a face. I had a glance in the paper this morning but they were blurry snaps. Overall, though, I've got a good head for faces. Professor Shedden, the one you want to visit, I've bumped into her. She's nice. They're all nice. Everyone here is nice."

"Hmm," Cinq-Mars says. He doesn't believe that last part, but as they encounter the professor in the corridor near her office, the guard is greeted by her first name and with a note of sympathy. "Roberta. How are you?" In the aftermath of the murders, personal exchanges are noticeably subdued. People are solicitous with one another.

"Good, Professor, good. This man is Mr. Cinq-Mars, I'd like to introduce. Some kind of detective. I brought him to see you." If she stops right there, Émile will be satisfied. In like Flynn. Unfortunately, Roberta continues. "President Palmerich asked me to show him around to do his investigating and he asked to talk to you."

"Me?" The blond woman looks up from the open file she's been carrying. Her eyes trip across Roberta and up to the tall Cinq-Mars. He's six two; she's a smidgen over five feet and stocky, yet exudes an attitude of physical strength and confidence. "Why?"

"People got killed," the guard explains.

The woman continues to study Cinq-Mars a moment, then gestures toward her office. She closes the file in her hands and Émile follows her to the door then goes past her as she holds it open. She's waiting for Roberta to come through as well but he intervenes. "This has to be a private conversation."

He's not averse to the security guard being in the room but wants to demarcate how their association will work. By ruling against Roberta's entry he elevates the importance of the proceedings. Striking an ominous note increases the gravity of the moment and hopefully that will provoke a desirable tension in his subject. A device that may or may not have value down the road. Professor Shedden shuts the door and the two plunk themselves down on opposite sides of her desk.

Posters are strewn on the walls, too untidily to be considered decorative. Most represent political postures. *Question Authority*. A policeman is viewed with antagonism in that one. *Seek Change*. A pair of urban squirrels are addressing rodent cousins from the countryside as though they're plotting to take over a park, then merge it with a dump site. The meaning is unclear to the uninitiated. Cinq-Mars is puzzled.

"Your name again, sir?" Professor Shedden probes. "I couldn't quite catch it."

"Cinq-Mars."

"Sounds French. Like the fifth of March?"

"Very good. That's it exactly."

"What significance does the date hold?"

"Nobody knows. Could be that my name is a corruption of Saint Marc, that's one theory. Another holds that a distant relation was the fifth son of somebody called March. Or Mars, in French. Or it's a corruption of another surname and somebody had five kids. Or an event occurred on the fifth of March. Lost to the veil of time, I suppose."

"I see. I detect an accent. Are you from France?"

"Quebec."

"And—you're a detective?"

She's asking, *Who are you to be here talking to me?*

He doesn't want to delve too deeply into that aspect. As well, he's the one who's supposed to be asking questions. "Sheriff Till of the Hanover Police Department—I'll remind you that that department governs the village of Holyoake as well—he brought me in as a consultant, an arrangement that has met with the approval of President Palmerich." An impressive introduction for himself, he concludes, one which should fly in any number of circumstances, as it does here. He has to hope she doesn't repeat it to Trooper Hammond, although he's guessing that the two won't have cause to meet.

"What I don't understand is why you're asking to speak to me. I presume the guard misspoke, that you're talking to various people at random?"

"Oh no," Émile counters, "I specifically want to speak to you."

She stares back at him. Her features invoke strength, suggesting a severity she can turn on and off. Her hair is closely cropped yet possesses a high gloss shine, at least in this light, the blond flecked with pure white.

Her clothing is relaxed for summer, highlighted by an embroidered thin yellow vest and a pair of mauve capris. Three tiny diamonds reflect from the lobe of one ear only.

"Why?" she asks again. Professor Shedden's tone sounds more genuinely curious than defensive.

"You knew the victim."

The silence in the room is not necessarily telling, but it is palpable.

"Given the bounty of your knowledge," she considers, the sarcasm in her voice sufficiently muted that it's difficult to confirm, "which victim are you referring to? I knew all three."

She has one up on him, and has surprised him more than he has her. Cinq-Mars battles back. "I don't want you to take offense," he warns.

"Why would I? Over whom I know? This is a curious conversation, Mr. Cinq-Mars. I confess, I'm more intrigued than offended. So far."

"You've given me a jolt. I hadn't expected to come across anyone who knew all three victims."

"I see. Okay. What am I supposed to be offended about?"

"For starters, I'll ask if you slept with all three." Since meeting her, he's struggled to take command of the talk. Without his badge and the authority that it signifies, he's been unable to deploy his usual methods. This is clumsy, he knows, but at least he's achieved his objective, which is to confuse her, to undermine her native poise.

The professor continues to glare back at him, as if they're combatants now, yet with lessening aggression and a deepening curiosity. She does not seem *offended*, although she remarks, "I can see where people might take exception to your phrasing, Detective. Shall I call you detective? Is that the correct salutation? You said you were working for the president?"

"With. Alongside. The president. Detective is fine. So is mister."

"In what capacity, exactly? You said, a consultant?"

"Did you? Sleep with all three?"

He's again caught off guard, this time by the naturalness of her laughter. He expected to have skidded more deeply under her skin by now. "Do I come across as some kind of slut to you, Mr. Cinq-Mars?"

She's decided not to call him detective after all. "You did sleep with at least one of the three, did you not? Which one?"

"I'm not going to answer that. If you think you know, say so."

"I'm curious. Why won't you answer?"

"For starters, I'm a professor."

"And Addie Langford was your student."

"Secondly, it's none of anyone's business."

"And Addie Langford was your student." He lets her know that the accusation is not going to go away.

"Not my student," Professor Shedden declares, as if on a witness stand, as though under oath. "She was a student. Here. Yes. But never of mine."

"You make that distinction, do you?"

"I don't have to if that's what you're saying. To be clear, I'm not saying that I slept with her nor am I denying that I did. I simply do not answer questions of that nature, no matter where they come from or in what regard."

"You make it sound like a— I don't know, like a virtue. Isn't it really a convenience?"

"What is?"

"That you don't answer questions of that nature?"

"As far as I'm concerned, there's a distinction to be made and I make it. Others might disagree. The sort of thing you're suggesting is generally frowned upon. Years ago, starting in the sixties if not before that, student/professor relationships were rampant. Times changed, although I have a suspicion that the old days are making a comeback. Nowadays, I suspect it's the students, more often than horny professors, who do the initiating. Just a theory. In any case, Addie Langford, that poor girl, I was very fond of her, but she was never a student of mine. I don't know where you're picking up your rumors, but . . ."

Cinq-Mars waits awhile. Then asks, "But what, Professor?"

"I was fond of her, that's true. She was murdered and that's been upsetting to say the least. For me personally. I've wept. Not because we were close or anything, but I knew her once and now she's dead just as her life was beginning. It's awful. Words can't say." She levels her gaze again. "Mr. Cinq-Mars, I don't wish to impede any aspect of your investigation, but you should know that I haven't spoken to Addie since last summer, maybe ten months ago. We haven't talked. I don't know what she's been up to. As far as an inappropriate relationship goes, I don't want to say and I hope that you won't ask, but in any case I won't answer. I never do. If I had a relationship with any student, male or female, who was not in one of my classes, I would consider that a union between consenting adults. Therefore, nobody's business. On principle, I won't answer. If you ask me if I've slept with Genghis Khan, I might point out the discrepancy in our centuries but I still won't deny it or say yes. If you consider that a convenience for me, that's not my problem. Addie was never in my class. She was not even in my department."

Having gone as far as he can with this line without making a dent, he senses that he's better off to reverse course and diffuse her fears. There's no virtue in antagonizing her any further, in large measure because he has no authority here and, sooner or later, that's bound to surface. "I'm not on a witch hunt, Professor Shedden. I'm interested in three murders and how they transpired. You're now on record. You've not had contact with Addie Langford in nearly a year. What about the other two?"

"If I slept with either of them, as I told you, I won't say."

"My question was out of line. I apologize."

"I know the woman by her first name—Malory—what's her last again?"

"Earle. Malory Earle."

"Yes. Only certain scholars are admitted to the seventh floor of the Lincoln Library. Special collections are kept in the stacks up there. The floor was part of Malory's nightly cleanup schedule. I often work in the stacks, and I have a tendency to work late. Sure, we came across each other."

Cinq-Mars is staring at her and appearing a bit wide-eyed.

"What?" she asks.

"Miss Earle worked on the seventh? At the entrance to the clock tower?"

"Do you think that's significant?"

"Don't you?"

"I hadn't thought of it. Now that you mention it, I guess, although it could be a coincidence. I mean, I don't see the connection."

"Two people die. One in a locked and restricted area. The other one has access to that area. That's a remarkable coincidence." Cinq-Mars breathes out heavily, and clutches his wrists behind his head and secretly gives his back a stretch. "Please. Go on. How do you know her?"

"That's it. That's all. Late night, friendly, quick chats. I do research, she takes out the trash. Sweeps up. In the daytime we might never speak, unless we pass each other in the corridors, but late at night, it's normal to say hi, how's it going? How're the kids? Exchange a few pleasantries."

"Was that the extent?"

"Are you insinuating something again?"

"Even if I am, it doesn't matter. Was that the extent?"

"Polite exchanges. That was it. The full extent."

"Ever talk with her when you weren't on the seventh floor?"

Professor Shedden thinks about it, her eyes going up to a poster condemning biologically modified food. "As I said, we bumped into each other a few times elsewhere in the library, of course. We exchanged a smile, once or twice said hello. Little more."

"Were you up there, on the seventh, the night before last?"

"I haven't been up there for a week or more."

"Okay. What about Professor Toomey? How well do you know him?" He's keeping his wrists crossed behind his head, extending his spine.

"I don't know him, actually. Biblically or otherwise. Whoops, sorry. I don't reveal that stuff. He sought me out, about a year ago. He wanted to be my date."

Another surprise. "Seriously?"

"In a way." She laughs. All in all, although he's tried to keep her off guard, he finds her remarkably relaxed. His detective status usually has people on edge, a trick that doesn't work in this room. "I don't hide my preference. I was amused initially. He didn't want to *date* me, just to *be* my date. There's a difference. Turns out I had an invitation to a cocktail party that he wanted to attend. He asked to be my escort."

Cinq-Mars drops his hands. He has an inkling. "Was this to a donors' party?"

"Could've been. I go to those. I think it must have been."

"Did you agree? To bring him along?"

"I did. Once inside, he pretty much dumped me at the door. Never saw him again, except across the room. Not that I cared."

"Did he take you home at least?"

"No way! Don't you get it? This was not an actual date. Which was fine with me. He was a busy man at the party, I noticed. Then again, I was, too. For me it's part of my job."

"For him? Not his job, then what was it?"

"Don't know don't care."

"Are you going again this year?"

"Every year. I expect a different tone this week though, given recent events."

"Toomey, also."

"Pardon me?"

"He was going again. This time, he engineered an invitation of his own."

She nods, as though to give him credit. "I guess he figured out how the system works."

"Hmm." Émile hesitates. He grips the arms of the chair. "Thanks for your time, Professor Shedden."

"About that," she says.

He stalls in pushing himself to his feet.

"Your thanks," she adds.

He's only clueless a moment. He says, "At this time, what some may deem inappropriate, even though you hold to a contrary opinion, needn't come up."

He appreciates the clarity of her gaze. "Tah," she says.

In the corridor outside, Roberta nearby, Cinq-Mars dials Chief Till's number. "How's it going?" he asks him.

"It's going." The policeman mentions that he has Addie Langford's parents in the backseat of his cruiser.

"Can I talk?"

"*You* can," Till tells him, with a tone that suggests that he's not free to reciprocate.

"Sorry to bother you, but can I get photographs of the deceased? All three?"

"Where do I send them?"

"Security at Dowbiggin. Have them addressed to Guard Roberta Dale." He reads her full name off the tag on her uniform. "She'll pick them up for me."

"You bet. Find anything out?"

"The custodial worker, Malory Earle, part of her job was to clean the seventh floor. The *restricted* seventh floor where the entrance to the clock tower is."

There's a silence, and Émile suspects there wouldn't be if Till was alone. The parents in tow, he must mute his response. "Interesting," he says. And asks, "Your take?"

"Another piece to the puzzle. Anything new at your end you can mention?"

"I'm not privy to ME reports from this side of the river. Trooper Hammond is keeping those to himself. From White River Junction it's more or less what we expected. Nothing too strange."

"What is more or less than expected? What's strange if not too strange?"

"Could be nothing. The medical examiner noticed radioactivity on Malory Earle. Specifically, on her chest. It's unexplained. Makes us wonder where she was, what she contacted. Otherwise, it's straightforward. What we saw is what we got."

"Radioactive. Was she, I don't know, dangerous?"

"Only a trace. The ME thinks it means she came in contact with something she shouldn't have. Hard to explain it otherwise."

"All right then. Okay. Thanks. I'll talk to you later."

Cinq-Mars puts his phone away in a hip pocket. "You can be the first to look at the photos, Roberta," he advises his official escort, "when they come in. You can tell me who you know."

"Probably nobody. A lot of people walk through this campus every day. I only know a handful by name."

"That's okay. The photographs aren't only for your benefit. If you don't mind, call your people. Ask them to alert you when the envelope arrives. Meantime, we're off to Professor Toomey's office. A visit on your *authorized* list. I know that will please you."

"Yeah, throw a dog a bone, why don'tcha?"

He likes this woman.

Rather quickly he finds out that he should never have been admitted to the room. State troopers shouldn't be allowed to enter either, or even some members of the FBI. This is a job for Homeland Security if he ever saw one, although he reminds himself that he's never actually seen such a job before.

Perusing Professor Phillip Lars Toomey's papers, he finds documents that should not have been left out in the open. Admittedly, much of it is old, but when he flips through a file and finds *Top Secret* stamped on certain pages, he questions the efficacy of secrecy these days. If they were old, secret documents may have been admitted to the public domain, but this easy access to anyone with a key to the room or a willingness to trip the lock strikes him as careless, at best. Even deliberately incendiary.

Roberta's phone rings a chime. The photographs have arrived at the front security desk.

"Do I leave you here alone?" she asks. "Do I trust you?"

"Not on your life."

"You're not trustworthy, you're saying?" That much probably does not surprise her. What does is that he admits to the failing.

"I wouldn't trust me if I was you, Roberta. But, we have no clue to what's already missing, if anything, or what might be construed as missing. We don't know what's here. I need you to be a witness to the fact that I'm not removing a speck of dust from this place."

"And turning the dust over very carefully." She's noticed.

"As such, you're my salvation. I wouldn't mind if no one, other than President Palmerich, because he's your boss, finds out that I was here. That's all I ask."

"My lips are sealed tighter than a jar of strawberry preserves."

The comment cheers him up. "What that means exactly I don't know, but I like it."

She stands watch while he carries on with his search, and is the most curious when he stops and does nothing. For a while he inspects no manuscript. He opens no drawer. He appears to draw no breath. It's spooky. She's feeling trepidatious.

"Sir?" she asks, but Cinq-Mars ignores her and carries on doing absolutely nothing. As if listening to the walls speak.

She waits.

He's acquiring a feel for the room. Sensations compete for his attention. An academic patina marks the office as different than an entrepreneur's, a businessman's, or a professional's. Yet the atmosphere feels borrowed from the institution and from previous tenants. He thinks this way because the library makes no sense, it's more of a grab bag of titles than indicative of any course the man may be teaching. As well, he's already cracked the covers of twenty books and no less than seven times has seen inscriptions to other people, as though Toomey purchased the collection at a secondhand store. For appearances sake, perhaps he did. Two such volumes are stamped to show that they belong or previously belonged to libraries in other states. If Cinq-Mars were to guess what courses the man taught based on his bookshelves, he'd fail.

Manuscripts, many lengthy, others mercifully brief, have been authored by the man himself. Often the attitude is readily identified as partisan, intended more to extoll a position than to examine various possibilities. To advocate, rather than inquire. Occasionally, in discussing different options, the diction falls to the pejorative. No academic distance or neutrality there. To the man's credit, his arguments at first glance are committed to his point of view, they're persuasive and intelligent. He sounds more like a smart, ardent lobbyist than any thinker of merit or active teacher. If there is a unifying theme to both the library and the unbound manuscripts, it's their geographic diversity and topical concerns, with books and commentary on issues current to Asia, Africa, Europe, and South America, as well as being germane to the United States.

The man got around.

As in his home, absent again are any indications of family or friends.

The guy was a loner.

A loner who got around and who poked his nose into current affairs and had a dubious connection to the State Department and received a professorship without a life in academia.

The guy was a spy.

"Can I help you?" Roberta's voice is loud and startling. He's shaken from his reverie. He hadn't noticed her leave the room to challenge someone in the hall.

Cinq-Mars takes a peek out the door to satisfy his own curiosity. Roberta has issued her combative question to a rufous-haired, tall young man, a bit scrawny, good-looking, who will fully count as handsome as he fills out. His eyes are darting around as though he's feeling cornered, for such is the sudden power of the guard's voice.

"I was walking by here, that's all."

"That's not all. You were looking in the room," Roberta points out to him. "You were snooping."

"No. It's Professor Toomey's office. I was curious, that's all. You know. On account of he's dead."

"You expected to find him in? Even though you know he's dead?"

"You knew Professor Toomey?" Cinq-Mars interrupts.

The boy shrugs.

"Does that mean yes?"

"Yeah. He was my professor once, that's all. Last year. Look, I'm sorry. I didn't mean to interfere with anything."

He seems a good kid.

"What kind of a guy was he? Professor Toomey?"

"Umm," the boy says.

"What does that mean?"

"He was a prof. It's not like we hung out or anything. I thought he was a pretty good teacher, though. On balance. He told a lot of good stories."

"What subject?"

"International relations."

"He told stories about international relations?"

"Life in the foreign service mostly. Stuff like that."

"Hmm," Cinq-Mars murmurs. Then he murmurs, "Mostly."

"Yeah," the boy defends.

"They were probably lies."

Roberta looks between the two, the fidgeting boy and the humming, hawing older man, and decides to dismiss the lad. "All righty," she says. "You can go."

The boy shrugs again, this time to indicate that he doesn't believe he requires her permission to walk away or stay, that it's his choice to carry on down the corridor. He's soon around a corner and out of sight.

"He was looking in," Roberta explains.

"You were guarding," Cinq-Mars comments. "That's what you do. Guard."

"I guard," Roberta agrees.

She locks the office again and they're walking away before she says something that Émile wishes had come out earlier. "Know what?"

"What?"

"I've seen that boy around. Don't know his name. But do you know who he knows?"

"Who?"

"The lady professor."

"Wait a minute." Cinq-Mars stops walking. "That boy, hanging around outside Professor Toomey's door, knows Professor Shedden?"

"I've seen them talking."

"When?"

"Not recently. A few times, I'd say. But a while ago."

The boy's long gone at this point. Émile is interested in him now, if only for whom he knows.

"Let's check out the photographs that've come in," Émile states. "We'll test your knack for faces."

She gets that he's teasing her, in a way, and doesn't mind.

"If I've seen them, I can tell you where. On campus. Oh that'll be a big help."

"You just never know, Roberta. By the way, that's a detective's mantra: you just never know."

They cut back outside, and are greeted by a lovely day after the thrashing the region took during the rainstorm. The humidity low and the sun high. Roberta waxes on about her kids and how she hopes to find a good university for them that doesn't cost an arm and a leg. "Or at least not too many arms or too many legs." She'll never be able to afford Dartmouth

down the road no matter what they say about bursaries and jobs, and
the governmental and international thrust of Dowbiggin doesn't interest them at all. Not that it's any cheaper. Émile plants a seed by suggesting she consider Canada. "Good schools, less money. They charge
Americans a premium but it's still a bargain compared to the cost down
here. Truth is, even rich kids go north." She's excited by that and goes
on about the student loan crisis, then, when she gets to the security desk
inside and is shown the photographs, she's unexpectedly intrigued.

"You're not going to like this," she says, then changes her mind. "Or
maybe you will."

Émile has spread out the photographs at the end of a long table intended for student study and quick lunches. Other students chat quietly
a short distance from them. He waits, sunlight from outside glowing on
his brow.

"I've seen this woman before," Roberta says, concentrating, trying
to sort through a distant memory.

"She worked here. Cleaning up," Cinq-Mars points out.

"Yeah. Yeah. Do you know who she was talking to one time?"

"Tell me."

"I remember this because it struck me funny. A woman from the
janitorial staff, a black woman like me yet, talking to a professor."

"What's unusual about that?"

"It did not seem like a friendly talk. More like they were arguing.
You know, a prof doesn't have much to do with someone who sweeps
floors. If they do, they don't have to argue about anything, know what
I mean? A prof is like management. If one wants something from the
janitorial staff, I don't see there's much to argue about. Get me?"

"I do. That might be odd. Do you remember who was the prof?"

"Sure do. Professor Edith Shedden."

Polite exchanges, she had said of her encounters with Malory Earle.
The terminology now strikes him as interesting, especially as a reliable
witness is now contradicting that characterization.

"This is Professor Toomey, I take it," Roberta goes on, looking at the
photos. "I've seen him around, too. More than once. I can tell you who
with, too."

"Who with, Roberta?" He wants to kiss her in the friendliest and most celibate of ways. He's delighted with the president's choice of accompanying guard.

"The same boy we just saw, snooping by his office. A lot of times I seen them. The boy's hard to miss, tall like he is. The prof, this picture of him makes him look bigger. He's a shorter man, on the dumpy side. More like me, ha ha. Walking together, they stood out in a way. Otherwise, there was nothing unusual about them."

"Except that you saw them together a lot. Wouldn't you call that unusual?"

Roberta agrees. "I could. Yeah. Definitely. Unusual."

"The boy held to a different opinion. Why? The university must have a computer file of all students, with their photographs."

"Sure do."

"I'm sorry to ask this of you, Roberta. I'll need you to look through those photographs until you find that boy's face. That'll give us a name and address, because we have to talk to him. He did say that he and the professor didn't hang out. That's sounding like a lie now."

"Don't be sorry, sir. Protecting the young ones. That's what I do. Anything related to that is fine with me. Do I start that job right away?"

He has to hold her back. "For now, I need you to take me to the clock tower. After that you can check the pictures. Roberta, you've said nothing about the girl." He points to Addie Langford's photograph. "Anything?"

"Sorry," Roberta laments. "Never seen her. Sure pretty, though. Know what? I've never been up the clock tower. Too bad it has to be for this sad time."

"You can sneak up after I come down," Cinq-Mars says. He doesn't explain himself. "I have to go up alone. I'll wait for you afterward." He returns the three eight-by-tens to their brown envelope, tucks it under his arm. "Lead the way," he instructs.

"You're a funny duck," she says. Roberta smiles, and leads the way.

SIXTEEN

After his visit to the clock tower, which offered no specific clues but left an impression that might prove useful over time, Émile Cinq-Mars gets in touch with Chief Till. They arrange a meeting, to be conducted in secret, along a deserted highway not far from Sandra's family farm. Both men hope the road remains deserted. State troopers are swarming Hanover, Holyoake, West Lebanon, and Lebanon; finding a side road where they can piss in a ditch without a SWAT team descending on them is dubious. Yet they do meet without being noticed and exchange information. Before Cinq-Mars gets away he receives a gem uncovered by the chief. In talking with Addie Langford's parents, Till learned that the day before she died she said she had lined up a dream job for the summer. "With a donor!" was how she had phrased the opportunity.

She didn't name her employer, not that her parents recalled.

"Put the word out that her folks want to speak to that individual, to say thanks," Émile instructs him, forgetting for a moment not to sound as though he's the one giving the orders.

Till forgives him. "How do you mean, *out*?"

"Through her friends. Through Dowbiggin. Through the local press."

"You think it counts?"

"If someone comes forward, we vet him. Or her. If not, we seek him out."

Sitting behind the wheel of his Escalade, the chief on the passenger side, Cinq-Mars dips his chin. He doesn't elaborate on why the news about the job offer is vital, but Till notices the man's heightened interest. He has more on his mind than a process of elimination. Lately, he's been provoked by news of interconnections and shared contacts among the victims. Nobody anticipated that, and it's not to be ignored, or kept to themselves. The hard part will be to share information with the troopers without them hearing of their clandestine, side investigation.

"Let's push on," Émile suggests, "before we dump our findings in Hammond's lap."

"He asked me to pick up the parents," Till gripes. "He did it to keep me out of his hair. Can he blame me if I kept my ears open?"

"Watch. He might find a way."

As Till drives off, Émile stays on the side road next to a frog pond, the big guys croaking away, amphibians and one pensive human peaceably pondering the universe. Bulrushes line the water's edge. He makes a crucial call to Palmerich, amazed to promptly be put through.

"Émile," the president remarks. First-name basis. Wow. He wants news.

"Sir, about that cocktail party we discussed."

"I remain exceedingly uncomfortable with the idea."

Exceedingly. Émile hadn't gauged the man's opposition to the concept as that trenchant.

"A few things have changed since we last spoke, sir."

"I remain to be convinced. What have you heard?"

"This year, as you know," Émile begins, "Professor Toomey finagled an invitation to the party. You mentioned that he wasn't an obvious choice of invitee. Sir, last year, without an invitation, he still wrangled his way into the party by pestering to be another person's date. Clearly, it's been a priority for him to attend these functions. We need to know who he knew and who he was interested in contacting. The party may give us clues into his life which are currently missing."

"Interesting." The president's words are noncommittal, yet a breath of compliance hangs in the air between them. Émile feels that he's gaining ground, and presses on.

"Sir, someone described as a donor offered Addie Langford a job this summer. Understand, this doesn't accuse anyone of anything or frame any donor in a bad light. Chances are, whoever offered her that job was simply doing the young woman a favor for all the right reasons. He may offer an internship every summer. As with Toomey, we need to know her connections, what she was up to, who she was seeing, where does this all lead. Two of the deceased may have had contact with a person or persons attending that gathering. That's compelling. As well, one of your professors was acquainted with all three victims. *That* professor happens to be going to the party. Again, nothing is defamatory, not in the slightest, but what your people know is important to us. The police need to expand their knowledge on that front. This isn't adversarial. We simply desire to know what the victims knew, with particular emphasis on what interested them. We care about who they talked to and why."

The other end of the line is dead air for what feels like a minute. All that time he can't even hear the man breathing.

"Émile," Palmerich comes back at last, "I appreciate that you're making progress with your investigation, at least with getting to know the victims. I don't wish to stand in the way of that." Émile is happy that he doesn't have to make that threat again. The president is bringing up the issue of interference on his own. "You've implicated an unidentified donor, not with the crime, but with knowledge of a victim. He or she might expect to be interviewed, as that will show that every stone is being turned over. In that sense, I have no choice. I need to show that we're doing things the right way." The argument is not one that occurred to Cinq-Mars—people familiar with the victims may expect to be interviewed, and wonder why not if they're ignored—and he's glad that the president has made it for him. "With your solemn vow to be circumspect, I will issue an invitation for you to attend the donors' party. With this proviso. I do not want you to discuss the murders at the event. Forfeit those conversations. Do you wish to be introduced as a donor yourself? As a disguise?"

"That depends on how much cash I'm obliged to contribute."

While the president doesn't laugh, he emits a sound which relaxes the tension between them. "Write a check for any amount you care to, Émile. I presume you caught my meaning."

"I'm not sure I can pull off being a financier. I'll dress well. Say I'm from Canada with a niece graduating, that's no lie, and that I'd like to help the school out. No lie there, either. I'll be a minor benefactor with a personal interest. I'll use my own name. These out-of-towners haven't heard of me."

"Very well. Thank you, Émile. You can pick up the invitation in a sealed envelope from my secretary. No one in the office will know what it is, for the sake of our ongoing discretion. Forgo the RSVP as well, as I don't want your name on any list."

Not a party animal by a long shot, Émile is thinking that he's never been as happy to receive an invitation. Then he reminds himself that it's probably all for naught, that nothing is likely to come of it. Typical police work. Scratch the sand in the hope of finding a buried clue, only to hit solid rock.

Or more sand.

He drives on home.

Émile Cinq-Mars has a hunch that his time in the clock tower will eventually prove beneficial, although he's admitted to himself that putting stock in such an opinion requires a leap of faith. Technically, Roberta was supposed to accompany him wherever he went, including up the clock tower stairs. Given that nothing existed for him to steal up there on high, and given that he was insisting on solitude, she let him ascend on his own.

"Don't," she warned him, "try to change the time of day."

She meant to be facetious, and was rewarded with a smile, yet her remark struck him as ironic. Time. As always, of the essence. Perhaps not in the traditional sense. He didn't need to accomplish anything specific in the tower, only to give silence and meditation their due. Time reveals secrets. Time extracts truth from infinite space and from the decay of physical matter. He was sensing a spiritual poke again, both in the clock tower and on his drive home after his talk with Till. So be it. Spiritual concepts were part and parcel of his hypothesis of the world, why not permit them entry into his investigative tangents? As he has pontificated to others, the mind possesses a core brain, thousands of times quicker in its computations than any conscious mind, and way too quick for the dragging effect of language. A thought that requires words is slowed down by that imposition, the brakes are on. Often perceived as *intuition*, or a voice from dimensions more esoteric than that, Cinq-Mars considers the core brain to be merely functional, though so wickedly fast that any insight or conclusion it might pass along to a wakeful mind arrives with such acuity, and with such velocity, as to knock the thinker onto his or her intellectual derrière. The unwary thinker is stunned and at a loss, as if from a blow. Stripped bare of a conscious process—the conscious mind too slow to register how a remedy was gleaned at full throttle when only the conclusion is offered up—the out-of-the-blue thought is as likely to be dismissed as welcomed. At least, by many. Which is when Émile's spirituality knocks on the door. Accepting a random, fleeting, and elusive thought as potentially valid requires the lost art of faith. For Cinq-Mars, faith is the least understood virtue. Shunned as being an excuse for superstition, or as a means of admitting ignorance into a religious catechism, further denuded by the adjective *blind* when in his mind faith requires acute vision, it is anything but ignorant. The contrary, faith is meant to be a resource for insight and thoughtfulness into what is temporarily or permanently inexplicable, or merely beyond one's ability to fully fathom or articulate. Which is what he was searching for in the quiet serenity of the tower. Insight into inexplicable murder. An unfathomable homicide reduced to its mechanics. Others might imagine he was listening to the walls speak or attuning himself to the distant voices of victims, when all he was doing was exercising patience. Thoughts knitted together a myriad of notations pertaining to evidence, then were mixed with a phalanx of possibilities. In turn, this abstract stew is spiced by suspicion and the whole batch cooked in the pot of his experience. Allowed to cool and set, the concoction, if it's a good one, might offer up a singular possibility. If one's faith in the process holds. Or not. In the tower, he was *listening*. To himself. Letting everything simmer. Giving it time. In the depths of a solitude.

At a bare minimum, no interruptions.

The quiet elegance of the clock tower, emphasized by the steady *shhlunka-shhlunka* of the mechanism, demanded that he be there alone, and in that vacuum he hears what he himself thinks, not the walls. How does he weigh an inexplicable murder where the victim is dressed up and *presented*, like a debutante at a ball? To understand any of that he lets himself slip back in time and space, sequestered in the tower but also in that part of his mind that is capable of not only fathoming but of engineering such a thing. He must believe himself capable, he must believe himself gripped by such a terrible impulse. He must allow himself to be irredeemable and loathsome and celebrate what is vile and secreted in every man's nature. None of that is easy in this circumstance for he remembers more the vitality of the bright young woman who was the victim here, and it's hard to get her out of his mind and draw the perpetrator of this crime into his consciousness instead. Details about what might have occurred do not rise willingly. As they trickle into his head, he finds them so troubling, ruthless, and intricately *sick* that he comes to doubt himself, his ability to do this, and entertains instead the notion that the walls, witness to this malady, this crime, are indeed speaking to him, shouting out in pain, for he cannot possibly be talking to himself.

If it was the walls or a distant voice or his own core brain at full throttle, he did listen, he did interpret what he heard, and Émile in the tower found himself growing increasingly troubled.

When Roberta, less patient, called up, perhaps to ascertain that he's still alive, a spell was broken, and for once he was glad of that, even though he hadn't lingered there long enough nor immersed himself deeply enough in this morass. He knew, as he came down the stairs, that he's on the run, that he's intent on escaping.

Roberta was expecting to go up, to take a turn in the clock tower.

"Another time," Émile instructed her instead, and the timbre of his voice, something in his overall attitude, convinced her not to protest. She passed up the chance to climb the stairs on her own to admire the view.

Coming away, Cinq-Mars carried a few revelations with him. Specifics he'll mull over time. One tells him that, beyond the usual horror that accompanies murder, the events that occurred there were intricate and more unsettling than the usual run of sordid crimes. He also learned of a surprise more mysterious and daunting. Namely, that he's afraid. He'd forgotten how deeply fear can slide inside a man. That reminder distressed him. He wanted to be back in the countryside. Out on the farm. To be breathing clear air.

SEVENTEEN

Upon his return, Émile finds that Sandra hasn't made it back from her sad errands. He warms leftover meat loaf for himself, enjoys a tossed salad, and washes it all down with a cold beer. The afternoon drink feels indulgent. On the job he'd rarely do that, and yet, as he tells himself, this is his bona fide retirement. Each sip warrants a smile, even if he is neck-deep in a case.

A case. Imagine that. At this time in his life.

This one's a puzzle.

A matter that confounded him in the clock tower was the primitive aspect to the space, which would have imposed limitations on any perpetrator. The stairs, railings, and platforms are of sturdy construction, meant to be functional rather than attractive. The angles are harsh, the wood unfinished, inhibiting movement. Even as a mere observer, he felt clumsy. At the apex, he dwelled upon the physical reality of a man who intends to commit rape and murder in that environment. Any attack would leave more traces of blood than were found and should have resulted in more obvious bruising on the victim. The perpetrator, if located, ought to show damage on his person, too, given that the rough edges and blunt ends to the woodwork are never more than inches away during the commission of his violence. Yet the victim, as far as he'd been able to see, showed only strangulation marks, and those were minimal. No cuts, no further bruising. How was that possible? In the narrow confines, a young woman was assaulted, probably raped, then murdered. She was undressed, then dressed again in different clothes. Judging by the chalk circles on the highest platform, forensics had discovered blood spotting and seminal or other fluid residue there—the state troopers would know, but he doesn't—which confirms that the attack had been carried out that high up. Yet it would appear that only trace amounts were found. Anyone being assailed and choked would have kicked and lashed out, causing injury to herself and to her attacker. Why was there no such evidence on the body, that he discerned? No cuts, no splinters, no scrapes to indicate that she'd been mauled and dragged across the rough-hewn floors. Why were blood smears not apparent on the posts, railings, and stairs? Somewhere? Anywhere? As he sat high up in the tower, suspicions arose all through his assessment, and Cinq-Mars wished he had the medical examiner's report in hand. He was working with only a fraction of the available knowledge and being deprived in that way was getting the better of him.

At home, one hand on his beer glass, Émile puts a call through to Chief Till.

"Hey, what's up?"

"Chief, we need a copy of the ME report on the girl."

"My hands are tied, Émile. You know that. I'm not privy."

"Get it," Cinq-Mars tells him, pausing for emphasis, "anyway."

"How do you expect me to—" Till begins, then checks himself.

Cinq-Mars fills in the blank space. "If Hammond won't release it to you, talk to whoever wrote it. Or typed it. You're bound to have a relationship with the ME or with a few people in his office. If necessary, do it unofficially, but we need a copy."

Chief Till agrees to undertake the attempt.

An old, and crude, crime-fighting adage is not holding true here: *follow the money or the honey.* If anything, the killer was willing to dip into his funds to adorn the victim with mild extravagance—clothing and jewelry. If money is not the guiding motivation, then count on it to include sex, at least the criminal's take on what constitutes sex. This is where the killer's attitude is puzzling, and possibly revealing. He's being unique, dressing and posing his victim, making an exceptional effort not to mark or wound her. The murderer wanted the killing to be as *gentle* as possible. Nothing about homicide is anything other than brutal, yet in this instance the killer seems repelled by his own deed, going to great lengths to cloak his true nature to suit an ideal of a superior aesthetic. A kind of whitewash of the murder even as it's taking place, as though he wants the act to be noticed as a work of art.

He wants others to declare it so.

As though he desires to be considered worthy.

Be mindful of that, Cinq-Mars instructs himself. Be on the lookout for a perpetrator with an inflated, pompous sense of his own artistic nature. Keep an eye out for a well-heeled gentleman who sees himself through rose-colored lenses.

While Addie's killer might suit that profile, he can't say the same for Malory's.

Perplexed, Émile guzzles beer as though to ease the pang of his frustration.

A call to Sandra puts him at ease with how she's getting on. She and her sister have taken lunch in town, moving on from coffee at the restaurant to cosmopolitans in a bar. "A few cute gents around," she intimates. He knows she's doing okay. The funeral arrangements are done and weren't complicated—she's predicting her arrival back home for later in the afternoon.

He's stuck with choosing either a nap or another beer. The nap idea holds sway momentarily, until, alone in the bedroom, strangely, the fear that overtook him in the clock tower insinuates itself again, rising through his bloodstream. He nixes sleep as a bad idea. Émile decides that another beer suits the hour. He'll down it slowly, not to be mired in his cups this early in the day. Given his wife's inclinations for the afternoon, it might be wise to remain the semi-sober one.

Mulling things over on the front porch, lazily swatting flies, Émile concludes that his problem may be both simple and large: between his current cocktail hour and the cocktail party a couple of days on, he lacks a next move. After his beer he'll drive back to the campus and pick up his official invitation to the gathering, then call it a day. He starts with that plan, but a third of the way through the beer he takes out his mobile phone and makes another call. He and a pal in Washington, a high-ranking special agent with the FBI, rely on voice recognition. They never repeat each other's names over the phone, in case a friend or foe nearby—such as an agent at the next desk over—can hear them. He had called him the other night from Till's squad car to do a background check on Professor Toomey.

"I'm upping the ante," Cinq-Mars stipulates. Not even a *hello*.

"How so?"

"Browsed the dead guy's papers. He had knowledge. Probably position. He's stepped away, but like me his switch never fully tripped. I suspect he's a closed circuit, plugged in."

"He was live when he was still alive, you're saying."

"In some respects. Maybe. I'm wondering what the connection was."

"Will get back to you."

"Say hi," Émile adds on. He isn't going to speak the man's wife's name, either.

"You, too." He'll say hi to Sandra from him.

He's left alone with his beer once more. A lonely old soldier of a bottle. Horses across the yard graze under a clear sky. Perhaps it's the alcohol in the middle of the afternoon but he finds himself in a particularly chatty mood. He calls his former partner, Bill Mathers, a younger man who remains on the force back home in Montreal.

"Don't recognize the area code, Émile. Where the hell are you?"

At least New Hampshire doesn't sound far away.

"Doing what?" Bill wants to know. If he's strictly on vacation he wouldn't be calling.

"Sandra's mom passed."

That changes the mood. "Sorry, Émile. My condolences to you both."

"Thanks." Émile heads back inside, where it's cooler. Fewer flies.

"That's not why you're calling," Bill points out to him.

Émile admits, "I'm investigating three murders. Don't ask how I got involved."

Mathers skips only a single beat before replying, "Of course you are. Do you need me down there?"

"That won't work. I've got an ally on-site, but there's a state trooper who'd consider it a provocation and send us both to Gitmo if another Canadian cop shows up."

"What then? What can I do to help?" Obviously, there must be something.

Émile is drawn back to the cozy kitchen and a comfortable stool there. "A heads-up, Bill. I have a bad feeling about this one. I'll try to acquire a list of charitable donors, rich men and women kind enough to give their money away. If you can use your powers to run down that list, see if any red lights go off, I'd appreciate it. Can't tell you what to look for because I don't know."

Bill Mathers understands as well as Émile does that he can call the FBI and have greater resources at his fingertips. At times, he chooses to do things more quietly, without the Americans knowing, and that's where Bill comes in. Or, he merely desires to revisit the association with an old friend and colleague for the ease and comfort that that provides. Bill wonders which one it is this time. Given that Émile is down in the States, he's guessing it's the former, although his tone suggests that he ought to keep an open mind about that. The death in the family might have instigated the call. Either way, he agrees. "Send it. I assume I'm not actually doing this?"

"Always the best option," Émile concurs. They exchange pleasantries and Bill repeats his condolences before signing off. Thoughtful, Émile Cinq-Mars quaffs the dregs of his beer. Now he's considering making a third phone call, a fourth if he counts buzzing his wife, and suspects that he's lost the will to resist the impulse today.

He's saved by the bell. In this instance, the doorbell.

A man steps back as Émile pushes the screen door outward. It's accomplished awkwardly. His eyes are slow to adjust from the dim light of the house to the brighter light of the porch and the still brighter glare of the yard beyond the visitor. He blinks several times before the new arrival comes into focus. That he's below average in height is accentuated by being a step down on the porch which puts him at a greater disadvantage to the tall Cinq-Mars. He's wearing a jacket and tie which comes across as a tad suspicious out in the countryside, as though he has stuff to sell that no one wants to buy. His spiky nose complements a tuft of beard that sharpens to a point. The facial hair changes from white at the sideburns, to salt-and-peppery across the cheeks and jaw-line, to mainly black under the chin. The man's eyes look frightened. He holds his hands in an attitude suggestive of either fear or prayer, one wrist raised high on his chest in the grip of the opposite hand as though he's wounded.

"Bollocks!" the man remarks. "I'm gobsmacked. Pardon me?"

Which not only sounds foreign it makes no sense at all.

"May I help you?" Cinq-Mars asks. The attitude inherent in his voice strikes a compromise between a welcome and a challenge.

"No way to do that. May I help *you*? That is the crux, I'm told, the genuine crux of the question at this moment. That's what she tells me."

Émile's confused. "What were you told? By whom? Who is *she*?"

"Me," another voice pipes up.

"Her," the man confirms. "I'm gobsmacked."

At that moment, his niece peeks out from behind the gentleman where she'd been crouching at his back, big grin on her face, mouth wide open in an attitude of clownish surprise, her eyes expressing tom-foolery. "My bad!" she exclaims, then marches right on past the visitor and Émile Cinq-Mars into the house. The door bangs shut behind her. Turning, she's surprised that the visitor is still outside. He seems to be turning around as though to leave. "Oh for heaven's sake," she mutters and repeats her entrance, this time holding the door open for her guest to come in as well.

"Who's this?" Cinq-Mars asks once everyone has filed indoors.

"This," Caro announces, "is Chuck Carpel."

"Mr. Carpel," Émile says.

"Charles," the man corrects. "Or CC, my friends say. My friends call me CC."

"I'm pleased to meet you, Mr. Carpel. I'm Émile Cinq-Mars."

"The detective."

"Retired," he adds.

"Really?" Carpel asks, and shoots a glance at the willowy Caroline. The look on his face expresses disappointment. "What? Why?"

"Not from this case," she assures him, and takes one of his arms in both her hands. *"Charles,"* she says, deploying the French pronunciation, rolling the *r* in an exaggerated way, "can help us. Can't you, Chucky?"

"Probably not," he tells her. "Not likely."

Émile has had enough. "Okay. What's going on?"

"Charlie's a gemologist," Caroline explains.

"Charles," Carpel insists again.

Caro doesn't release her grip, as though she believes that she has hold of someone who's slippery. "Okay, I'll CC you later, but for now, *Chucky's* the man of the hour. Not only a seller of jewels, but a gemologist of considerable renown."

"They say that," Carpel qualifies. "I say that, too."

"He can tell us stuff about the necklaces."

"Please," Émile says, still unsure of this meeting, "have a seat."

They move into the living room and sit. Carpel adjusts his position to be more forward in his soft chair than seems natural. The stance suggests that he might bolt.

"I suppose," Émile remarks, "I can describe the necklaces to you. Better yet, I have a small photograph on my phone."

"He's seen one already."

"I can describe the necklace to *you*," Carpel says, and Cinq-Mars puts his finger on what's odd about the man. He talks as though no one else is in the room, as if to the walls, and it's never obvious that he's listening. As though he perpetually inhabits his own mental shell.

Perhaps that's why Émile addresses his next question to the college student as if Carpel is absent. "Did he make the necklace?"

"Inferior, no," Carpel answers. "Too inferior for me."

"It's not a valuable item, given its inferiority, is that what you're saying?"

"Stones have value, of course, always. The design. Over the top. Inferior."

"He's a bit odd," Caroline states, also as though the man is actually not in the room. She says more loudly to Carpel, as if he's hard of hearing, "You agree with that, right? You're a bit odd?"

"Odd duck, yes. My mother says. Odd duck, she says."

"See? His mother runs the store for him, but apparently," Caroline explains, "Charles is an extraordinary expert in his field."

Émile puts up both his palms. "Okay. Let's slow down. What do you mean when you say that you've seen the necklace? Where and when?"

"Uncle Émile," Caroline explains, "sorry to barge in on you like this. But look. I saw the police—state troopers—go into Charlie's store. Didn't think anything about it, right? A thief shoplifted a brooch, what's the big deal? But it's right across the street from this sandwich shop where I was having a bite, and I noticed that the trooper who came back out of the shop was the same guy who interviewed me yesterday and, you know, who chewed you out this morning. The big green cheese."

"Hammond?"

"Him," Caroline confirms.

"That's his name," Carpel says. He's scanning the mantel.

"He's got three murders on his hands and he's spending time in a jewelry store over a stolen brooch? How does that make sense?"

"Nothing's stolen," Carpel says. "Inventory intact."

"That's what I'm thinking. Nothing's stolen. If Hammond is going around town, it has to be about the murders, right? After he leaves, I finish my lunch, go into the store, and that's where I find our leading expert on precious stones in the north country—"

"*World* expert," Carpel corrects her.

"Our world expert, Mr. Charles Carpel."

"That's me. Charles. CC."

"That's him." Caroline confirms. "What was Hammond talking to Mr. Carpel about, do you ask?"

"The necklaces," Cinq-Mars catches on.

"One necklace," she trumpets. "Which he showed to him. In the flesh."

"I see." Émile looks the man over again. "Good of you to come by to see me, Mr. Carpel."

"CC," the man says.

Émile gathers that he wants to be friends.

"There's a reason he came," Caroline points out.

"What's that?"

"He didn't listen to me," Carpel maintains.

Émile immediately comprehends what that means. He offers his niece a sly wink, a quick thanks for her initiative. "Charles," Émile invites, and sits back. He has a hunch that this might take a while. If Hammond didn't listen to what he had to say, he can guess why, and doesn't want to make the same mistake. The man's peculiar speech patterns require patience. "What can you tell us about the necklace?"

"Purposeful," the man postulates.

"Ah, purposeful?" Émile inquires.

"With purpose. Not a proper combination of gems."

"Amateur work, then, would you say?"

"I would not say that. A professional job. Quality workmanship. The secret to jewelry is to have no purpose, except for beauty and mystical projections."

"Does the piece have mystical projections?"

"No. It has a *purpose*. Not the jeweler's vision. A client's requirement. Guaranteed, I say. A client should never guide the artist's hand. But he did. That's who had a purpose for every stone. Not the jeweler. The client."

Cinq-Mars appreciates what he's getting at. "You've concluded this through your observations. You are clever. In a sense, the gems were put together to say something, to signify a message at the cost of the aesthetic virtue of the piece?"

Not only does the man appear not to listen, he hasn't made proper eye contact since his arrival. Until now. He seems to be appraising Cinq-Mars as he might a diamond.

And takes his time with that.

Cinq-Mars undertakes an evaluation of his own. For a man whose life revolves around gemstones, Carpel is not extravagantly adorned, although he's chosen a ring of choice with care. Suddenly inspired, Cinq-Mars asks, "May I see your ring, sir?"

The man continues to eye him, then looks away, then offers his hand as a giddy bride-to-be might show off her engagement diamond, her head turned away in shyness. Cinq-Mars stands up to view it properly, and holds the man's hand over his own. The band is hammered gold. He compliments him on the stone. "That's a fine star sapphire, CC."

He smiles. He beams. He blushes.

"I have looked at stones all the world over," Carpel tells him. "Many very fine, but I cannot afford them. This one, though, is special. Didn't know until I saw it, but this is the one I most desired. My life stone. Took me a while, hard bargaining, a lot of dealing. Wrangling favors, flattery, many dinners. The seller knew that he would sell to me. I believe that. But. A game to play. He wanted me to seduce him. To prove my fidelity to his star sapphire. I could not offer him only crass money. Not for such a luminous stone. If I was going to acquire his beautiful star sapphire, I had to find an equivalent stone for him to adore, one that impressed him and replaced the stone he'd be missing from his collection. That took years. But I found it. A ruby of such exquisite color that I bought it at a premium on the spot. I knew it would win over my man with the star sapphire. It did. We traded."

Carpel is beaming. Cinq-Mars asks, "Where was this?"

"Istanbul. I earned a lot of air-miles points."

"An amazing story."

Cinq-Mars resumes his seat again, confident that he has gained what a man like Trooper Hammond never could: this fellow's respect. All he'd done was listen to his story, and appreciate his ring, all that this man requires of anyone.

Caroline has noticed. In life, she's relied upon a high IQ and her innate fierce determination, and along the way she has not denigrated her good looks, either. In this instance, she used all three traits to lure a man out of his shop and down a highway to visit a foreign detective in a farmhouse. No mean accomplishment that. She knows how to make her skills work for her. Yet Cinq-Mars, she marvels, has won the guy over without an ounce of cajoling, merely by paying the stone that he loves best its due. She crosses her ankles and sits back in the corner of her sofa and waits to see what else he might accomplish here, taking mental notes as though she's still in school.

"Why the Berman topaz?" Carpel asks, as though someone else posed the question first and might be willing to hazard a guess. "From Brazil. Aesthetically, ask yourself, does it complement the piece? In terms of its meaning, nothing stands out as signifiers. The Berman encourages this and that, fortifies the body against disease, the mind against greed, but none of that reflects well with the companion stones. Who would put these together? No jeweler." He does a mock shiver, and concludes, "Crude."

"Such as?" Cinq-Mars asks.

"Excuse me?"

"What companion stones?"

"The kunzite. These particular stones are from California. That's a guess. A good one, probably. They are the light purple gems, set off center on four sides. Significant to the piece. Kunzite opens the heart to all forms of love."

Caroline relates, "CC told Trooper Hammond exactly that, and Trooper Hammond said—"

"You don't say," Carpel interrupts, meaning to quote Hammond.

"What you believe, if you will forgive me, isn't relevant," Cinq-Mars points out. "What matters is what the client who had the necklace made believes. That's what counts."

"Exactly," Carpel concurs. "Take a look. True carnelian sardonyx. Brazil–Uruguay border. Can be either country. Usually it's heat-treated to bring out the color, but the beautiful color in this talisman is natural. Natural and exceptional. Therefore, of value."

"All these stones, placed together, do you think it's a code?" Émile asks him.

"I think it's a map," Carpel stipulates.

"A map."

"Places have importance. Impact."

"They do. Yes. What other places are involved?"

"Hammond didn't care to know."

"I do. That's why I'm asking the question."

"But you're retired, she said. She didn't tell me that before. It's significant."

"Retirement is a state of mind, that's my thought. I don't seem to be in that state yet. What other countries, CC?"

"Russia."

"Which stone?"

"Stones on the outer rim. Travel off the centerpiece, partway up the chain. Patterned agates. Could be from anywhere but I'm betting on

Wyoming or Montana. American is a good guess. Because we're in America. Why import what you already have? Understand? But really, it's the stones. Can't explain that to you. Not what my mother says. Intuition. The best word I can say is *experience*."

"I believe in experience. Intuition, too. What do we have?" Émile tries to summarize. "California. Wyoming or Montana. Brazil. What's Russian, CC?"

"Don't forget the lapis lazuli. How can I be content with the aesthetic? I am not gobsmacked. From Afghanistan, that's a hunch. Touching the lapis, we have amethyst. Go figure. Those two together. Not a jeweler's hand. Unless he's a lousy jeweler but I don't think that. The client. The client made him do it."

"What's the problem with those stones touching?"

"Amethyst protects against being killed, essentially. The lapis protects the dead. It's like they're at war, one with the other one. Do you see?"

"A contradiction. One for the dead. One to keep from dying."

"Yes!"

"And the Russian stone?" Émile presses him once more.

"The charoite. From the Charo River in Eastern Siberia. Only place on earth you can find it. High spiritual energy and union with love on earth. A talisman about letting go. Giving it up. Moving on. In Russian, *chary* means magic. A stimulant, this stone. Promotes dreams. Inner vision. True, in combination with amethyst it helps the sleepless get through the night. Maybe that's how the amethyst was supposed to behave."

"How?"

"To help a murdered girl enter her deepest sleep."

That mention casts the three of them into a somber aspect, and they each inhabit their private thoughts a while. Caroline gives her bare arms a rub. Sifting through what he's learned, Cinq-Mars ponders, "Is that the theme then? Jewelry to assist the victim to cross over into death?"

For once, Carpel is less emphatic in his response. "Close enough," he says. "A bit muddied, the waters, but close enough as a theme. I think it's a map. A guide to death. A bit of a mixed bag between love and death."

"Bearing in mind that we are dealing, most likely, with a radically sick individual, love and death may well be intertwined in this case, no?"

Carpel considers that as well. He nods his agreement.

Cinq-Mars isn't convinced that he's an inch further ahead with his investigation, except that he knows a tidbit that he didn't before. Sometimes usefulness lags discovery. On the off chance that something has been missed, he asks another question.

"CC, is there anything that you didn't tell Trooper Hammond, largely because you weren't getting along with him, that you might have told him otherwise? That you haven't noted yet? It doesn't matter how insignificant the point may appear on the surface. You never know when a notion might count."

Carpel knows exactly what he wants to say. "Hammond cut me off. Done with me at one point. Tick tock. *Whish! Whoosh! Wants to go! Ho-ho! Off with my head!* He's one of those. I wanted to say a curious note. He was too impatient to hear it."

"What was that? What was the curious note you wanted to pass along?"

"Russian stone. Charoite. Color a deep, very deep, purple. Beautiful, lovely. Intensity very strong. Unusual. Special. Easy to think it's a synthetic. That intense. I can give it a study with my eye to make sure it's not a synthetic, but I have another method. One I use. Quick. Foolproof."

"What's that?"

"Scan it."

"Scan it?"

"For radioactivity."

Émile is promptly alert and keen. "Radioactivity. How can a gemstone be radioactive? Wouldn't that be, you know, dangerous?"

"Often stones are radioactive. Emit a trace, we live with that. One way to know they are not synthetic. The readings can be high. Too high. It depends."

"I see. And this sample?"

"A few years ago. I need to Google it. Two thousand seven, or eight, around then, a train is traveling into Russia. From Siberia. It got checked for radioactivity. Ask me why, I can't tell you. Russia is Russia. Have their reasons. Worried about plutonium on the run, maybe. Anyway, I'm glad they do that."

"As am I. What happened?"

"One boxcar ticked high. *Highly* radioactive. They looked inside and found a load of charoite. Way more radioactive than usual. Way more than what is legal or safe."

"What happened to that shipment?"

"The Russians, bless them, God bless them! They separated the car from the train, sent the train on its way. The charoite was banished. Who knows where? But."

"But?"

"This is Mother Russia, hey? Charoite stones aren't diamonds here, but they can be there. Know what I mean? Depends whose hands. They're not sapphires even. But a boxcar load? Good charoite, with only a trace of radioactivity, is worth twenty to thirty-five thousand dollars, wholesale on the cheap. Maybe forty."

"Highly radioactive it's worth nothing."

"Except!" Carpel states.

"Except on the black market."

"Where nobody cares, nobody checks. Smuggle the charoite into the U.S.A., the gemstones get distributed, nobody the wiser. Who checks stones with a Geiger counter? Some do. Most don't. Not a ton of money, but in poor countries, it's a fortune. Like they're diamonds. A semiprecious stone to a poor man is not semiprecious. It's like gold. Like a diamond."

"You've been more helpful than you know," Cinq-Mars says, and he means it, too. Carpel shrugs, happy to say what he wanted to say. He stands in a manner that suggests he's leaving.

"Can I fix you a drink?" Émile, the tardy host, inquires. He doesn't want to appear impatient to this man.

"Back to work. Do that sober. My breath can't smell like mint. People think I'm crazy. Okay. Don't want them to think I'm drunk, too. When I'm not. Not good for business. My mother says. Gobsmacked! Don't drink!"

They are moving toward the front door and their good-byes—Carpel drove his own car with Caroline the passenger, so she'll be staying behind—when the young woman speaks up.

"Uncle Émile?"

Both men give her their attention.

"Look. It's my friends, coming up the driveway."

"Good."

"Not good. A state trooper's behind them with his lights flashing."

EIGHTEEN

Whoever's behind the wheel of the lead vehicle is ignoring the flashing lights of a patrol car in the rearview mirror. Both vehicles splash through deep puddles on the long and narrow road. Upon entering the wide area by the stables, the lead car stops in the middle of one big enough to fish in. Whether she's done this purposely is a matter of conjecture but the driver is fanning the ire of her pursuer. The squad car pulls up and Trooper Hammond plunks on his Smoky the Bear hat as he climbs out. His companion officer emerges as well and hangs back, his hands under his biceps, his butt resting against the car door. Maybe he wants his feet to stay dry. Both men wear reflective sunglasses and it's the friend whose name is Anastasia who winds her window down and waits for the senior cop to wade up to her.

He gazes in. A snarly look.

As Émile and Caroline walk up at a good pace they see Hammond gesture for Anastasia to move the car onto higher ground. She demonstrates that her nerves are frayed by causing the car to lurch forward, then stall. She starts again and lurches forward a second time, as if she's learning to drive a standard shift.

To Émile's surprise, Hammond has only a quick word with her before he opens the rear door. That's curious enough: When a tall young man steps out, he's taken aback. He's seen him before. The security guard confronted the student on campus when he was loitering near Toomey's office. He had denied that he knew the murdered professor except in passing, which has since proven to be a lie. He also knows Professor Shedden, who was on speaking terms with the other victim, Malory Earle.

"Who's he?" Émile asks Caroline. The Dowbiggin security guard was supposed to scour pages of student portraits to find his name, so far to no avail. Émile is already guessing that he's heard it mentioned before.

"Vernon," she confirms for him. She quickens her pace alongside him to keep up with his naturally long strides. "Addie's boyfriend. Ex, I mean. Her previous boyfriend. One of. Vernon Colchester."

"The one who'd rather not be an ex," he recalls.

"We all like him. Vernon's a good guy."

"Maybe he is," Cinq-Mars says, although he sounds skeptical. He's now loosely connected the boy to all three murder victims.

By the time they reach the car, Hammond has the young man's biceps in the firm grip of his left hand and is guiding him around the pool of water toward the squad car. The patrol officer intercepts them halfway, takes over, holding the boy's opposite arm, which frees Hammond to spin on his heels to block Émile's progress.

"Police business," Hammond states, to put him in his place. He stands with his thumbs tucked into his gun belt. Cinq-Mars is tempted to laugh.

"You're on private property. My property. Only natural that I take an interest. You can't fault me for that." The girlfriends are climbing out of the car, realizing that they can, that they are neither under police edict nor in a pool of water. They're upset that Vernon is being led away.

"*Your* property?" Hammond mocks him.

"The farm belongs in my family. My wife is about to inherit. Half of it anyway. Moving here is a consideration. Do you live in the area, Trooper Hammond? We might be neighbors one day. In any case, I'm representing the family with respect to the property. I'm asking about a warrant and wondering what's going on."

"Not your concern."

"I agree with you. To a point. You can appreciate that arresting people on my property who are connected to my family—that's getting awfully close to being my concern. Don't you agree? Especially when I still haven't seen a warrant."

"Don't get wise with me. I followed him here because the driver didn't stop. Or do you want me to arrest her, too?" Hammond looks back at the patrol car, to check how his officer is getting on. He continues, "Anyway, I'm not arresting the boy. No warrant necessary. He's being picked up for further questioning."

Émile smiles. That's all he wanted to find out. Vernon Colchester is being handcuffed and the back of his head receives a downward shove as he crawls into the patrol car's rear seat. To the lad, this will feel like an arrest. All the trappings.

"Glad to hear it. I'm curious, though. How'd you know he was in the car?" The trooper is under no obligation to answer him, so he tries to keep the talk easygoing.

"We had him under surveillance. New information came in. I decided to reinterview. We were keeping tabs on his whereabouts."

"Right. He knew the victim. Makes sense to keep an eye on him."

"Then you know what that means."

Cinq-Mars sees himself reflected in the officer's glasses. "Not particularly. What?"

"Think about it."

He knows what he wants him to say. Cinq-Mars won't give him the satisfaction. Instead, he shrugs.

"If we had an eye on him, who else do you think we've seen strolling around the Dowbiggin campus?" Hammond raises his right index finger, holds it aloft for dramatic effect, then stabs Cinq-Mars lightly in the center of his chest.

He should take offense. Since there's nothing Hammond would enjoy more, Émile adopts a different tack. "Whoever your track dog is, keep him. He's good."

"I'll let him know you approve. He might say *whoopee*."

Hammond is spoiling for a fight. Not finding one he's set to proceed to a reprimand, except that his gaze appears to hover over Émile's left shoulder. He might be looking at Caroline. As the gaze is prolonged, Émile suspects that he's found someone else to stare down behind him.

"What's he doing here?" Hammond inquires.

Cinq-Mars grasps the locus of his interest. The gemologist. Charles Carpel is ambling their way, although he exhibits no discernible sense of direction or interest in anyone's conversation. He appears to be sleepwalking on a sunny day.

"Ah!" Cinq-Mars exclaims. "An old, dear friend of the family. Right, Caro?" She backs up his lie with an enthusiastic nod. "He happened to drop by. Don't worry, I wasn't—what did you call it?—*muddling*. He did mention that the two of you spoke, yes? And he said something quite interesting. But I'm sure you caught all that in your interview."

"Caught what?" Hammond wants to know, rising to the bait.

"Oh, you know," Cinq-Mars says. He's quite sure that Hammond has no clue. "The radioactive thing."

The trooper rocks his chin back as if expressing comprehension. "The radioactive thing," he mutters. "Yeah, that."

Carpel, having identified that it's Hammond on the premises, chooses not to join them, wandering over for a chat with a spotted white and brown mare leaning her head over a rail fence.

"Yeah," Cinq-Mars quips, "that. It's amazing how things can come together. I'm sure you found this out on your own, but if I hadn't been over—*muddling*—on the other side of the river, I might never have heard back about the Vermont ME's report. I mean, the coincidence! Then Charles drives over and talks about seeing you and brings up the necklaces and the radioactivity—"

"Coincidence?" Hammond ponders.

"I don't know when you figured it out, probably when you talked to Charles. Given that the necklace is radioactive, and Malory Earle's neck showed unusual traces of radioactivity—"

"Oh yeah," Hammond says. "Oh yeah."

"Which links the three murders together through the three necklaces—"

"Ah, three?" Hammond interrupts.

"I'm counting the radioactive necklace around Miss Earle's neck, if you follow my drift. Obviously, one of those necklaces, or one similar to them—similar in radioactivity, anyway—was around her neck recently, which links all three murders. You're probably way ahead of me on that."

Behind his sunglasses, Hammond is hard to read, although his silences are telling. "What—" he starts to say, then stops, then tries again. "I meant to ask him. What's the level—? I mean, how dangerous is the level of radioactivity, do you think?"

"Charles!" Cinq-Mars suddenly barks out and he can feel Hammond jump an inch. "The radioactivity! How dangerous?"

Carpel puts one foot up on a crossing brace as if he's a cowboy. In that suit and in that pose he looks ridiculous. "Won't kill a man in one day," he hollers back. "Prolonged exposure, different story. Skin damage. After that? Who knows?"

"Have you run that test yet?" Cinq-Mars asks the trooper.

Carpel isn't done, and barks out to Émile, "Not a story where you want to find out the ending!"

"What test?" Hammond asks.

"To see if both necklaces are radioactive."

Carpel shouts out, "Two years might kill you! Meantime, keep your testicles away!"

"Ah, yeah, the results aren't back yet," Hammond says, faking comprehension to the bitter end. "Or I don't think so anyway. Been on the road."

"Right. Right. Of course."

"Not my area of expertise!" the gemologist lets it be known.

"Thank you, Charles!" Émile shouts back, hoping he'll be quiet now. To Hammond he says, "Sorry."

"Sorry?" Hammond asks.

"I've been muddling. Meddling, anyway. Can't seem to help myself.

You're right, you're right. I'm old, I'm retired, it's your case, go for it and good luck."

"Yeah," Hammond says. "Right. Thanks."

"Is that boy a person of interest?"

Cinq-Mars is looking out across a pasture when he asks the question, as though his lack of eye contact paints his query as casual, offhand, and therefore insignificant. Hammond patiently waits for his wandering gaze to return to their jurisdiction, and the two men study each other. All Émile can read is his own reflection.

Ignoring the question, the trooper asks another. "Anything else you found out, from when you were snooping?"

Émile understands that if he is going to turn a corner with the man, then this might be his lone opportunity. "Maybe. Look, the boy's a good friend of the girls. They speak well of him. Do you have anything on him? A heads-up, just in case?"

"He told us he didn't know Toomey. We checked. He took a class with him."

Cinq-Mars nods. "That's funny," he allows.

Hammond detects the new gravity to his demeanor. "How's that?"

"I overheard him say that he *did* know Toomey. I'm surprised he denied it to you when he says something different to other people."

"That's why I'm bringing him in. To talk about that sort of contradiction."

If he was still a cop, Cinq-Mars well knows, working this case, he'd bring the boy in himself and give him a rough ride. He can't hold it against Hammond if he's thinking about doing exactly that.

"So," Hammond says, "you said 'maybe.'"

"What's your rank? How do I address you?"

"Captain."

"Yet you're a detective. In uniform."

"That's how it goes sometimes."

"Captain, something fell in my lap that maybe you don't know. I found it out by accident. I wasn't muddling."

"We both know that's bullshit. Or maybe, out on this farm, you want to call it horse manure. Either-or. What was it that fell? Into your lap?"

Émile has to consider the remark. If they both know when he's talking bovine or horse droppings, they might manage a meeting of the minds. "The boy knew Addie Langford," he sums up. "They were intimate at one time. You know that. He also knows a Professor Edith Shedden. Might not mean a thing."

"Okay. But you think it might mean something. Why?"

Émile's thinking that he might be able to get along with this guy, once they both get past their mutual antagonism. "Edith Shedden knew Malory Earle, okay? I'm not saying there's any connection at all, but if you're going to question the boy, if he already has a history of fudging the truth, you might want to keep that in your hip pocket. In other words, he's connected, if only loosely, to all three victims."

Hammond's wheels are churning, Émile can tell, perhaps so rapidly that he's unable to articulate a reply. A slight nod of his chin is probably meant to indicate thanks, or perhaps he's broaching an outside perimeter of appreciation.

"Can I talk to him?" Émile requests.

"The boy? No."

"I don't mean as an investigator. He's connected to my family. As a family friend, can I have a quick word? He's just a scared boy. You know I'm not working against you here. I just gave you good material."

The trooper mulls it over. Hammond may be a bright man, and a stubborn and insecure one, a combination that causes him to flail his way through certain complexities and come across as awkward and slow. Though Émile's initial impression of him as being incompetent might not stand, either.

"One minute, max," Hammond stipulates.

Émile casts a glance back at Caroline and the girls as he walks over to the patrol car. Huddled together for mutual support, they seem relieved that he's involved to some extent. The back door is opened for him by the patrol officer and the two cops move off a short distance. Émile waits for them to attain the furthest distance they're going to permit him before he leans down and looks at the boy. Vernon is putting on a brave front. The retired policeman has seen that attitude frequently enough in his career that he knows instantly that the lad before him is frightened half to death.

"We meet again," Cinq-Mars says.

"You're the uncle?"

"Go figure, hey."

"Yeah."

"You know you're in trouble, right?"

"Why am I in trouble? They want to talk about Addie, they said."

"You lied. You lied and you're trembling because you're afraid of something that you're hiding that you want to keep hid. That's obvious to any cop."

"I'm not trembling." The boy looks away. He swallows hard. Asks, "What lie?"

"Do you mean there's more than one?"

The question sets the boy back in his seat a little. He looks up.

"How many? If there was only one you should be able to recite it back to me."

The question is tricky, and the boy knows it. "Maybe there's more than one. I didn't feel like talking to them, you know? Some things in life are personal. Which one do you know?"

"You told me you knew Toomey."

"Oh yeah," Vernon says.

"Not very well, you said. Which was a lie. You told *them*—" Cinq-Mars lets his statement hang in the air, for Vernon to accept or reject.

"That I didn't," he admits.

"That you didn't know him at all. You doubled down on your lie. Why?" Émile asks. "They found out on their own what's true. You told me one thing—"

"I didn't know who you were. The security guard, she was aggressive. I had to give her an excuse for being there."

"What was your real reason for being at Toomey's office?"

He doesn't want to say.

"Were you having an affair with him?"

Vernon scrunches up his face in a look of contempt. "No way."

"They're going to ask," Cinq-Mars points out, indicating the troopers. "You might as well get used to the question."

"That's not it."

"They'll want to know what *it* is. Why'd you hang out with him?"

He's pushing past his level of personal knowledge. An old ploy. Increase the level of agreed-upon knowledge and mere supposition soon becomes an acknowledged fact. "I think I told you," Vernon reminds him, although he doesn't sound convincing.

"He tells good stories," Émile remembers.

"I was interested in what he taught, that's all."

"Yeah, but he's dead now, Vernon. Why visit his office?"

Hammond is returning. "I'll take him in now," he says. "We'll have a long talk downtown." Then he smiles at the boy with what seems a threatening grin. "Won't we, son?"

Vernon, Émile notes, refuses to look at the trooper.

"One more quick word in private."

"You've had that quick word."

"The time it takes for you to go around and get in the driver's seat."

Hammond makes a show of his impatience. He agrees with a shrug and starts around to the front of the car. His subordinate clambers into the front passenger seat and slams the door a whole lot louder than necessary. The conversation isn't private.

"You lied," Cinq-Mars whispers in Vernon's ear. "You're in trouble. Answer as honestly as you can. Don't get upset if they're aggressive, that's their job. If you feel they're trying to pin something on you, whether you're guilty or not, lawyer up. Put in a call to one of your friends here, and we'll get a lawyer in to see you right away. We'll even get one ready to go, just in case. Understand?"

Vernon nods that he does, and with fright showing in his eyes he meets Émile's gaze. "I didn't kill anybody," he says.

"Then what are you scared of?"

"Shut the door, please!" Hammond calls out, bossy again now that his patrol officer is nearby.

Knowing that he's been granted considerable license throughout the exchange, and has won a speck of ground, Cinq-Mars obeys.

————

Evening falls with casual grace and a relaxed melancholy. Shadflies panic in the high dim lamps that illuminate corners of the yard. Frogs croak by the large pond. A couple of field and barn laborers and a horse handler pack into their cars, heading home, save for the resident Mexican foreman who can walk a path through the tall grasses to his cabin by the edge of the woods. He's an older man, made lethargic by the passing of his longtime employer and friend. The sun absconds early due to the affront of Vermont mountains to the west; in the morning the sunrise will be postponed by these New Hampshire hills. As it sets, mosquitoes intensify, and Émile and Sandra take their leave of the front porch and retire to the family den.

For Émile, the familiarity of the evening has been striking. A lot like home. Changing one horse farm for another, he's thinking, may not be the new direction he and Sandra have been searching for, notwithstanding the move from one country to another. He's not sure that he wants to read *Live Free or Die* on his license plate. Not that he doesn't believe in the sanctity of freedom, or in defending a homeland, but the phrase seems rife for spoofing. For him, as an outsider, the line conjures boys on the backs of pickups firing their rifles into the air expressly to prove they can. They embolden their sense of freedom through misbehavior while the real seriousness of freedom—an interest in intellectual rigor, scientific and spiritual exploration, speaking a difficult or unpopular truth, or countering a lie—is not considered. On this side of the border, freedom often seems reduced to a right to stash cash without a thought to the family that has nothing, or to promote conspiracy theories, such as that men never landed on the moon but surely aliens have spawned a superspecies on earth, and *freedom* is the right to mock those who think otherwise. Freedom is the right, apparently, to take a knee-jerk position with respect to absolutely everything, whether it be a favorite hypothesis of the left or of the right, and call it thoughtfulness. Odd how *freedom* often engenders a belief in dogma. He fumes to himself at times. Does everyone holding to a batty or nonsensical or even a perfectly reasonable position need to take up arms for being mocked in public? That's not the meaning of the rallying cry, surely, *Live Free or Die,* but it's not difficult to imagine the words being reduced to a comic outcome. Does he want that around him? he ponders. Should he live here? Is it even a threat or just a slurry offered up by his fertile imagination? Émile doesn't know. It's difficult to fully conceive of moving to this lovely place.

Live free or die.

How free were the victims struck dead? They were never able to raise that flag when a killer approached.

Under the gloom of such contemplations, the evening passes.

Early to bed. Uncommonly for summer, Sandra pours herself a cup of ginger tea and honey which she sips sitting up under the covers, pillows bunched up behind her.

"You okay?" he inquires.

"Fine. Just beat."

Grief, they both know, can be exhausting and seditious.

This is a small, charming room, and of course if they ever bought this place they would sleep in Sandra's mother's bedroom, rather than this spare one which was once her sister's and even, for a time, where the two young sisters slept in bunk beds. The room has been refashioned for guests, and no longer evokes childhood memories, or not sharp ones. As old as the house may be, it's suffered the passage of time well, and has been kept up. Charming as all get out, it speaks to them with muffled aches and pains the old timbers expand and shrink and sigh. In moving here, that's worth considering on the positive side of the ledger, the charm of the place, and the affection they both feel for the rooms, for the intimacy of its nooks and crannies, the warmth and patina of the old wood.

Though the wind whistles through in winter. Which is Sandra's exaggeration, or old memory, although the home can still be drafty and the wind outside fierce.

One thought Émile must abide by, as it's persistent, one which he's unwilling to speak aloud, is that in choosing a home for his retirement, he's choosing a home that Sandra may live in long after he's gone. That's simply a reality of being nineteen years her senior, and it's a compelling consideration. If she wants to return to her roots—and why not? It's both a lively and a peaceful place—then living freely and dying there might prove to be his lot. He's not one to stand in the way of her interest in this regard as she has more at stake.

She has more life to live. More lovely years.

He eases over to her.

"What's in your craw?" She's suspicious.

"I want to hold you. What we call cuddling. Have you heard of it? You've been through so much the last two days while I've been off solving crimes."

"Tilting at windmills, more like. What crime have you solved?"

"Making progress. Give a guy a chance."

"Okay, but don't cuddle out of guilt. I'm onside with this, Émile."

"The cuddling?"

"The crime-solving. One of Caro's best friends was murdered. I'd be upset if you didn't stick your nose in."

"Leave my nose out of this. It draws enough barbs in life."

She kisses it, gently, in case he needs to feel better about his huge schnozzle.

"Had an interesting chat with the girls today," Sandra says as Émile moves off to get into what he wears to bed these days. "Nothing to do with murder or death."

"What else is there to talk about?"

"They're anti-Ivy League."

"A little late for that, no? Now that the privilege of being graduates is upon them?"

"They *love* their educations. Wouldn't change that part of it for the world. Technically, of course, Dowbiggin is not in the Ivy League, but culturally it's close enough. They were going on about what happens to graduates after they leave school."

"One of them wants to feed the starving. I overheard something about that."

"Caroline doesn't plan to be just any CEO. She intends to make things happen."

"Good on them. How does that make them anti–Ivy League?"

Sandra sips her tea, and peruses the naked form of her husband before his loose-fitting Jockeys go on for the night. He doesn't believe her when she tells him, but his body moves her still. The size of him counts, his height, girth, the inherent strength through his chest, those big hands and the veins that trace the line of his forearms. She feels that his weakened back has caused him to see himself as less attractive, and Lord knows confidence is half the battle. Yet she admires him still, and she's seen women—admittedly, mainly those older than herself—admire him also. The authority he bears naturally does the trick, she figures, in any case she's not complaining. Long ago when she'd look ahead to such a time, trying to imagine herself in her midforties and him in retirement, she painted a picture duller than this reality. Not bad, she's thinking, and is it the recent death in their household that has her waking up just as they both prepare for bed?

"They were extolling a theory that the Ivy League is about privilege and prestige. There's been books, apparently, the idea doesn't originate with them. But it's earned their attention."

"Nothing new about privilege and prestige."

"Their point is—all the girls think this way, apparently—that smart, privileged, affluent Ivy League graduates study and learn well but they still don't have a clue. They go from here to Wall Street or on to another existing platform and ride that gravy train for all it's worth. Their complaint about it is, Ivy Leaguers don't innovate, they don't create, they don't redefine, quote, 'the paradigm of modern complexity.' Quite the spiel."

"They plan to save the world by re-creating it. I'm all for that. Those kids won me over from the get-go."

"You're an old goat. You've got a crush on them all."

He pulls the covers back. "Don't old goat me. I'm relieved to find the world in good hands."

"Speaking of hands." This time, she sallies over to his side. "I will not be made to feel guilty about this. I will not allow myself to feel guilty."

"Okay. About what?"

Her hands, under the covers, tell him about what.

"I know, I know, you need to take a pill," she says.

"Keep that up, you might disprove the theory."

They kiss, and feel the ominous depth of the night and the empty space of the country house, the darkened fields with their night critters on the prowl and the stars above in their austere splendor. Time goes by, and life is fleeting, a parent dies, yet moments occur when life yields to this serendipity, and time, then, for the moment, stands still. Then they sleep until the morning.

PART 4

NINETEEN

At precisely 11 A.M., a weary, shaken Vernon Colchester is released from police custody. A trifle disoriented. The bright sun hurts his eyes as though he's been squirreled away in a grotto for a week. He'd expected hard questions. He'd not expected Captain Hammond to put a hand on his kneecap and hold it there, squeezing intermittently, and he had not expected him to insist that the first word out of his mouth anytime he spoke had to be *sir*.

"*Sir*, I didn't kill anybody."

"Sure you did, son. Absolutely you did."

At the end of the first sentence that Hammond spoke he would always say *son*. Vernon detested that word as much as he hated having to say *sir*.

"I loved Addie. I'd never hurt her. That's a crazy idea."

"Say that again properly, son," Hammond instructed him, and squeezed his knee.

"*Sir*, I loved Addie."

"Nobody doubts that, son. Why did you dress her up?"

"Sir, I didn't!"

"Speak the truth, son. You'll see. Things will go better then."

"*Sir—*"

"We know you loved her, son. Love can take a man into strange places. You agree with me on that, right?"

He didn't know what to say.

"Don't you agree, son? You've been in strange places. If you admit to that, at least, you won't be admitting to anything much. We can agree on that, can't we?"

"Sir, agree on what?" He was confused.

"That love can take you into strange places, son."

He could admit to that, but he wouldn't.

"Sir, I don't know what you mean."

"Oh son." He squeezed his knee again.

Vernon didn't know what he hated most, saying *sir,* being called *son,* or having his kneecap squeezed for no reason. None of that felt sexual, he couldn't fight back at him on that, and yet the cop was trying to dominate him, to wear him down that way.

He just wanted him *off.*

He slept in a cell.

Outside in the bright sunlight, he finds himself at a loss, wanting to run, hide, wanting to scream at passengers on a city bus who presumed to glance his way. He reaches out to a friend instead, calling Caroline, who texts Anastasia. One girl arranges to pick the other up, then the two girls drive over a few blocks to meet Vernon in the center of town. He calls back once to see where they are and when they say they're nearby he departs the coffee shop to wait on the street. The girls are slowing down, looking to park, when a large black SUV ducks ahead of them and stops just past where Vernon's standing. In the wink of an eye, a heavyset man emerges from the backseat, leaps onto the curb, and before Vernon can react grabs him by the front of his shirt and by his belt and half hurls, half squashes him into the backseat of the vehicle.

The door slams shut on its own as the SUV speeds off.

At the wheel of her car, Caroline goes comatose, shocked. The scene has been previewed a thousand times in movies she's seen, but this is real, this is happening to someone she knows. She feels unable to breathe, her chest clogged.

The moment falls to Anastasia to revive her.

"Get after them! Caroline! Caro! Get after them!"

The black SUV is speeding away.

"Caro!"

"He had a gun!"

"What?"

"He had a gun!"

"Fucking go! Drive!"

Traffic has already come between the two vehicles and Caroline can't bring herself to drive that aggressively despite Anastasia's protestations. Soon they're leaving town on the highway and catching a glimpse of the vehicle as it outruns them and reappears and vanishes up and down hills and frequently around bends.

"Hurry up!"

"Oh my God oh my God!"

"Get a hold of yourself!"

Caroline does just that. "Call my uncle!"

"What?"

"Now!" She barks out the number as she careens around a corner.

"Careful!"

"Too late for that."

Anastasia calls the farmhouse. Caroline, one hand on the wheel, seizes the phone from her. When Sandra answers she falls back into being polite yet demands to speak to Émile immediately. Apparently, he's doing his exercises and is slow to make it to the phone. She's screaming into the phone to hurry, not knowing that Sandra has put the receiver down and wandered off.

Finally, Émile answers. "Yes?"

"Uncle Émile, for God's sake, it's me!"

"Caro? What's going on?"

"He's been abducted! Vernon! They grabbed him right off the street!"

"The police?"

"No! Not the police! Or maybe. I don't know who! Two guys with a gun! He just called me to pick him up because the cops let him go. They released him. Somebody else grabbed him!"

"What do you mean grabbed?"

"They threw him into the back of this big van thingee."

"SUV!" Anastasia shouts out.

"Did you see which way they went?"

"Yes! Uncle Émile, we're following them right now! Anastasia and me! We're chasing them!"

"Oh no. For God's sake be careful. Who's driving?"

"I am!"

"Then give the phone to Anastasia. Right now, Caro."

Partly to comply, more out of physical necessity, Caro flips the phone to her friend as she grips both hands tightly to the steering wheel. The other girl makes a miraculous catch before the phone falls between the seats, and shouts into the device, "What!"

"Anastasia," Émile calmly directs her, "tell me exactly where you are and what direction you're headed. Be as precise as you can be." He then shouts through the house, "Sandra!" Back to his caller, informing his wife at the same time, he explains, "Sandra will call the Hanover Police Department on my mobile. She'll speak to Chief Till. We'll get a patrol car out to you right away. Tell Caroline to keep her distance."

"No, I want her to hurry up, we're falling behind!"

"Fall behind! We don't want an accident. Do they know you're chasing them?"

"I doubt it. Caroline doesn't drive fast enough for them to think that."

"I'm glad she doesn't. Good for her. Okay, Anastasia, we have Chief Till on the other line. Now where are you?"

She knows the road. At that moment they happen to pass a highway sign and she doesn't have to think twice. She spots a civic address and relays that number as well. "Add on, I don't know, a quarter mile, maybe more, heading south, that's where they are, ahead of us."

"Keep your distance," Cinq-Mars instructs her, although Anastasia hears him talking to Chief Till as well. His voice is calm, directed, and she tries to emulate his tone in repeating the message to Caroline.

"We haven't seen them for a bit," she gets back to him a moment later.

"Steady on. Keep looking down side streets and driveways to see if they turned off."

"Vernon must be terrified." Suddenly, Anastasia is excitable again. "What're you doing! What're you doing!"

"What's going on?" calmly, Émile is asking in her ear.

All that Anastasia knows is that Caroline is pulling over to the side of the road for no reason of which she's aware without slowing down and not in a good spot, either. The shoulder is hazardous and the ride violent. The old jalopy Ford bucks like a crazed bull. Anastasia prangs her head on the ceiling then hits her chin on her own kneecap. In the chaos she sees a Hanover police car, lights flashing, siren off, roaring past them at the speed of sound and by the time their car fights its way back onto the roadway, rocking from side to side, the patrol car has virtually vanished. They spot it around a curve through trees, at bullet speed.

"My God, will you stay on the road, he would've gone around you, Caro!"

"Just—" Caroline thinks of what to say. She's staring straight ahead, driving as though she wants to choke someone the way she holds the wheel.

"Just what?" her friend asks.

"I don't know. Just, shut the fuck up, I guess."

"Tell her I heard that," Cinq-Mars says. "What's going on?"

"The police are here. They're ahead of us. They're after them."

She hears Émile convey the news to Chief Till, and she relays his message, then he advises the girls to pull over and come home. "Let the police take it from here." He waits a moment.

Caro asks her friend to use the speaker phone, then speaks to her uncle while she drives. "Uncle Émile, seriously, there's no place to turn around here, it's too dangerous to stop. We have no choice. We'll go straight until it's safe to turn."

He suspects that he's being played, and knows there's nothing he can do about that. "Stay on the line," he advises her, "until you start heading back."

"If you don't mind too much, no. I'll call you if something happens."

A young person with a willfulness all her own.

"Be safe," Émile warns before the connection goes silent.

———

In the rear seat of the vehicle being pursued, Vernon Colchester resists. He knows what's coming. The big man has the advantage of size and positioning and uses it to pummel him without mercy. In the limited confines they compete to a moment when the student submits, it's useless to fight on. He answers their questions. Not like they want him to. He's wedged against the door with the heavy man almost entirely on top of him, still punching and demanding different answers, when the door is opened, his head falls back, and as they speed along the highway his scalp dangles a foot and a half above the pavement although it feels more like an inch, and he's being shoved, incrementally, out the door. Toward, he believes, a certain death. Fiercely he kicks with his one free leg, grips whatever he can hold on to. Their stalemate persists until the heavy man squirms off his chest, yet still pins his hips, and the man yanks Vernon's torso up by pulling him by the hair then aims a pistol between his eyeballs.

That gun again.

Vernon is looking at the man's fat finger on the trigger.

"Motherfucker, jump!" commands his attacker. He's breathing heavily from the exertion of punching him, his voice succinct. "Jump or die for sure. You got that one fucking chance I give you here."

Not much of one. *A fat chance,* Vernon thinks, he doesn't know why.

The door keeps swinging open, then closes partway. The car careens down the highway in excess of seventy miles an hour. Vernon looks out. The shoulder of the road a blur. He's permitted to slip out from under the heavier man and with a gun to his head Vernon Colchester tries to leap but in the end merely stumbles out of the car.

He suffers a ferocious wallop as he hits the side of the road.

The officer in the gaining patrol car sees him bounce once, twice, lifting high off the ground, then hit the grass hard again before his limp form cartwheels down an embankment. The cop needs to make a choice in a hurry—and quits his pursuit to come to the aid of the injured boy.

He hopes that he's merely injured anyway. As opposed to dead.

———

Caroline sees the flashing lights of the squad car, now stopped by the side of the road. She pulls in behind. Anastasia can see down the embankment and puts both hands to her mouth. Caroline opens her car door.

"Caro. No. Stay here with me."

The words, the look on her friend's face, are too much for Caroline; they provide her with the necessary impetus to clamber out of her seat. This time it's Anastasia who's frozen in place. Caroline steps to the side of the embankment, sees the two cops, one next to Vernon, the other still working his way down the hill. The embankment is mostly shrub grass and gravel. There's blood. There's a limb akimbo. There's a motionless boy. Way, way in the distance, she hears the initial wail of an ambulance, she hopes, or more cop cars. Or both. When she turns back to inform Anastasia of what she sees, both their faces are cracked and broken.

Before his surgery, Vernon Colchester's friends are informed that his chances of survival are touch-and-go.

The pressure on his brain must be relieved. A broken arm and leg are repaired and placed in protective removable casts although his broken ribs interfere with his ability to breathe. Three fingers are reset on the tip of the arm that's not broken as has been the kneecap on his good leg. The broken leg has three pins embedded in the ankle now. They're worried about a hip but can't deal with it yet. His face has suffered a few serious lesions, one quite deep. He looks as though he had a bare-knuckle brawl as an amateur featherweight against the heavyweight champion of the world. They address his face with bandages.

After surgery, one of the attending physicians calls him lucky. Even so, everyone can tell that the doctor remains worried.

TWENTY

Émile Cinq-Mars stays behind at the farmhouse. For a short while, he's alone, as Sandra has chosen to include herself among the young women holding a vigil for Vernon Colchester at the hospital. He doesn't tell her what he's up to, and wouldn't want anyone to know his own take on the matter. Essentially, he's rummaging around the darker terrain of his thinking. Begging old grievances to rise from their fallow to fuel his emotions. To seize this day and kick the bad guys' collective ass. Something. Anything. He needs to get churned up. He speaks to his God in his way, though with less passion than he'd prefer to summon, and wonders if this is an old-age thing, if time is sifting through the hourglass and with its passage go his better observations and sharper concentration.

He stretches to keep his back limber, wishing he could do the same for his mind.

During his brief time on the case, he believed he was merely investigating the arcane circumstances. He never suspected that further risk was in the offing, or that his real task should be to protect others. He feels shoddy and incompetent now. That a boy he doesn't know has

been severely injured is bad enough, and gives credence to the accusation that a young woman, his own niece, whom he idly sent off on a
mission, is at risk of being victimized. That vexes him no end. Especially
because he's already thinking that he might do it again. He imagines
that this may never have occurred if he was a younger man or merely in
a workday groove, although he's still cogent enough to doubt that excuse. Now, he awaits the top cops, the principals from various forces—
having had to do *something,* he's called a meeting—and blithely he
grumbles to himself in a rehearsal of what he might say. They've been
incompetent, too, yet how can he disparage their work when he's been
equally inept? Still, things need to be said. The matter has been plowed
over and judged. Blame will lie where it falls. Hopefully, everybody gets
that. Hopefully, they're ready, as he is, to cooperate.

As the headlights appear of a car turning onto his driveway, Émile
acknowledges that he's secretly playing favorites. He's hoping that
Chief Till shows up first, as being in his company may help him relax.
He's nudged, then, by disappointment, when left with no choice other
than to invite Trooper Hammond into the house. Awkwardly, he offers
him tea or coffee and a slice of the coffee cake a neighbor brought over
to help ease Sandra through her bereavement.

If Hammond prefers, he's welcome to a shot of hard liquor.

"I'm drinking scotch myself," Émile admits.

The drink a calculation. He figures he needs to loosen his synapses.

Hammond has slumped through the door looking like a dog checking out which table leg to piss on. He seems his usual gruff self, with
nothing to say at the outset, not even to answer if he'll accept a bever-
age. The man peruses the front room with a thumb tucked in his gun
belt as though expecting to draw his pistol in the next few seconds. He
glances at Cinq-Mars, then says, "You got the governor's ear."

"Me? Not really. Not directly, I wouldn't say."

"Pretty straight-on direct to me. You ask me over. I say no. The governor phones and look where I am. I'm hearing that it's not in one state,
either, but two. You got two governors on the line. Fucking impressive
for a retired foreigner."

"I've had a long career."

"Balls," Hammond attests. Today, though, he's inclined, and perhaps compelled, to rethink his response. "What's that supposed to mean?" He keeps himself turned away.

Lacking an audience, Cinq-Mars shrugs anyway. "Connections?"

"That high the motherfuck up? With governors yet."

"With colleagues who have sway. I know who to call, let's say, if the homeland requires a measure of security. Let's put it that way."

"Sure, let's put it that way. Why not? Don't tell me it passes the sniff test. Not close up. I detect a whiff of bullshit in the air. Anyway, like I said," Hammond grunts, "impressive. It's like you're holding on to the governor's balls and asking him to cough. He coughs for you. I'm trying to compliment you here. Seriously, is it the homeland? You can spin that with any kind of sincerity?"

"Trooper Hammond, I need you to be here today. It's that simple. You said no, sir. I took measures." The conversation needs to turn, Cinq-Mars believes. Among other issues, he senses that his personal outer limit for civility is fast approaching.

"You made the arrangements."

"I did," Cinq-Mars confirms.

Hammond grunts once more. Possibly, in appreciation. Then he says, "Sure. Coffee. Thanks. Why not? I got caffeine seeping out the corners of my eyeballs, what's another drop?"

At least the request separates them into different rooms for a minute.

By the time Émile emerges with two cups, having decided to forgo more whiskey for coffee himself, another cop car is on its way up the drive, with a third making the turn off the county highway.

"Company's coming," Hammond mentions, an attempt at a joke that misfires. He's as uncomfortable being alone in the room with Cinq-Mars as is the retired detective to be entertaining him.

Putting the coffee down, the host tries to improve the situation. "I respect you," Émile says. "I respect your authority in all this."

"That's in major fucking doubt," Hammond contends. His tone, though, seems friendly enough.

"We've got a young woman killed and a young man badly injured. Not to mention the other murders. More forces are at play than we're able to get a handle on. You've got to agree with me on that part. I'm not saying that it makes anything easier, but you've got to agree with me. We need to clear the air. Everybody has to start sharing what they know before more young men and young women get hurt or killed. That's just a plain fact and nobody wants more deaths around here."

"I'd probably trust you more if I knew where your weight comes from," Hammond points out. "Share that."

"The FBI will be here. They can share."

"The FB-fucking-I? Are you kidding me?"

"Why would I? Three people are dead and a boy is in hospital. One of the dead was an intelligence agent. You thought the FBI would stand down?"

"What? Who? Toomey? Intelligence?"

"Yes. What. Who. Toomey. Intelligence. Don't you think you need to know that sort of thing over the course of your investigation? Toomey might've described himself as a *former* agent to his friends. I'm not sure it applies. Not sure that that can ever be the case. Look at me—I'm supposed to be retired. Why am I standing tall in a heap of dung here?"

"Not a professor?" Hammond is still stuck on this one gem of information.

"Not entirely, anyway. What's he been up to? Besides teaching? What's been his purpose in being here, do you think?"

"Fuck if I know," Hammond mutters, loudly. He's peeved to be finding this out only now.

"My point," Cinq-Mars tells him. "People need to know things. We all do. Even, and I know this won't sit well with you, Captain, too bad on that, even me. I need to know a few things. I understand if you don't like it. I wouldn't like it in your shoes. In a roundabout way, I have the ear of the governor—"

"Two governors."

"Both of them, sure. Suit yourself. You don't have to like it—that's how things stand. You found out what you need to know, and guess what, Captain, there's a whole other boatload of stuff to learn. I'm certain of that. If we don't share information, everybody might as well retire to Canada, not just me."

Outside, the next cop to arrive has been waiting for the one who followed him in, then the pair stride up to the house.

"How's that boy doing?" Hammond asks.

"You don't know?"

"I hear one thing. You got ears on the ground. That girl tribe of yours."

"Which includes my wife." He can get to like this guy for a while, but only so far. Then it's as if he spits out the side of his mouth during a polite conversation. "The boy's head trauma is delicate. He's in an induced coma for that. The prognosis is fair. A full slate of broken bones. Do you want the list?"

"That's okay. I got the list. Listen," Hammond says.

On the way to the front door, Cinq-Mars pauses, and turns back. He waits to hear what the trooper wants to tell him.

"I'm onside with what you're saying. So you know."

Always it's up and down with him, a roller coaster. Yet Émile appreciates the comment, and indicates as much with a slight, yet meaningful, nod, a gesture that Hammond returns. As much of a bond as these two men are likely to manage together.

Chiefs Michael Till of Hanover, New Hampshire, and Roy Horriza from White River Junction, Vermont, are at the door.

Another car turns up the drive behind them.

Once everyone has arrived and gotten settled, Cinq-Mars inquires of Till, "Did you get the ME's report?" His way of both initiating the discussion and making a point.

"You know I'm not privy," the chief remarks. With Hammond present, he doesn't appreciate being put on the spot this way.

"Did you get it anyway, like I asked you, find a back door?"

Hammond is interested in the answer. Six men are seated around a coffee table with their cups in front of them. They could as easily be a group of philatelists at a monthly meeting. The fifth man who has joined them—by walking downstairs—is Michael Hartopp, an FBI special agent with whom Cinq-Mars has worked previously and who provides him with assistance on occasion. Hartopp considers a favor to the Montreal detective—for rooting out a corrupt element in the bureau—a bottomless well, so never begrudges lending a hand. Such as talking to people who can talk to governors who can get things done. The others in the room were introduced to him and a line drawn from his work in the FBI to Homeland Security, and they're already aware of his pull in high places. He's accorded authority in the room. Émile's connection to the man allows the retired Montreal cop to be in the room himself, as he has no official status and normally his presence would not be tolerated. Mainly, that's why Émile brought him in. To lean on his authority. Hartopp is slim, bony of visage and body, with a knack for getting others to feel at ease around him. Consequently, in answering Émile's question, Till is more concerned about Hammond than the outsider from Washington. He gives the trooper a hard glance, yet comes across with the truth.

"Hey, I tried. But that's a locked shop."

"You tried," sneers Hammond, the sarcasm easing through his veins like an IV drip. "You damn well know you're not privy but you tried anyway."

"Why am I not privy?" Till is set to blow a gasket. He's not afraid of Hammond, just frustrated by the protocol that exists. "It's my town! Holyoake is part of my jurisdiction. Two of the three dead are on my turf. That boy was thrown out of a speeding car on my turf."

The last man who showed up is a state trooper from Vermont investigating Malory Earle's murder. His name is Archie Leopold and he's the youngest of their bunch. His youth marks him as the least experienced among them, a supposition that holds true. When it comes to serious crimes he's remarkably inexperienced for his rank and has relied more heavily than might be the norm on the advice of Chief Horriza. In this company, he's comfortable to be present and on the sidelines.

"Gentlemen," Cinq-Mars begins, and his tone, at once serious, cordial, and authoritative, commands the room. "This is why we're here. Three dead, one injured, and nobody has a clue because nothing is shared among us. I've worked with multiple departments all my life. Where I come from it was Mounties at the federal level, plus provincial cops and city cops. Always, every agency claimed that cooperation between the forces was exemplary. Departments won extra government funding to make that point, to assure the politicians that cooperation was seamless and computer friendly. None of you have worked in Canada, yet would any of you be surprised to learn that cooperation between jurisdictions was virtually nonexistent? Bogus. Nothing more than PR, and after the official PR was out of the way every police force in the land went back to keeping its information to itself and not communicating a damn thing. The more precious the information, the tighter that news was kept. Anybody here surprised?"

They indicate that a similar regimen conforms to their own experience.

"You're sitting in a farmhouse today because we have got to agree that this can't happen right now. Too much at stake. When this is over, go back to your Neanderthal ways. I don't care. Nobody does. With three people dead and a young man in hospital we cannot afford the status quo. Who knows who else is at risk? Nobody in this room does, I'll tell you that much. We're all ignorant."

The policemen are feeling a trifle sheepish.

"Incidentally," Cinq-Mars continues, "Special Agent Hartopp has agreed that if you guys say you'll cooperate, share information, then don't, the FBI will take complete command and boot all of you off your stumps in the blink of an eye." They know that he's continuing to declare his own status: he can use his influence to have them booted if they don't want him around. "I hope that's understood. Now. Brass tacks. I informed Captain Hammond a few minutes ago that Philip Lars Toomey was an operative throughout his working life. Secret service although I think I know which branch. Special Agent Hartopp will enlighten us as to what that entailed. Take it as one example of information that needs to be shared, and if it's not shared, we're either working in the shadows or in a pitch-dark room. Captain Hammond. Since you've already been granted information that you didn't know, give something back. The rest of us haven't even heard yet if Addie was raped or not. Start with the ME report. What did the medical examiner say that we should all hear?"

Émile has thrashed a stick around: This is a carrot. Hammond gets to take over the room and say what he knows, a salve to his ego, and Émile can tell that the opportunity suits him. By being the first visitor to speak, he's content with his lot, and less concerned with being under this outsider's thumb.

"Real sick," he lets them know. "Addie Langford was raped. You probably figured that. It's been confirmed and gets worse. She was strangled. It's believed that she was strangled with the same nylon stockings she ended up wearing. Both stockings, bound together for extra strength, I guess. And then, quite dead, this is the thing, her corpse was raped again."

They let the unspeakable settle among them.

"Time of death?" Hartopp inquires. His voice is scarcely above a whisper.

"Between 3:30 and 5:30 A.M. That's about three to five hours before the body was discovered. The first rape possibly occurred between eight and ten hours earlier. Our ME doesn't consider himself an expert in that regard so he communicated the data to others who concur. Rape was inflicted sometime before death, and one crime did not immediately follow the other. Yet her disappearance, as far as we can ascertain, occurs hours before that. A prolonged misery. She was under the perpetrator's control for many hours."

"What's the basis for estimating her time of disappearance?" Émile asks.

"Cell phone use. When did she stop answering her texts and stop checking status updates on Facebook? That's constant for her during the day, every day of her life unless she's in a class or sleeping or both, then stops suddenly the eve of her murder around 9 P.M."

"Have you found the phone?" Till wants to know.

"Left behind in the clock tower. Upper level."

"You checked for fingerprints, of course."

"Wiped clean. Partial traces match her own prints. Mostly it's been cleaned. That suggests that the killer was handling it and made sure to wipe it afterward."

"He didn't phone home, I presume," Hartopp says.

"We're not that lucky, no."

"Blood? Bodily fluids?" Cinq-Mars asks.

"Very little blood was found and most of it was the victim's. This is where we do get lucky. A bit of tissue and blood was left behind which is not Addie Langford's. ME's best guess is that it came off the elbow of the assailant."

"The elbow?" Horriza speaks up.

"That kind of tough skin got left behind. Quite possibly this was during the rape, which lets us place the rape at the highest point in the tower. A trace secretion, from the girl's anus, matches what remained in her lower bowel. Someone, undoubtedly the killer, cleaned it up. A fraction slipped down between the cracks into the grain of the wood up there. We've run the DNA, of course, of the foreign skin and blood. No matches."

"If we catch the guy, we have evidence to convict," Horriza notes.

"In that direction, for sure."

"I didn't see damage or blood on the girl," Cinq-Mars recalls. "Except for the ligature marks on her throat."

"She bled a little out an ear. Then the guy cleaned her up, to look nice. I can't tell you if he did that before or after he had at her again, postmortem."

The comment brings on another contemplative silence.

"She's brought up to the highest point in the clock tower, probably lured there," Cinq-Mars begins to summarize.

"Why lured?" Trooper Archie Leopold interrupts, speaking for the first time. He looks around nervously, hoping his question isn't inane.

"No signs of a struggle on the way up," Cinq-Mars points out to him. "Surely the rough surfaces of the stairs and banister would have picked up traces of fabric and/or skin and at least a drop of blood if a struggle was going on. Besides that, she brought her phone up there. It's not conclusive, but presumably the killer would have taken it from her before going up the stairs if the attack happened earlier."

"How'd they even get in the clock tower?"

Hartopp's question elicits no response from anyone.

"Possibly," Cinq-Mars suggests, "that's where Malory Earle comes in. Since we don't know that yet, let's stick with Addie. No signs of a struggle on the way up, not much evidence of a big struggle once there. That suggests a pacifier."

"Drugs," Hartopp imagines.

"Or a weapon," Till adds.

"The ME didn't mention drugs," Hammond says. "It's not on the tox report. In conversation, he mentioned that she was probably as squeaky clean a college student as there is in the nation. Drug-free. Not even marijuana. She just says no."

"Then it's a weapon," Till concludes. "A gun to the head or a knife to the throat can buy a certain amount of silence and a fair amount of compliance."

Émile is tugging on an earlobe, which others think might be significant. It isn't. He spies no clear path through this. "Two things," he mentions. "A calling card was left behind to a cocktail party for the very well heeled on campus tomorrow."

"You don't think it was a decoration?" Hammond asks. It's not hard to tell that that's exactly what he thinks of the invitation. "Or maybe an attempt to throw us off?"

"Toomey was going to that party. Toomey, in fact, went to considerable lengths, this year and last, to make sure that he was getting in the door. The boy who's lying in a hospital bed as we speak, he knows a professor who's going. That professor, Edith Shedden, always attends the party, it's part of her job. And—keeping this in the room, I'm not supposed to let this out—that lady professor probably had an affair with Addie Langford."

"The victim was gay?" Hammond asks. "I don't get that. I've got a list of her boyfriends. Not one or two. A list."

"Girls at that age, the promiscuous ones perhaps, experiment. Or that's what they call it anyway." Cinq-Mars raises the index finger of his left hand. He wants to issue a warning, such as, Don't say something you'll regret two seconds later, then edits himself. He has to keep all these egos in the fold and it's no time to warn Hammond not to be vulgar. Instead, he talks right through whatever he might say. "The point is, it's a cocktail party for rich donors, and that brings us to the next item of interest. The necklace. What killer provides his victims with gifts? In my experience, usually they're takers. What's more, the necklace worn by Addie Langford is a close match to the one in Toomey's glove box, and they're both exceptionally radioactive. Radioactivity was found around the throat of Malory Earle."

"Those two were lovers," Archie Leopold pipes up.

"Malory Earle and Addie Langford?" Hartopp inquires.

"No, no. I meant Malory Earle and Toomey."

"What makes you say that?" Hammond barks at him, almost as though he'd like to see the young man cower. "How can you know?"

Although Leopold may be quiet, he's not timid. "His picture was on TV. Professor Toomey's. People in Malory Earle's neighborhood recognized him. He paid visits to her all the time. A few think she was earning a little extra on the side. If that's true, she had only the one client. What folks do know is that when they parted for the afternoon, she'd wave from her window. She wasn't wearing a whole lot of clothes, and seemed, people say, happy."

"Her body wasn't typical for a girl working that way," Horriza says. "I vote for happy lovers."

Cinq-Mars is about to speak, then yields to Special Agent Hartopp who wants to run with this one. "So, Toomey goes to see Malory Earle. She's wearing the necklace. He takes it off her. Why?"

"Before or after he kills her? Not that it matters much," Hammond says.

"Not likely that he killed her," Cinq-Mars stipulates. And explains, being careful not to insult him, "You saw his clothes. Clean. Wet—he was out in the rain—but clean. Malory died violently. That scene was a mess. No killer walks away from that one without bloodstained clothes."

"Okay, what if he finds her dead," Hartopp is wondering. "He takes the necklace for an unknown reason, then goes home and has a shower? He's got a note in his pocket that proves to be good advice. *Breached Run!* Does he run, after his girlfriend, or his consort, gets slaughtered? No, he gets into dry clothes and waits for *his* killer—who may be *her* killer—to knock on the door. If the guy's a professional spy, like you say, he's not without instincts. Resources, even."

"Tell us about that part," Cinq-Mars suggests. "His history, his resources."

When first they met, he noticed the FBI agent's narrow nose, yet the wide flare to his nostrils. A thought at the time, which perseveres, points to a touch of the dragon within his genetic code. In the way that birds are probably descendants of dinosaurs, in Émile's mind this demure, thin, crafty fellow has a secret link to fire-spewing mythological beasts.

The link requires a leap of the imagination, and is both ridiculous and crazy, yet for him it's there. He's glad to have him on his side.

"His record is absent from computer screens where you expect it to be located. What I mean is, now you see him, now you don't. His record is on file. It can't be opened, and where corollary evidence should exist, it's missing. That usually points to CIA. I made a few calls."

Hammond is nodding aggressively. "You're the guy, aren't you? You've made the calls."

"We all have bosses," Hartopp admits. "They can all be contacted, that's true."

"Get over it," Émile bursts out, speaking in Hammond's direction. "You're here. That's all that counts."

Hammond throws his hands up. "I've got no problem with it. I'm just impressed, that's all. You guys can move mountains. That's all I'm saying. Go ahead. What about this CIA guy?"

"Not CIA. That took time to figure out since we were sniffing the wrong hydrant. Military Intelligence. Army. He worked on the ground. He's been in tight spots in his day. It makes little sense that his lover is murdered and he responds by letting nobody know, by going home, taking a shower, getting into fresh duds, then he waits to be shot in his living room without even turning his head away. Explain that to me in plain English. Anybody."

"Cinq-Mars here is the genius detective. Let him explain it."

Cinq-Mars might have expected such a comment from Hammond, but it's Horriza who spoke. He doesn't mean anything by it, he's not picking a fight, and merely looks away in response to Émile's sharp glance.

Till takes up an initiative. "Captain Hammond, what did you get from the boy? You interrogated him for hours, correct? I know you released him. Anything interesting?"

When Hammond takes time responding, the others study him more closely to see if he's hiding something. That doesn't appear to be the case. He's formulating his response, which takes time because he's drawing conclusions he hasn't previously articulated, not even to himself.

"In a way, he was not forthcoming, the boy. In another way, I have to say that at times I believed him."

"Believed what?" Hartopp asks.

"That he didn't know anything. What I did notice in him was fear. He was afraid and at first I thought he was afraid of me. I changed my mind on that. Tried a different approach. Father figure. The kindly cop. The gentle pal. Maybe I'm not good at those roles but worth a try. They didn't work out, either. He gave me nothing. But the boy's afraid."

"I don't suppose," Cinq-Mars says, and rather wearily he draws both his hands down over his face, then lets them drop into his lap. "I don't suppose that you acquired a search warrant to visit his home. His apartment or his dorm or whatever."

"I did actually."

Cinq-Mars catches himself being more impressed than he should be. "And?"

"Nothing. No speck. I don't get kids today. Neat as a pin. What's up with that? In my day, we tossed our stuff on the floor. We didn't keep our underwear all folded in a drawer, or hang up our pants like we were in the military."

"Don't . . ." Émile starts, then pauses to make sure that Hammond processes his next remark ". . . take this the wrong way."

"Fine," the trooper says. "I won't. Don't you be so goddamned condescending, how about?"

He lets that pass. "Would it be all right if I visit his place? Is the warrant still active?"

"I won't take that the wrong way. Move in, for all I care. The warrant's active. I have to go with you, though. When he wakes up you'll want to interrogate him again, I suppose. You don't trust what I did."

"No, I believe you got out of him what he knows."

Hammond stares at him a moment, then, because he's not sure, he finally asks, "Is that sarcasm?"

"Not meant to be. Look, he was thrown out of the car by guys who wanted to stop Chief Till's men from chasing them. Throwing him out alive caused the patrolmen to stop and take care of him first. Which was the right call, by the way. Probably saved his life with all his internal bleeding. If they found out, in the bit of time they had with him, that he knew what they didn't want him to know, would they've risked taking a chance that he'd survive the fall? They could've shot him first."

Nobody's quite sure they're following him.

"What I'm saying is, I have a hunch that the bad guys found out what Trooper Hammond found out, that he doesn't know what it is they were afraid he knew. They let him go."

Others nod. They know it's a stretch, and the comment seems to demonstrate how thin the fabric of their investigation has become. Feeling that way himself, Cinq-Mars looks around the room, and asks, "What else we got?"

Not much, all told. Going forward, Special Agent Hartopp agrees to run down the necklace as best he can, find out if anyone has reported radioactive charoite. Cinq-Mars reveals that he's in possession of the guest list for tomorrow afternoon's cocktail party.

"Who'd you get that from?"

"President Palmerich."

"Of course. Yeah. Who've you *not* talked to, I wonder."

"We're past that," Cinq-Mars reminds him, and surprisingly, Hammond seems to agree. "A colleague ran down the names for me, to see if any bells went off. So far, nothing. Rich people and their racehorses and yachts, that's all we know. Special Agent, I wonder if you can't have your people do a rundown. See if any names pop out for you."

"Sure thing."

"I was thinking," Vermont State Trooper Archie Leopold says, and people look to the quiet one in the room, "well, what's our next step?"

Each in their own way, they've been asking themselves that.

Basic procedure will be observed. Small-town New Hampshire is not lousy with security cameras; the ones that exist will be examined again, to see if they might catch sight of the vehicle involved in the abduction of Vernon Colchester. Friends and neighbors of the victims will continue to be canvassed, often for a second and a third time. One person who knew everyone was Professor Edith Shedden, and her background will be checked, her movements covertly traced. Hammond will talk to her. FBI forensics specialists will be brought in from out of town, with the emphasis on Malory Earle, as her murder was the messiest, and messy usually garners the most abundant clues. Chief Till, after a modicum of resistance, agrees to look again at the previous issues with rape on campus, to determine if there is any possible link. And Émile states that he has the boy's digs to examine, in Hammond's company, and that he'll be attending the donors' cocktail party tomorrow.

"What's the point to that?" Till asks. "I mean, the killer left an invitation with the girl, but seriously, do you think he's deliberating dropping clues, asking us to chase him down? Doesn't that only happen on TV?"

"Partly I'm going," Émile informs him, "because it's almost all we've got. Another aspect has to do with what Special Agent Hartopp was saying. Why did Toomey hang around, and do nothing, and seemingly wait for his killer to ring the bell? Then why answer that bell? What could have gotten into his head to behave that way? Maybe, I'm thinking, just maybe he was guided into waiting. Led to be there. Maybe something indicated to him that he should wait."

"Despite," Hartopp asks, "the warning about being breached, the edict to run?"

"That I don't know. Just as he decided to hang out at home after seeing the body of his butchered girlfriend—assuming I'm correct and he didn't do it himself—in the same way it's possible—not likely perhaps, but possible—that we're being led to the cocktail party. That's where I'll be. Maybe no one will know I'm there or for what purpose. They'll expect you, at least one of you, to be there. There's no other reason I can think of for Toomey to stay home except that he was guided to do so. We're being guided to the party. We have to go."

A consensus permeates the room: No one seems particularly upbeat about the tactic. If they took a straw poll, they'd probably find that the consensus expected the party to be a necessary waste of time. Émile chooses to buoy their spirits a little, and reveals more about his thinking.

"Look, I spent considerable time in the clock tower, trying to get a feel for this guy, for a sense of the terrible events there. I got scared while I was up there, because I felt something sinister, and the news that Addie was abused even after death confirms that for me. I also caught a glimpse of our killer's weakness."

"Seriously?" Archie Leopold's query isn't negative. Perhaps it's attributable to his youthfulness that he expresses a thrall that everyone is feeling, if only a little. "You're in an empty room and you detect a killer's weakness? That's pretty cool."

"Not cool. A bit of a misery, truth be known. Consider: raping and killing Addie Langford wasn't enough for our guy. Raping her again after death demonstrates his contempt for her and for civilized society. That wasn't enough for him, either. He had to put her, and by extension, his crime, on display. That's how I guessed that whatever he'd done had to be especially wicked. Because having committed his acts, he then needed to turn his crimes into an exhibition. Everything about that crime, as opposed to the other two murders, was planned in detail and executed, pardon that word, with precision. No weaknesses there. The display, the need to turn the murder into a performance piece? That's a crack in his psyche. What does a performance require? Or a gallery vernissage?" He waits for a response. The men are waiting for him to answer his own question and one or two of them wonder what the French word means. "An audience. That's his weakness. He seeks an audience. Is it enough for him to imagine our reactions, our take on the situation? Maybe. More likely not. This may be wishful thinking on my part. I'm guessing that he might want to encounter his audience, which is who *we* are to him. He may want to witness our reaction, to hear our applause. He may even want to talk about it and hear our comments. How does he do that? This killing was infinitely well planned, planning may have included an invitation to discuss his genius. History is full of criminals who permit themselves to be caught merely to gloat over what they've done. If I'm right, this man is intent on keeping his identity secret, he's not looking to get caught. Having us attend a cocktail party, though, may be his way to covertly receive our applause, to pick up nuggets of our admiration for his expertise, and for his artistic flourish. At least, what he would call his artistry. He'll even want to hear public admission of our impotence in the face of his genius. We need cops at the party, and they need to feed his ego, admit our incompetence, our admiration for his expertise. They might even drop a comment about the beauty of the presentation of the corpse—we can be incredulous that the same person could commit the crime then arrange the body artistically—and after that we need to be alert to whoever's soaking it all in, getting a charge. Our killer may be there, people, because he *needs* to walk among us, to *gloat*, if you will, before he can be satisfied with what he's done."

The men are more excited now. Cinq-Mars is not done with pumping them up.

"How's our perpetrator feeling right now? The way he dealt with the body, he's not feeling guilty. He's euphoric. I guarantee you. He planned it, he carried it off perfectly. He's over the moon. Of course he wants to celebrate by chatting with the flummoxed investigating officers at a cocktail party. What could be more delightful? He *needs* to celebrate. Some of you will play the roles of baffled police officers, and I'll be there trying to pass myself off as a superwealthy philanthropist. We'll see what we can root out. Okay. What else do we have?"

Horriza wants to know what campus cameras revealed. That's one job that Hammond was willing to share with Till, and both their departments have been scouring through the footage. Nothing yet. The pending stormy weather on the eve of the murders and on the morning after didn't help. A majority of people were wearing rain hats and hoodies, making identification difficult.

No cameras were up in the stacks or on the floor where the clock tower is entered.

"Who had keys to the tower?" Hartopp wants to know.

He expects to find out how many people and how long is the list and how have they been checked out. Cinq-Mars gives him just the one name that's telling. "Malory Earle. Once in a while she used to go through the tower to brush away cobwebs."

"What's her time of death? Before or after Addie Langford?"

Neither Horriza nor Leopold know.

"See, that's the sort of thing we need to know and share," Hammond points out to them, thereby giving his formal stamp of approval to the entire proceeding. In another ten minutes, Cinq-Mars expects, he'll take credit for calling the meeting.

"What has surprised me since I've been in town," pronounces Special Agent Hartopp, "is the apparent lack of public information. Why isn't this twenty-four/seven on the local news?"

In tandem, Till and Hammond sigh, and shoot a glance at each other.

"What?" Cinq-Mars asks.

"That's tricky stuff," Hammond says.

"It's the culture here," Till adds.

"What is?"

"The colleges are the power in this town, and in the state. President Palmerich wants all this kept as quiet as possible. He especially doesn't want to look bad in comparison to the bigger university in town. His authority takes precedence. Maybe you can arm-twist a governor again?"

"How well did that strategy of keeping things quiet work with respect to the rapes on campus?" Cinq-Mars puts to them.

"Not so hot," Till admits. "Still. The colleges are not merely the power in these towns, they *are* these towns."

Cinq-Mars takes his turn to sigh. One place in the world is pretty much the same as any other. Throughout his career, local politics have always been at play. He comes up with an idea, though. "How about this? Chief Horriza and Trooper Leopold go back to Vermont, and in White River Junction they hold a press conference about *their* murder. About Malory Earle. Only, they make allusions back to the murders in New Hampshire. Now you have people talking, tips might come in. We need the public's help here and shutting them out is definitely a negative. Doing it that way, Hammond and Till are off the hook with the Dowbiggin School. It's the grubby White River Junction people who are messing it up, and you guys can push aside any criticism by blaming Vermont. By then, it won't matter, the news will be out, people will be talking on both sides of the state line. Talk should help."

Everyone is onside with that, which assists their group to congeal. They're making headway.

"With respect to the three different killings," Hartopp muses. "The White River one makes a point of being brutal. Blood everywhere. It's a mess. Toomey's murder was efficient. A shot through the throat. Slightly messy, but it's over and done with. Ballistics are in—a different gun. Then the first murder you came across strikes me as being a glorification of death. The neatest, it's psychotic. I think we have to be willing to separate the three from one another, even if we may want to link them."

"Link them?" Leopold repeats. "Different killers, from the same group?"

"Or one action trips another, is a consequence, or a logical sequence, that sort of thing. One action might support another. Keep an open mind because we understand little about this. A universe of possibility is out there. Personally, I believe we have three killers, but at the same time I can't segregate one crime from the next, especially given the necklace connection. That binds them, and we've generated links between the three victims."

"I wish we had one solid link we could talk to."

"We do," Cinq-Mars contradicts Hammond. "Vernon Colchester. Too bad he's unconscious for the time being."

The implication hangs in the air that he wasn't unconscious when Hammond interrogated him.

"I got nothing out of him," the trooper points out.

"You didn't know what we know now," Cinq-Mars says. "No fault of your own."

"Good to have this meeting," Hammond concurs. "Émile, you and me are going to his place, but I can't go yet. I've got a press conference scheduled. One where I'm not supposed to say much."

"Once you've frustrated those reporters, take one or two of them aside, suggest that they attend a press conference across the river. Give them a wink. That way, Chief Horriza and Trooper Leopold might have a good audience for what they say. TV. Radio. Big press. Until now, that murder has been overshadowed."

Another plan they can agree on.

Once they decide to curtail the meeting, they break up rather quickly, with only Special Agent Hartopp, who'll be staying on at the house, remaining behind with Cinq-Mars. He agrees, now that the others are gone, to a wee dram of good scotch.

"What else are you up to, Émile?" Hartopp puts to his friend. "It's not only what you said."

"I hate to do this," Émile answers, and sips. He examines the color of the liquid in his glass.

"Do what?"

"Put the kids at risk."

"Then don't."

He shakes his head, tries to agree with him. In the end he concludes, "I have to involve my niece and her friends. A cop is expected at the party. Even an undercover cop or two. I can play the rich man role. I might not get away with it, and anyway, I can't be everywhere. The undergrads, working as servers while being our ears, no one will expect that. Not in that room. Attractive young women may elicit attention we'd like to see play out. Sorry, Michael, but this party is all I've got for now. That, and the visit to the boy's house in the morning."

"What do you expect to get out of that? Hammond may be right, you know, your legendary powers of observation notwithstanding."

Cinq-Mars blows air as though scoffing at his legendary powers. "Feeble is the better adjective for those so-called powers. These days, anyway. What do I expect?" He seems to be addressing the scotch in his glass. "Anything. Something. We're looking for a guy with a scrape on his elbow and a sense of euphoria. I better find something. Face it. We don't have much else."

TWENTY-ONE

Another fine day. In the morning, Émile Cinq-Mars is in possession of the Escalade again, with Sandra, a day before her mother's funeral, willing to be chauffeured by her niece if she needs a ride. Émile drives straight to the dorm where Vernon Colchester normally resides, where he'll meet up with Trooper Hammond. The campus security guard, Roberta, has been invited to join them. Émile explained to Hammond that a noticeable police presence will attract the wrong sort of attention: They need someone other than a cop to guard the door and their privacy. To his surprise, when he arrives, he discovers that Hammond has invited Chief Till to pay a visit, as well.

"New leaf," Cinq-Mars presumes.

"He's embraced team play for a day," Till whispers. "Go figure."

"Before we're done, he'll say he invented it. Good morning, by the way."

"Back at you. How's it going, Émile?"

"I slept. You?"

"I always sleep. My mind is constantly at rest, my body's never far behind."

"Too modest."

"We all have our ways. You think things through. I think about maybe thinking about thinking. Works for me, now and then."

The banter brightens Émile's outlook. As Till seems to have that effect on him, he supposes that the man's technique does appear to be working. He introduces him to Roberta and those two revisit occasions in the past when they may have met. They recognize each other anyway. Then Hammond swings around the corner, and due to a shortage of parking spaces pulls in down the block. So much the better, as his squad car half a block away won't draw attention to the building they enter.

Vernon's room is on the top floor, the fourth, of his dorm. They ascend the stairs without running into many students. Most residents have packed up and left for the summer. A few have returned for convocation. Roberta was able to quickly secure the keys—the room's been entered by police previously, the administration knows that the boy has been hospitalized—and after opening up she stands outside while the men enter, and closes the door behind them.

Inside, Till and Hammond, accepting that this is Émile's walk-through, hang back. The chief of the Hanover police has not been in the room, either, and takes a look around while standing out of the way. Hammond ascertains that the room is exactly as he left it a day ago. Satisfied with that, he studies the retired Montreal detective while pretending that he's doing no such thing.

Émile stands, oblivious to the attention.

Once again he wants to be quiet, to permit the air in the room or the spaces in his head to have their say, to refine initial impressions to an essence. The process usually strains the patience of any observer and today is no exception. Till shifts his weight from foot to foot, then from his heels to his toes and back again. Guilty of tilting his hips one way, then the other, Hammond perseveres, trying not to stare but at the same time gawking at whatever Cinq-Mars looks at, then sneaking a glimpse at the man's face to see if he can snag a reaction. Émile remains impassive throughout, and after prolonged immobility becomes more active. He opens and shuts drawers, casts a long glance into a closet. He peers up onto a high shelf and tests the surface for dust. Clean. The bed, he notes, is precisely tucked, pulled tight to the corners, not a wrinkle to be observed on the blanket. Twin pillows look as though they've been prepared for inspection, smooth as curved glass.

When he's done, he says, "Okay, let's go."

Hammond chooses not to stand aside. Cinq-Mars looks at him, to see what's up.

"Share," Hammond says.

"Excuse me?"

"That's what we're doing now, right? Do it. Share. I've been through this place. Didn't find a thing worth mentioning. You? Any different?"

Cinq-Mars considers the challenge, flexing his lips a little.

Hammond encourages him with a more conciliatory tone. "You and me, we got off to a bad start. My fault. Fine. I admit it now. You've got a bit of game. Educate me. Is there anything you're taking away from this room?"

The older detective concedes with a nod. He notices that Till is waiting for him to speak, as well. "Open the door," he instructs them both. "Let Roberta in."

Till does that and the woman takes her place beside the officers.

"I asked Roberta in because she was probably eavesdropping anyway."

She's about to protest before she notices his slight grin, and smiles instead.

"Frankly, she should know how we're thinking. She's on campus. She sees and hears what we don't. The more she knows, the more she can help, and I happen to know that Roberta wants to help."

If she felt trepidatious entering the room with the experienced policemen present, she's beaming now.

"Trooper Hammond, I'm seeing exactly what you said you saw. The military perfection. The unstudentlike, undormlike attention to keeping one's quarters to a pristine tidiness that would be bizarre if it wasn't so telling."

The trooper reflects a certain pride that he saw what he was supposed to see, until he realizes that he doesn't know why—in the mind of this city detective—that's *telling*.

"Now we know," Cinq-Mars reveals, "what Toomey was doing here at Dowbiggin."

As neither of the men respond, Roberta takes a stab at it. "He was teaching."

"He was teaching, of course. Not only that," Émile says, not taking his eyes off Hammond, as though he's waiting for him to get it.

Hammond admits, "I don't get it."

"He was recruiting," Cinq-Mars tells him. "Teaching, in order to recruit, then training his recruits. Look at this room. Vernon Colchester was clearly being trained. Which means he has already been recruited. He was being taught and tested and made to modify his natural behavior. He's left absolutely nothing lying around that would point to any activity he's involved in anywhere at any time. There's not even a clue as to what he's studying—the books are off the shelves. This is a young man learning to live his life in secret. *As* a secret."

"I think I get that now," Till mentions, and Hammond nods.

"Of course, he wasn't going to tell you anything. What spy talks?"

"Poor kid. He's bitten off more than he can chew," Till adds.

"An old saying is often used," Cinq-Mars muses aloud, "in describing American covert agencies. I don't know where I heard it but it's undoubtedly valid. American spies are 'male, pale, and Yale.' Composed, that is, of white men from Yale, the latter school being its major supplier of personnel. *Yale,* however, apart from being the most prolific supplier, has been understood to refer in general, and more so over time, and in this instance in particular, to the Ivy League. Toomey's life as a spy came to a close. He was handed this post at the Dowbiggin School, which draws students interested in a future in the diplomatic corps, or international trade and finance, where he can teach from his lengthy study of international relations and from his considerable experience in the field, and where he continues to serve as someone who recruits and trains star candidates—bright, patriotic, idealistic, impassioned young men—and nowadays, young women—to be the next generation of intelligence gatherers. In our times, a growth profession."

"I get it now," Hammond says quietly.

"I don't," Cinq-Mars contradicts him, and contradicts himself. "I don't get how all this came crashing down." Then he looks at Roberta and gestures to his eyes, his ears, and his mouth. Over his mouth he draws closed an imaginary zipper.

"No problem," she states.

The four of them are exiting the building when Trooper Hammond's phone vibrates in his pocket. He takes it and reads a text to himself, then asks, "Anybody ready for good news?" The others wait expectantly. "Vernon Colchester. They brought him out of the coma they induced. The boy's awake. He's sitting up in bed."

TWENTY-TWO

A doctor cautions them before they go inside, which provides an opportunity. The physician wants them to keep it quiet, and not upset his patient. After he steps away, Émile takes advantage of the pause to ask of both Till and Hammond, "Who talks?"

"Oh, Christ, do I need to pull rank again?" Hammond objects. He considers the issue a closed subject.

"Your pretty face alone will upset him. Doctor's orders, we're not supposed to do that. That's all I'm saying."

"He has a point," Till agrees. "I can be up front here."

"In that uniform?" Cinq-Mars challenges him as well.

"What's wrong with my uniform?" Till can't resist looking down at his shirt and trousers, wondering what's the deal with his look.

"It's a uniform. Chief Till, come on, the kid's been through hell. Interrogated by state troopers, then abducted, then thrown out of a car during a high-speed chase with police sirens on his tail. Probably there's nobody he'd rather *not* see right now than a cop in a uniform."

"Get off the pot." Chief Till mounts his defense. "You're making a case for yourself."

"Sure I am. Look, I've talked with Vernon on a friendly basis. I'm practically a friendly face. Hammond, you saw me when he was taken in. Tell the man. I comforted him. I gave him good advice. My niece, her friends, are part of his crowd. I have an *in* which isn't a negative, and given the circumstances, who better than me? My gentle touch. This has nothing do with evaluating one guy over another."

The three men know that it has everything to do with evaluating one guy over another, and that Émile thinks he's the best man for the job. Yet he receives backing from an unlikely source, even though it doesn't come as a total surprise. Hammond recognizes that he's already gone a few tough rounds with this kid, and tried various techniques on him, to no avail. The last thing he wants now is for another officer from a different force to show him up. Better to go with the retired and apparently famous detective from a foreign country. Plus, there's honor in standing down. If Cinq-Mars succeeds, Hammond can be thanked for his magnanimity. If the outside guy fails, then stick him with the blame while the local cops are off the hook.

"You go, Cinq-Mars. See what you can do." Till looks as though he intends to object before Hammond silences him. "My call. That's it. That's all."

They enter the young man's hospital room.

Curtains on the windows have been drawn, the lights dimmed low. The television that sits high on a corner shelf has not only been switched off but unplugged as well, perhaps to foil a bored visitor curious about what's on. Vernon Colchester sits propped up, one arm in a sling, the other bandaged, his battered face partially covered. Both eyes are visible but one is red and the eyelid is puffy. Both his upper and lower lips are sutured where his teeth chomped through them. The bedcovers terminate at his armpits, concealing other injuries down his torso and legs and their wrappings. One leg appears to be elevated by several inches.

Cinq-Mars looks him over and the boy glances up.

"None the worse for wear," the detective kids him.

That may be a faint smile, the best he can muster across his mouth and swollen cheeks.

"Seen," the boy says, then wets his lips. "Better," he adds. Then concludes, "Days."

"Hmm," Cinq-Mars notes. "We all have. It's touch-and-go with you for convocation."

A slight bob of his head suggests that that's not the boy's main concern.

Cinq-Mars pulls up a chair. The two policemen in uniform hang back. They notice that the boy takes note of their presence. His eyes move across them. Warily.

"Vernon, all kidding aside, we're sorry for what happened to you. We're concerned, of course, that you were abducted and treated horribly. We believe this relates to the deaths of Addie and Professor Toomey, and even to a member of the custodial staff. What do you think? Do you think that's likely?"

He rests his forearms on the boy's bed, and speaks softly near his ear. The other two officers move in a little closer if he's going to talk that quietly. They see the boy nod slightly, agreeing with Émile's hypothesis. He completes that concession with a modified shrug, as though to suggest that he's not sure.

"They grabbed you off the street. I know things are probably a bit fuzzy for you. Do you remember that part? Just blink your good eye slowly, once, to say *yes* if that's easier than speaking."

He blinks the eye slowly.

"Do you know why? A slow eye blink for a yes. A slight move of your head, or rapid eye blinks, to mean no. Do you know why they snatched you, Vernon?"

His *no* is perhaps more emphatic than Cinq-Mars had in mind, as he doesn't want the boy to stress himself with either head shakes or eye blinks. The young man does both.

"They wanted information, do you think? Were they asking you questions? I'm sorry, that's two questions. But maybe it's the same question."

He slowly opens and shuts both eyes.

"What did they want to know?"

Vernon moistens his lips again, then requests water. He's satisfied with just a few sips through a straw as Émile holds the glass. He answers, "If I knew. Who did it."

"The murders? Addie's? Or all three?"

He's shaking him off, to indicate no. "Didn't seem to know. I mean . . . they didn't . . . know . . . what *it* was. Never said."

Émile takes a moment to consider his next question. "Okay. You're saying that you think they didn't know what they were asking you for? You mean, like they were on a fishing expedition?"

He makes the mistake of looking at the two policemen in the room and Hammond takes his glance as license to speak. "That doesn't seem likely," he says.

Cinq-Mars won't make that error again. Vernon is busy shaking his head, they assume in response to Hammond's comment, but at the moment everyone's lost. The retired detective tries to stitch their conversation together again, to make it just between the two of them, the approach slow, careful, and intimate. He's already thinking that the apparent ignorance of the abductors marks them as hired henchmen, which means that in all likelihood they were outsiders who have fled the region.

"Go on," he encourages the boy. "Take it easy. Give us your impressions."

"Looked surprised. Real surprised. I said . . . I didn't kill. Anybody. Same thing. I told. Trooper Hammond." He's getting agitated.

"It's okay. You told them you didn't kill anyone."

"Yeah. But. It's like. They're not asking me that."

"What are they asking about, then?"

"No clue. With them. It's like. Why say that?"

"They don't get it?"

He's trying to shake his head.

"Take it slowly."

"Like. All of a sudden."

"Yes?"

"They're shitting themselves."

Cinq-Mars takes that in, and waits as the boy sips water through a straw. He holds the glass. "You mean, it's your impression, that this is more than they bargained for, those men, that type of thing?"

"Yeah. Like. Like. Shocked. Weird, for me. At the time."

He coughs, and Cinq-Mars helps him take a few more sips.

"Do you think they were wondering if maybe they picked up the wrong guy?" Cinq-Mars asks.

"Maybe. More like. They didn't want. To do. What they're doing. Argue. Talk about. Letting me go. Like. Remorse."

"They found themselves in over their heads."

"Yeah. I tried to get out. Big guy. Starts hitting me. Cop car wailing. One guy. Says jump. Or die. Or he shoots me. I jumped. Sort of jumped."

Cinq-Mars needs a breather to process what he's heard. He leans back and rubs his hands a few times over his thighs. Then leans in again with his elbows on the side of the mattress. "When you said you didn't kill anybody?" he asks.

"Yeah?"

"Did they believe you?"

Vernon thinks about the question. "Yeah," he says eventually. "I think so. But. More like. Why say that? More like. Who died?"

Hammond mutters at his back, "Just like you said, Cinq-Mars."

"Not exactly," Émile remarks. Looking into the boy's eyes, he addresses him directly, in a way that gives him no place to hide, nowhere to turn.

The boy tries to elude him anyway. He asks, "What day is it?"

"Don't worry, Vernon. It's only tomorrow. You only lost yesterday. It's tomorrow. That's not too bad. Now, Vernon, I believe you. You didn't kill anybody and you don't know who did. They believed you when you had a gun to your head and the pavement screaming by. I believe you now. They might have thought you knew stuff, even if we don't know what stuff, because you are a candidate to know stuff. In a sense. Am I right? Vernon, what made you a reasonable candidate to know stuff?"

Along the mattress and through the covers he can feel the boy stiffen up. He's clamming up. "Can't say."

"Sure you can. We know about you and Professor Toomey."

The boy almost laughs. "Right. Think I. Sleep with him."

"No, not that, Vernon. You loved Addie Langford, we know that. In a way, though, Professor Toomey seduced you. Nothing to do with sex. You're in training for a secret service. You want to be a spy and you've been developing techniques under his tutelage. You see, we know that. What we don't know is what you stumbled upon during your training, what worried some folks. What was it that lit up a few switchboards, if you take my meaning? What worried some folks enough to have you picked up and interrogated all over again? Then, when you didn't give them anything they could hang a hat on, except the possibility that a man was involved in murder, and that man might have been one of them, only without knowing it, they tossed you in a ditch to live or die. Whichever it was, they didn't particularly care. But you lived, Vernon. You're going to be fine. Now we've got to flesh out the story of what happened and why. We know you didn't kill anybody. Let's start there. What I have to ask you today, and what you have to provide—and this doesn't go against your spy training, this is what it's for—is to help out the good guys. Toomey's dead. What were you two into? What were you talking about? What was being revealed? What would you be saying to him if he was sitting in this chair at this moment under these circumstances? A spy doesn't merely keep secrets, Vernon. A spy moves secrets along. Up the ladder. Into the right hands. Now is the time for that."

In fits and starts, between sips of water and bouts of coughing, once pausing to close his eyes and hold his forehead with his bandaged hand, Vernon Colchester recites a story. His speech is governed by his breathing, as though a word can only be emitted on a conscious exhale. Inhaling hurts. Chief Till moves around to the side of the bed opposite Cinq-Mars to hear the boy better, and Trooper Hammond pulls up a chair. In the sleepy darkened room, as light bothers him, the young man talks about a day he drove out to the airport to meet his parents flying in from California, a year ago. He neglected to call ahead and, once there, learned that their connecting flight was held up at Logan Airport in Boston. They wouldn't be landing for another two hours at the earliest. He had options, but couldn't afford the taxi back into town then back out again, choosing to kill time by hanging around the terminal, watching people come and go. That's when he noticed three men.

"How old?" Cinq-Mars inquires. His senses are alert. He doesn't know the story yet but this tale of three men must be pivotal. Vernon puts one in his forties, another in his fifties, the third in his sixties. Despite the difference in their ages they come across as solid friends. Vernon's descriptions, slowly extracted from him, are of generic white men for their age groups, except that one man had a sickly look to him. Like someone who had recently undergone chemotherapy or a major operation.

"Not oldest," the boy recalls. "But. Gray hair. His skin. Looked gray."

"Go on. How did you come to notice them?"

"Taking. A leak." The three men landed in the men's room where Vernon was urinating, each arriving separately. Once inside, they fist-bumped and tapped one another's shoulders in greeting. Rambunctious, giddy to see one another. "Finished up. Washed hands."

"What caught your attention?"

"Nothing. Yet. Except. Mentioned Dowbiggin. Me. I wanted. To call out. Like. A preppy. Idiot. That. I go there. But. Restrained. Myself. They mentioned. Meeting up. At cocktail party. *Donors' bash.* They call it. Around now. This time. Of year. Lots of parents. Alumni. Arrive in town. Thought. Nothing. About that. Dried my hands. Under. Hot air. Machine. Went back. Out. To terminal. Took a seat. Stared into space."

"What changed?" Cinq-Mars inquires.

Vernon reports that the three men came out of the room as they went in. "Separately."

"Separately," Cinq-Mars repeats.

"No contact. Don't. Acknowledge. Each other. They're buddies. Going to. Same party. Soon. But. Outside. Men's room. They don't know. Each other. Anymore. I am. Committing. To. A life. Checking people out. Right?"

"That's right. You're committing to a life as a spy. Your curiosity was aroused. You kept an eye on them."

"For all I know. Could be. Toomey testing. Me."

"I see. And?"

Two men took separate cabs into Holyoake without saying good-bye to the other, and the third rented a car, without offering a buddy a lift even though they were going to the same small town. A village, in fact.

"Strange enough," Cinq-Mars agrees.

"Toomey thought so. I told him. He got excited. Wanted to go to. Party. Check them out. And. He did." To be in on the action, Vernon arranged for a friend to bow out of serving at the party and to suggest Vernon as his last-second replacement. "That way. I can. Point out. The three guys."

"And?"

"Toomey. Impressed. Said they. Up to something. Went out of. Their way. Not to be. Seen together. Toomey said. One man was sick."

"The man you mentioned."

"He meant. Sick. Like mentally."

"How did he know?"

The boy manages to approximate a shrug. "Recognize. He said. To me. Evil. When it stands. Beside you. In the room."

"Vernon," Cinq-Mars asks him, and takes a deeper breath, "did you get their names?"

He gave him their names, but Vernon dipped and faded badly after that. A nurse arrived, then the boy's physician came in and ushered the men out. "He needs rest."

"I need five more minutes," Cinq-Mars protests. "Doctor, this is a multiple homicide investigation, it's important."

A sigh, and a decision. "If you wait outside for ten minutes I'll give you three. Maybe. We'll see. Go easy on the poor kid."

Till, Hammond, and Cinq-Mars wait in the quiet corridor.

"We have enough, don't you think?" Till remarks.

Hammond agrees. "Names. What more do we need?"

"This and that," Cinq-Mars attests, and declines to be more forthcoming.

They wait twenty minutes before they're permitted to return and take up their positions as before. The boy has more color in his face. His body is relaxed. A different drug or a fresh dose has come to his aid.

"Pain. Killer," he says. "Won't. Let me. Press my own button. Age discrimination. My opinion. They think. I'll overdose."

His voice seems more fluent, and more clear.

"Vernon," Cinq-Mars begins, once again with his forearms on the edge of the mattress, leaning in close. "I'm sure that Trooper Hammond has already asked you this question. Where were you the night that Addie was murdered?"

"You think it was me? Still?"

"Actually, I don't. That doesn't particularly matter because I don't know who did. Which means, everybody in this room and beyond this room, including these guys, including you, has to account for their whereabouts. I know where I was. I'm the only person alive whom I'm pretty sure didn't do it."

He's satisfied with that approach. "Saw Addie. Around seven. For ten minutes."

"Where?"

"Lincoln. Downstairs. We had a quick coffee. Quick because. She was half finished. When I got there."

"What were you meeting about?"

"Not planned. Bumped into her. Seemed nervous. New boyfriend. I figured. Didn't want me there. We drank coffee. Addie took off."

"Where did she go?"

"Upstairs. I stayed down." They can feel his disappointment from that time. "Didn't want her. To think. Stalking."

"Okay. Did you notice anything unusual at all? Maybe regarding her appearance, other than nervousness? Did she seem distracted?"

He thinks about it, not coming up with anything. "Same."

"And why where you there again? Were you hoping to bump into her maybe? People do that. Pretend a meeting is accidental. Were you stalking?"

This time, Vernon is reluctant to answer the question. "Didn't want. Meet her. Dumb. But. I had a job. Interview. At the Lincoln. Next day. In the morning. There. Night before. Get a feel for the place. To help imagine. The interview. Rev up."

"What kind of job?"

"Secret stuff."

"Who with?"

"Don't know. But. Secret."

"Who set up this meeting?"

"Call. Came in. I assume. Professor Toomey. He trained me. I'm graduating. Call comes in. I guessed. Through him."

"But you didn't ask him about it?"

"I did."

"What did he say?"

That reluctance again, and the boy casts his eyes around the room once more.

"Vernon, Professor Toomey is deceased. The secrets the two of you shared must become public knowledge, at least privileged knowledge among these officers, if we're to track down his killer. You want that, right? To track down his killer? Addie's, too?"

"Sure I do."

"Then let's get on it. What did he say?"

"Nothing. Didn't get the chance."

"But you were talking to him."

"Not. Talking. We had. A method. To commun—icate. Part of. Training. We exchange. Messages. Regular basis. He said. Do that. So the process. Second nature. Learning. How to. Disappear. On people. So. They won't think twice. We have a tree. On campus. Down by river. In the woods. Put messages. In the bark. That's how we. Do it. Communicate."

"I see. You asked, in this tree bark, if Toomey was behind the job interview, do I have that right?"

Vernon affirms that with a slow blink.

"He never answered you? Did you get any message from him after that?"

"Yeah. Not related. Hypothetical. Test case. Just an exercise. In code."

"What about after Addie's death? Did you communicate?"

"No. Missed morning message. Due to. Her death."

"Picking it up or dropping it off?"

"Pick up."

"You were supposed to pick up a message early and instead you picked up a hypothetical message later on. Vernon, did you write *Breached Run!*?"

"What's that?"

"It's a message. It means nothing to you?"

He shrugs, although the movement causes him to wince in pain.

"Maybe it was meant for you. If a message was left in the tree trunk that said, *Breached Run!,* what would you have done?"

He gazes back at his inquisitor without comprehension. "Assume. Found out. As spies. Hypothetical. Test. Stop messages. Run. Maybe. Probably. If that was. The instruction. Yeah."

"You were late for a pickup in the woods. That's what we know. When you did pick something up, it was nothing germane to what's happened. That's what we know, right?"

He nods slightly, blinks an eye.

"Did you know that Addie was in line for a job interview?"

He looks up, his brow knitting over a lack of comprehension. "No. Who with?"

"A patron. Apparently, it was also a secret. Maybe it was the same job you were going after. Maybe you were in competition. Maybe she knew that and maybe she knew that you didn't. Do you think she might have been nervous when she met you because of a job interview? That she might have been nervous the same way you were nervous?"

"Could be," he admits. "Don't think so."

"Think back to her appearance. You suspected she might be meeting someone because she was nervous. Could you have thought that because she was dressed up for an interview? Is that what made you think that way?"

He thinks it through, and after a few moments his chin begins to nod. "Yeah. Looked nice. Extra makeup. Nice blouse. Blouse. Not shirt. Noticed. She showed. Hint."

He pauses longer than usual, repeatedly swallowing but declining more water.

"A hint?" Cinq-Mars presses him.

"Cleavage. Thought. Dressed for hot date."

"You're a young guy, you're allowed to notice a little cleavage. Maybe you're supposed to notice. I'm not clear anymore on what's appropriate."

"Jewelry, also. Forgot. She wore big. Necklace."

Cinq-Mars takes out his cell phone and starts tapping buttons. He shows him a copy of the necklace she was wearing when her body was found.

"This one?"

Vernon says, "Yeah. That one."

"*Before* she was dead, she was wearing this?"

"Yeah." The boy is confused by the question, and notices that the two uniformed officers appear baffled.

"Did you ever see her wearing it before?"

"No. Afraid a boyfriend. Gave it to her. Didn't want. To ask."

Cinq-Mars needs a moment to reconstitute his thoughts. In the interim, a nurse appears in the doorway, set to shoo them on their way. Hammond, seated in his chair, plants an authoritative hand in the air to stop her. He doesn't bother to even look in her direction. In the face of such disdain, she hurries off, no doubt to fetch the doctor.

"Did Addie want to be a spy, too?" Cinq-Mars asks him. The query is out of the blue. The confluence of the two young people entertaining job offers, both in the library, possibly, and both with a person or persons unknown, prompts the query. They were both enrolled in a school for international studies, where many students were interested in diplomacy. Among those, might not a few have been interested in something more exciting? Conversely, both Vernon and Addie may have been guided to meet with the same person for different jobs entirely, or different reasons entirely.

The boy seems flummoxed. "Never said."

"Did you ever? To her?"

"No."

"Well, then?"

He shrugs. He sees the possibility. "Addie. Wild girl," he acknowledges. "Very wild. Except for drug thing."

"What drug thing?"

"Never did any. Stayed clean. As a whistle."

"Wild enough to be interested in spy craft, like you. Not so crazy as to do drugs."

"She made. A vow. To her mom. Help her through. Dowbiggin. She stays clean. She held up. Her end."

"Okay. Vernon," Cinq-Mars encourages him. "You're doing great.

We're almost done here. Just a few more things. Where else were you that night, after seeing Addie?"

"The guy I said. Like he had chemo?"

"Yeah, sure. What about him?"

"Saw him. Coffee shop on New Hampshire Avenue. Just hanging. I didn't want. To talk. To anybody. Interview. To psyche up for. But. Didn't want. To be alone. Either. Had coffee. Read a mag. Saw chemo guy there."

"From a year ago. And?"

"There awhile. Like me. From nine. Or ten. Stayed after. Midnight. Followed him out. Then."

"Why, Vernon?"

"Just. Practicing."

"Practicing?"

"Spying."

"You spied on him. What happened?"

"Went to Holyoake. Inn. Looked inside. He chatted. Hotel night guy. Then went up. I went back. To my place. To bed. Until morning."

"Okay. Good. About the morning. Why were you on campus when Addie was discovered?" He knows why, but needs to see if Vernon can step his way through this as naturally as any man could who's telling the truth.

"Told you. Interview."

"It was to be on campus?"

"At Lincoln, yeah. I said. You. Are. Cross-checking me. Why? I told you. The truth."

"It's an old habit, Vernon. Sorry. Where at the Lincoln?"

"Ground floor. Main entrance. At first."

"At first?"

"Got a text. Switched. To basement room. Where sculptures. Are."

"Same place you were with Addie the night before. How long were you there?"

"About an hour. Second text. Police on campus. I should go. To seventh floor. It said. *Death @ Dowbiggin.* Find out. What's going on. I took it. As a test."

"What did you do?"

"Went to the sixth. Seventh is segregated. Found out. Female student. Dead. Clock tower. Contacted Caro. Heard. Addie missing."

"You were being set up, did you know that?"

"What? Do you mean?" He's wide-eyed now. "What do you? Mean? Set up?"

"You were supposed to run. Your whereabouts puts you on and about the scene of the crime, planning to go to a meeting which you'd never be able to prove was anything other than a fiction. Then you were supposed to go to your communication tree—to run to your mentor, as it were. Also, to keep up your daily habit, you were supposed to be on time—and there you were supposed to read a signal that said, *Breached Run!* And you were supposed to run, Vernon, because that would have contributed greatly to your guilty demeanor. Lucky for you, you never read that message. Your balls would've been in a vise if we had to pick you up in Boston. Problem is, Toomey went to the tree before you did, and instead of getting a message *from* you, he got a message intended *for* you. You were supposed to run, Vernon, thereby confirming you to be a likely suspect for the murder of Addie Langford."

The doctor is in the doorway.

"Failing that, partly because the police let you go, you were picked up on a busy street then dropped out of a car to prove, to cast an aspersion at least, to incriminate you, to show that you consort with the wrong people on a semiregular basis. The specific people who did that didn't even know why. They were following orders. They didn't count on a couple of brave young women to be on their tail and then the local cops." Cinq-Mars drops his voice to a whisper. "Do you want to help us out?"

Vernon Colchester nods. He has something to say first. "Sir."

"Tell me."

"Virtual. Spy. Exercise. I have. Safe house. Place to go. If. Toomey. Simulates trouble. I would not run. Like you said. To Boston."

"And that was where?"

"House of. Malory Earle."

Chief Till can't help himself. He whistles.

The doctor announces his presence and intentions. "Guys."

Hammond says, "My God. I hate to contemplate what would've

happened to you there. I'd have hung you by now. Found a stand-in for your trial after the fact."

"The sickly-looking guy," Cinq-Mars inquires, "that night at the coffee shop, what was he doing all that time? Like you, reading, drinking coffee?"

"Talked. Lots of people. Flirting. With baristas. People. Students. Talked politics. Sports. School. Stuff."

"Okay. Thanks. Now play along, okay?"

Cinq-Mars whispers a plan to the boy. He appeals to the spy in him. Vernon nods consent to his part.

"Trooper Hammond," Cinq-Mars instructs in a louder voice, "arrest this man for the murder of Addie Langford."

He winks at the boy and the boy winks back.

Catching on, Trooper Hammond issues a Miranda warning while the attending physician shoos the others along.

TWENTY-THREE

Even though the preparation has been extensive, the best that he can do under the circumstances, in the end everyone is obliged to wing it. No road map exists for their endgame—they don't know if this is an endgame or another blind alley. They can only hope. Throughout the case they've been traveling blind, as if caught in the full throttle of a storm cloud while flying a glider, and still there is little distance that they can view. Nowhere to land.

Hammond, Till, Hartopp, and Cinq-Mars converge on the campus well away from the location for the late-afternoon cocktail party. They need not rototill the same ground: New developments have been coming in, to be shared, and everyone is eager for the updates.

Cinq-Mars begins by remarking on their clothing. "You fellas clean up good." Till and Hammond are out of uniform, a last-minute choice to don suits and ties. Shoes are polished, cuff links gleam.

"My one chance to hobnob with the stinking rich," Till remarks. "I want to at least pretend I'm equally odoriferous."

For his part, Hammond smiles, a rarity for him, and wishes he'd said that.

They get on with it, and Chief Till reports that, as a result of the press conference in White River Junction, two credible eyewitness accounts place Addie Langford in the vicinity of Malory Earle's house in previous months.

"Okay, that's freaky," Hammond acknowledges.

"Interesting," Cinq-Mars evaluates. "Only the vicinity? Not inside the apartment? She could've had friends in the vicinity. She's allowed to have friends across the river."

"Not a student destination particularly," Hammond points out.

"True enough. As I said, it's interesting. What else?"

Till talked to the Langfords regarding their daughter's vow to live drug-free. Naturally, they were pleased that that was the case, yet they had no memory of any such promise.

"The boy said she made a vow with them," Hammond blurts out. "How could they forget? What parent forgets something like that?"

"No such vow," Cinq-Mars concludes.

"The boy said there was. Vernon."

"That's because Addie told him that. She lied. We're all capable of lying, Trooper Hammond. The question now begs to be asked, did she make up a credible lie to give herself ammunition to just say no to drugs, which is commendable, I suppose, or did she make that vow, only to someone else? Such as to a recruiter of some kind."

"Secret service? CIA?" Till suggests.

"Or an unknown version of which she could never reveal. Legitimate or not. Which might have been a false front anyway."

"For what purpose? If it's the latter?"

"To kill her, I suppose. Or one of her friends."

The others consider this, and Tills steps back, having exhausted what he can offer.

Special Agent Hartopp's report is more elaborate. While his people have perused the entire list of donors attending the cocktail party, nothing about them jumped into plain view. Country club folk with deep pockets. "Theoretically, an upper tax bracket, although every last one of them successfully avoids exorbitant taxes."

Hammond objects to the content of that information. "Personal stuff like that is supposed to stay confidential."

Hartopp glares back at him and the trooper shrugs, backing down.

"Nothing significant there," Hartopp carries on. "We put special emphasis, obviously, on the three names the boy provided. Same deal. This is what's interesting. One guy, his name is Ben Havilland-Clegg—a mouthful, right? I haven't said it all yet. His full name is Bennington Orion Marshall Havilland-Clegg. Good luck finding the space on a check to sign all that. And he does sign checks. He is a philanthropist, not only with respect to Dowbiggin. Throat cancer a couple of years ago. An ongoing problem for him. Ben, for short, an alum, has been contributing for years to Dowbiggin, and years before that his father did the same. Our Ben is an inheritor of riches. He doesn't run anything or make anything or work himself. He lives off the family's extensive trust."

"I'd like that job. That's nice work," Hammond rhapsodizes.

"Here's where it gets interesting," Hartopp goes on. "A year and a half ago, no longer than that, the other two names on our list start contributing to Dowbiggin. They are men of means who have no connection to the college of which we're aware. That's fine as far as it goes. Good stuff happens. Conversely, Ben has lowered the amount he gives from what he used to contribute. The annual contribution that the endowment is now short from Ben, the other two make up for to the dollar, and no more. Those two gentlemen, Hanson Parker and Al McBride, have no history of being generous to charities."

He glances at Hammond as though daring him to challenge his knowledge.

"I hate to stain your innocence," Hartopp continues, while staring down the state trooper. "A suspicious mind might want to believe that Ben got his friends onto the donors' list with his own money."

"I, for one," Cinq-Mars attests, "have a suspicious mind."

"Okay. Why do that?" Hammond asks.

No answer is immediate in the air. "I think it's our job to find that out," Hartopp comments. "All we know is, being on the list of donors gets all three into the cocktail party. It brings all three up to Holyoake. For what it's worth, we haven't been able to link them together. They come from different cities, different backgrounds. Hanson Parker is in the financial services industry in New York City these days. Initially, he worked in the diplomatic corps. I'm told that he's a bright man. Al McBride owns a network of tire shops in Tennessee and Kentucky, expanding into western North Carolina and Virginia. He sells a lot of tires, especially for trucks. The youngest of the three, probably the least bright, he's second in wealth."

"He could contribute to a lot of universities between here and his old Kentucky home," Till muses.

"Do you have pictures of these guys?" Cinq-Mars inquires.

"Thanks to the almighty Internet, of course we do."

He shows their faces on his tablet and the officers commit them to memory. They receive copies onto their own mobile devices. Cinq-Mars adds, "I have a few other e-mail addresses to forward these to."

Hammond wants to know who he has in mind first.

"I'll keep that to myself."

"I thought we were into universal peace and love by now. All set for another Woodstock. I thought we were sharing."

"Trooper, there are matters you can know about and things that you can do that other people cannot know about or do. You get to know about them and do something about them because you carry a badge. Am I right?"

"Aren't you always? What's your point?"

"There are things I can know and do now because I no longer have a badge."

"How's that? Like what?"

"I'll put it another way. There are things you can know and do that won't get you into anything other than hot water. Maybe boiling oil. There are things in life you'd rather not know about if it can be helped."

The trooper checks with Chief Till to see if he gets this riddle, and apparently he does. "This is an ignorance-is-bliss type thing?"

"That's the type of thing it is," Cinq-Mars sums up, and Special Agent Hartopp goes ahead and sends copies of the photographs to Caroline, Anastasia, and Kali who are already at the party, unknown to Hammond and Till, preparing for their guests. Bringing in civilians would be a liability to the officers if they knew about it. This is not the case with Émile, while Hartopp knows he can easily wiggle free from any culpability.

"One more thing," Hartopp instructs them. "This may prove significant down the road. My people located the charoite. The wholesale distributor, on Amsterdam Avenue in New York, didn't know it was radioactive until he was informed of that fact by one of his clients, a jeweler. He did the right thing. He took the stones off the market. Ordered back the stock he'd sent out. This is way before we made contact, so he's on the up and up. He knows who bought the stones from him previously, including one who made a significant second purchase for smaller charoite stones. That jeweler hasn't indicated he's sending anything back. We'll be speaking to him, of course, to see who his client or clients are who have such a demand for charoite gemstones."

They are each impressed.

Till, though, nurtures a lingering doubt. "Honestly, Émile, do you really think our bad guys are at the party?"

"I like our chances. Think about it. *If*—and this is not the only big if—*if* our bad guys are donors, they have to show up at the party, otherwise they'd be missed. *If* their cover is to come here as donors, they have to follow through. Besides, they may have planned that all of us would be hot to trot for Vernon Colchester by now. We've led them to believe we are. They think they're in the clear. *If* it's them, or if it's not them, they'll show."

"All right," Till agreed. "Let's party."

"Gentlemen," Cinq-Mars announces, "have fun. If we're missing the boat here, barking up the wrong tree, some cliché like that, at least the drinks are on Dowbiggin."

TWENTY-FOUR

They arrive in the midst of a throng.

A technique utilized for this event, when much is at stake to keep donors happy and, by extrapolation, generous, is to invite a select group of cohosts and guests to be on hand early. The party, then, is in full swing and lively by the time the larger contingent arrives at the appointed hour. From the outset, the room is boisterous.

Laughter and cheery voices echo off the stained-glass windows.

Émile Cinq-Mars withdraws to the sidelines to peruse the gathering. While elegant, the room is formal and austere, one that would serve equally well for funerals. The vaulted ceiling is high, the dark mahogany dominates, the sense of age-old privilege remains wholly intact. Life-sized portraits of early presidents and benefactors point to the future by drawing attention to the past, yet the atmosphere is energized by an abundance of living, breathing young people. Many are working as servers, others as articulate representatives of the graduating class, on hand to illustrate the virtue of their elders' munificence. The cocktail party constitutes an exercise in unabashed ego-stroking, and the attendees, like kittens being petted, purr with delight.

The first person with whom Émile Cinq-Mars speaks is Professor Edith Shedden. She crosses the room to confront him, and notes, "Ominous. The cavalry has breached our defenses."

"If that's a euphemism for barbarians at the gate, then yes, we're here. Please don't blow my cover." He says this with a smile, to imply that he doesn't care what she does with her knowledge.

"My lips are sealed," she vows, with a smile. "Are you here for our protection or do you hope a murderer will leap from behind the curtains to confess his sins? Will he beg to be arrested?"

"Stranger things happen. Keep your eyes peeled and your ears alert."

"You almost sound serious."

"I almost am. I'm that desperate."

She gives him about twenty seconds of her time which apparently is more than enough. "I've done my bit here, Detective. You may not know this: The attention I've paid to you has increased your standing in our rather insular community. Our guests are wondering about the newcomer. Either you are a contributor of high standing or an academic of great renown. Whichever it is, you are now an entity who must be met. Not to mention, a few of our diamond dowagers, as we call them, will have noticed by now that you are tall, handsome, and a stranger, with the face of a renegade academic, or a hermit crab billionaire. What shall I say when the wags inquire?"

Émile smiles again. "Professor, my expertise in life doesn't add up to a hill of green beans. I expect to fail any academic test going. Better to paint me as a man of means. Let's see if I can pull that off. I've had little practice."

"Oh, just condemn the President of the United States for every problem on earth and you'll do fine."

"I'm in trouble then. The cost of gas is so cheap in the States I can't find anything worthwhile to complain about while I'm down here."

"Cheap! Now you're behaving like a misfit. That works, too. See? You can't lose. Have a good day, Mr. Cinq-Mars. Good luck with your work here. I'll get back to mine."

They formally shake hands before parting. As she moves on, he's feeling a trifle guilty for revealing secrets about her that she had wanted protected. Hopefully, those remarks will remain where they lie now, although his experience in life suggests otherwise. People's *stuff* seeks the light, and breaks through at inconvenient times.

He continues his study of the room. Eighty are present, and while that's not a significant crowd, people are knit tightly together making it difficult to pick out individual faces across the broad bay of humanity. Caroline, smiling, swinging a tray, tracks him down to ask if he'd like a drink.

"Whiskey, Caro, neat. The best available, if you please."

"Like I know the difference." She's teased him in the past for being a lush, and as she leans into him to whisper he's expecting more such commentary. Instead, her voice is urgent and insistent. "Find Anastasia. Like now."

Caroline dashes off and he goes on the hunt for her friend. Anastasia is probably pushing the boundaries of her job here. Not merely serving drinks and canapés, she's doling out wit, wisdom, and favorable impressions of Dowbiggin along the way. Émile spots her from a distance, at her back, and draws closer while trying not to make it appear that she is the object of his intentions. Before he arrives, the girl turns, clutches an empty glass on the tray to keep it from toppling, and in the same motion indicates the bar. They'll cross paths there.

She's emptying her tray and simultaneously imparting her order to the bartender as Émile comes up behind her a second time. Spinning around again, Anastasia offers a mock smile, and states, "Check out what I'm wearing." She lowers the serving tray.

The necklace. An identical facsimile to the one that adorned Addie Langford both before and after her death. If he was standing on a rug, Émile can imagine it yanked out from under him. As it is, he feels the floor give way, and he's floating.

"Where the hell did you get that?"

"Here, is where. Why, is my question."

"All right then, how did you get it?"

A charge shoots through him. An invitation to the party was placed between the fingers of the dead girl—cynical and challenging enough—and now a signal of the murderer's presence has been put on display. Instinct tells him that this is not a diversion, rather that a challenge has been laid down, and redoubled. Worst case, it's not a challenge at all, but a serious threat.

"This thing arrived in the kitchen inside a chocolate box with my name on it. With a decorative bow. A card inside. I kept it, it's in the back. The message explains that the necklace was found on campus and may belong to someone at this party. I'm to wear it—me, specifically—to see if its owner responds. That answers where I got it and how, Mr. Cinq-Mars. My questions still stand. Why? And why me?"

He realizes that his cover may have been blown. That he has now been identified.

That might be the whole purpose of the necklace this afternoon.

Anticipating delivery of her drink order, the coed turns away from him. Cinq-Mars appears to be waiting on something. The answer to her question, perhaps. They hope to present a posture to the room that suggests they may not actually be talking to each other.

"It's possible, Anastasia, that you've been marked. You may have been identified as the next target. A choice has been made and they might want us to know it. Or want us to think that way. More likely, someone is trying to identify who takes an interest in you now. My anonymity may already be compromised, as of this moment. *C'est la vie.* Something else is curious. The three people we're tracking make a point of not communicating with one another. They don't acknowledge one another's existence in public. I'm wondering if perhaps they chose to identify their quarry without a word passing among them. You know?" She doesn't know. He's mainly talking to himself now. "If true, that sets up an interesting possibility."

"I wear the necklace around the room and killers get to see that I'm the chosen one? Something like that?"

"Maybe exactly that."

"Lovely. I'm a marked woman for perverts. How sick is that?"

"Not to worry. Nothing's going to happen. I won't let it."

"No, I mean, it's *sick.* That means good. They have targeted someone who's out to get *them.*"

"All right, then. Sick. Don't be overconfident. They seem to know more about the people up against them than the other way around. Be careful."

"Here's your drink, sir." It's Caro, and he turns to receive his glass. "Everything okay?" she whispers.

"Have you seen the one called Bennington et cetera et cetera, the one with the double-barreled last name?"

"Turn straight around. Sixty degrees on your left, toward the back of the room."

He's had junior officers who would not have been that precise or quick with directions. "Thanks. I won't turn to look just yet. Bye."

"Bye," Caro says.

"You go, too," Cinq-Mars advises Anastasia.

Loaded up, the young woman heads off. Cinq-Mars keeps his back to the room, sips, and recognizes that the drink is Laphroaig. Without turning or going the way that Caro indicated, he heads off in a nearly opposite direction from his quarry, intending to circle around.

The party has grown festive as more people arrive, although here and there through the crowd he picks up inklings of conversation that have to do with recent dire events. While the mood is far from somber, it's not thoroughly jovial, either.

About a hundred and twenty people are present now and he wonders what the bar bill will be for that.

Cinq-Mars passes the youngest of the three persons of interest, a tire mogul from Kentucky. Chief Till, comfortable in his civilian duds, chats in the mogul's vicinity to an elderly matron with diamonds around her neck. They discuss the value of an older building, such as the one they're standing in, during modern times.

"Irreplaceable," she contends.

"Invaluable," he calculates.

Cinq-Mars smiles as he entertains the thought that they might both be referring to themselves.

He physically bumps into Kali, the other of Caro's friends working on his scheme. She passes him a canapé. Realizing that he's famished, Émile takes two. Walks on, munching. He smiles, nods, keeping up a cheerful front, his look suggesting that he has a destination in mind. He does not appear to be in search of a conversation to join just yet and that helps him avoid being drawn into any. He passes Hammond, who has his eyes on Émile's target as well, yet stands twenty yards away.

Émile presses on.

Through a shift of bodies, a convergence of interests, a dispersal of hangers-on, Émile discovers that the man he's after, Bennington Orion Marshall Havilland-Clegg, is now engaged in discussion with the president of the Dowbiggin School, Joshua Palmerich. As he approaches, he catches the president's eye.

"Émile Cinq-Mars." Palmerich lights up. "How are you?"

"Very well, Mr. Palmerich. Yourself?"

"Tip-top. May I introduce Ben Havilland-Clegg, one of our most ardent and faithful alumni. A third-generation alumnus. Ben, this is Émile Cinq-Mars, one of our newest contributors. His niece is graduating this year. Mr. Cinq-Mars has expressed his appreciation by making a significant contribution to our general endowment."

"Wonderful, wonderful, that's much appreciated, Mr. Cinq-Mars— am I saying that correctly? I'm not familiar with the name."

Palmerich didn't say it correctly either, and Cinq-Mars repeats his name for the benefit of both men. "It's French. I'm French-Canadian."

"I thought I detected a slight accent. Congratulations, sir, on your niece's success."

He seems about to pull away, disinterested in continuing with their introduction. Or perhaps he wants to leave Palmerich to his duties. Émile, though, hopes to snag him for a minute more. "Sorry to have interrupted," he jumps in. "You two were quite engaged."

"That nasty business on campus," Palmerich says in his silky, cordial, official voice, "of which you are, no doubt, aware. We don't wish to seem callous, and yet we were reviewing scenarios that might allow us to recover from our sordid circumstance."

"Tragic for the family," Ben Havilland-Clegg tacks on. He wants out of this quickly, as he's clearly uninterested. "Nevertheless, the school must consider its PR. We must move on, pave the way for others to enjoy an exemplary education at Dowbiggin."

"Rapes and now a murder. Yeah, I'd call that a PR challenge."

The sardonic note in Émile's voice is intentional, which finally prompts a reaction in the gray-haired man. He respects attitude. He tilts his brow back, the gaze narrows, and the pursued takes an interest in his pursuer.

Palmerich has his own reaction. "I cannot speak to the murder of a student on campus, Mr. Cinq-Mars. That's an unfathomable tragedy. Perhaps, in due course, we can look back on these events as representing a turnaround. Don't single us out, sir. Rape is epidemic on university campuses across America. I know. I've been studying the situation. Perhaps Dowbiggin can now lead the way toward a culture that repudiates rape. Not to be cynical about it, such a movement may be the backbone of our PR, going forward."

Despite the president's insistence on how they treat his initiative, both Cinq-Mars and Havilland-Clegg choose to regard it cynically.

"What do you do, sir?" the benefactor inquires. "In life? If I may ask?"

The former cop has noted the man's attraction to jewelry. Three rings, two bracelets—one medical, the other an adornment—cuff links with diamond studs, a lapel pin with a setting of minute gemstones amid gold. A bias toward topaz. The man's question is one that Cinq-Mars considers quintessentially American. Canadians tend to judge the query as rude, an intrusion, an invasion of privacy; Americans find it an ideal icebreaker.

"I was in wire," Émile tells him. "Now retired." A standard he's used before. By virtue of being dull, the nature of the business provokes no curiosity or corollary question. The formula works in this instance.

"Wire," Havilland-Clegg repeats. "Fascinating." Satisfied that he's spoken a virtual benediction, he makes a slight bow, and departs their company.

The look Cinq-Mars grants the university president has the man both uneasy and inquisitive. "What now?" Palmerich presses.

"He's involved."

"Excuse me? Ben? No, he's not *involved*."

"Yes. Ben. Your wonderful third-generation alumnus and donor. He's involved."

"Impossible. I knew this was a bad idea, you being here. Why would you entertain such an absurd line of thinking?"

"I can feel it. In my bones."

"That's balderdash. Or arthritis. Or a change in the weather. You cannot go around making outrageous accusations," he hisses. "Not in this room. Nor on this campus. May I remind you that you have no standing in this *country*. You're putting a strain on my confidence in your project, Mr. Cinq-Mars."

"As demoralizing as this may be, sir, why don't we discover the truth? Find a side room. Ask him to join us. We'll have a talk. If I'm wrong, feel free to demonize me, hoist me on my own petard. If I'm right, you can immediately start work on your PR."

"This is outrageous."

"No, sir. What's outrageous is a student of yours being slaughtered on campus. Then raped, not for the first time, after she's already dead. Now what's it going to be?"

Palmerich studies Cinq-Mars's gaze awhile, taking note of his conviction, then looks across at Havilland-Clegg, and back again. "If you're wrong, it's not a matter of taking out my revenge on you. The consequences to this institution can be significant. Please appreciate my position and my responsibilities."

"Again, your constituency will praise you when the criminals are caught."

"Don't count on that. That might be true only if my constituency *approves* of the criminals who are caught."

So that was it. Arresting one of their own garners no reward.

"Okay, sir. I get you. I can be circumspect. Do it in such a way that an innocent man won't be too put out. He won't know enough to put up a stink. I'll assure him that you have no choice in the matter, that it's all common procedure. I'll bring in a couple of other men as well; he won't feel singled out. And then, if he's guilty, you'll have a different sort of PR job on your shoulders."

"I recall that you are university educated yourself."

"I am."

"You sound like it. In animal husbandry? What is that?"

"I'm not sure that it exists anymore."

"How did it ever?"

"I believe it has a fancier name these days. After I swore off the priesthood, I wanted to be a veterinarian. A long time ago now."

"You became a cop instead."

"Another form of herding cattle."

Palmerich releases a sigh. "I respect you, Cinq-Mars. Nonetheless, what you are wishing for is not going to happen. We won't bother with any part of it." He keeps his voice low and urgent. "Let us endeavor to contain the damage, shall we? Bring me hard, virtually irrefutable evidence, then we'll talk. Until then, what's in your bones, stays in your bones. Period. Should you or the real police override my authority on this, you shall be persona non grata on campus. You may not care—why should you?—except that your investigation will be impaired. Check with Chief Till to see if he wants to override me in this town, or Trooper Hammond in this state. Both gentlemen will come to blows with their political bosses should you overstep your bounds. They don't doubt it, why should you? I sincerely wish you well in this difficult undertaking, make no mistake, we are on the same side. And yet, you must stay within the lines. Stay there! Now, if you'll excuse me, sir, I have important people waiting with whom I must touch base."

The retired detective wonders how well the criminals know this president, if they were able in advance to predict his reactions and depend on them. Another speculation that he *feels in his bones,* as well as taking the university president at his word, is that Palmerich is not his foe, and covertly looks upon his involvement with favor. Still, the man simply cannot tolerate offending a contributor. The thought has probably occurred to him that citing even one member of this entourage as a rapist and a killer undermines the group. Many, for no logical reason, might then lose their taste for funding the institution. One sick puppy, let alone three amid the throng, might leave a score of others feeling ill. Historically, and for the time being, the members are buoyed by the prestige of their private club. Tarnish that image, and important associates might choose to disperse. He comprehends the president's dilemma—perhaps more than the man believes.

When these folks learn that one of their number rapes, kills, then abuses the corpse, how will they view their privileged retinue then? They'll want out. To disavow themselves of any connection.

Émile mulls it over as he wanders around.

He observes Chief Till, who continues to impart a favorable impression. Working the room, he's located himself in a circle with the youngest of their suspects, Hanson Parker, the forty-something financial services adviser and former member of the diplomatic corps.

Cinq-Mars puts him at about five foot five, probably no more than a hundred and fifteen pounds. Many of the female students in the room are both taller and carry more weight. He sports a mustache that he maintains with vigilance. This attention to grooming is evidenced as well in his haircut, the trim of his eyebrows, the perfect knot to his mauve tie. Given his distance, it's impossible for Cinq-Mars to declare that the scent on his nostrils derives from the man's cologne, but if asked, he'd take that bet.

Till and Parker stand with seven patrons, men and women, while Till holds court. He has let them know that he's an officer of the law working the campus murders, and successfully he recites the company line, that the crimes are as sophisticated as they are heinous, as puzzling as they are diabolical. "We've imported the best minds in our business," he elaborates, perhaps to pull the Montreal cop's leg, "yet they've been stumped. The FBI is at a loss. I'm sure they expected to show us country bumpkins a thing or two. This is not simply a violent crime. A mastermind lies behind it."

Responses converge on the notion that Dowbiggin is not to blame, that the murder of the young woman is a symptom of the modern world visited upon a community where it receives neither welcome nor nurture. A list of towns where mass shootings and other horrors have occurred gives credence to the veracity of the claim. Soon Till is offered encouragement, including from Hanson Parker, to be neither deterred nor disheartened in his relentless pursuit of the killer.

"Leave no stone unturned," Parker instructs him.

Till assures him that he will not, and thanks him for his moral support. "God knows, at this stage, we need it."

"Thank you for coming to our wee party," a handsome lady proffers from her elaborate, amply cushioned wheelchair. "You have restored our confidence in a single bound. We place our faith in you."

Cinq-Mars has not planned his next move, and has no time to think it through. In a trice he seizes an opportunity. "Well put, ma'am. I was speaking earlier to Chief Till when he made an interesting observation. He mentioned that the police do possess one significant clue."

The circle of the rich look to Till to reveal it to them as well.

Blindsided this way, the chief is stymied. "Clue, sir? There are a few. I don't recall—which one are you referring to in particular?"

"The one about the elbow, and the killer leaving his DNA behind. What Chief Till said to me was—I'll paraphrase. Please, correct me if I'm mistaken. He mentioned what a shame it is that he can't require everyone in town to show him their elbows. I don't see why not. I'm willing to show Chief Till my elbows."

The lady in the chair, who's wearing short sleeves, has no problem revealing hers immediately. She points both of them upward, and rotates her torso for everyone to see. "The only people who ask to see a body part of mine these days are doctors, and they have *instruments*. Yes, please, Chief Till, examine my elbows if you will. Clear my name of this terrible crime! I can't imagine that anyone, other than the killer, wouldn't want to put his or her elbows on display."

Cinq-Mars is delighted. Those in the circle take up the task, the men removing their jackets and rolling up their sleeves, which causes a bit of a stir in neighboring cliques. No scrapes. No dried blood. Not even on Hanson Parker's elbows, although he does seem a bit more put out than the others to be showing his off.

Cinq-Mars is hoping for a miracle that's not forthcoming. Their sport fails to catch fire through the room and remains limited to the original select circle.

Trooper Hammond, Cinq-Mars sees as he checks on what he's up to, has inched closer to Bennington Havilland-Clegg. He's not confident that he wants him there. Leaving Till in the company of Hanson Parker, he moves across the room to intervene, yet before he manages to get there Hammond is distracted by Anastasia. The student is sprinting quickly between clients. Spotting the necklace, the trooper fails to conceal his sudden interest. Cinq-Mars worries that Havilland-Clegg will take note of the man's reaction, too. He's wearing a conceited grin. Diverted in his pursuit of Anastasia now, Hammond changes direction, and Cinq-Mars lets him go.

Within his range is the tire mogul, Al McBride, forty steps away. Should he invade his vicinity, it will mean that he has found himself in talks with the three suspects in short succession. Any keen observer, and Cinq-Mars suspects that Havilland-Clegg qualifies, could identify him as a person who has linked the three men together and not deem that a coincidence. Rather than revealing the suspects, he'd be further revealed himself, and he'd be surrendering a key aspect of his knowledge: that he's aware that a trio may be up to the dirty work. Émile moves away from all three, searching for an innocuous huddle where he might be embraced and from where he can maintain a close eye without arousing suspicion. He chooses a destination, and on his way there taps Caro's shoulder and whispers for another scotch.

And delivers a message.

"Pass by Trooper Hammond. Tell him I know about the necklace. Ask him not to let on. Then ask Kali to tell Chief Till about Anastasia's necklace. Have her ask him not to let on, either. The key thing is, I don't want you to talk to both officers yourself, understand? One each. Then catch Anastasia's eye. Ask her to return the necklace to its box. After that, when no one's watching, give it to President Palmerich yourself. Tell him to keep it safe for the police. He's free to look at it if he wants to."

"Not for me to question why, I suppose."

His facial expression confirms that. He adds, "This is important, Caro."

"I know," she says, and dashes off.

Now that he's set matters in motion, Cinq-Mars retreats to what seems to be the most mundane of groups and infiltrates their number. That's not difficult where one matron, into her cups, thinks that everyone is somebody else. She mistakes Cinq-Mars for her old friend Wesley, who also has an accent apparently, albeit from Cornwall.

"I'll call you Wesley, too," a gentleman with a bright red face offers. "Makes things simpler in the long run. My name's Harold. How do you do? Mrs. Shimon has taken to calling me *Ron*, for reasons no one can quite discern. At this point I answer to either appellation."

Included in their group is an academic representing the college, who remarks that two years ago she called him Fido. "Consider yourselves fortunate. I was mistaken for a Pekingese."

Mrs. Shimon seems not the least put out by their remarks.

It's an interchangeable group of eight to fourteen people who are enjoying themselves, and Cinq-Mars happily shelters himself within their midst. No one questions his identity and at least five people now refer to him as Wesley.

Attention is drawn to the dais in a corner of the room where a lectern with a microphone has been erected. President Palmerich is about to be introduced, and while it does not seem to be the best time, Caro successfully places a hand lightly on his wrist and draws his attention to the wee box, which he covertly drops into a jacket pocket. During the introductory remarks, Cinq-Mars sees the man's hand slip into the pocket and remove the contents. He makes a quick study of the necklace inside, and it's easy to tell that he cottons on to its significance. He might now believe that the murderer is in the room.

Discombobulated, he's called upon to speak.

Palmerich issues a warm welcome to his distinguished guests. He follows with a few sly jokes about the necessity of asking for money and receives a few chuckles of appreciation. Everyone accepts that they are here to drink, laugh, and have their bank accounts pilfered. He then delivers solemn remarks that acknowledge the tragedies of recent days and the loss of a beloved student, a brilliant professor, and a hardworking custodian. He emphasizes that the three events are disconnected from one another and merely incidental to Dowbiggin, although the investigation is ongoing and "who knows what might turn up." He parlays that shocking report into a talk that portrays the challenges of the present time as an incentive for generous donations, as the events will have consequences to be combatted and overcome. He envisions a Dowbiggin that will emerge from these tragedies as a beacon of peacefulness and respect. Palmerich concludes by offering his thanks, introduces a few key colleagues around the room, including Professor Edith Shedden and the man who once accepted to be called Fido, and with a flourish urges everyone to enjoy themselves this afternoon and through the following days amid a plethora of commencement activity.

Although skeptical of the man's ambitions for peacefulness, Cinq-Mars evaluates that he would hire him at his university if he was on the board of directors.

He wonders how Havilland-Clegg is doing and finds him either miffed or confused. His demeanor suggests a slow burn. Cinq-Mars casts his eye around the proceedings and draws the assumption that his suspect has spotted Anastasia—now without her identifying necklace. Havilland-Clegg has been in control of the game until this moment— and a small voice whispers that he has to keep in mind that he may not be part of this game or any other. Cinq-Mars ignores the minority opinion in his head and sticks with his stronger judgment—the man has been defied and feels the effects. Anastasia has removed the necklace and he has no clue where it's gone.

Cinq-Mars moves close to him again.

"Ah," the philanthropist pipes up, "here he is, our man of steel." His supercilious grin can as easily undermine the former policeman's agenda as would another man's confession to the crime. Émile's being goaded and he's not inclined to accept such treatment from this fellow. For now, he must. "Sorry, sir. Not steel. My mistake. Wire. Same difference, no? The man of wire. The wiry man. Are you enjoying yourself?"

"Are you?"

"Immensely. Then again, I always do. Oh, good—my drink."

Caro is delivering it.

"A Manhattan," the man exults, to Cinq-Mars and to others in his fledgling niche. "Was a time when good rye became less available. Quality rye is back, the comeback booze, and with it, the classic Manhattan. Yummy. Friends! May I introduce Mr. Cinq-Mars. He's from Canada way. A maker of *wire*. Isn't that grand and exciting?"

Many agree.

A man unknown to Cinq-Mars has a question. "What kind of wire do you manufacture, Mr. Cinq-Mars?" The man's eyeglasses appear to be made from sea glass, a mauve hue, as thick as a windshield on an armored car. He has wide, rather unattractive lips. The detective would rather not wade through a pedestrian conversation with him to engage Ben Havilland-Clegg.

"Barbed," he replies.

The man adjusts his glasses a notch higher on his bulbous nose. He's an unfortunate-looking fellow. "Barbed," he repeats.

"Barbed," Havilland-Clegg says also.

Cinq-Mars shrugs. "I do prisons."

"Except that you're retired," Havilland-Clegg reminds him.

"Except that I still work as a consultant."

"For prisons?"

"One way of putting it. I also used to sell to ranchers and the military. It seems that people always want to hear about my visits to prisons."

"I'll pass, if you don't mind."

"Don't blame you one bit. Dreadful places. Repulsive. I wouldn't want to live there."

The man who is observing him through sea-glass lenses remarks, "We were discussing our president's homily, regarding the dreadful business. What is your opinion on the matter, Mr. Cinq-Mars? Will Dowbiggin recover from this dark day?"

Havilland-Clegg answers for him. "Mr. Cinq-Mars believes that we have a PR catastrophe on our hands, sir. He spoke previously. He believes we're doomed."

"I'm inclined to believe him," the sea-glass man allows.

"Cynics! I'll leave you to it, then. Would either of you like a Manhattan, by the way? I've taught our man how to concoct a good one. The Manhattan was the first cocktail to introduce vermouth, did you know? A classic. It deserves a revival."

Cinq-Mars knows the technique well. While he may not have invented the tactic himself, he's not sure that he hasn't perfected it in his day. Confuse an adversary with a variety of topics until his head spins. In this post and riposte, he's very much at home, and gives his foe a nick with his own rapier.

"I like my whiskey neat and not be rye," Cinq-Mars attests. "Which is how I prefer my criminals."

"Ah, pardon me? You like your criminals not to be rye?"

He fails to observe the third man in their conversation scratch his head. After giving his scalp a good mauling, he takes a step back.

"I like them neat. Tidy. All the facts in a row. Like ducks. I like my criminals, I've known a few, to be tidy ducks in a row, their grand schemes brought to dust and suctioned up with a vacuum. Then, when all the nasty criminals are sleeping, lying on their cots, I ship my barbed wire around them to keep them docile. It's my contribution to society."

The third man is committed to his escape now and Cinq-Mars notes that Havilland-Clegg wants to flee as well.

"We did a little experiment across the room— Mrs. Heidl!" Cinq-Mars calls out, catching a break here. "Tell this man what we did across the room to help out the police in their investigation."

Mrs. Heidl is beaming, delighted to be called upon. "We exposed our rusty elbows. You must do it, too. We must all! Everyone must expose their elbows!"

At the very least, Cinq-Mars has managed to get Havilland-Clegg to wear a frown.

"We both have double-barreled names," the detective goes on. "I find it to be a nuisance, don't you? People think the humble hyphen is anything but, that its very existence indicates a declaration of superiority. I mean, I was born with it, it's not my fault. It's not as though we had any say in the matter."

"Quite."

Cinq-Mars has his suspect entirely to himself.

"One thing about barbed wire, it does a lot to keep criminals in their rows. Nobody likes to mess with it. Nobody likes to cross it ever."

Hammond and Till are closing in. They sense that an action is afoot.

"I'm glad that your life's work gave you satisfaction. Now, if you'll excuse me—"

"What was *your* life's work?" Cinq-Mars puts to him.

He smiles. Deflects the question.

"Another topic. Another time," Havilland-Clegg begs off.

"I admire your jewelry."

"Do you? Thank you. I see that you're bereft of trinkets yourself."

"Trinkets! No, sir, I'm sure that you've adorned yourself with the finest of gemstones. May I see them more closely? I'm keen."

As if offering his arm to give blood, Havilland-Clegg permits Cinq-Mars to examine a bracelet. "You can help, you know. With your expertise. With your knowledge."

"Help? Who, you? To buy jewelry? Are you sure you wouldn't rather start with something more conventional. Such as tattoos. Or a nose ring."

"You jest!" Cinq-Mars exclaims. He's never had to play the fool to this extent before—he's enjoying the role. At the very least, he'll give his wife a few laughs with the retelling.

"The police—that one over there, he's in plainclothes, the rank of chief—he said the dead girl was wearing a necklace. He's certain that it harbors clues. What do you think? With your knowledge? I'm certain of it, you can help the case. Are you willing?"

"I'm not a jeweler, I only wear attractive gemstones."

"You see? You know the difference. What did you say you did again?"

"I didn't."

"Oh, sir, don't make me guess. What did you do? Shall I guess? Shall I? I'll ask others to join us. Or perhaps they already know. I'm the newcomer here. I told you. I'm in wire. Fair is fair. What's your profession?"

Havilland-Clegg's smile wavers, vanishes, then repeats itself. While he revels in being rude, he is unaccustomed to being the object of even mild derision, and finds Cinq-Mars's behavior objectionable.

"I spend my father's money," he lets him know. "If anyone has a problem with that, they can damn well see my lawyer."

Cinq-Mars lifts his head back to laugh. "You're a hoot," he says.

"I'm glad to be such an entertainment to you, sir. Perhaps I've missed my calling."

"Jeweler?"

"Comedian."

"Perhaps you have. Will you help? Let me call that nice policeman over."

Havilland-Clegg cranes his neck to peer over a few heads. "Which one is he again?"

Cinq-Mars moves close to him, their cheeks almost rub, and points. "That guy there."

"Oh sure. Call him over. Anything," he says, rocking back on his heels, giving himself personal space, "to get me out of this."

"You don't mean that."

"I do."

"You're a kidder. A frustrated comedian."

"Oh, sir, one thing I am not, is frustrated."

Cinq-Mars is waving Till their way.

"How kind of you to help our local constabulary."

"Not at all. I merely wish to be informed. I hate being left in the dark about all this, don't you? If we're to overcome our PR catastrophe, and I agree with you, it's a catastrophe—"

"I think those were your words, Mr. Havilland-Clegg."

"Now who's the kidder?"

"They were!" He cannot press the point, as Chief Till has arrived. Addressing him, he says, "Chief, Mr. Havilland-Clegg is an expert on gemstones."

"An amateur, truth be told."

"I explained about your interest in the necklace that you told me was around the young woman's neck. I believe—Mr. Havilland-Clegg believes—that he can be of assistance to the police. I thought the two of you might like to go off for a chat. Please, I hope you don't mind my initiative."

Till and Havilland-Clegg nod to one another, and both seem to indicate that they agree—that they are in the company of a nitwit.

"Perhaps, in a small way," the benefactor suggests, "I can be of assistance. I do know this and that about gemstones. If I may take my Manhattan away with me, *and* if this man promises to replenish with another before it's done, then yes, perhaps I can be of minor assistance."

"A Manhattan," Till replies, a rejoinder so perfect that Cinq-Mars could kiss him, "My God, I haven't had one of those since I was in the army on leave."

Havilland-Clegg seems perfectly content now. Excited, even, as a liveliness returns to his eyes that was absent a moment ago. "Why don't we find ourselves a cozy little alcove, I know a few, where we can arrange for a steady stream of Manhattans to arrive as we enjoy our conversation. I want a leather chair, though. I insist on leather chairs whenever I return to Dowbiggin."

"I'll arrange for the drinks," Cinq-Mars offers.

"Fine," Till concurs while meeting Havilland-Clegg's glance. "You understand, Mr. Cinq-Mars, that this is police work. It will be a private chat." Excluding him suits their suspect's sense of entitlement.

"Sure, sure," Cinq-Mars agrees, playing the dunce who doesn't understand what's going on. "I'm just the wire guy," and he's off to flag down his niece for the Manhattans. While he's at it, he'll have a word with Palmerich, to assure him that the conversation taking place at that moment between the police and Ben Havilland-Clegg is not only voluntary on the part of an enduring Dowbiggin benefactor, it's the man's own idea. He is prepared to quote Havilland-Clegg verbatim: "I can be of assistance." His very words. All is aboveboard.

Besides, Palmerich has the incriminating necklace in his pocket and Cinq-Mars must retrieve it from him now. It's evidence.

TWENTY-FIVE

Cinq-Mars and the police devise a plan. Their target has taken leave for a washroom visit, and in his absence Émile has a word with Hammond, specifically, before whispering a straightforward strategy to both him and Chief Till. The latter is assigned to take the lead in the interrogation—ostensibly, a chat—with Bennington Havilland-Clegg.

"Keep it neat, keep it cordial," is the gist of his suggestion.

"I'll stroke the prick's ego," the Hanover police chief promises.

"But not the ego's prick," Hammond mutters, and the others give him a look. They're amused. That was fast, and they didn't know he had it in him.

The trooper, of course, is free to pull rank at any moment. To secure his secondary support, Cinq-Mars makes the case that the suspect's personal radar will be thwarted if the humbler police force is out front and visible. Fearing Till less makes Havilland-Clegg more vulnerable. "What he can't see coming stays invisible."

"Gotcha." If anything, Hammond is annoyed that his colleagues are making allowances for him. He's excited, and part of the kick derives from their collaboration.

The next shoe must not fall from the benefactor's foot until he himself kicks off a leather penny loafer and hurls it across the room. In the interim, the interrogation will benefit if the man's supercilious demeanor remains intact. A devotee of precious gemstones, he's been touted as an asset: They need him wholly convinced of that fib. By hook or by crook, they must delay revealing to Ben Havilland-Clegg, and even to themselves, the depths and contours of his own depravity.

Provided, of course, they've got the right guy.

"Shit creek if we're wrong," Hammond notes.

"You guys will be up it without a paddle," Cinq-Mars points out. "Me, I'm retired."

Their suspicions run deep, yet they have no way to validate them. Havilland-Clegg must do that on his own. As police work goes, their case is flimsy, at best, and Till treads lightly, aware that the man harbors an alibi in his hip pocket.

Their suspect returns to the selected venue where Cinq-Mars and Hammond leave him alone with Till.

"Thanks for this, sir. Appreciate it."

"Do I call you 'Chief'? I wish you were called 'Sheriff'. *Chief* feels Native American to me, doesn't fall off the tongue in a natural way. I feel I'm disparaging you."

Already he'd like to smack him. "Please, sir, call me Alex."

"Glad to. Alexander, is it?"

Till nods. They seat themselves in a small antechamber where the green-shaded lamps are dim, in part to keep the aging oil paintings of the school's founding fathers from damage by light. Portraits dominate three walls, the fourth faces a corridor and is mainly glass. A quiet, if public, place to study. Anyone walking by might imagine them on a stage. The interview can be conducted at this time of year with little or no interruption, yet it's still a public place and therefore seems safe. The guest is content to ease himself farther back into a plush leather chair, careful not to spill his drink.

"As I was saying, I appreciate it. We have no suspects. We can't hang our hat on a single significant clue. I hate to admit it, the guy we're looking for must be a mad genius. All we can do is go over the same ground, try to shine a light, see if we can't trip over our own thumbs, you know?"

"How may I be of assistance, Alexander? I heard mention of a necklace?"

"We'll have a copy for you shortly," Till lets him know. "We showed it to an expert, got nowhere. Maybe the more people who take a look, the better our chances. A shot in the dark. Oh. Pardon the expression. My mistake. I didn't mean it that way."

Havilland-Clegg smiles in sympathy of the faux pas by the bumbling officer. "No problem. You're hoping the gems have meaning, is that the idea?"

"If they offer any clue at all, we'll take it. If not, no harm no foul." Till extracts a notebook from his suit pocket. "I don't usually do this out of uniform, Bennington. While we're waiting for the necklace—"

"Not to mention my Manhattans, they're on their way, as well." He claims a coaster from the drawer of his table stand, which he tests by placing his current glass down gently. Then he promptly retrieves it for another sip.

"While we wait, if it's all right with you, protocol, procedure—a formality—for the record, can you account for your whereabouts on the night in question?"

Havilland-Clegg peers over his lowball glass at him. "What night in question?"

"The night Addie Langford was murdered."

He smiles, and knits the fingers of his hands together. "Am I a suspect here, Alexander? Such a question."

"Heavens, no, Ben! Procedure. That's all. Formality. Frankly, if I had my way, I'd know what every person from three states around was doing on that night."

Till hopes that he hasn't pushed him too far too quickly: The man appears compliant. "Of course." He puts his glass down and considers his response. "I had a rather long evening, Alexander. Not unlike today. By the way, would you mind calling me Mr. Havilland-Clegg? Ben and even Bennington are reserved for only my closest associates. I believe in restoring a proper formality to American discourse, you see. Or perhaps you don't."

"Certainly, sir, not a problem. Your whereabouts and activities at the time in question, sir?"

A gesture with a hand dismisses the worth of the question. "A few drinks in the late afternoon, through the cocktail hour. Over dinner, a bottle of fine wine. Perhaps a second. Shared with friends, of course. I was feeling a trifle tipsy. After dark I chose a coffee shop to sober up and while away the time. I hate waking up inebriated, don't you? Anyway, it turned out to be a congenial evening, Alexander. People saw me there if I need to provide you with an alibi. Isn't that exciting? Being required to state an alibi! Many of us in the coffee shop conversed. I spoke to a barista at length, a delicate young woman, full of ideas and ambition, and a waitress, as well. I'm sure they'll remember me. Patrons, also. I don't imagine I can find the latter unless it's their habit to show up there again. The young people who work there, they'll vouch for me."

"Sorry," Till intrudes, "the coffee shop crowd doesn't strike me as being your usual sort."

He smiles. He feels complimented. "A nostalgic hour, in a way. A sensibility takes hold of me when I come up here. Old reveries from college days. I step back in time, talk to young people, feel like a kid again myself. I forget the name of the coffee bar. It's new, I can point it out to you. After that I went across to the Holyoake Inn, where I'm staying—"

"What time do you think?"

"After midnight." He picks up his glass, without sipping, then puts it down again as he remembers. "Closing in on one. Does that take me off the hook or put me on it? When was the crime committed?"

"Ah, the murder occurred during that hour, actually. The rape, a while before, we believe."

"Then I'm standing in the clear light of the sun! Multiple witnesses will confirm my whereabouts through the late afternoon, evening, until the witching hour. At the inn, I had quite a lengthy chat with the desk clerk. I guess that cinches it. Then I went up. Sorry, Alexander, no one can say whether I snored or not."

Till chuckles on cue. "Thank you, Mr. Havilland-Clegg. I've often wondered, away on my vacation, fishing in the north woods, what would happen if I was accused of a crime elsewhere at that moment? Who would vouch for me, off on my lonesome like that? You've got it covered; that's great."

"I hear what you're saying. I'm a social animal, Alexander. I usually have it covered. Certainly on that terrible night I do."

Hammond arrives with the necklace. A door opening and closing down the hall releases a burst of party sound. The event is still going strong. Hammond offers a perfunctory smile, removes the necklace from the box, places it on the coffee table at their knees, then sits in the big armchair beside Till as if he's hardly interested. He wears a placid expression and intertwines the fingers of his hands.

Bennington Havilland-Clegg picks up the necklace to examine it at close range. His eyes squint, emphasizing the wrinkle lines on his face. When he puts it down, he takes up his glass again, and laments, "A bit clumsy overall, don't you think? The gemstones themselves are interesting. Not without value. Pretty enough, I'd say. On the busy side. I prefer a necklace on a woman to be more delicate. That said—and I'm being picky, I admit—it's interesting. On the right neck, with the right dress, the right cleavage, shall we say, the right atmosphere, proper lighting, it could be lovely on certain women."

"It's radioactive," Till tells him.

"Pardon?" He seems taken aback, then recovers. "Obviously, many gems have a faint trace of radioactivity, that's to be expected—"

"More than a trace in this instance. The charoite—do you know which stones they are?"

He nods that he does.

"Normally, they're slightly radioactive, a trace, as you say. These happen to be highly so, to a degree both harmful, I'm told, with prolonged contact, and illegal. Can you imagine? The Russians. What a society. Chaos. Anyway, a party from there shipped them here. Callous bastards, hey? Fortunately, we've determined that the American distributor wasn't part of the scam, only a victim. Once he caught wind of the problem he stopped his sales before too much of the supply hit the streets."

"A break in the case, actually," Hammond inserts.

"How so?" Havilland-Clegg is smiling still, pleased to be included in their enclave. "I have to say, this is fascinating!"

"Only a scant few jewelers," Till lets him know, "received the charoite from that shipment. We know who they are through the distributor's records. The FBI is contacting the individual jewelers as we speak to see who among them made the necklaces that were oddly included in two murders."

Their suspect raises his chin in curiosity. "Two? Which other one?"

"The necklace wasn't found on the other victim. Only its radioactivity remained. We assume that the custodian was wearing one. Then that necklace, if it was the same one, showed up at her boyfriend's house."

"You've arrested the boyfriend, then. This is fascinating!"

"We can't make that arrest. He's one of those killed."

His chin drops a notch. "The professor, you mean? *He* was the boyfriend? Getting it on with a custodian? My God. I expect hanky-panky at a university, lots of it, only that's not the sort of liaison that pops to mind. To each his own, I suppose."

"Of course, we're hoping that when we locate the jewelers who made the necklaces, they'll give us the customer we're looking for."

Havilland-Clegg nods his chin thoughtfully. "I commend you," he says. "This sounds like excellent police work to me. Now, how can I be of service? Ah!" he suddenly exclaims. "Further help is on the way. My fresh Manhattan!"

Émile Cinq-Mars has chosen to bring it along himself, and takes the opportunity to ham it up.

"Flurry of activity in there. I think a few of the old biddies will soon be dancing on tabletops. The FBI showed up, talking a blue streak to President Palmerich. I get the feeling that our host is at his wit's end. He can't take more police action on his campus without busting a gut."

"FBI?" Havilland-Clegg says. "I didn't know that they were here."

"Everybody's here," Till mentions. "They're stumped, too. Although they might have information on who bought the necklaces."

Hammond plays along with Émile. "Did you eavesdrop?"

"They weren't speaking to my ears, no."

"Even Homeland Security is on this case," Till tacks on.

Havilland-Clegg reacts. "Why them?"

"The professor," Hammond explains. "He has a spy background."

"Really?"

"No limit to police activity on this case," Till points out to him, "until it's solved."

"Is that the necklace?" Cinq-Mars asks, and he leans over the coffee table for a closer look.

Havilland-Clegg warns, "Watch out. It's radioactive," and Cinq-Mars jerks back.

"Shouldn't you put it away?"

"A box won't help," Till explains. "The damage is done. We'll need a lead safe for this thing."

"You know, I'm a little leery," Havilland-Clegg admits, looking as though he's about to make a beeline for an exit. "I recovered from cancer in the last year—"

"I'm sorry to hear that, sir," Till sympathizes. "I mean, I'm glad to hear that you recovered. Sorry that you had to go through it."

"Perhaps the necklace can be taken away? I've said all I can about it."

"Do you think it tells a story?"

"No, I don't think it tells a story. Better yet, since I can't help you, perhaps I'll just remove myself back to the party. I wouldn't want to miss the octogenarian tabletop dancers."

"Hmm." The utterance that Émile Cinq-Mars emits has the odd effect of stopping everyone right where they are. As though no one will take a breath until he has revealed the objection on his mind. His sudden rise to authority countermands his earlier persona as a retiree devoted to wire. He flashes a smile, before taking it back, looking stern again, and says, "Not just yet, Ben."

Havilland-Clegg stares back at him a moment, then checks quickly with Hammond and Till. Returning his gaze to Cinq-Mars, he corrects him, "It's Bennington. Not *Ben*. At the party, I may permit a compromise or two. Here, I shall ask that you call me Mr. Havilland-Clegg. Thank you."

Cinq-Mars murmurs to himself again.

His adversary continues. "You have an interesting face, Mr. Cinq-

Mars. I'd pick you out as an academic long before imagining you to be a manufacturer of wire."

"Book by its cover," Cinq-Mars cautions him. "I'm not an academic. Although I do have a degree in animal husbandry."

"Seriously? What is that? Are you the wife? That's unkind. The midwife, then? Yet you made wire for a living? Who are you?"

"Émile Cinq-Mars is my name. But you know that."

"You don't make wire."

"Metaphorically I do."

"FBI?"

"No, sir."

"Homeland Security." Havilland-Clegg speaks the words as though they constitute a joke.

"No, sir. Although I've worked for both the FBI and your Homeland Security."

"In animal husbandry?" He snorts.

"The question of the hour, sir, is not who am I, the question is, who are you? And what have you done? What have you done, Ben?"

Their suspect hardly skips a beat. "Gentlemen, a delight and an education. Thank you for serving as the day's entertainment. You should go on tour! Unfortunately, I'll be on my way now. Ta-ta."

Although he is standing in the man's path, Cinq-Mars deigns to sit down, in one sense giving him an open exit. He sets up an obstacle to his escape route, however, by what he says next. "Palmerich has had a change of heart."

Havilland-Clegg, hands on his knees to give himself a push to his feet, stalls. "Excuse me?"

"I don't know if you are aware of this. President Palmerich has been sheltering you from us. He didn't want his old-boy benefactor being upset by the scrutiny of ragamuffin police. The sophisticate from Virginia and Washington being bothered by local yokels—not acceptable. I understand. Your money is important. Nobody denies that. Still, he's had a change of heart. Apparently, the FBI has told him a few things."

"You do realize that you're starting to tick me off."

"Brace yourself, sir, because we have a long way to go down that road."

"I'm outta here," Havilland-Clegg states.

"What a thing to say!" Cinq-Mars challenges him. "First of all, *Ben,* you haven't touched your Manhattan. I'd expect you to say I shall take my leave, or I can assure you that my departure is imminent or any one of your annoying locutions. I would not expect you to say 'I'm outta here.' Before you know it, you'll be telling us that you have to split, or head back to the 'hood."

Till and Hammond chuckle, for they know now that they've been given permission to needle their man.

"Chief Till," Havilland-Clegg instructs, his voice monotone and ir-ritated at last, "please advise this man that my alibi for the time in ques-tion is airtight."

"I haven't investigated your alibi," Till reminds him.

"It's airtight! The three of you are making fools of yourselves. Tell him. I can produce one witness after another to demonstrate that I could not have been in the clock tower while that poor girl was going through her ordeal."

"Oh, we already know that," Cinq-Mars scoffs. "You were being watched at the time, didn't you notice? By the boy who was tossed out of a car. Or is that why he was tossed out of a car? Or did something go terribly wrong with that abduction, which led to the boy being tossed out of a car? Which was it? The FBI," Cinq-Mars tells his newfound colleagues, "have located the two men who were involved, as I pre-dicted they would, actually."

Hammond whistles. "That's major," he states.

"A breakthrough," Till agrees.

Havilland-Clegg is wearing that supercilious grin again.

"What is it, Ben? You don't seem pleased that we've found the two culprits?"

"What? No. I'm delighted. In fact, if you've just arrested the two men, pin the crimes on them. They've got nothing to do with me."

"They may talk. Aren't you concerned? They may have a lot to say."

"Don't know them. They don't know me. Why should I be concerned?"

"What've they told us?" Hammond asks.

Cinq-Mars punctuates the air with a finger. "You see, that's a good question. Why didn't Benji ask that question?"

"Duh. Because I'm not a cop?"

"Possibly. Or—?"

"Or? Or because . . . I think this is a policeman's silly trick where you invent a discovery to fool your witness into believing that the jig is up. Well, I'm not guilty. I didn't kill that girl. I have absolutely nothing to admit. And yes, I will take a polygraph if you like. My alibi is simply that I was with a *lot* of other people at the time. *If* these two fellows that you say you have located said anything detrimental about me, then I'm quite certain that you put the words into their mouths. *Or* they never said anything at all because you haven't found them. You just made that up."

"Or?" Cinq-Mars asks him again.

"I have nothing to add."

"Or," Cinq-Mars explains to Till and Hammond, "Benny is not concerned about what the two men might've said because he knows that they are both quite dead. You know that, Bens, and now we know it, too. I predicted things would turn out this way."

Hammond takes out his wallet, extracts a twenty-dollar bill, and passes it over to Cinq-Mars, who holds his palm up to receive it. Havilland-Clegg observes the slow-motion transaction played out for his benefit.

"I shared that prediction with President Palmerich, as well. Now that the FBI has confirmed that it's true, he's more impressed with me, less impressed by you. Of course, I bit my tongue earlier, about what the agents said. I was permitted to listen in. A jeweler gave the FBI an excellent description of the man who commissioned the necklaces, and that description was relayed to President Palmerich. Of course, you looked different then, less hair, you had your cancer at the time and it showed, although the president remembers how you looked back then."

"Are you full of shit from the knees up or all the way down from your nuts?"

"Cute," Cinq-Mars says.

"Mind your manners, please, sir," Till suggests.

"Fuck you."

"Let's keep it civil," Hammond warns him.

"Or what?" Havilland-Clegg fires back.

"Or I'll take you in, lock you in a cell, and have my guys beat the living crap out of you. Then, we'll talk again. Your choice. Which do you prefer?"

Havilland-Clegg briefly waves his hand in midair. "I get this now," he says.

"Do you?"

"You've got nothing, so you're trying to pin it on a rich guy. No wonder our prisons are full of people who never committed a crime. All due to police incompetence and pure laziness. Well, sir. Think again. They say that money can't buy happiness but it sure as hell can buy the best lawyers in the land. By the time they're done with you, you'll be two scrambled eggs"—his eyes take in the police officers—"on toast," and they get who *toast* is supposed to be.

"Think so?" Cinq-Mars presses him.

"For starters, I know President Palmerich. He's a brilliant man. He has no reason to believe that two dead ruffians means that one of his most faithful benefactors is guilty of a crime. Get real." To Cinq-Mars he adds, "Pardon me for using the vernacular."

"There is the matter of the description."

"Lots of people with cancer look like me with cancer."

"Who said the jeweler described you?"

"Go to hell. I know what you implied."

Cinq-Mars adds, "Oh, and the FBI had one other thing to say to him. I asked the president this morning if he might permit the FBI to search through school records. He acquiesced. He's not going to stand in the way of justice if none of his money people are inconvenienced, now is he? What they found out—tell me. Can you guess?"

Havilland-Clegg makes a face and indicates that he cannot.

"Yeah," Cinq-Mars says. "It's been a while, Benji. Easy to forget these tiny loopholes in the perfect crime. Is that what you were after, by the way? The perfect crime? How to be vile and vicious and commit murder and confound the authorities into submission? Nice effort. Anyway, what the search of school files indicated—you may not have known that the archives carried such information; they do, and we hired a number of students to help us cull through the records on microfiche. Old technology is slow. They culled the records on behalf of the bureau, and those records indicate that when you were at Dowbiggin, a long time ago, during the Winter Festival, when the public is permitted to go up the clock tower, for three years running you were entrusted to be the Guardian of the Tower, which means that you were in possession of the keys. Do you remember that?"

"Nice try," Havilland-Clegg tells him, although he does seem more subdued now. "Those keys are not the kind that can be duplicated, and of course I returned my copies."

"Oh, please, a young man of your wealth and cunning, you could have had the keys cut. Unscrupulous people exist in the world, some are locksmiths. Don't tell me you haven't met an unscrupulous person willing to break a rule for cash."

"Why are we even having this conversation? Check out my alibi! And seriously, do you think I planned a murder thirty years ago?"

"I don't give you that much credit, no. I think you planned escapades in the clock tower, with your private keys, while you were a rambunctious student, and over the years. Your personal den of iniquity. Or maybe you used it as your own private study hall, who knows?"

"As I said. My alibi is airtight. This conversation is over. Talk to my lawyers. I'll bring in a truckload."

"You were being followed that night, Benny! By the boy who was thrown from a moving car! We've interviewed him. We know where you were when the girl was raped. We know where you were when she was murdered. Stop fretting about that, please."

"This is ridiculous. Can I go now?"

"Nobody's holding you," Cinq-Mars tells him, and the man stands. "Of course, you have to understand that whether you are guilty or not, you are going to be accused of raping the poor girl's corpse, which occurred at a later hour when you have no such alibi, unless it's being alone in a room, and even if you are entirely innocent of the crime, it is going to stick to you like glue, like Krazy Glue, that accusation, and you know how hard that stuff can be to get off. Intimate relations with a corpse. Chances are, the stench of that will hover around you for life. You might want to consider talking to us now to see if you can't wiggle free and persuade us otherwise."

Havilland-Clegg stands over him as though he's been walloped by a telephone pole. Teetering, he absorbs the blow.

"Seriously," Cinq-Mars puts to him, "how willing are you to take that polygraph now that you know what will be the key question? Did you rape the corpse, Bens?"

In apparent slow motion, he sits down again.

An innocent man, Cinq-Mars believes, would not have bothered. While he's still relying on gut instinct, and evidence that only barely qualifies as circumstantial, although it's growing, he feels more certain than ever that he has his man. This far, anyway, his one lie has worked, as the FBI has no report from a jeweler. Not yet. He got away with that one, as he believed that only Havilland-Clegg could have designed and overseen the creation of the necklace.

"That's a terrible thing you said," Havilland-Clegg contends. "A sordid accusation like that will carry repercussions in public."

"I realize that I just threatened you, Ben. I accept that it is your pre-rogative to threaten me back. Tit for tat. A retaliation. I'm not an officer of the law, nor even a citizen of this country, so good luck with whatever legal maneuver you have in mind to come and get me. No, no," Cinq-Mars says, interrupting Havilland-Clegg before he can get a word in edgewise. "I'm giving you this one. You don't need to object. I expect you to be angry with me. As I said before, we have a long way to go down the road toward me ticking you off. Or to put it another way, the road to your perdition is long and bumpy, and yet, we're going down it. That is our final destination."

Havilland-Clegg stares back at him. "The road . . . to my perdition? Gentlemen," he asks the others, "who's the madman? What's he doing here? The road to my perdition? What fucking train to the nuthouse did you leap off of, Cinq-Mars?"

The former detective nods, as though agreeing with the man's objec-tion. "You're right," he says. "Are you a religious man, Benji? Probably not. Most killers lack both an efficient conscience and the spiritual consciousness that's required to be a religious man. I am, oddly enough, exactly that. Religious. I know! Incongruous, isn't it? In my profession. In this day and age. It takes all kinds, even to be a detective."

"That's what you are."

"A detective, yes. Retired, though. That part, at least, is true. A retired detective and a religious man. I apologize, you see, for my language. *The road to perdition.* You're right. Way too formal, too orthodox, too *religious*, for the circumstances. After all, we're not here to consign you to hell, sir, or even to pass judgment. We're here merely to compile evidence sufficient to see you convicted and incarcerated. For life. I don't suppose New Hampshire has the death penalty?"

Hammond confirms that his state does not.

"What a shame. Life imprisonment, then. That's what we're here for. I'll retract the bit about perdition. Not my domain."

Havilland-Clegg has gone both cocky and amused. "Oh, bring it on, sir. Show me what you've got. Tell me how you're going to convince a jury to convict an innocent man, with an airtight alibi, of a crime he did not commit when that man is rich, with great lawyers in his corner—that's inevitable—*and* who is a veritable pillar of the community. You've got your work cut out for you, I'd say."

Cinq-Mars returns his amused manner. "I knew you'd enjoy this. Why else tempt us by introducing yet another necklace to the afternoon party? You're here, in part, for the sport. That's a given, and that's a weakness I'll freely exploit. If," he finishes, and lets the word linger in the air between them.

Havilland-Clegg cannot resist. "If?" he inquires.

"If . . . if you don't mind," Cinq-Mars says.

"Why should I mind? Fire away. Give it your best shot."

"Thank you, Ben boy. I shall."

He waits while Havilland-Clegg sips.

"Religion is a strange beast, don't you agree? Immediately, people always think in terms of an orthodoxy, or a fixed set of beliefs. Yet the history of spirituality indicates that it's in continuous flux. Pretty much like everything else in the universe. We keep learning. Many would like to stand still, no doubt. Say this, do that, call it a religion, brand it as being the truth, and if you don't believe it, rot in hell. Nevertheless, the history of spirituality shows that change occurs, and when it does the era of change can be confusing to people."

"I feel like I'm back in school. At a lecture. I liked school. Not the lectures."

"Touché. I'll cut to the chase. Right now, we're going through an-other sea change. What science brings to our knowledge of the uni-verse boggles the mind. What we forget, of course, is that that's exactly what happens anytime spiritual development occurs—the mind is boggled. Make no mistake, the understanding that's arriving about the universe is spiritually transformative, for those inclined to take it that way. Usually, when a new religion comes along, it attempts to obliterate what's gone before, and that's happening again. History is repeating itself. Monotheism obliterates polytheism, Christianity seeks to obliter-ate paganism, and so on. That's all political, you understand, and what was previous survives in its way. The previous is incorporated to a certain extent within the new. You see, the past becomes manifest in the present in interesting ways."

"You are going on about this why?"

Cinq-Mars opens his hands in a posture of togetherness. "Because, Benny, it's fascinating. Don't you think? Like you, I get distracted be-ing at a university. I start having big ideas. Maybe it's the books every-where, the discussions, the very idea of an institution dedicated to learning and evaluating and to purposefully challenging the mind. That's all glorious stuff. Of course, people might think that I'm trying to distract my suspect's mind by talking like this. It's true that I do that sort of thing. The more intelligent the person, the more complex are the notions that arise, in large measure so that I can squirm my way under the hood, and mess with the person's head. Not to you, Ben. I'm not doing that to you."

For once, Havilland-Clegg gulps his Manhattan. He wets his lips as he puts the glass down. "Or are you?" he asks. "Doing that here?"

"You're right," Cinq-Mars muses. "You're right! You're clever. I could be. Maybe I can't help myself. Maybe it comes from wondering why you would introduce the necklace to the gathering this afternoon. To experience that, to better understand it, I introduced you to an as-pect of my method. I'm saying to you, I'm messing with your mind to get under the hood, and you—for the moment, indulge me, let's say that it was you—did you not have a girl today wear the talisman to show off your *power*. Your attitude is: *I show you what I can do, and I can still do it, because you can't stop me.* You show me what you can do, because you don't think you can be stopped. We're a couple of egomaniacs, Ben! Do you think?"

Havilland-Clegg seems to be getting his footing, and recovers. "I see. You're messing with me. What good did it do you?"

"What good did it do you? The necklace? Here today?"

"Ah, but it has nothing to do with me, you see."

The comment provokes a smile from the detective. "Yes, Benny, and my interest in cosmology and spirituality has nothing to do with you. Except for this. We understand now that all carbon forms, not just people, carry knowledge that they pass along. Evolution and all that. Matter carries and transmits knowledge on many levels including the molecular. Through atoms and microbes and other elaborate and invisible forces, matter learns as it progresses. The quantum of our personal and paltry physiques carries knowledge! Mind-boggling. You, Bennington Havilland-Clegg, transport knowledge, every atom in you does, and my job is to extract that knowledge, to reveal it to the light of day."

That supercilious smirk is back. Perfect.

"Go ahead, Cinq-Mars, tell me what you know."

"If you insist. So you know, Ben, when they leave today and find themselves off campus, wondering where you are, Mr. Hanson Parker from New York and Mr. Al McBride from Kentucky will be placed under arrest and questioned at length. Be comforted, knowing that you're not in this alone."

The smugness abruptly vanishes from his visage, and his skin tone is pallid. This is the first mention that his possible coconspirators are known to the police.

"I know that you wrote the directive. *Breached Run!* Trouble is, the perfect crime becomes imperfect here. The message was meant for the boy, for Vernon Colchester. Did you know? That's why he never showed up at his safe house, to be caught with the shot and butchered body of Malory Earle. I suppose your thugs were going to bop him on the head. Smear his hands and clothes in the woman's blood. Report him. He didn't get to the tree on time, where messages were exchanged. Professor Toomey got the message instead and I think he was flummoxed by it. A kid disciple of his says something has been breached and he's supposed to run? What's that about? Ah, but if the boy had received the message, that would mean his mentor was either in a jam or merely wanted to test him, so he'd run to the safe house. That's how things went awry there."

Havilland-Clegg permits his hands to rise slowly. "Safe house? Messages in a tree stump? Is this supposed to mean something to me?"

"Tree bark."

"Whatever. This has nothing to do with me."

"Of course it does, Benny. Didn't you recruit someone to spy on Vernon Colchester, to figure out why he was spying on you?"

"Who did I recruit?"

"Seriously? Do you think I don't know?"

"If I don't, how do you?"

"Addie Langford."

"Who's that? Oh. Oh. The dead girl. I see. She was my recruit, was she? Precious."

"That's how you gained her confidence," Cinq-Mars reveals, and it's questionable as to who is listening more keenly, the accused or the attending officers of the law. "That's why she revealed Vernon's secrets to you. That's probably why she had an affair with Vernon in the first place. Boys weren't her thing, you know, appearances to the contrary. That was how you were able to send her up a clock tower to meet a stranger, her future employer, she thought, without putting up a fight. Why did she carry on with Vernon, then break his heart, when she'd rather find a woman to love? She liked her hetero identity, always talked about her boys, then took her girlfriends to ground because they mattered more to her. Or maybe she was genuinely bisexual. The thing is, she was being recruited by *you*, just as Vernon was being recruited by Toomey."

"And what, pray tell, was I recruiting her for?"

"What you told her is between the two of you and doesn't interest me. You seduced her with an adventurous idea for a life of undercover work that captured her imagination. Young people are often susceptible to that sort of offer. You were the person she was relying on to give her a job. She probably crossed the bounds by telling her parents that she had a job lined up. All hush-hush, mysterious. As to what you were *actually* recruiting her for, that's obvious. To die. To be your victim."

Havilland-Clegg laughs a little, sips his drink again. "If it were not for the sordid accusations you could bring upon me, which I admit give me pause, I'd almost enjoy being in court while you attempt to make such a case."

"You won't. Enjoy it. Trust me. As we said, Homeland Security is involved, as well as the FBI. Can you honestly say that you and your pals haven't left a digital trail behind? In what sour, perverted little chat room did you find one another? The small, frail, hand-shaking diplomatic, now financial adviser, with the strength of a mouse, the runt of the mouse litter, too weak to fulfill his rape fantasies without help. The tire man from Kentucky with the strength of an ox who wants to murder women, yet who isn't willing to do it on his own because he has too much to lose and he's smart enough to know that he's not smart enough to get away with it. And then there's you, the genteel heir, who could, if you wanted to, pay for sex in any of its myriad forms. Except for the one form you desire most. Your bout with cancer creates urgency, life is short and unpredictable, if you're going to do what you most want to do then you have to get on with it. You don't have it in you, nor do you have the desire, thankfully, to kill or to rape a living, breathing, fighting-back woman. Any physical engagement with a living person makes you ill. But you can now indulge your deepest desire, to love in your own sick way, a girl, a beautiful woman, who is comfortably, conveniently, dead. Not breathing. Inert. A woman who does not respond to your touch in strange and frightening ways. You arrange to have one man abduct, and another man rape, leaving each of you with airtight alibis if the crime is viewed as a single event committed by one person. Then the first man returns to commit the murder. In this scenario, you are left with the remains to abuse to your heart's content."

"It wasn't like that."

"Of course not. You have a different aesthetic. You doll her up, dress her up, put on her makeup, grace her throat with a talisman as tribute to your own brilliance and possession of her. Perhaps to hide the ligature marks, the only imperfection."

"That's not what I meant. I meant that I wasn't involved."

"You rape the dead, Benny. It's what you have always wanted to do, and now you've done it. Do you care to explain yourself, if you can?

You're not spiritually inclined. I am, and Benji, you may feel the need to unburden yourself of your loathsome desires."

For a few moments, the combativeness of the man's nature is evident, lurking under the skin, ready to jump. He takes a moment to regain his self-control, and with it, reverts to being smug.

"What?" Cinq-Mars asks. Seated beside him, Chief Till has been sitting back, observing this play out, beginning to grasp how the whole dire crime was orchestrated. Yet he's aware that the premise has holes.

Their suspect brings one up. "I'll grant you that your theory is elaborate, Cinq-Mars. I'll admit that what frightens me here is that it just may be compelling enough to have people believe it. Fair-weather friends, for instance. This story goes out, I may not be trusted again. I'll grant you the power that you have over me at the moment. However—" He pauses for effect. "I point out again, that the total lack of hard evidence won't allow this *innuendo*—it's no better than that, you're aware of that yourself—your innuendo won't pass muster in a court of law, if your charges even get that far before being tossed. I am innocent of these outrageous accusations, Cinq-Mars. What you're doing is hoping that you can scare a guilty man into a confession. That won't happen, not because I'm not scared, you do frighten me, but because I happen to be completely, and utterly, and totally innocent."

In receiving the statement, Cinq-Mars rocks his shoulders, neck, and head slightly from side to side, and checks with his two colleagues. Then all three stare back at their suspect.

"Benny, no one is. Innocent," Cinq-Mars attests. "Captain Hammond has a request."

Havilland-Clegg looks at the trooper.

"Would you kindly show us your elbows?" Hammond asks.

"What? No. Why? I'm not showing you anything."

"Sir, I can easily have the sleeves of your jacket and shirt cut off, if you prefer."

That threat hangs in the air a moment.

Cinq-Mars says, "I'm pretty sure we can make it easier on you, Ben. Show us only your right elbow. I remember the circle made on the platform by the forensics team. For the live rape, I believe her hands were tied to the railing, so we know the angle of the body. A jury will be impressed by these details. Since you were dealing with a dead body, it's likely that you untied her. To allow her to be more loving with you. But still, it's in a certain position. Your right elbow should suffice. Ben. If you please."

He takes his time. Removing his jacket, he folds it over his seat back, careful not to create any creases. He unfastens a cuff link on his shirt, which he tucks into his jacket pocket for safekeeping. Then he says to Cinq-Mars, "It's Bennington. You can call me Mr. Havilland-Clegg."

"I know. Speak the truth, I'll use it."

The man's right elbow is exposed. Hammond leans in close to it.

Cinq-Mars, as well. "Partially healed. Only partially."

"A skimmed elbow is not a sign of guilt," Havilland-Clegg remarks.

Without him noticing, Hammond has taken out a penknife, which he flashes quickly and takes a speck of skin and a dribble of blood from the man's elbow.

"Hey! What the fuck! You can't do that!"

"We just did. Relax. Elbows don't hurt. Anyway, if you're innocent, your DNA will be your best defense. You only need to be concerned if you're guilty. This isn't for the courts. Just for us."

He has no argument to prevail in the matter, and the man unrolls his sleeve. Before he attaches the cuff link again, Cinq-Mars asks to see it. He examines it under a lamp. Then hands it back to him and watches as the man attaches it.

"Berman topaz," Cinq-Mars says. "From Brazil. That's the one stone that makes no particular sense in the necklace. The stone in your cuff link is the same. Berman topaz."

"Coincidence."

"Hardly. It fortifies the body against disease. You've been feeling the need in the past year to take help wherever it can be found. The rest of the necklace is a paean to love, death, and crossing over. My expert calls it a map. Maybe. We might study its geographic notes to see if they conform to times in your life. I think it's about death, and love, and love in death, loving death, and equating death with love. I guess I was wrong, huh? You're a spiritual man in your own way. In an evil way."

He sits again and, with a rather stunning display of confidence, sips from his drink. "I could use another."

"Enjoy. It may be your last ever."

"I think not, Cinq-Mars. Let's say, for the sake of argument, as absurd as your argument may be, that I am guilty of what you're accusing me of."

"Sure. Let's say that."

"Which means I'm guilty of abusing a corpse. I agree, that puts a dent in the social calendar. Fewer invitations. And yet, ask yourself, how much time do I get for that? Five years? Max? Three? First offense, how about fourteen months? Ah, with a great lawyer? Thirty days and time served. Time off for good behavior. Community service?"

"Conspiracy to commit murder," Hammond adds, a remark greeted by a scoff.

"Yeah. Good luck proving anything close to that. My lawyers against your district attorneys. What are the Vegas odds, do you think?"

"Ben," Cinq-Mars advises him, "and you'll be Ben with me until you speak the truth, I understand that that was your plan from the get-go. McBride murders both women, one for you, one for his own pleasure. Parker kills Toomey. You gave him an assignment. That's the price to pay for raping a beautiful young woman if he wants to get away with it, scot-free. Squeeze a trigger. Put a bullet in Toomey's brain. He's all paid up."

"If this—Mr. Parker, is it?—killed this guy Toomey, that's on his head, not mine."

Cinq-Mars rocks his shoulders as though taking that into consideration. "Yeah. He only got him in the throat anyway, but still, he did his part. It's on his head. Lets you off the hook. Agreed. You're in the clear, except for the abuse-of-corpse issue."

"Hypothetically, if I'm convicted on that bogus charge, if things don't go my way, I'll probably be out in six months. Worst case."

"Hypothetically. Give or take. Yet the matter has gone awry, Ben. You didn't pin suspicion on Vernon Colchester, as planned. That was meant to cover your three asses for as long as you were up here in the north country. You were forced to put the necklace into play at the cocktail party, it wasn't only for ego. Apart from everything else, Plan

B, you cooked up a conspiracy where a couple of thugs did it. Pin the blame on two dead ex-cons. A good lawyer can swing that if you got into trouble. After all, you had the thugs deliver the necklace the other day ahead of the cocktail party, you made sure we picked that up on a camera, then you had them throw a boy from a speeding vehicle. They were being set up, all part of your perfect crime. That's done with now."

"Your avid imagination."

"You don't like my theory?"

"Doesn't hold water."

Cinq-Mars chuckles. "What does, hey? After all the rain we've had. Okay, another theory goes like this. You put the necklace on the neck of another young woman to tantalize the senses of your coconspirators. How's that? Keeps them interested. They get keen on a next time and that keeps them under your thumb today. You bastard. Of course, that's not going to happen now. Benny, I'm going to suggest to my esteemed colleagues that they pursue murder charges on the three of you."

"Fat chance," Havilland-Clegg determines. He bolsters his opinion with a grunt.

"McBride," Cinq-Mars continues, "for Addie Langford and Malory Earle, Hanson for Lars Toomey, and you, Benny boy, for your two henchmen who have gone to their negligible reward. Before you bring out that smug, very unattractive grin, may I inform you of something that you don't yet know? For a change of pace?"

The man stares back at him, confident still. "Just don't bore me."

"I promise. Benny, when you arrived back at your little hideout in the woods, one of the men recorded your arrival on his smartphone. He spoke into it as well. *If shit happens here, this guy did it.* That's what he said. I don't know why he didn't trust you, Ben. Do you? What possible cause would he have? He recorded that message, took his little video of you showing up, time stamped, that was a bonus, then he put the phone out of sight. My God, but that's going to impress a jury, don't you think? You'll like this part, too, it may be a comfort to you. The index finger of his right hand was on the trigger of his gun. No kidding. When we found him. Good thing you shot him first, Benji, because he was ready for you, he was wary. He nearly saved us a lot of trouble. Fortunately—for you, not so much for us—he hesitated."

The four men remain seated in a circle, and for a full two minutes, no one utters a word. The silence seems to fill the space with a sense of grief mixed with jubilation, by some, and by a joy that now bleeds into an agony for one among them.

"And the second guy? You'd already shot him. He was lying in plastic in the trunk of your rental," Cinq-Mars says.

He rises. He leans over Havilland-Clegg, placing his hands on the armrests on both sides of him. He has not commonly given suspects a verbal comeuppance. This time is different, a privilege of his retirement, perhaps. He's no longer governed by any professional code of conduct, or by a superior's guiding hand. He's wanted to give many criminals a talking-to in his day. Now's his chance.

"What was the problem with you, Benji?" he taunts him, his voice a notch above a whisper.

They're nose to nose.

"Tired of blow-up dolls?"

"You turd," the killer talks back.

"Move too much, did they? Squiggled around? Bounced?"

"Get away from me."

"Was it like they were breathing? The way they moved? Was that getting to be too much for you? Too much like the real thing?"

"Get off me. You're an imbecile. You'll never know what we— What we had."

"What were you going to say? What you what?"

"Shut up."

"What you what? Say it!"

Havilland-Clegg thinks it over, then speaks calmly, even thoughtfully. "What we shared. All right? What do you know?"

"Oh, I'm missing out, am I? Go ahead. Tell me what you *shared* with a dead girl."

Havilland-Clegg looks away, agitated again, set to strike.

"She was dead, Benji. Don't you get that yet? Your great passion was for death. You were mated with death. A real woman? Life? For you? Impossible. What was it, an effect of the cancer, couldn't make it anymore with a blow-up doll? They weren't perfect enough for you anymore? I'm curious. Do you own a blow-up harem? Keep them in a closet? Or under your bed? Is that it? Did you pay girls to do it with you without moving? They'd always make a sound? Or breathe? You got greedier, wanted the more perfect doll."

"Shut up with that."

"Why?"

"Shut up with that!"

"Tell me what it was. What did you share?"

"You'll never know. You're not the least bit worthy to know like that. You'll be ignorant forever, like the rest of the world."

"Too much bounce in your blow-up dolls? For that, a girl had to die."

"Up yours. Or is that too parochial a phrase for you?"

"Go ahead. Tell us what you shared raping a dead girl."

"SHUT UP!" Havilland-Clegg is on his feet, knocking the taller man back a step.

"What's the matter, Ben? Put off by the word? Rape? You rape the dead. That's your thing. Do you honestly think it was something else?"

"You don't know fuck-all! I saved that girl!"

"Oh! You saved her?"

"I rescued her! I saved her from this fucking world! You'll never know what ecstasy is! You don't know the meaning of the word. You're not capable. You'll never know what we shared!"

"Tell me. I'm all ears."

"Fuck you."

"Tell me!" he yells. "Now! What was great? What did you share?"

"I said fuck you!"

"TELL ME!"

"Rapture!" He holds his gaze and his smirk returns. "Go ahead. Laugh. Imbecile. You'll never know the meaning of the word. Few ever will. We shared rapture. What do you know anyway? About anything real."

Cinq-Mars shakes his head slightly. "No, Benji. She was dead. She never knew you were there. She shared nothing, absolutely nothing with you. Not even a word. You had more communication with your blow-up dolls. Though I'm glad to hear—rapture, huh?—that you're religious, too." Cinq-Mars lowers his voice. "Did you get that?" he asks, but he's no longer talking to Havilland-Clegg, and the man looks around, confused.

Coming to his feet, Chief Till shows off his mobile device. "Thanks for sharing," he says.

"Abuse of a corpse, Benji," Cinq-Mars tells him. "That was your escape hatch. Problem is, that hatch won't stay open. We have video of you showing up to kill that man in the woods and now we have your recorded confession on the other charges. To top it off, we're just beginning to collect evidence. Yet, you still don't believe in God? You must. Rapture? Seriously? Come on."

Captain Hammond is the last to rise. He'll be professional now, and resorts to being polite. "Mr. Bennington Havilland-Clegg, turn around, please, sir. You will cross your hands behind your back."

The man looks at him, glares at Cinq-Mars, then numbly complies.

TWENTY-SIX

Fair-weather clouds sail effortlessly across a bright azure sky, intermittently casting a welcomed shade upon the cemetery. This is a day for funerals. Sandra Cinq-Mars has buried her mother, and later a memorial service will be held on campus for Addie Langford, although her body is to be returned to Michigan. Malory Earle will be eulogized and buried across the river in White River Junction. Rumor has it that a jazz band will perform. Partly for that reason, a diverse group of people are planning to attend. She had many friends. Professor Toomey's body has been claimed, although no one can say by whom. Neither a service nor a burial has been arranged for him in New Hampshire. His nearest relative, who did not claim the body, is a distant cousin who suggested to one of Special Agent Hartopp's agents that perhaps he should be buried with his lover in Vermont. That hasn't been worked out with Malory Earle's family as yet. The bodies of the two dead thugs have undergone autopsies and, unlike the others, await the claim of a relative, a friend, or an associate. If none comes forward, they will be interred without ceremony at the state's expense.

Sandra and Émile catch a moment alone. Upon departing the house in the morning they've stuck close to each other, yet private moments are rare. He stretches an arm over her shoulder to give her a hug, for about the twentieth time.

"You okay?"

She seems distant. "Sure. Not having Mom at the other end of a phone line seems strange. Still unreal, I guess. Too real. I don't know what it is."

"Takes time."

"I was thinking . . . in an odd way, I finally feel like an adult, and also like a kid again. You know? Like a little girl who's missing her mom. This is hard, Émile. It's not sad, it's time. Still, I'm sad anyway. This is hard. I suppose it helps to know that my grief is nothing compared to what Addie's poor parents are going through."

"Hmm," Cinq-Mars says.

"You don't agree?"

He has to work through what he's feeling himself. "I do agree. Of course. But . . . this isn't about them, is it? It's about you. Your grief is perfectly natural, understandable, also it's *yours*. You have to go through it. I don't want you to slough it off now because someone is suffering more, only to find it working through you in a different way later on. That won't be good. Someone is always suffering more. You're hurting. I know it sounds like a trite thing to say: You have a right to grieve. Along with death, that's natural, too."

She nods. She understands.

He shakes his head again.

"What now?" Sandra asks.

He stops shaking his head to emphasize his words with hand gestures. "Part of it is, you're being stoic. While you are strong, you're not naturally stoic. I'm worried about you, San. The other thing, a chunk of this falls on me. I don't have the right to pontificate here. I haven't given you the attention you've needed over the last few days. Truth be told, I'm feeling guilty about that."

"Émile, please."

"It's true."

"I've missed you, too. Look, we have our troubles. I'm not holding recent days against you. Okay? You were justified. I always knew you were with me. Never doubted that. Besides, I had good sister-time. Niece-time, too. What I need you to understand is, under the circumstances, this will also sound trite, I wouldn't want it any other way."

This time, their hug is mutual. He draws her shoulders toward him, she pulls his waist in close to her side.

"What'll we do?" she whispers, still holding him.

"Stay together," he suggests. His breath on her ear.

"Okay," she whispers, as simply as that, and it feels like a resolution, a new start. "Where?"

"I like it here," he admits. "The mountains. The rivers. The fishing. The hiking. The fields. I enjoy the towns. Some of the people."

"Only some?"

"Oh, sweetie, with me, that's the way it is. Staying here doesn't have to mean your mom's house. A farm is a lot to take on, as we know. There are other properties. We can look around. Take our time with that."

"Or go home?" she suggests.

He's a bit startled, and pulls back to look more closely at her. "To Quebec?"

"Don't sound surprised. It's been my home for a while, too. We don't have to stay on the farm. We can look around there. Like you said. We can take our time."

He touches her neck right below her left ear as he gazes at her. "But stay together?" He wants to hear her confirmation repeated.

She knows he's asking for what is large, definitive, and uncompromising. She can see in his gaze that he, too, has had enough of their troubles. "It's true, Émile. I'm tired of working it through. Worrying about it. Fretting. I'm sick of the spat. Tripping over ourselves at home. I'm exhausted. These last few days, on my own, with everything, Mom dying, my emotions have been right on the surface. I'm not used to that. In a way, I needed this." She brushes his cheek with a kiss. "I've been thinking about things and talking to my sister—getting drunk with her, which probably didn't hurt." She smiles. "It's not only that I'm tired of our difficulties, Émile. That's not the only thing. I feel I've come out the other side. Maybe it's the age difference that hit me unexpectedly. I needed to get through a few things. Especially now that you're supposed to be retired. What a lie that's turned out to be! Brother! Still, I've come through stuff on my own without you and the odd thing is, more than ever I want us to be together. Even if it means you're off chasing killers— don't give me that look. Come on. Face it. It's inevitable. Murder traipses along beside you like a plague. Fine. That's how we'll live."

She's half serious and half teasing him. The part that counts most— wanting to remain with him—prompts them to kiss.

People are moving toward the couple on the curving, rising path through the cemetery, and while the kiss pleases the onlookers, they have no concept of its singular importance in the life of this pair. They cheerfully interrupt. Sandra is gently drawn away to other discussions and reminiscences. Many folks will be coming back to the house, the young graduates are soon to prepare for Addie Langford's memorial. Having had his wife taken from his arms at a decisive moment, Émile sees that others are now set to overtake him, beginning with Special Agent Michael Hartopp.

"Bone to pick with you," he says. A smile may not be on his lips but Émile can see it in his eyes.

"What else is new?"

"The grapevine tells me that the FBI authorized a scrutiny of school records. That you had students foraging through Bennington Havilland-Clegg's history at Dowbiggin on our say-so. That's a crock, Émile. Once again my name was taken in vain by you. I don't hire amateurs. I authorized no such forensic study."

"Michael, consider, the girls wouldn't be permitted to look through the files without your official request, I merely authorized it on your behalf, knowing that deep in your heart you'd agree."

"Émile, seriously, you never asked. And you didn't ask because I would probably have said no, notwithstanding whatever the hell goes on in the depths of my heart."

"Didn't want you to feel conflicted, Special Agent. I know what it's like to breathe bureaucratic air. A man can gag on the lack of pure oxygen. Time was of the essence."

Hartopp extends his hand. "Speaking of time, I'm off. A plane's waiting. It's been a slice, Émile. One day we should do this without dead bodies lying around."

"We must. I appreciate your help when they're close by, though."

Émile feels a pang, a sadness to see him go. The man's headed back to work, and he wishes he could do that, too. Hop on a plane and be back on a case.

In his wake, Captain Hammond ambles over. He seems a bit shy to speak what's on his mind and nudges a stone on the ground between them. Cinq-Mars assumes that he has a bone to pick, and is surprised when it's the contrary.

"What you said once, that we might be neighbors one day." He reaches down and picks up the stone, examines it in his fingers. "Just wanted to say, I hope that comes to pass. You should move here, Cinq-Mars."

"What's gotten into you, Hammond? You want to keep an eye on me? See me get my just deserts?"

"Sure thing. Why not?" The stone holds no meaning for him. He flips it a short distance down the path. "In the meantime, if some weird case comes up, we can have a beer and talk it over. I'm looking good on this case. Not saying I'm not giving you all the credit, maybe I'm taking a few brownie points for myself. Anyway, you know what it's like being a cop."

"Meaning?"

"It's not easy."

They make eye contact, and for the first time a genuine connection passes between them. They will never be more emotional than that with each other, which Cinq-Mars confirms by giving the trooper's elbow a quick tap. Another reason to stay, he's thinking.

Till ambles over to join them. A bit tentative, he's concerned that he might be interrupting. Both men welcome him, putting him at ease.

Cinq-Mars asks, "How've you guys come along with the other two?"

"Easy pickings," Hammond is proud to say. "Hanson Parker is under the impression that his life is in ruins. No remorse. Not a speck. He's devastated that he got caught. Blames our boy Ben. Can't stop getting back at him. Can't figure out why he had to show the necklace off at a cocktail party. He thinks that did them in."

"It helped do them in," Cinq-Mars believes.

"I ran both your theories by him. That Havilland-Clegg was trying to pin the matter on his goons. He didn't bite. Then I suggested that he wanted to entice him, to induce him to stay interested, and I detected a change in him. No admission, an awareness. As though it was dawning on him that he might be the author of his own demise."

Although he seems to agree, Cinq-Mars is focusing on other things. "Benny boy's genius seduced his stablemates. Happens all the time. It's not true genius, in my book. He mistakes complexity for genius. He wanted his life's work to be a Gordian knot. The more elaborate the crime, the less chance any dumb cop can figure it out. That was the plan. The others bought into it and, of course, Ben knew how to keep them onside."

Hammond has been wondering about things. "They didn't have to kill Malory Earle? That was to be complex?"

"Hmm," Cinq-Mars comments. They detect that he disagrees.

"Yeah, I get that," Till concurs, as if he has a new thought, and both men look at him to continue. "Captain Hammond interviewed Parker. I took McBride. He wanted to show that he was the tough nut in the clubhouse. That he'd never break. That's his weak point. His pride."

"In what way?" Cinq-Mars asks.

"Parker and Havilland-Clegg met at a financial services convention, see. They met in a bar when they were already two sheets to the wind. Neither expected to ever see the other again and it came out when they were hammered that Parker fantasized about rape. The idea got him off. He needed his victim tied up and incapacitated first because he can't handle the rough stuff himself, he's not strong enough or fit enough to wrestle with a frightened woman. Benny boy let it slip that he wanted his victim dead first. After that, they let it drop, according to Parker. But as the years went by they circled around each other. I'm getting this from what Parker told Trooper Hammond and what Ben told you. I passed it by McBride. Tough nut had to say it. That he was the linch-pin. That they needed him to do their dirty work. They needed him to kill."

"What about the abduction?" Cinq-Mars wonders.

"Addie was given a key," Hammond explains. "She trusted Benny boy enough to go up the clock tower on her own with him. A secret meeting about a secret career. Instead, McBride was waiting for her."

"But he didn't kill her immediately."

"His job: subdue her, incapacitate her, gag her, tie her up. Then take off the necklace she was given, place it in the library in a certain spot for Hanson Parker to know that the coast was clear, that their victim was bound and gagged. They never met during the process. That way they were always in three places at once. Part of the plan to keep themselves neck-deep in alibis. After Parker did his dirty work he planted the necklace again to let McBride know it was time for him to return. He goes back and kills her. The deal is, he has to kill her tidily. No mess, no bother. Then dispose of her old clothes."

"Benny could lay claim to a pristine corpse," Cinq-Mars puts in.

"Exactly," Till concurs. "McBride is into slaughter. He does the tidy killing as a favor to the other two, but gets to do his thing with Malory Earle. Like you said, Parker had to shoot Toomey. That was easy. They'd met the previous year. Toomey pretended to befriend him while trying to find out what the three secret pals were up to. He answered his door, Parker shot him, nothing physical required, a bullet to the head that went through the throat. You thought he didn't shoot him again because he was a pro, Émile! Ah, but the great detective screwed up. What you didn't know, Parker badly had to piss all of a sudden. His nerves went south. Toomey gurgled and croaked while Parker was in the bathroom."

Cinq-Mars poses a different question, although he assumes he knows the answer. "Why Malory? Why not someone else?"

"She'd be in the way, up where the clock tower entrance is located. Cleaning. They had their comings and goings all planned. McBride removed her early, violated her in her own home early, then left her with a necklace around her neck to confuse the issue, to confound us."

"Which it did," Cinq-Mars allows. "Especially when it wasn't there. You've gone over the film from Dowbiggin? What does that show?"

He learns that the men traded clothes. McBride arrived in one disguise and departed in another. Parker showed up in another outfit then left looking like McBride did when he first came in. Then Havilland-Clegg went out the door looking like Parker. They knew how to avoid the cameras except for the odd glimpse, and the disguises initially worked to confuse their arrivals and departures.

Hammond assures them both that before this goes to trial they'll have run down every detail and timed each second. For now, it's clear what the men did and how. A year ago, Havilland-Clegg noticed the boy lurking on the periphery, spying on him. He returned the favor. He spied on Vernon. Had him tracked. He traced back the lad's connection to Toomey. Rather than abort their mission he chose to include both in his plan. When he figured out Toomey's role, apparently by using Parker's old contacts in the State Department, he duplicated his ruse, only for personal, rather than governmental, effect. They tested several young female recruits. First, they asked them to seek intimate secrets on different professors they chose, and Addie Langford won that contest by sleeping with her target, Professor Edith Shedden. After that, they directed her attentions to Vernon Colchester and discovered how things worked between him and Professor Toomey. Addie found out that they exchanged notes placed inside a tree's bark, and the two of them never discerned that their correspondence was being monitored the whole time. What she gleaned was passed on to Bennington Havilland-Clegg. She knew enough to do everything in secret, delighted that she was outfoxing another pair of wannabe spies. Havilland-Clegg not only figured out Vernon's spy education, he was provided with the ideal victim, one who was secretive, loyal, and trusting. Not to mention beautiful. Addie Langford was doomed. When he explained the workings and ramifications to his cohorts, McBride and Parker were both dazzled, they believed they had thrown in with a master magician, neither could imagine being caught. Both reveled in the prospect of unleashing their personal villainy with impunity, not only this once, but on down through time.

"They planned to rape and kill again," Cinq-Mars says.

"Repeatedly," Till confirms.

"Of course," Hammond points out, "once McBride and Parker started yapping, Benny boy couldn't hold back his contempt for both of them. Called them out for their cowardice and stupidity. He even referred to them as 'sick,' as if he's in the pink of mental health. I asked him if he didn't think he was a little sick in the head himself."

Cinq-Mars smiles imagining that exchange. "How did Ben respond?"

"Unloaded on me. Every cuss imaginable. I told him, I didn't think his language was worthy of a Dowbiggin alumnus."

They're quiet, mulling things through. Till sums up his general feeling about it all. "What a world."

Hammond concurs, "Yeah. The world we live in."

Cinq-Mars murmurs, "Hmm."

They look at him. They know he doesn't fully agree.

Sandra is returning up the walk in the company of her sister and niece. The men wait for her, then shake her hand and kiss her cheek and utter a few final words of sympathy before taking their leave. Hand in hand, Émile walks on with his wife. The other women follow a step behind. A reception is on tap back at the house, then two more services. Neither Sandra nor Émile are feeling as though they can do this, and might beg off. Up ahead Caroline's friends are waiting. Anastasia and Kali contributed to the investigation of their friend's murder and are devastated by the prospect of saying their final good-bye. It's not mere obligation that carries Sandra and Émile forward after that. The company of the young ones invigorates them, and gives them hope, even as their hearts go out to them in a time of sorrow. Buoyed by that, they will attend the other sad events, before finally calling it a day and collapsing into a long and necessary sleep.

In bed, they kiss good night.

Lying there, thinking of Malory Earle's funeral, Émile remarks, "Wasn't that band something? They seemed inspired."

Sandra agrees. "The band was great. Know what? I felt Mom listening in. Thought I did anyway."

"You not going religious on me, are you?"

"Can't say. Except she loved their sound."

They fall from this world awhile. When they awake, they will begin the exploration to find where it is they might live, where it is they might make their way again.